Roland,

Always go to the left....

B~
A~

"Find your Happy"

Roland,

Always go to
the left...

Today the world ended.
Not by war, plague, fire or famine.
That death would have been too fast.
Too humane.
No, this death would come like a lion in the night
from the first sweet breath of a newborn child.

RED SKY RISING

Prologue: In Bloom

Murder is a lot like dancing with a stranger. At first, there's this awkward period of struggling to discover each other's rhythm; several clumsy moments are spent just trying to learn this unknown person. You lean in, they lean out. Both of your hearts race as the anxious pace picks up. You lead, they follow. Each of you are desperate to anticipate the other's next move. You share this intimate, almost romantic moment, except only one of you will survive the encounter.

Now, people automatically assume that all death is the same, but there's a subtle beauty hidden behind all that violence—depending on your motivations. Death can be necessary, senseless, immoral, vengeful, or even merciful.

I've been responsible for all of the above.

Tonight's kill should land somewhere in the middle. I mean, there's a reason for it, but how ethical it is probably depends on who you're asking.

That brings me to where I am now; silently gliding over a dense line of trees with my victim in sight. The intense glow of a burning moon highlights the steam erupting from my mouth after each long jump. Every tense muscle flutters from the biting combination of frosty midnight air and my own growing excitement. The mixture forces me to pause while the bittersweet pain sets my insides on fire. The brief delay gives me time to embrace the raw beauty of this place from atop my sugary sweet pine.

All around are the subtle sounds of a forest in full bloom; an entire symphony of creatures that have finally been released to explore their nocturnal world. Lingering in the far distance is the heavenly scent of a smoldering campfire that will later guide me back to my temporary home. But for now, all these brilliant things pale in comparison to the intoxicating aroma of my prey below.

I feel a wicked smile stretching across my face as the familiar adrenaline rush kicks back in. The power from these tense, drawn-out moments before a kill always leaves a tightness in my chest. It's as if I've taken an extra-deep breath and my lungs refuse to release the additional air. It leaves my heart feeling trapped up against the inside of my unforgiving ribcage, where it can only swell instead of taking a full beat. The only possible relief could come in the form of a belly-emptying scream, except that would instantly alert him to my carefully hidden location.

We're *far* too deep in the game for that.

He's gone for miles trying to escape me, instinctively running from darkness, unsure what it is he fears in the shadows. Every now and then, his eyes will nervously search for the invisible monster tormenting him. He knows I'm here, of course, senses I'm coming, but can never find me. I've done this far too long to ever let one of my prey actually catch me.

Not even a stray crinkling leaf will give me away tonight. The only thing he'll hear is the carving wind as I soar above him. You know the inescapable feeling in the back of your mind when you're being watched? It lurks, nags, and refuses to leave until the source of constant torment is finally found. Well, that's because of *me*.

And this upcoming kill will be the result of weeks of work. Time that's been spent patiently waiting for just the right moment. This moment.

Time spent relentlessly studying every aspect of his life. He has no family that will miss him. No one depends on him. While he's lived a long life, his best days are far behind now. The only thing remaining is the inevitable pain time brings to a withering body.

That's a pain I'll never know.

Time and death have long forgotten my name.

His nostrils flare from the panicked run. Like me, he also struggles with the cold, damp air. I could end this now, but choose to remain on my perch while he enjoys the last few moments of life. He deserves that much.

However, I feel the monster inside me start to rumble around. He's not nearly as patient or sympathetic as I am. The beast only wants his kill. So, before he takes over and things get... *messy,* I begin my cautious descent. Slowly, branch by brittle branch, until I'm close enough to be his own shadow. So close that I fear what will give me away is the pounding of my anxious heart. Before going any further, I enjoy one more lingering smell of his inebriating fear. Then, before the steam from his last breath can even fade... it's over.

He never saw me coming, only felt the cold embrace of a ghostly shadow, before a slight constriction around the throat ended his life with a simple twist. Let's be very clear, I kill because I have to, not because I want to. That impatient monster living inside me would force this lifestyle on me if he had to. So instead of letting him control me, I've simply made killing my job.

I kneel by the body for a silent prayer, *"This is a good death, an honorable one. Death itself is the gateway to an eternal life. I have not chosen to be the lion any more than you the lamb; however, the circle of life demands us both."*

My hands move up his neck to find veins still throbbing with hot blood. From here my teeth can easily pierce the soft outer skin of his throat. When the surge of salty blood hits my lips, the entire world disappears. The merge begins and his simple life plays out like an endless movie throughout the halls of my mind. I witness every emotion, every buried memory, as his blood fuses with mine. His entire life soaks in to become a part of me in the truest sense.

The lives of thousands of creatures, plus far too many people, exist inside me now. That's the unfortunate result of what it takes to live for far longer than a human has the right to. Hundreds of years longer than a righteous person ever could. At least with my inner beast satisfied, what little is left of my fading humanity is finally free to return. The veil of hunger lifts so my mind is, once again, my own.

Thank you, Mr. Stag.

Chapter 1: Call of the Wild

Slogging back to camp with a lifeless, bloodless sack of deer meat is always a tedious task. Fortunately, it's a financially rewarding one. Well, not that rewarding; as is painfully clear to anyone who sees the the wimpy motor scooter now loaded down with several slabs of fresh-cut meat. The bike's weak springs clatter constantly under the weight of the heavy load.

Their relentless rattling has me dreaming of a day when I'll be able to cruise back to our Colony on a big black chopper instead of this tiny red scooter. Its booming exhaust would rumble off the outer walls and make the ladies swoon. Well, maybe I'm getting a bit ahead of myself on that one... I mean, I'm dead, or whatever people consider vampires these days, but that doesn't mean I can't fantasize a little!

Until then, I'll just have to settle for my shabby old scooter, affectionately named "Ol' Red". On the bright side, she's never let me down. Sure, she barely makes it over even the most modest of hills anymore, but the engine starts every time I turn the key. I try keeping that in mind while pushing the heavy bike over the top of this steep mountain road.

Thankfully, she still coasts down the other side like a dream. A slow dream, but a dream nevertheless. The leisurely pace allows me to enjoy the relaxed serenity of abandoned country roads at early dawn. All the way out here, there's little evidence humans even exist. I'll occasionally pass by an old rotting shack or the crumbling remains of a long-forgotten life, but nothing that could really be labeled as a home any more.

Still, it wouldn't surprise me if people still lived in them. This far outside the colonies, life can be dangerous, but some will gladly risk it all for some small amount of freedom in this restrictive world. I try imagining what this abandoned place could have looked like before the war. How many smiling faces called it home? Did they all end up like me?

Sometimes imagination and curiosity are great! Other times, you're the cat...

When I spot two cryptic figures walking in the distance, I have to wonder how many lives I have left. The real trick is going to be assessing their risk without looking like a threat. A few quick glances reveal the one out back is a stick-thin man, and the other appears to be a much smaller woman. She's almost completely buried underneath a bulky robe that hides everything except the burlap sack on her back. It appears to be lightly weighted down with their latest kill, while he carries the weapon responsible for it. That seems to be nothing more than a small wooden bow with an almost empty quiver of arrows.

Judging by the smell, their catch couldn't be much larger than a rodent or squirrel. Maybe a few, if they're lucky. Even though they look harmless, I would never risk trying to talk to them. They're far more likely to shoot me dead than ever take a chance on some pointless conversation.

I settle for a respectfully lowered head while cruising on by. Sadly, even going downhill, my bike refuses to pass quickly. Ol' Red only has one speed, and it's slow enough to take in every last detail of the mystery couple. The man is far larger than he appeared from further up the road, standing at least 6'10" on an amazingly lanky frame. Hundreds of sunspots cover his bald head from far too many days in a tree stand.

His cracked bow is of the homemade variety, and its crude construction probably contributes to their extra-thin bodies. As the woman gently leads him up the side of the narrow dirt road, he looks unwillingly dependent on her gentle touch. His vision is most likely fading from some disease that would have been easily curable not long ago.

The young lady, on the other hand, is visually his complete opposite. She has jet black hair that peeks out to reflect the early morning sun like diamonds. Her fair skin appears as if it could be made from the purest poured milk. Despite her noticeable beauty, those bright green eyes are drowning in deep pools of sorrow. There's a genuine sadness rooted in every line of her solemn face. My eyes struggle to watch her clutch the bloody sack that leaks crimson death behind her. Someone so pure should never cling to something so filthy and vile.

Safe to say, she captivates me, although not in the way you might think. It's not her raw beauty or obvious tragic state that haunts me. It's how she looks through my soul in a way only one other person ever has. *"Dru,"* the name barely rolls off my staggered tongue. It's a word that struggles to even make it past my trembling lips. It also hurls me back into a life buried long ago. Long before the uprising and vampire revolt. Before our world became nothing more than scattered Colonies ruled over by tyrants. These warlords are only fueled by an insatiable lust for power, stature, and greed.

Fear is our true currency now.

She forces me to remember what it was like to be a real person, instead of the ghost I've become. Dru was the compass that always kept me sailing straight. She could calm my fears with a voice as warm as an August sunset. She was there for me, even though I didn't have the maturity to appreciate it way back then. She was my best friend, my confidant, my twin sister.

See, I was born human (as I suppose we all are), and enjoyed a very normal life in the soaring mountains of West Virginia. In fact, the rich green trees here remind me of that magical home. They're also a constant reminder of a time when forests were for playing instead of killing.

Of course, I wasn't always this monster. In fact, my life was probably quite similar to yours. My sister and I were a total surprise to our parents. I say "surprise" because we arrived almost a decade after they'd given up hope of ever having kids of their own. Mom was in her early 40s and dad was already well past 50. I guess this unique perspective made them appreciate us even more. And they showed it every day.

We lived a blessed life, filled with cookies for Santa, roaring campfires, and competitive Easter egg hunts in the backyard. Every year they would cheer me on from the football stands while I rode the bench. It's safe to say they were my biggest fans. I guess we were the stereotypical family: a dog, two cats, and purple bastard of a parakeet that bit me every time I walked near its cage. I even had a typical job in a sporting goods store. Aisles 12-17, "Camping & Outdoors", were my domain. If little Johnny needed a sleeping bag, or you wanted to know the difference between nylon and canvas tents, I was your man. It was a simple life for a simple guy. I had a few friends that, in retrospect, were only people to surround myself with. But that's what life was all about back then.

Right up until the very eventful evening of July 2, 2023. That's the exact date my world decided to come crashing down around me. And as cliché as it sounds, it happened by walking down the wrong dark alley, at the wrong damn time.

There was nothing unusual about that Saturday night. It was a typical night of closing down the local bar, just like every other twenty-something I knew. A hard night of drinking, laughing, and flirting with anything that came within shouting distance had led me down that alley in search of my *"lost"* car. Now, I'll admit to being *fuzzy* about the details, but what I do remember has proven impossible to forget.

There was a very pale, grizzled old man stumbling up the street toward me. Of course, I didn't think much of it at the time. After all, I was young, dumb, and drunk as all hell, but I could feel his penetrating stare burn right through me. It was a bitter poison that forcefully invaded every wrinkle of my inebriated soul. His pale, hollow blue eyes sat inside a body so sickly, it was almost translucent. I'll never forget how the long blue veins crawled along his forehead like burrowing worms.

The last thing I recall was the overwhelming stench of rotten flesh wafting off his breath as he passed. He looked right at me, just as my world went dark.

My life was over.

…Until it wasn't.

Chapter 2: Shovels & Dirt

There are a few universal fears we all share—terrors that have been the foundation of vivid nightmares and far too many bad Hollywood movies. But none are worse than the agony of waking up to find yourself trapped in a wooden box buried six feet deep. I can personally guarantee it's not as mind-numbingly terrifying as you think.

It's far, *FAR* worse.

You're engulfed in an ocean of the deepest black imaginable. While your body is trapped, your mind is free to conjure up the worst ideas possible. I had never experienced true helplessness until that exact moment. The most frightening part was pushing against the cold wooden walls and feeling the weight of the smothering earth pushing back.

All my other senses were completely useless. My nose had become saturated by the stench of damp mud and stale air that had been buried along with me. Unlike those B-movies, there was no hidden flashlight to light the corners of my tiny tomb. There was nothing other than the sprawling, endless void. All I knew, or cared about, was that I couldn't move and breathing was getting harder by the second. My mind was consumed by a desperate need to survive—to escape.

So, I did what anyone would do: thrash about hysterically, rip at everything within my confined reach, and shout until my lungs burned and mouth went bone dry. Hell, I probably pissed myself. And, because every single minute could've been measured in decades, I can't even tell you how long I was down in that pit.

My bloodied fingers eventually tore at the lining long enough to find the impenetrable lid. I remember the wood splintering as I beat my forehead against the impenetrable wall. Then, somehow, through the echoes of my screams came a faint crumbling noise. This was accompanied by several damp clumps of dirt finding my tear-slathered cheeks. All my frantic writhing must have created an opening somewhere— I just had to find it.

Turns out my painful efforts had only created the tiniest of cracks, but it was all I needed. From there, my mind latched on to that glimmer of hope like a bulldog with a meaty bone. It brought an intense calm that allowed me to methodically bash against the lid, instead of just randomly thrash around. The more focused approach eventually widened the gap enough to begin pulling in dirt with my hands. The idea was to make some room for the hefty top to slide all the way open. *Hopefully,* I could then burrow out like an anxious mole.

I repeated the tedious process over, and over, and over again. Each time, I would drag in another small fistful of mud to pack into the farthest corner. Hours of this tedious work had left only my face and one hand free from the crammed dirt. Because I was completely out of room, and almost out of air, I once again tried to unleash my bottled-up fear onto the unyielding ceiling. This fierce violence sent orange fireworks exploding across my vision every time a fist landed on the splintering wood. Unfortunately, all this tiresome work only freed up a few inches of space, but it had to be enough.

At first, it was. My head and shoulders fit through nicely. The rest, however, was a different story. Squeezing my chest out would require bending ribs so far inward that they smacked against my heart. Safe to say I was totally unprepared for the amount of pain it would take to leave that hole.

The biggest test of my resolve would come with the first shattered rib. All I really remember about it was a lightning bolt of pain seizing my entire body, causing me to accidently bite off the tip of my tongue. The crippling agony made me want to just surrender and die down in that hole, but I didn't. I was already stuck halfway between freedom and a torturous death, so my *only* choice was to spit out the severed tongue and prepare for the rest of the bones to break.

Which they did.

One.

By.

One.

So many bones snapped that it sounded like walking on dry autumn leaves. My body couldn't even comprehend this amount of mind-numbing pain! A hundred years later and it's still the *second* most painful experience of my life. Then, mere seconds later, came the *absolute worst.*

My air-starved lungs eventually had to stretch back out, and when those dirty bastards did, they pushed every crushed rib right along with them. It felt like someone had ripped open my chest, replaced every organ with broken glass, and sealed it back up with hot lava. What's worse, I couldn't just stop breathing. The agonizing process had to be repeated every few seconds. Through it all, my stubborn legs never stopped pushing, my terrified arms refused to rest, and my weary fingers flung dirt aside—even as rocks cut large chunks from them. The farther up I burrowed, the more the narrow tunnel wanted to collapse back in. Most of my energy had to be spent simply trying to keep the loose soil from clogging my blood-filled mouth.

However, *nothing* would stop me from finding the light again. I ripped, pulled, punched, and fought back the devil himself to be released from that tormenting hole. When the moment finally arrived, I burst through that final dark barrier with a scream that must have shook the very pillars of heaven. It terrified even me as it echoed off the distant mountains.

Immediately, my feet scrambled to leave the messy pit. They slopped through the thick mud and driving rain to be free from my self-desecrated grave. I stood there, triumphant, as the gods welcomed me back with crackling voices. I watched their long, glowing fingers stretch across the patchy grey sky. My mind craved to scream back at the raging storm. It wanted to declare my defiance to the angel of death and that menacing hole in the ground, but all my fragile body could do was fall face down into the sloppy mud.

Wha—what had happened?

Nothing seemed to work anymore. My arms had become unmovable slabs of concrete. My legs were fallen tree trunks. Even my face had somehow become permanently glued to the ground. Every ounce of life had been left down in that hole! Merely flopping over onto my back required Herculean effort!

There was plenty of panic in this paralyzed state, but also something spectacularly new. The world I came back to was completely different than the one I had left! Everything was now magnified as if the volume of life had been turned up to eleven. Every drop of rain now sent shockwaves rattling throughout my motionless body. The tiny droplets collided with the weight of mighty boulders! And not only could I hear the squirrel scurrying in the pine fifty yards away, but I could *feel* every single needle scrape its fur.

The massive variety of sounds allowed me to paint a vivid portrait of the world in my mind. The longer I listened, the clearer it became. It was both astonishing and confusing at the same time! I laid there, lost in the soundtrack of life, as if I were hearing it for the first time. It was *that* much different from everything I'd ever known.

Of course, since everything in life comes with a price, I was about to discover mine. At first it was only a faint whisper that blended in with all the rest.

Thump, thump.

Thump, thump.

Thump, thump.

But it quickly built with my own racing heartbeat.

Thump, thump.

Thump, thump.

Thump, thump.

Thump, thump.

That simple sound transformed me into a mindless beast. It instantly unlocked some long-forgotten piece of savage DNA. Those feral new instincts made saliva drizzle down my chin simply from the creature inching closer. Tiny tremors shook the ground as his claws dug into the spongy dirt. I could feel them trying to shake off the little clumps of soft mud.

His pulse accelerated from drawing closer.

So did mine.

My once-useless muscles roared back to life as his hot breath steamed up my left arm. The smell from his last putrid meal, still lingering in matted fur, raised my excitement level to staggering new heights. His rough nose tickled the delicate skin surrounding my locked fingertips. I remained frozen while the mysterious creature continued circling me. The growing anticipation had my heart pounding so hard, it became the only thing I could hear anymore. That was the very moment my life was changed forever. Boring old Hayden Archer Flynn became something far more...*complicated.*

That was the day my monster was born.

Acting on uncontrolled instincts alone, I hurled myself on top of him. When I did, the entire world burst into the brilliant colors of a waking dream. This intense new reality made it seem as if I'd been living in black and white my entire life. Standing directly in front of me was my soon-to-be prey; a Creole mustard-colored mountain lion with terrified eyes. Before that day, I would have feared his teeth and claws. Now, all I saw was a fresh new toy to play with.

Tunnel vision hid everything except his frightened face and exposed throat. An addictive inebriation spread quickly over me. Anything resembling morality, or even humanity, was washed away by the raging flood of unadulterated insanity. Hayden Flynn was gone. All that was left behind was a snarling beast with an insatiable appetite for violence.

What happened next, I'm not particularly proud of, but I'll admit because it's part of my story. One that's been repeated many times since. I sat hunched over him like a wild animal for what felt like days. When he moved, I moved. I did everything to keep enjoying the sweet intoxication of his fear. That was also the first time my monster found his fangs.

It's impossible to describe the insane rush I experienced as they sank into his furry throat. Let's just say it was powerful. Life-alteringly powerful. It wasn't about the blood; it was about the control. I pulled back to find that a patch of the cat's flesh had returned with me. It tried to cower in pain and run away. However, by then it was too late... I already had fresh blood on my lips. That first taste took our cruel game to a place that could only be called pure madness. I would let him bite me just to feel it. That searing pain only drove me deeper down the rabbit hole of insanity.

I'll never forget the pure terror locked in those yellow eyes. As shameful as it is, my heart still races at the sick thought. My fingers still itch to feel his wet fur running between them. I'll spare you the worst details, but, needless to say, we continued on like feral dogs for a heartless amount of time. The only thing that finally stopped the madness was sinking those new fangs in a little too far. My inexperience ultimately saved that poor creature from an even more gruesome death.

While the physical rush was intense, the resulting mental fallout would break me for decades. When the fog of hunger eventually lifted, reality was free to rush back in. Each second that passed made the mangled carcass more *real* to me. More shameful. The taste in my mouth, which had been wonderful seconds ago, now ripped my heart open with a guilty torture. I stared down at my stained hands, covered in matted fur, as if they were no longer mine. They couldn't be.

I basically shut down while watching the blood and rain pool in my hands. It wasn't just because of that one guilty act, it was because I knew there would be more.

Many more.

All I could do after that was run. Not just from the field and stone with my name carved into it, but my *entire* life. Away from Mom, Dad, and the joyous holidays. Away from Dru. After all, how could she see me like this? Hayden Flynn died. Whatever crawled out of that hole didn't deserve the happiness my family would surely bring. So that long, brutal night was only the beginning of a new life. One filled with a mindless thirst for violence and a hunger that would haunt me for several lifetimes. It was a drug that latched onto my very soul. I tried absolutely *everything* to kick it: starved myself until the monster would take control, lived as an outcast on the fringes of society, ate rodents, ate people... everything.

The ghost of my parents' oak door would torment me to come back home every night. Stepping through it would surely make everything all right again. Our mangy old dog would be there, warming her soft pink belly by the fire. The sweet smell of caramel-glazed apple pie (Mom's specialty) would welcome me back. Sometimes the dreams were so vivid that I woke up still feeling Mom's gentle touch on my shoulder. But eventually, those imaginary worlds, painted with the rich colors of love and acceptance, would be replaced by whatever filthy alley that had served as my shelter for the night. The heavenly aroma of apple pie would become the smell of stale urine wafting up from my newest dumpster blanket.

How many times did I almost go home? Thousands. Each time, I would talk myself out of it for one reason or another.

"What if I lose control?"

"I need to get better first."

"I'll do it tomorrow."

Well, twenty years passed and "tomorrow" never quite came. So eventually, like everything else, that option was taken from me as well. The war between vampires and humans burned across the globe until nothing good was left. Those of us who survived were only charred husks of our former selves. We occasionally sifted through the ashes to see if there were any long-missing pieces left behind, but rarely found any.

And I'm ashamed to admit it, but not even after the fire did I have the courage to discover what happened to my missing family. I didn't need to. I knew they didn't stand a chance against an army of creatures like me.

After that, I wouldn't even allow myself the comforting dreams anymore. That final sliver of hope, just like Dru's warm voice, was silenced forever. All that's left now is the heartache.

Chapter 3: Tin Pan Alley

The dirt trail gradually becomes enough busted concrete that it might be considered some kind of crude road. Mother Nature and all her woody pines is eventually replaced by the mismatching walls of our little Colony. This patchwork metal is supposed to create a barrier between the dangerous world outside and the relative safety within. Although I technically live inside them, I only feel at home while surrounded by the smell of budding leaves and a smoldering campfire as I listen to animals chirp the night away.

But there are certain things, like selling the meat from my latest kill, which can only be accomplished by going back inside the restrictive walls. And that must really be a sight to see. While I'm not a huge guy, anyone would look stupid riding this dinky scooter. Especially when it's been packed down with camping gear and a full slab of deer.

Although I might find me a funny sight, the guards greet me with their usual indifference. After years of passing through these same gates, you would think they might just wave me on through. Well, no. I still get the same extensive full-body scans as everyone else. After this, they're going to toss my meager equipment around for no apparent reason. Thankfully, when you don't have much, it doesn't take long.

I shouldn't complain about living in a place where security is still valued. Most of this rebellious world is filled with outlaws, thieves, V-heads, and blood whores. Our Colony, Cedar Points, is around a 60/40 split of humans to vampires. That would normally leave me in the minority, except this place is motivated more by money than food preference.

The gates only swing open after the exhaustive pat down is complete. I affectionately blow a kiss to the guard who did the deepest part of the search. He quietly slinks away without making eye contact or accepting my offer to finish his search over a romantic dinner. The way I see it, if you're going to toss my junk around, I get to have a little fun with you. Judging by the cold-shouldered response, he has no interest in taking our relationship to the next level.

Anyhow, navigating the points is a breeze. It's basically a three-acre sized hand with five fingers of housing radiating off the central palm. The nicest homes are found up in the thumb area. Unsurprisingly, that's _not_ my section.

My kind sticks to the skinny pinky known as "Tin Pan Alley." That's where those of us who trade... um, less civilized fare, go to make a living. Believe it or not, I'm actually considered a high-ranking trader since I mostly deal in stag and rabbit. Maybe a squirrel or two occasionally, although I find the blood to meat ratio is usually not worth the time. Most of my fellow traders prefer rats, rodents, or even hobos who've passed out in the wrong place. Of course that's illegal, but completely overlooked by the ruling class, who consider it a cost-effective way of controlling the miscreant population.

Our de facto leader is the man in the green shanty at the very end of Tin Pan Alley. His real name is John Buttonfold, though I prefer "Old Man Buttons." Over the years, we've set up a pretty fair deal: I hunt the game, take the blood for myself, then sell the meat to him. Good deal, right?

The portly old man rushes up to greet me with typical wide open arms. His enthusiastic tone is much higher than you might expect to come out of such a round and robust body. Honestly, he's probably five feet tall and six feet wide.

His wardrobe is always flashy, as any good trader should be, so he stands out while peddling his crap to you. That being said, today's outfit is particularly bad. Only people who've lost a bet should wear a knee-length velvet coat with bright purple trim. Normally, the vanilla shirt tucked underneath would be considered a reserved choice, except this one has ruffles that would put any Victorian nobleman to shame. The icing on the old-fashioned cake are the impenetrable mounds of grey chest hair bursting out from between every button. Each one has been perfectly trimmed to resemble miniature snow-covered hedges. They could easily be confused for tufts of fluffy white cotton balls.

"Good day, kiddo!" he eagerly squeaks. Of course there are two things wrong with this statement.

First: it's *night time.*

Second: I'm more than 90 years *older* than he is!

That's just one of the many special treats that come with not aging past twenty-two. No matter how much older you get, you'll never get the respect that comes with a few wrinkles and silver strands of hair. He knows how old I am, of course, but this is the first of many bad jokes still to come. It's also my cue to put on my normal forced smile and banter back, "Hey there, old man. How's today treating you?" I can already tell you his response word for word. It's been the same since he was young man Buttons. "Still warm!" he playfully delights. That's his gentle stab at us cold bloods.

Side note: A vampire's blood is not cold, nor are we dead, despite what I said earlier. This is a damn dirty stereotype, so don't believe everything you read!

We wrap up a few minutes of casual conversation by moving around back to wait for the metallic clunk of a dead bolt before I unload my latest kill. One new addition to our old routine is me having to help the frail man slide the heavy door open. I joke, "About time to get an electric opener, isn't it?" He boasts in return, "Why would I do that when I can make you work for your money?" Touché, old man, touché.

"You know the worst thing about buying your venison?" he asks while I sling the deer onto a set of massive scales.

"No, Buttons; what's wrong with my meat?"

"I ain't had a juicy steak in over 40 damn years! Hahahaha!!!" This isn't a new joke, but I've only heard it fifty or sixty times, so it's better than most. Something about it must really tickle him though, since he's laughing way harder than a person ought to at their own joke.

"Yeah, because I drain all the blood. Good one, Buttons." My painted-on smile fades a bit more each visit. Don't get me wrong, he's a nice guy, but I've grown far more comfortable among the trees than socializing with people these days. The monotonous politics of navigating society just don't have the same appeal as they used to.

We continue laughing on through a few more bad jokes until he pays me my *"ransom money,"* and I'm free to scooter off into the night. Luckily, I don't have far to go. Only a few buildings up is my favorite watering hole, Pandora. It's nothing special during the day, but for a desperate man, she looks real good at night. Especially since there's a parking spot right up front that should be easy to stumble back to. Today was a particularly good hunt, so that's reason enough for me to celebrate.

One of the biggest advantages to being of the vampire persuasion is that sleep hasn't been a major concern of mine in over a hundred years. My state of mind is only relative to my hunger level, and with a full belly, I'm ready to kick off the party with a squirt of *special occasion* cologne. You know, in case someone in there wants to keep me warm tonight.

These are the optimistic hopes that launch me through both double doors to make a very grand entrance. Sadly, not a single interested head turns my way. Disgruntled but still determined, I casually stroll past each table slow enough to make one man threaten to kick my ass. I keep walking since it's some old guy that strongly resembles a wrinkled bulldog. After that, I really start putting maximum swagger into each confident step. And still my trip ends without a single lady's eye caught! A more realistic scan of the room reveals that nearly every table is filled with grumpy-looking dudes! Suddenly, my spirit, outlook, and crotch deflate like a shriveling balloon. This night is definitely not going the triumphant way I hoped. I eventually have to resign myself to a lonely place at the bar up front.

That's when my evening takes an unexpected, but very welcome turn when a long-lost voice calls out, "I didn't know we let people like you in here!?" The smiling face of one of my oldest friends happens to be working the bar tonight!

"Well, if it isn't the man, the myth, the legend Shepherd Roberts here to fill my belly with his finest ale!" This is a not-so-subtle hint for some of the private reserve he keeps stashed behind the bar. "Where have you been? And why haven't you been here?" I ask because it's been years since I've seen him.

"The normal bartender was a no-show, so here I am, pedaling booze to the likes of you!"

"Whatever it took to get you here! I'm just thrilled to see you after all this time! What's it been, almost fifteen years?"

"It's definitely been far too long, my friend!" he warmly replies while giving me an awkward man-hug over the wide-top bar. He continues, "I could never keep up with your crazy ass! Remember the last time we hung out? You ended the night butt-ass naked with a stuffed monkey so you could shout, *'touch my monkey'* to everyone stupid enough to pass by!"

"Oh, that's right!" I vaguely recall. "Man, it was the absinthe. I swear that stuff was mean! Where did that monkey come from, anyway???"

He laughs, "It was some teenager's Valentine present that you apparently wanted more than she did. Don't forget you *still* owe me for the *'donation'* it took to get your wobbly ass back home that night."

Shepherd's a good friend. As a person with very few of those, it's safe to say he's my best friend. I don't say that lightly either—it was a lesson learned long ago. Our friendship goes way beyond keeping me from making a drunken ass out of myself. We fought side by side during the vampire uprising and spilled a lot of Mongrel blood together. That's what we called the rebel vampires, "mongrels," because they had lost touch with their humanity like dogs without a breed. They believed they were somehow superior to humans. Shepherd and I strongly disagreed with them. We believed that no matter what the virus made us, we were still the same people.

He was motivated by protecting his loved ones. I was driven by a rage so pure it simply obliterated every other emotion possible.

I was utterly numb to everything except unadulterated anger. It became comforting to force all those raw emotions through a filter of pure hatred. I channeled the loss of my family into a long string of violence that made me a valuable soldier, but absolutely *terrible* person. I could physically see Dru in every fanged face I slaughtered; that's how messed up I was. Not knowing how they died let my madness run *wild.* It drove me to do things that wouldn't be acceptable in even the bloodiest of wars. My morality was gladly sacrificed at the altar of uncontrollable violence and rage.

Let's just say he fought the better war. While Shepherd's kills were swift, mine were not. I wanted to share my pain with them. I needed to fill this personal void with their suffering. It's certainly not something I'm proud of, but it's true.

Thankfully, those are not the stories we share this evening. Tonight is filled with fantastic tales of great victories and many terrible jokes. I make fun of him for living on the top side of the Colony, up where the grass is *actually* greener on the other side. Far away from Tin Pan Alley and his own bar. We aimlessly chat away the night while knocking back beer after beer. Our stories devolve from genuine memories, to *slight* exaggerations, to *outright damn dirty lies*, all in an attempt to remember what it was like to be something greater than ourselves.

When one of the other bartenders makes the mistake of stopping for too long, she gets to hear the story of the first time I met young vampire Shepherd Roberts. "Now picture this, it was the battle of Golden Gate, and hundreds, *NO,*

THOUSANDS of blood-thirsty Mongrels were pouring across the bridge. They swarmed like rabid cockroaches to overtake a defenseless downtown San Francisco.

Our unit had arrived too late to do anything other than burn down the bridge to keep them from crossing. That would at least save the city and a hundred thousand people. Well, unfortunately, those bloodsuckers hurled themselves across the wires in never-ending waves to slaughter our entire unit within minutes! There were only about a dozen of us left by the time someone got the bright idea to rip the cables out and finally take the fight to them! We swung out over the bridge, down the sides, under it; wherever they went, we followed. As good as the Mongrels were that day, we were better.

We searched out every set of snapping teeth and smashed right through them. They just kept coming, diving from cable to cable, so we kept pushing them back in the most gruesome cirque performance of all time. Anything that got in the way was quickly ripped apart.

Everything was going perfectly as we fought our way toward an unexpected victory! All that remained was for our explosives expert to reach the last set of pillars, then we were home free! I tried to do my part by tying myself onto a cable directly above him and destroying anything that came within a hundred feet. That was the plan, at least... all it took was one sneaky prick slipping by to make the entire house of cards fold.

Maybe it was due to my over-confidence, perhaps it was just my destiny to fail that day, too; either way, I never even saw the mongrel until he had already ripped the kid's head off. All I could do was watch the poor solider melt into a lifeless puddle of bones. Sadly, I never even knew his name.

Being tied to the steel cable kept me from doing anything to keep the explosives from tumbling into the bay. Then, out of absolutely nowhere, came a young Shep Roberts to snatch the charges right outta midair! It was an act of courage so fantastic, so unbelievable, that it could only be matched by the sheer amount of ironic bad luck that would strike next.

He was so focused on saving the day that the brave guy never saw the concrete pillar waiting at the end of his wild swing. It also meant he never saw the violent collision, either. While the bombs didn't detonate, the wall pulverized the entire left side of his body. Believe it or not, that mangled soldier, screaming in agony, never stopped for a second. He couldn't even stand, yet somehow managed to arm every explosive with three working fingers! That day, I witnessed one of the bravest acts of heroism no one will ever know about.

I pause the story to boast to the impatient waitress, "Bet you didn't know your boss was a hero, did you?" An eye roll is all I get in return. Anyhow, "So there he was, propped up on a shattered shoulder, waiting for the end to come. Any sane man would have run from the armed bomb. Not Shep! He knew there was no going back, and seemed completely fine with it! He sat there, looking out over the city, with a steady smile as if he were watching a tropical sunset in full bloom.

Something inside me clicked while watching him happily waiting to die for complete strangers. It made me realize why I was actually there that day. He was who I should be.

After that, the suffocating anger didn't go away completely, it just died down far enough to let me feel something again. I forced my monster to remain with the wounded hero when he tried to run. He wanted survival; I craved redemption. Either both of us made it back—or no one would.

While I had been a deeply cruel person, I was a smart soldier. I knew there was no going back through the impenetrable Mongrel horde. Our only real option would be to dive toward the bay and pray nothing too big followed us in.

So, that swell of righteous inspiration launched me in the direction of the mangled hero. I began by swinging high on the cable before dropping like a rock from the high heavens. One thing you gotta understand is that the lip of the pillar was only about two feet wide and completely covered in shattered concrete. Logically, I should have just slid right off into the bay, except the laws of physics must have taken that particular day off. My scrambling feet stuck like hot glue!

I had that broken man scooped up within seconds. The poor guy screamed bloody murder the instant my arms wrapped around him. It must have felt even worse when I had to sling him all the way down into the icy water! And we weren't even under by the time the entire bridge exploded in a spectacular ball of fire! I'm telling you, I felt the red-hot flames licking my feet just as the shockwave rocketed us toward the muddy river bed. Dozens of flaming spears were shooting by on the way down. Only one managed to clip the inside of my shoulder, but their main damage was turning the entire bay into a giant hot tub. The immense heat released millions upon millions of tiny steam bubbles to keep us from being able to see anything other than the boiling blizzard.

Soon, the pillar-sized boulders began crashing down. While we couldn't see them, we could definitely feel them! Have you ever been sucked under an extra-fierce wave at the beach? You know how the tide tries to rip you in a thousand different directions at once? Well, it was like that... but with boulders.

By the time we were done bouncing around the extra-large spin cycle, most of the initial explosion had passed. For us, at least. Back on the bridge, things were really starting to go south for the Mongrels.

Literally.

The entire structure had become a long wave of rolling steel and concrete. It kicked like a bucking bronco with each new snapping cable, flinging mongrel after mongrel off its arching back. Hundreds were catapulted from the mighty bridge as it collapsed into the furious waters. Their screams, even if they were Mongrels, still haunt me to this day.

It didn't take long for the rapid current to sweep us downstream onto some dilapidated old fishing dock. There were no cheering crowds to greet us as I pulled Shepherd's twisted body from the muddy water.

No one praised us for our courage.

No tears of pride were shed.

All we got was a burning bridge and bodies drifting by like logs caught in a flood. As amazing as this battle was, our contribution would be nothing more than another link in an endless chain of war." Although it does makes for one hell of a drinking story.

Chapter 4: Only the Good Die Young

The night grows long as stories flow across the beer-soaked bar. "...so the bartender says, 'I was talking to the duck!!' Hahahaha!!!!" My insane laughter is fueled by one part liquor, two parts old-fashioned nostalgia, and four parts genuine happiness. Despite all my foolish joy, Shepherd abruptly takes on a much gloomier appearance. His sudden mood shift has me rushing to figure out how he could have been offended by the lame duck joke.

In an attempt to defend myself, I start to say, "See, it was mainly about the duck..." though his grim look shows just how disinterested he is in hearing what I have to say. He marches away without another word and leaves me totally staggered.

"Come on now, it was just a stupid joke!" I try following the mysterious man until my drunken feet decide to send me to ground instead. The unexpected fall manages to avoid all tables, people, and bottles so that (for now) only my pride hurts. Judging by the size of the growing knot on my arm, tomorrow may be a different story.

It takes a small miracle to finally wrestle my feet back under me and after I do, the entire room is spinning. Finding Shepherd suddenly takes a backseat to simply finding the closest chair. It takes several more failed attempts to line my blurry ass up with the elusive seat. Even then, I'm kind of ashamed by the sense of accomplishment I get from completing the otherwise simple task.

Although, ultimately, it's a short-lived swell of pride.

An invisible hand shoves me back down almost immediately. From the ground, I get to watch the unmistakable power of a major explosion rip across the tiny bar. The unstoppable force hurls a sharp wave of glass through like a shotgun blast without bias. It begins up front and takes everything in its path (including me) with it.

Next comes the ringing ears that keep the screaming crowd down to a muffled growl. The shrill silence drowns out everything except my own growing panic. In an ironic twist, the chair I fell from actually shields me from most of the debris. For once, I'm thrilled to have drank myself under a table.

I struggle to comprehend exactly what's happening because of a mind that's as fuzzy as my eyesight. Could it have been a bombing raid? We haven't seen one of those since the war ended! But when I find the entire front of the room missing, that appears to be the leading candidate. The idea seems to be spreading over the rest of the terrified bar. They swarm like bumblebees to Shepherd, who's hastily waving them through the back exit. Not me though; I'm aimlessly wading through the scrambling people as if floating through a waking dream. None of it seems real yet, even as I find myself up by the disfigured lump in the center of all the rubble.

Wearily looking at the fleshy mound reveals a scarred badge belonging to one of our Colony's guards. There are no burns or any other telltale signs of a bomb apparent. Besides being horribly disfigured, his body is still in one piece. That's when it hits me—this was no explosion at all. This, all THIS, was caused by something using a human body as a wrecking ball. But what could have the strength to do it?!?

The terrible question forces an expedited sobriety over me. My mind strains to piece together all the improbable facts. The alcohol-induced curiosity, along with a habit of making poor life choices, pushes me closer to the mystery instead of following the tide of people going the other way. I'll forge my own path! Even if it's with great hesitation...

As my feet exit what used to be the front of the building, I expect to find a rampaging war. Us against them. Our massive collection of guards against a mighty unknown foe. Instead, there's only me.

Alone.

How?

Where's the attack?

WHERE'S ANYONE???

The only evidence of this not being a normal evening are the blaring sirens and the one dead guard. Maybe the battle is somewhere else? Maybe this is just a small piece of it? Getting up to the roof should answer some of this. Although, as soon as I try, I realize that I may have overestimated my sobriety when my wobbly legs can barely make it halfway up the short jump. This results in me having to use the narrow lip of the building to pull myself the rest of the way up. And that's when my problems really begin...

As soon as my drunk body pours onto the rooftop, I'm thrown across the roof like a ragdoll. It happens so fast that all I can see is a blurry grey hand before taking flight. Granted, my senses are not a hundred percent... or sixty. Maybe forty? Most likely mid-twenties. Anyhow, I'm pretty sure that whatever it was wasn't human.

The abrupt trip ends in a harsh meeting with a solid wall. Any bricks not broken by the impact immediately fall on top of me. The ones that crush my fingers hurt, but the ones that smash into my forehead do the real damage. After that, I have to stay moving to keep the world from folding in on me. Everything except the area right past the tip of my nose has already gone black.

Before the tunnel vision gets even worse, I pull myself from the wreckage by basically feeling around for something that doesn't crumble. I eventually find a vent that's wedged against so much other broken stuff that it becomes a solid handle. And that's when I see it...

It can't be.

A pair of unnaturally red eyes scowl at me from across the rooftop. It's letting out a low, clicking growl from its shadowy lips. And the smell—God help me—the smell hangs in the air like a mildewed blanket. Standing only a few feet away is a living nightmare in the rotting flesh.

A Eutherian.

A creature so mind-numbingly terrifying that you can't breathe and look at it at the same time. He literally takes my breath away. It's also disturbing because, as a vampire, that's my future. This devil is where we all end up. They're just our natural evolution. And that thought burns like a cheap shot of whisky going down. Much like all vampires used to be humans, all Eutherians used to be vampires. These monsters are the horrifying result of when we live too long. No one knows why our bodies mutate into actual demons, but they do. Your nose really falls off, and then you sprout giant car-sized wings!

But wait, *there's more!* Next, your skin turns a dark scaly grey with bristly hair that could scrape paint off a house. That's all before your fingers stretch into these long, webbed spines, and your mind loses the ability to think far beyond the concept of *"meat"*.

All traces of humanity disappear because you're nothing more than a hunter. Like this guy. He's a hunter that has me anxiously searching for the quickest way out of here. My feet try inching backward but they're already against the wall with nowhere else to go.

His first move is to unleash a mind piercing scream that crumples me to the ground. The powerful waves bounce around my skull and leave warm trails of blood leaking from both ears. As brutal as it was, that wasn't even a real attack. It was merely a warning to leave him alone. The reason why quickly becomes clear.

Wrapped in those grizzly arms is a girl that couldn't be much more than eight or nine years old. She appears to have fallen asleep with eyes wide open. Given the horrifying situation, that's not likely. I've heard of vampires who can enchant, but never seen it in person.

What's left of his upturned nose is busy sniffing to decide what kind of threat I could be. Before the kid, not much; I would have gladly left him alone, but after her... still not much. He must feel the same way since his bristly ass is already heading toward the outer wall. He obviously isn't overly concerned about me.

My bruised ego decides to hurl a couple of busted bricks to make him quickly reconsider, but (of course) my drunken hands miss by a country mile. Still, they do manage to get his attention.

He pauses to spray me with another one of those mind-scrambling wails, then casually turns back around. My only defense against the sonic assault is to clinch my head and squeeze tight. I've fought vampires of all shapes and sizes, won countless fights I shouldn't have; however, these things are a different kind of beast. They don't fight with strategy or tactics. They're simply exaggerated versions of my own inner monster —only released out onto the real world.

Looking at all his broken teeth, somehow, makes the idea of being mauled to death even less appealing. That fear causes me to hesitate just enough to allow the big bastard to make it off the side of the building. By the time my feet are ready to move again, he's almost across the entire courtyard and getting ready to clear the outer wall!

Well, damn! I'm pretty confident I couldn't make this jump sober, but one way or another, the head-splitting, wobbly-kneed version is going to have to. It takes so long to talk myself into a heroic leap of faith that the bat has already disappeared over the wall by the time my feet agree to move. I have to shove the nagging doubt aside and leap into an epic moment of greatness before he gets away completely.

So, that's exactly what I do! And I (predictably) make it less than halfway before crashing into a rickety old fruit stand. At least the landing wasn't all that painful. The squishy foods did a great job of cushioning most of the clumsy fall. On a relatively good note: squashed citrus smells *MUCH BETTER* than the rancid beast.

I roll out of the colorful wreckage to find a small group of guards already gathered at the gate. The way they're lazily standing around only adds to my growing confusion. Am I the only one who sees what's happening here? I scream for them to open the gates, using authority I don't actually have. Despite their uninterested attitude, they don't argue, and the gates creep open. Having others will certainly help in our search for the devil in the trees. I shout out more commands on the way up the steep hill. They trigger old instincts that resurface as effortlessly as breathing. The thrill I get from solo hunts is nothing compared to leading a pack into battle.

Before entering the first row of trees, I turn back to see that not a single person had even followed me in the first place. The entire group remains stuck back behind some imaginary barrier at the gate! I can't believe it!

I shout in genuine disbelief, *"You big bags a' dicks!"*

Well, with or without them, I'm going. I bark at the cowards a few more times before returning to the line of dense trees hiding a killer.

Alone.

Chapter 5: Mouth of Madness

It's been a half-hour since I've laid eyes on him. That's not really much of a problem since a blind man could easily follow his foul stench. It's also pretty hard to miss the large trail he's cut into the mountainside. Broken branches, entire trees, and dead animals litter the ground in a straight line.

Does he know I'm following him?

By the look of it, he doesn't care.

Passing a sloppy mound of shredded flesh is a powerful reminder of what efficient killing machines these things are. It also makes me curious why he didn't do that to the girl back in town. Why drag her all the way up here when he could've just finished her back in town? He could have even grabbed a few more on the way out. Not that that would have been a good thing...

The questions linger, but at least the maddening night has drawn to a merciful end. With dawn comes a chilly morning and a dense fog to add to my rising level of discomfort. It also coincides with the cozy dirt path, becoming an endless series of limestone boulders. Just knowing that each step is bringing me closer to a cave full of demons has me wanting to run—not walk—back home.

There is one quirk about this place that helps distract from the thought of my impending grizzly death; all the trees here are completely lopsided. The branches only grow from the left side of the trunk. An evolutionary change to survive the high winds up here?

Seriously, the breeze has two speeds, "freeze your ass off" and "blow you back down the hill". Fortunately, the sun eventually rises high enough to help compensate for the freezing winds. It also cuts through the thick blanket of fog. This will be especially important when I finally find this creature. While sunlight doesn't bother me as a (relatively) young vampire, those things are so deteriorated that it sets their skin ablaze. Like, actually on fire. That's why they hide away in caves and only terrorize people at night.

So, it's safe to assume he's been home for a while, since the sun is up and I haven't seen any animals in over an hour. Although there have been plenty of those little pools of meat. Chunks of sheared fur are stuck to most of the sharp rocks, and there's enough blood splatter to qualify this entire mountain as an abstract painting. One thing is becoming painfully clear: I'm not at the top of the food chain anymore.

NOT. EVEN. CLOSE.

After another hour, the random pools merge into one long crimson trail leading to a place God ignores. Carved into the side of the mountain is a hole filled with the vilest creatures to ever walk Earth. The massive, gaping entrance makes it appear as if even the rocks are screaming for me to turn back. Stone spires guard the entrance as if they were the snarling teeth of a crazed wolf. The tops have been stained a dark cherry red from all the unfortunate souls that have passed through them.

Endless waves of putrid breath are spewing from inside the screaming mouth. The smell of rotting death rapidly brings out all my crippling insecurities. To describe how it feels standing at the front gates of Hell is impossible. Small. Weak. Powerless.

I don't even know this girl! Why should I risk everything for her? She means *absolutely nothing to me!* I try convincing myself that turning back is the only rational choice. There are actually muscles twitching to yank me away from this nightmarish pit. Only the lingering image of the girl keeps me here. Her helpless eyes say that leaving would be the same as killing her myself. And that's a guilt I can't live with.

Again.

Walking away would plunge me into the deepest, darkest depression possible.

Again.

There have been points where I couldn't even stand the sight of my own face. My overwhelming shame was as visible as a black eye or bloody nose to me. I can never go back to that. Besides, I'll have daylight on my side for several more hours. There will be no need for a fight at all! I'll be able to sneak in and out before they even know I'm there! Just stroll into a thick den of monsters, in complete and utter darkness, to steal back a hypnotized girl! No problem!

An odd laugh, treading the uneasy line of humor and panic, leaks out. The brave thought brings a temporary swell of courage, but not enough to actually make me believe the hopeful words. However, the false optimism does give me the required motivation to finally get moving.

First thing I do is grab a big handful of the chunky stew covering the ground. The thick slime seems to be made from every creature that's ever been here. Purposely covering myself with the foul-smelling ooze may sound crazy, but it should easily cover my scent while I'm in there. Even if I do make a pretty big mistake by looking at it...

It appears to be nothing more than hunks of fur and meat collected into squishy piles. Since it would be suicide to walk in there without it, I reluctantly smear the rotten goo over every inch of exposed skin. Having an enhanced sense of smell certainly isn't helping the situation. A few dry heaves later, and I'm completely covered in chunky bat poo.

With the new suit of putrid armor in place, I'm free to search the gnarly teeth for the best way into the dark cave. Sadly, they reveal absolutely nothing about what's hiding inside. The bright mid-day sun makes it impossible to see anything beyond the black hole. By the looks of it, I'll be going in blind. Maybe it's best I don't know what's hiding in there??? *Ha!* Not even I can sell that load of crap to myself! There's never a good time to jump into a blender, especially when you don't know if it's running.

Since the rationalizing isn't going particularly great, I simply quit trying and immediately dive into the belly of the beast. The abrupt jump doesn't give me time to regret the impulsive decision. It also leaves my feet soaking wet and completely eyes shut off. They'll only show the blue sparkles of trying to adjust to the infinite darkness. I'm barely inside the entrance, yet I might as well be drifting in outer space.

Regrettably, my ears are working just fine. They easily hear the countless Eutherians and whatever squishy pile I landed in. I decide not to move while waiting for the dark to share her secrets with me. But as it does, *hundreds*, maybe *thousands,* of devil bats come into gradual focus. Directly above are massive swarms of hanging giants, still dripping gore from last night's feast. I can hear their heavy drool and chunky leftovers raining down from the high ceiling.

Most are bundled up in fleshy wing cocoons to keep away what little light can survive in here. I can't tell exactly how many are up there, but it's enough to make it hard to tell where one beast stops and another begins. They make the entire ceiling appear to be a living, *writhing* creature.

Surrounding my feet are the remains of decades of brutal hunts. Heaping mounds of freshly chewed bodies and bones; deer, cattle, rabbit, birds, and humans of every age and size imaginable. Most of them are so mangled that it's hard to tell what they could have been. The variety in this room is as endless as it is frightening.

My eyes can't escape one old man in particular. Something about his terrified appearance really draws me in. What little skin he has left is bleached the kind of white usually reserved for ghosts and bed sheets. It's so pale that it's almost the same shade as his silver matted beard. The dried blood in his wrinkles exaggerates his pained expression and glues him to the floor. The few rays of light seem drawn to him as well. This man, and the horrific moment trapped in his eyes, become tattoos on my already-stained soul. His agony will surely remain with me until the day I die. Which, *hopefully,* won't be today.

I have to shake it off and get back to what brought me here. I try compensating for the low light with the rest of my senses, except in this rotting place, they're useless too. The only smell is death. The only sounds are of the rough claws scratching against coarse skin. As far as touch goes, since everything is covered in decaying flesh, they all feel the same way too; wet and slimy.

In short, this place is *overwhelming.*

It's virtually impossible to do anything in here. When I mistakenly move one toe an inch too far, it knocks over an entire stack of bones! Since I'm not immediately eaten, I have to assume that the rattling of bones is not an unusual sound around here. I force myself to keep moving while trying not to make any more stupid mistakes. That means taking one cautious step at a time during my search of the mangled bodies. It's an extremely slow and very disgusting process, because there's barely enough light to see a few inches past my nose.

Examining these mounds tells me several things about the Eutherians:

1) Nothing that comes within miles of this cave lives.

2) All who come here die horrible, fiendishly gruesome deaths. Huge pieces are missing as if they were pulled apart for sheer entertainment.

So, the deeper I get into the massive chamber, the more I fear what I'm gonna find. I can't help it. Sort through enough severed arms and legs and you will, too.

Finally, after who knows how long, a single clue floats in while I'm elbows-deep in what, I think, used to be a baby deer. I catch only a brief whiff of the undeniably sweet smell of berries and honey, but even the faintest scent of something pleasant is startlingly out of place in here.

I immediately drop the slab of meat to follow the heavenly fragrance, off wherever it may lead. That turns out to be a very distant rear wall where absolutely no light can reach. Back to where only the sweet smell will be able to guide any me any further.

Without eyes, I have to feel around in the shadows. It's mostly the same old slime and gore, except for the one thin crack that leads off to who knows where. My heart pounds at the thought of blindly following the scent into a hole that's barely wider than a barstool. It won't stop me, but my inner voice is going hoarse from all the shouting.

My hands cautiously lead each apprehensive step I make away from the main chamber. After reaching the first corner, the narrow tunnel abruptly opens up, which this is somehow much, much worse. Without being able to touch both walls, I suddenly find myself hugging every rock to slide along. Half the time, the darkness is smothering; other times, I'm floating in a vast abyss. It's a nerve-wracking rollercoaster that's far too reminiscent of the last time I was buried alive.

It helps to pretend to pull myself along with an invisible rope. The imaginary life-line allows me to cross the black pool in search of the elusive berry smell. Other things begin to appear in the suffocating darkness: a bullseye, my purple bastard of a parakeet, an old remote-controlled truck, several bouncing soccer balls; whatever my worried mind can fill the emptiness with. My imagination paints the blank canvas with memories so vivid that I would swear I could go pick them up. In fact, I walk toward an actual beam of light for almost five minutes before figuring out that it's real. I had just assumed it was another one of those random things my brain had spat out. But no, it's an actual, real, colorful ray of light! Eventually enough of them join so that I don't feel as if I'm suffocating anymore.

My lungs ache from filling with the first breath they've had since entering the long hallway. If I weren't already, I would be breathless after seeing all the magnificent lights dancing along the walls like magical red, green, and blue fairies.

One thing's for sure, they're the life raft my sanity needed to pull me back ashore. I will follow these mystical creatures wherever they want to take me. Although they don't lead far, and end up going to the last place I ever expected… A river of gold spilling out of a dreamlike doorway. Waiting inside are stacks of coins, gems, and treasures piled so high that I have to climb to even get inside the dazzling room!

Why would this be here? What good is this to creatures that live as the Eutherians do? They're animals! No, that's an insult to animals! These things are straight out of a nightmare's nightmare! Then, the obvious truth hits harder than the brick wall from earlier. A shark is always a shark. While all these creatures used to be men, locked inside those grotesque heads are the uniquely human cravings for wealth and power.

I scoop up a fistful of the glistening fortune. It's a fascination that I confess I've never really understood. I suppose it's been easy to avoid since I'm paid by the pound, and profit margins aren't high in the squirrel game. Still, as the shiny treasures slip through my fingers, I begin to understand it a little better. One piece really catches my eye. It's an intricate golden owl that dangles playfully on the end of a twisted chain.

Dru loved owls.

I remember Mom redecorated her room for her fourteenth birthday. It suddenly went from bland yellow walls to having chubby owls everywhere; stickers on doors, the colorful outlines of a tacky bedspread, porcelain figures watching from their place on high bookshelves, and they all stood just as proudly as this little guy. His broad shoulders flow effortlessly into the fiery ruby planted deep in his chest.

I raise him to the light and watch the entire chamber burst into glorious red flames. The fire spreads quickly from coins, to jewels, to walls, and back again. I suddenly realize that I'm not standing on a mountain of gold, but atop *every dream I've ever had!* The possibilities fill my mind as fast as the coins fill my pockets.

My hands tremble from excitement. It gets so bad that my shaky fingers are knocking out more coins than they put in! Nevertheless, they methodically fill each pocket before moving onto the next. When there's absolutely no room left, I feverishly tie the arms of my jacket and load it up like a backpack. Instead of what could I do, what couldn't I do???

One thing I can't do is take it all in one trip, but so what? Who cares?!?! I can come back every day for the rest of my life! No one else knows about this place! My first purchase is going to be a replacement for that spring-sticking-out-of-the-seat ball-poking red scooter! I want something fit for a king!

A shiny statue unexpectedly tumbles to the ground while I'm loading my makeshift bag. I quickly rescue the treasure, only to find it's a graceful dancer craved from the purest silver. Pouring over her shoulders is a silky rose-colored dress that plunges down the slope of her deeply arched back. I admire the intricate craftsmanship it must have taken to sculpt such a wonderful work of art.

However, I begin to notice that the longer I look at the elegant outfit, the more it changes. How could my touch alter the silky gown so drastically?

The mystery of the flowing dress is only solved by peeling my fingers away from the thin silver waist. Left behind are long, juicy waves of red slime that drip down to the floor. It was never a dress at all, merely a thick coating of blood from my guilty hands.

The awful truth rushes in. My chest tightens from the realization that the gold I've lusted after has been mixed with the fresh remains of death. All those coins are glued together by an unholy mixture of blood and ripped flesh. The results of my greed have turned into a tormenting red river, steadily flowing down my forearm. Everything I've touched is now painted with bright crimson fingerprints! The long trails of gore that lead into each swollen pocket send me reeling in horror. My disappearing balance, along with a wildly spinning room, turns the wickedness I was so blind to into all I can see.

Those devils bring their prey here to devour on top of a mountain of gold. This new comprehension causes the self-loathing and toxic disgust to explode in the pit of my stomach. I begin flinging the bloody coins before ever thinking about the consequences. In a more rational state of mind, I would know better. They're bouncing off the tight walls and making such a ruckus that every bat should immediately be drawn here. How there isn't a swarm by the time the last coin drops is a total mystery.

And the worst is yet to come.

I finally find the little girl lying on a dense pile of treasure. Her young chest has been split right down the bloody middle. The only piece not covered with splatter is her innocent face. The image of these monsters feasting on her, like the cherry on a shit-covered sundae, has a physical effect on me.

If you've never seen vampire vomit, trust me, it's not pretty. Collapsed in a puddle of cherry-red puke really forces me to digest (for lack of a better word) the bitter unfairness of it all. These abominations have lived dozens of lifetimes, while she didn't even get to live one.

I grip her cold fingers and try taking comfort in the fact that her expression never changed. Her haunted eyes don't show even the slightest hint of pain. If nothing else, the trance kept her from suffering. I brush the loose strands of hair away from her face, then gently close her eyes for the last time.

There's still no way she could ever be returned to her family. It's best for them to remember her how she was, not like *this*. The only good to be found in this dark moment is the fuzzy brown bear next to her. Sure, it might be a silly thing, but it helps to know that he will always be with her. No one should die alone. Thanks to her fluffy friend, she never will be.

Sitting in a puddle of vomit, clutching the lifeless girl, is not the way this should've ended. My emotions sway between hatred toward an unfair world, and grief for a family that will never heal from this, with a bit of self-loathing thrown in for good measure. You would think after all these years I would be better at accepting defeat. After all, that's just who I am. But holding another failure in my arms makes every one of those old scars bleed again. Even the motivation to escape seems missing in the face of this latest disaster.

That is until my ears pick up the one thing you never want to hear in a place filled with death.

Breathing.

Chapter 6: Thief in the Night

Buried in the dark, inky gloom are long chains of slow, torturous breathing. Have they been here the entire time? Did they just show up? I guess it doesn't really matter—they're here now. All that's left is to remain still as a corpse and listen to the silent visitor.

My monster, on the other hand, is much less patient. He's already rattling his cage with the idea of going out in a blaze of glory and dead bodies. The only way to restrain him is by pointing out the obvious differences between this gentle breath and the choppy Eutherians. They snarl and snort in very disgusting ways. You can actually hear the wind swirling through the crushed bones of their faces. The breathing I hear is calm and smooth, without any of that nastiness. So, this leads me to believe it has be something else. Hopefully, something with a lower rage-to-fang ratio.

The intrigue lures me closer to the gloomy shadow, instead of scrambling for safety. Hidden somewhere behind the thick blanket of darkness is the source of all this gut-wrenching inhalation. I do take a few precautions, you know, just in case I'm completely wrong about this not being a giant bat. Mostly by wedging myself against a heavy box that should give me the necessary footing for a quick exit. Then, I have to sit and patiently stare into the unforgiving void. After allowing my eyes a few minutes to adjust, a vague silhouette begins to form. It's a thin shadow that seems eerily darker than the rest. Neither of us budge while waiting for the other to move. It sits with saintly patience, but I'm releasing enough sweat to form a small river flowing down my back.

I eventually break our stalemate by tossing a large coin at it. (What can I say, patience has never been my best trait.) The heavy treasure manages to land without causing any visible change to the steady breathing. This consistency gives me the courage to lean in a little closer so the dancing lights can be used to help piece together a more complete picture. And though I can't make out the exact details, it appears to be a silent girl leaning against the rough cave wall. That's it; I've completely lost the desire to move any further.

Or blink.

Or breathe.

My hands can't decide what to do, either. One is balled into a tight fist, while the other is reaching for the nearest exit. They're completely split on my upcoming fight-or-flight decision. That is, until our standoff comes to a very abrupt and unexpected end when my (apparently not well) anchored foot slips one of the loose piles of coins. It sends me tumbling toward the very last place I want to go—toward the girl. We end up as close as two lovers preparing to kiss. So close, I can taste the leftover apple skins on her breath.

Somehow, none of this causes the statue-like girl to budge. If this display of grace didn't move her, nothing will. I decide to throw caution to the wind by practically dragging the mute kid out into the light. At first, it's by the ankle, then wrist. I'm practically carrying the petite girl in my arms by the time she makes it all the way out.

Her eyes have the familiar blank stare into nothingness. She doesn't appear to be nearly as young as the girl who brought me here. If I had to guess, she looks to be in the awkward age right before full adulthood. Most likely around seventeen or so, but with soft features that make her seem younger than she is. The real giveaway is her hands. They have the rough pads of a person who's had to work to survive.

Everything about her is a simple kind of charming. While her outfit is nothing fancy, just a humble beige dress, she makes it seem far more elegant than it really is. One thing's for sure, she wasn't taken in her sleep like the last girl. Her outfit is far too proper to have been something she was simply lying around the house in. It has the appearance of a formal uniform without any of the identifying badges. It also offers zero clues as to where she might have come from.

I brush loose strands of blonde hair away from her face. They barely reach the tips of her shoulders and have recently been done up in soft curls of a special occasion. While she's dusty and covered in dirt, there's not a single claw mark on her! It appears, against all odds, she's completely unharmed! Her unbelievable condition leads me to believe she did not arrive here via wing or talon. So, how then?

In any case, one mystery gets solved. Drifting up from a shirt pocket is the same sweet smell that led me here. Squirreled away is a small batch of candied blueberries that had been tucked away for a later time. I remove one to lightly dab on the tip of my tongue. Its sugary skin is a welcome distraction from the oozing disgust of literally everything else in here.

"Hey! Can you hear me?" Whispering in a low voice, *"Are you in there?"* Snapping fingers are followed by a swift slap across the cheek. The only results are long red smears across her face from my bloody fingertips and a huge guilt trip for doing so. A growing sense of urgency raises my voice to a muted yell, *"Hey! Seriously kid, it's time to wake up!"* She remains a breathing statue.

She might not have been the one that brought me here, but nothing will keep her from leaving with me today. After all, something good come has to come from this. My heart begins hammering out a new kind of anxiety. This one is from the reserved optimism that's rapidly spreading no matter how much I try to contain it. That hope, combined with nerves fraying faster than a thread on fire, begins a new chain of rushed events.

I swallow the last of the sweet berries whole. It's a shame not to be able to enjoy the candied treats, but I can't spare the precious seconds it would take to chew them. Next comes the unenviable job of grabbing another pile of disgusting goo to cover every inch of her soft skin, so she'll be just as disguised as I am. The foul mixture has a texture somewhere between warm yogurt and decaying vegetables as it glides on.

The final step is throwing her over my shoulder like a rotten sack of potatoes. This results in one very unpleasant "smoosh"ing sound, as all my sensory organs die at once. I thought you were supposed to go "nose blind" to smells after a while? Well, that definitely hasn't happened.

I start stepping lightly but swiftly over the river of gold to avoid another clumsy slip. By the time we make it back to the dark hallway, it's even worse than I remember. My eyes start trying to fill the deep emptiness with the memory of all the vibrant colors they saw locked inside the treasure room. The light ghosts keep me moving in all the wrong directions. Every step seems to lead into a hidden wall or other unseen object. It gets even worse when the hall opens back up again. I stop running into things and get so completely lost that I end up heading back toward the gold river again.

After course correcting for the fourth time, I eventually find myself in the tight squeeze leading back to the front room. The girl in my arms has to be cradled like a child to squeeze us both down the narrow hallway. I seem to find _EVERY_ stray rock while attempting to fold myself into increasingly difficult shapes. My first priority has to be keeping her vulnerable face away from the jagged rocks. The best way to do that is to lead with my shoulders. Several potential scars later, the full-body origami ends and the exit is in sight!

...or, more accurately, isn't.

Even though freedom is right around the corner, it might as well be a thousand miles away. A raging storm has devoured what little sunlight we ever had. It also took away any remote hope we had of making it of here out alive. The once-empty cave floor is now filled with giants, sifting through the scraps.

I stagger back into the shadows to finish my not-so-mild panic attack. _Ugggggghhhhhhhh..._ think... THINK... _THINK!!!!_ Leaning against the wall is the only way to keep my numb legs upright at this point. It feels as if the entire lower half of my body has abruptly gone missing.

So, what now?

Outrun them over a ground of shifting bones? _No_

Retreat back to the treasure chamber? _No_

Fight my way through? _HELL NO_

There's no world in which any of that works. I don't stand a chance by myself, let alone protecting an unconscious girl.

DAMN! DAMN!! DAMN!!! SHIT BALLS!!!!

Descending further into the cave will only lead to me starving or being eaten. I've barely seen what's prowling around back there, and we can't simply stumble around, hoping to fall out of a hole.

Unless?

No...

Well, maybe???

In theory, a merge would allow me to know this cave as well as they do. I could swallow enough memories to navigate us to some secret exit or unknown tunnel. Sure, I might lose my mind from having to experience several lifetimes of unspeakable horrors at once. That could certainly be an issue. Plus, it's not like I'll get to pick and choose which Eutherian memories to take. I'll get all of them. Do I really want that becoming a part of me?

Yes.

Yes, because it's the only chance we have. I've got plenty of bad rolling around in there already, so what's a little more? Every drop of blood that's passed these lips has left a scar. People, animals; all of them are a part of me now. Of course that's led to some pretty bad merges before. Some of them have even screwed me up for an extended amount of time. It can be as small as picking up a bad habit, or completely life-altering on a foundational level. You don't just get memories; you get beliefs, values, and emotions as well. Sometimes it's a struggle to keep from becoming a totally different person. But compared to becoming bat food? Well, it's time to quit debating and just deal with the consequences later.

So, how do I actually make that merge happen?

First thing is to free up my hands. All that takes is planting the girl in the darkest place I can find. So dark that it might be tough finding her again. Next is to locate one single bat away from the group. Far enough that a little noise isn't going to bother anyone. My eyes won't be able to help with any of this. All they see is patchy blackness and a bunch of shifting shadows. Certainly nothing worth risking a blind jump.

I creep slowly along the edge to listen to the rustling herd. Even sealed in their wings, they leak all kinds of disgusting noises. Trying to focus on one turns out to be impossible since they're absolutely *EVERYWHERE!* Every direction is the filled with the sounds of scratching rough skin, crunching bones, high-pitched squeals, flapping wings, cracking jaws, tearing meat… *Aaaagggghhhhhhhhhhhhhhhhhhhhhh!!!!!*

I CAN'T DO THIS! It's like being trapped in a field of crickets, while trying to pick out a single one! My monster demands to fight through the giant herd of devils. He insists the exit isn't too far for him—of course his plan doesn't include the girl. She'll be fed to the bats as a diversion. No, I need to stay smart. Wait and be patient. Realize that I'm not looking for a sound in the crowd, but for sound in the silence. I need to find a place without any noise at all. My mind begins by constructing an imaginary grid over the blank ceiling. Instead of tackling the whole thing at once, I'll work through the smaller sections one by one. This will help break the problem into pieces that are *much* less overwhelming.

At first, the boxes click off slowly. Five becomes ten, ten becomes twenty, after twenty-two, each one raises my pulse a little higher. I have to pause at thirty-three when the sound of my heartbeat gets louder than the bats.

*One.   Two.   Three.   ...*relax and exhale.

Eventually, all the way in box fifty-five, is the sweet sound of silence I've been desperately searching for. I pause to wait for the most important part before getting my hopes too high.

1.   2.   3.   4.   5.

Damn.

6.   7.   8.   9.   10.

DAMN!

The lump seals my throat closed to any air that might want to come visit.

11.   12.   13...

On lucky number thirteen comes a single stream of labored breathing.

It's my single cricket.

I let another minute pass before declaring total victory. When no other sounds pop up on either side, I decide it probably won't get much better than this! I want to take advantage before the winds of chance can shift again. This is good, as my monster was already steadying for the jump.

He shuts off the entire world except for the sound of isolated breathing above. His focus is so intense that I can hear the hairs vibrating on the bat's upper lip, feel the tips of his jagged claws dragging against his course, leathery skin, even taste the meaty remains spilling from the corner of his bloody mouth. His grinding teeth give me a good target to aim at.

A quick flick of the ankles sends me straight up toward the hanging devil. Midway through the jump, I flip over so my feet should land on the ceiling next to him. The extreme lack of light makes it impossible to know how well I've actually accomplished my goal. And while it doesn't have to be perfect, the closer it is, the quicker the kill should be. I start frantically reaching out as soon as my feet touch the stone ceiling. Call it luck, or maybe fate, but waiting at the end of my fingertips is a thick batch of bristly hair.

HELL YEAH!!!!

It takes unbelievable willpower not to release my bottled-up enthusiasm. Since shouting would certainly lead to a super quick death, I decide to direct all that energy into holding onto the leathery sack of skin for dear life. My priority has to be finding his mouth. He can't be allowed to make a single squeak, let alone one of those damn banshee wails.

I'm going to go ahead and assume the hole my thumb slid into is his mouth. Actually, since several rows of jagged fangs are currently biting into it, I know it is. The resulting pain causes me to release a muffled cry that shouldn't alert the others, but signals the need to work a whole lot quicker.

One arm clamps around the jaw to keep it quiet. The other rips through the thin wing membrane. Both hands sink into the rotten flesh far enough to grab the slimy bones and organs hiding inside. Unsurprisingly, the big brute begins bucking like a wild bronco to fling me off. When I dig in deeper to keep hold, he fights back and my fingers have to sink in further. So far, he's still attached to the ceiling—I just don't know for how much longer.

I have to go ahead and bite down on whatever's in front of me. Of course, when the teeth slide in, his feet release. The countdown to finish the merge has officially begun.

His curdled blood triggers a tidal wave of unrelenting emotions that absolutely rip through me. First comes the anger; feelings so penetrating that they attempt to paint over me with his rampant fury. Then the memories flood in and shit _really_ hits the fan.

The year is 1734. His well-to-do childhood begins in a proper London borough. Burnt coal from the nearby train yard is permanently rooted in the fibers of his wool jacket. In spite of a privileged life, he suffers from a debilitating speech impediment that separates him from the rest of the boys. This one small difference will make him a perpetual outsider and mold the rest of his isolated life.

In a flash, the smooth sensation of plush velvet envelops me. It tickles my toes and shortens my breath. I lay in a luxurious maroon room that's scarcely lit by the oil of a dying lamp. My naked body is spread out over an indulgent bed in a secret brothel. Crawling up to me is a seductively exotic woman with dark lips. She's bound by a tight corset that draws her waist into a perfect hourglass. Her wanton eyes declare their boldly wicked intentions.

My muscles quiver at the sight of the raven-haired beauty. _Every_ piece of me longs to be captured by her dangerous seduction. When her strong, supple lips lock onto mine, they set my body on fire. Her delicate fingers slowly trace my inner thigh and hurl me into uncontrollable fits of pure ecstasy. The buttons of my ruffled shirt sail away from the force of her tug. I'm suddenly enveloped by the syrupy-sweet smell of lavender and jasmine as she pulls me into her heaving chest.

Before I lose complete control, she shoves me back down into the cavernous pillows. Her strong hands are applying a firm constriction to my throat. She lures me further into her world of seduction with a fingernail gently tracing my wanting lips. Carefully hidden behind her sly smile is the reason I'm here... Waiting impatiently is the sharp point of an extended fang. It will surely bring the power I crave.

I've sought out this stunning woman because she has the power to transform men into *gods*. I'll never again be the scrawny man with a broken tongue. The delightful pain of her bite launches me into a brand-new memory. This one is at the base of a golden tree. Leaves are drifting along a cool autumn breeze.

Then another.

And another.

My feet now teeter along the edge of a precariously sharp cliff. Far off in the distance is a menacing storm that's as purple as an October plum. Every few seconds, electricity lights it up like a beating heart. It hangs menacingly over a sprawling town made of glass. Above it all is a burning red sky.

The memories are starting to fly by without rhyme or reason, like papers scattered on the wind. Time is jumping randomly across a lifetime that spanned hundreds of years. Some of the most vivid are recent ones from his life in the cave. And yes, hunting after a wounded elk is just as disgusting as you would imagine. The images of fresh kills have my monster salivating enthusiastically. I'm used to his voice in my head, but now there's an unwelcomed third—the devil bat. Between it and the gluttonous monster, there's hardly any room left for Hayden Flynn.

I come out of my head long enough to see us hurtling toward the ground in the real world. Not that it matters much; I'm totally powerless to do anything about it. My mind seems to have come completely detached from my physical body.

The internal power struggle only allows me to aimlessly drift from one memory to another. This time, landing in a calm summer day with a lumpy pile of fresh mud. My hands are dirty, but the girl across from me is absolutely covered from head to toe. Her messy mop of hair is pinned up top like a spiky pineapple. She's shoving a cracked plastic shovel in my face, insisting that I fix it. Her glassy eyes warn me of the sad consequences if I can't.

Wait, I remember this day! That mud-covered girl is Dru!

My brain can't control the mammoth excess of information being dumped into it! The walls separating my life from his are rapidly coming apart! I'm *remembering* far too many new memories at once! Since only the deepest, harshest emotions stay with you, those are the scars I experience. Several lifetimes of love, pain, and tragedy are condensed into a single wave that sweeps me up and washes me away.

Chapter 7: Bat Out of Hell

Loose flaps of leathery wings are plastered to the side of my face when I finally come to. They're the direct result of a plan gone tragically wrong. It's safe to say the idea to merge and run has gone laughably bad. Well, it would be funny if I weren't now trapped underneath a prickly sack of warm jelly that hasn't bathed in a hundred years. Oh, and the awful memories are still clicking by like old films.

There's no way of knowing exactly how long I was out. Probably not long, but long enough to have gained a small crowd. I can hear the other bats stumbling around the body lying on top of me. They're poking at the fleshy meat sack as if it were an overflowing piñata. At least they don't seem to know about me—yet.

The ruthless memories make it hard to concentrate on anything other than endless blood and guts. No matter how disgusting I believed Eutherians were before, experiencing their intense pleasure while hollowing out the carcass of a dead animal takes it to a whole new level.

Ahhhhhhhhhhhhhh!!!!! My thigh burns from an errant talon sinking in right above the knee. It releases a sharp scream that—if they weren't onto me before—obviously lets them in on my secret. The thumping claws begin picking up both their speed and brutal force. It also appears that my shelter is quickly disappearing now. The sound of crunching bones and ripping flesh ignites a panic like no other. The only thing I'm certain of anymore is my desperate need to escape Meat Mountain.

But then what? I'll be balls-deep in a horde of cannibal monsters! On a slightly positive/relevant note: the merge did allow me to know several other ways of getting out of here. Although, actually reaching them might be the hard part.

Another claw tugs at my right shoulder. It's not close enough to cut, just provide the needed motivation to begin the trip back to the tunnels. They're not very far, and it might be possible to bottleneck the bats in the entrance. It's more of a *really* bad idea than actual plan, but it's all I've got.

I quit wasting time and hurl the remains of the big bastard into the air. The force of the shove, combined with how little is left of him, sends pieces flying off in every direction. The surprised creatures scatter away from the ruckus for a brief moment. This is probably the closest I'm gonna get to having any kind of head start.

Sure enough, before the bloody bits even land, every corner of the room explodes in ear shattering cries. The repeated screams hammer into the base of my skull like rusty nails. The pressure feels as if it wants to burrow out from underneath my eyeballs. It also causes me to have to crawl on my hands and knees over to the girl.

My mad scramble for her has to begin before even reaching the wall. I scurry around in complete darkness, trying to grasp in every direction at once; slime, bones, rocks, and *eventually* soft cotton! I tug at whatever my fingers have found, then take a quick glance at the forming wave of Eutherians ready to crash down. They're already stacking on top of each other to create a solid wall of impending death.

It appears my head start is over.

With only a loose grip on the dangling girl, I have to just charge into the tight corridors like a raging bull. There's no time for safety or caution with the herd closing in so quickly. We have to bounce wildly from wall to wall while attempting to stay driving forward. Of course my eyes are still doing their part to fill the darkness with gory pictures of several ruthless murders. There's an endless slideshow of severed limbs and slaughtered people playing on repeat. The worst part is the sick joy that comes with every kill. I feel an irrepressible smile stretching across my face.

HOLY HELL! THIS HAS TO STOP!!!

It's bringing me *thisss* close to feeding myself to the bats, just to get the twisted memories to stop! The only thing that keeps me going is the weight of the girl on my shoulder. Her life saves my sanity from going straight over a cliff. It's *right on the damn edge,* but still...

The brutal images, bubbling fear, and constant banshee wails burrowing in my brain complete the trifecta of misery. I can only shout back and run harder. Somehow the physical pain of crashing into the walls helps me to deal with the rest of the mental madness.

When a violent pounding starts in the center of my chest that isn't wall-crashing related, I have to assume the lifeless girl is awake and beating me with her fists. The violent drum solo helps to loosen my already insecure grip. As a result, she tumbles away and all my fumbling hands can do is cling desperately to whatever they can find. That ends up being a handful of cotton and what might be an upper thigh. It could be an ass cheek for all I know, but I'm going to have to just keep holding on and running!

"PLEASE, PLEASE, PLEASE STOP KICKING ME!" my lungs explode from shouting at the wiggling girl. I doubt it will do any good, I can't even hear myself over the bat screams. I yank the petite girl in closer, *"Seriously, kid, you gotta stop! I'm the good guy!"* and she kicks harder than before. Not that I can blame her, I would be shitting myself if my ass weren't puckered so tight.

With no real hope of calming her down, I simply pin her against my chest so she *can't* move anymore. A few bruises are better than becoming bat food. And there's no need to check how close the monsters have gotten—their nipping claws say more than enough. Occasionally, one will grab hold of my jacket and cause a hiccup in my steps. There's nothing I can do but try to charge on through the dark a little faster.

Momentary relief comes in the form of an extra-sharp twist in the tunnel. We happen to ricochet forward while the pack gets tangled in a mess of twisted bodies. They clog the narrow tube and the delay allows me to find a better grip on the girl. While rearranging her, I notice some of the screams behind us are shifting to cries of pain. It seems the vile things are so frantic to continue the chase that they're chewing through the fallen front line. But it doesn't matter, we're so close to the exit now that a faint light is cutting through the void.

I can finally see the terrified face staring up at me. Her innocent blue eyes trigger a brand-new memory that consumes my world. This one begins with the pudgy smile of a newborn baby. His soft pink cheeks are wrinkled into two round dimples of joy. He's a bundle of perfection wrapped in equally impeccable white linen. His hand-carved wooden crib looks oddly out of place in the cold steel room we're in.

Gathered around him is a diverse crowd of important-looking people. All of them are decked out in spotless uniforms and perfectly pressed suits to showcase their important status. They're undoubtedly mutts; they all have a permanent smirk of arrogance and vampire cologne (AKA blood).

This has the distinct feeling of being a marvelous occasion. One of those where only quiet conversations and polite compliments are allowed. Everyone takes their turn hovering over the small child. If they're planets, he's the sun. All of them are gathered into tight groups except one lone man, and he's a crowd all to himself.

His broad back is turned so all I can see is a smooth, bald head and rich chocolate skin. The dark leather coat over his broad shoulders perfectly reflects the bright over-head lights. His solemn mood doesn't seem to fit the casual celebration, either. He never even touches the baby, only stands in trance-like adoration over him. The child responds with a confident stare that's far beyond what a new born should be capable of.

Their unspoken bond seems to ignite something in both of them. The baby's vibrant golden eyes shine unlike anything I've ever seen. They bristle with what appears to be an almost electric spark. The power radiating from inside him is as undeniable as the blistering sun on a hot day.

Then I discover the disturbing truth in the face of the woman next to me. What I originally took for admiration, is actually concentrated terror. The false beauty of this fake place melts away instantly. It suddenly feels as if the entire world teeters along the crumbling edge of a steep cliff. Whatever this kid is, he's something alarmingly new.

A stray rock unsympathetically rips me from the unfolding memory before I get my answer. Even in the dim light, I can see the considerable chunk of shoulder that's gone missing. The rock's jagged teeth have bitten off more than enough to leave the useless arm dangling by my side.

The girl still won't quit struggling, and now, with only one good arm available, she's quickly slipping toward the ground. I have to awkwardly twist around to regain even a loose grip. At least I can actually see her this time. I manage to wrap a hand up in the folds of her dress before she makes it all the way to the floor. This move has left me running backward while barely clinging to her with my one good arm. There will be no pulling her up, or even turning around, so I have to remain focused on merely getting us through that exit. We've gotten so close that daylight is tickling the hairs on the back of my dangling arm!

Running backward while dragging a pissed-off kid has allowed the bats to make up almost all of their lost ground. Several sets of eyes and claws have already begun snapping eagerly from the black void. The growing light gives the kid her first real glimpse of the creatures chasing us. Her reaction is to try to kick the tenacious devils away. That makes it even harder to keep a grip on her.

The frustrated bats unleash several more war cries, each filled with spit, rage, and large chunks of freshly-chewed meat. From this close, their breath is almost as bad as their mind-piercing wails. Almost.

I slide sideways to bring a foot down on the skull of the lead bat. It drives his face into the rocky floor and begins a new chain reaction of bodies flipping end over end. As before, the beasts are torn apart by the more eager ones in the back.

But no matter how fast they chew and tear, it won't matter. We're so close to the exit, I can lock my arm around the girl, then hurl us toward the sunlight! As we burst from the jagged mouth of the cave, a whispered named echoes down the halls of my mind, "Samael."

Only a few rays of light are brave enough to pierce the pregnant storm clouds. They bring with them the Eutherian's most captivating memory yet. Overlapping the bright sun is the warm, happy face of the infant shining down, his pudgy cheeks folded back into two wrinkly mounds of pure joy. Concealed behind his captivating smile, just barely poking out behind thin lips, is something that will change my life and our world forever.

A subtle little fang.

Chapter 8: Misfit

Time and space warp chaotically throughout my fractured mind. While my body is free to soar from the mouth of the cave, my brain is still struggling to live in a reality where a pure-blood vampire can actually exist. The shock of seeing the tiny fanged infant has thrown me into a world without sound, gravity, or physics. It allows me to casually drift along, floating weightlessly in the swirling wind and rain.

There are times in life when you know everything's changed. That *everything* that comes after this will be different. You know, the famous "where were you when" moments? Well, this is one of those.

Clinging to the girl becomes a forgotten concern during my suspended animation. She drifts away freely as the cave, and all the horrifying beasts trapped inside, slowly fades into the distance. All that remains now is my inevitable meeting with the solid ground.

Slammmm!!! My bones rattle off the hard rock floor. Naturally, it's my mangled shoulder that lands first. That's immediately followed by the girl collapsing my lungs under her full weight. Every ounce of oxygen squirts out, and life zooms back to full speed with a thunderous new fury. Breathing is suddenly as useful as sucking on a collapsed garden hose. The harder I try, the less it works. I'm stuck alternating between the exasperated heaves of trying to regain the missing air and fighting against the images still playing through my faulty vision.

And if I weren't already breathless, after seeing a rogue Eutherian bust out of the cave, I would be. He soars from the hole like a jail broke lion. His wings unfold into massive walls that hurl a flurry of rocks while hovering directly over me. The dust doesn't bother me much, but the pebbles shoot out like miniature baseballs that leave behind instant bruises.

Even with my eyes covered, I can tell where the beast lands. His considerable impact slams down just off to my left side. Unfortunately, I can't see much more than a vague outline due to my double vision. It appears the nightmares in my head are visibly overlapping with all the real-world terrors. Of course, this means I can't really see *any* of them well. The one thing that's becoming abundantly clear is the large amounts of steam rolling off him. The sizzling water gives him a look that's an odd combination of anger and confusion.

It gets worse when blisters begin appearing all over his body. Even through the driving rain, his dark grey skin has become a disgusting patchwork of puss-filled sores. The wounds rapidly fill the air with the revolting stench of boiling flesh. My unfortunate opponent is obviously suffering from the Eutherian death ray known as "the Sun". Even the heavy storm isn't enough to shield him from its poisonous effects. The only mystery is, *why isn't he running for shelter?*

"You need to take your gross ass back into the cave." As soon as the words "gross ass" leave my confident mouth, hateful canyons carve across his brow. They begin over his stubby nose and stretch all the way down around a deeply scowling mouth. Puffs of white smoke steadily pour out from between the cracks in his peeling skin. And absolutely none of this affects him; he hasn't flinched or backed down in any way.

I believe my overconfidence might have been a bit premature. And exactly one second later, I'm proven right in the worst possible way. The giant bat ignites as if drenched in *gasoline!* Where there was smoke, there's now an all-consuming blaze devouring his entire body! Those giant wings have become nothing more than mountains of flames soaring in the air! And yet, still, none of this makes him run, scream, or even break the unflinching gaze he's held on me the entire time.

Instead, his response is to smother me with another one of those concussive roars. My ears throb from the sonic hammer bashing against the insides of my skull. This one feels far different than all the others I've felt today. It's filled with the defiant rage of a cornered grizzly bear.

Now I've seen a lot in my extended life, and many things have tested the boundaries of my courage, but absolutely *nothing,* prepared me for the sight of a flaming giant hurtling down on me. A seven-foot-tall, twenty-foot-wide, burning tower of meat with a death wish and vengeance in his eyes. It's more than enough to make me reconsider all the terrible life choices that lead up to this horrifying moment.

The fiery martyr's first attack is deadly fast. His piercing claws miss, but not by much. His flames reach out to nibble my shoulder as they pass by. The glass half-full part of this is that his momentum sends him sliding pretty far down the gravely mountain. From here, he resembles a drunken bear trying to stand back up. His clumsiness gives me the extra time to either find a rock to throw or maybe bury in the side of his thick skull. Unfortunately, my busted shoulder refuses to let me lift anything larger than a softball. I assume that would only piss him off, so we're not off a great start here...

Well, at least I'm not on fire.

The tide turns when the brute attempts to fly. Since the thin skin of his wings were the first to melt away, he can only fall clumsily out of the sky. He has to settle for a lightning-quick jump to make up the extended distance between us. Without much time to get away, I throw myself on the ground to compensate for the wounded arm. The plan was to use my legs to absorb most of the impact—which would have been a wonderful idea if the fiery bastard didn't crash down like a speeding train. It's sudden, violent, and everything you wouldn't want it to be. He lands so hard that my knees shoot all the way up past my ears.

Now he's got me pinned down with massive weight and a bad attitude to match. I'm having a hard time doing anything other than merely keeping the snarling, biting fangs away. And they aren't my only problem, either. The all-consuming flames are snapping like rabid dogs every time he moves. They wilt my skin and fill the air with the smell of burnt hair. When I mistakenly reach into the blaze, the searing pain quickly forces me to reconsider.

I settle for some good ol' fashion knuckles to his melting face. I'm not going for bone-breaking power this time around, just pure speed. My fists dart in and out before the flames can do any more physical damage. The result is each punch sinking a little further into the disgustingly soft flesh. Burning hunks of meat fall from the bone with every new blow. My knee-jerk reaction is exactly that, a donkey kick that sends the howling creature flipping up the steep mountain.

Even on the brink of death, he manages to land on his feet. Those oversized claws are digging a deep trench that helps to slow down his wild, uncontrollable slide. The farther he goes, the deeper it gets. He's almost buried up to his thick waist by the time he stops.

Waiting at the end of the ditch is a crazed bulldog, hunched over on all fours, sitting inside a self-dug crater. Even with one eye missing, he keeps his hateful gaze permanently fixed on me. The smell of burning, rotten skin makes it unbearable to breathe around the roasting bat. Not even the driving rain can make it through his impenetrable flaming shell.

Only a crackling whisper leaks out when he releases another war cry. The sound gets lost somewhere on the way through his flaming throat, likely due to the missing skin revealing all the exposed muscles underneath. The muscles twitch and quiver as the flames lick them. He spreads his once massive wings and they're barely more than a loose web of bones anymore. Even though flames have chewed throughout his *entire* body, he still won't stop! That thing craves *my* death more than his own life! It's hard to imagine having sympathy for something actively trying to kill you, but watching his leg muscles snap like guitar strings is heartbreaking!

This needs to end.

Now.

I immediately charge the hulking monster. Not wanting to repeat the scalding mistake from earlier, my shirt will be used for the flaming head this time around. That should save me from the fire, but not those damn swinging claws. Even though both eyes have already melted away, I have to flip over his backside to escape them! I use one long motion to tear off my t-shirt and wrap it around the burning skull. From there, I whip his skull back and forth savagely, trying everything possible to either break it, or pull it off his damn shoulders. My fingers sink in far enough to reach bone, and still, nothing works! No matter how hard I twist, pull, heave, or snap, those infuriating claws never stop trying to find me!

I grab the scorched shirt to use as leverage to flip the son of a bitch over my shoulder. The only option left is to end this with my bare hands. What follows is an intense release of every emotion built up during my trip through Hell:

The **FEAR** of standing at the icy mouth of the cave.

The **ISOLATION** of wading through the darkness.

The **DISGUST** of the treasure room.

The **HELPLESSNESS** of failing the lost girl.

The **HORROR** of endless stolen memories.

The **INCREDIBLE** sight of a baby that shouldn't exist.

All of it is discharged in a relentless barrage of bound fists. By the time it's done, my hands rain spilled blood over the tainted ground. And his head, still wrapped in my shirt, is hardly recognizable as ever having been human. My arms can't even lift after I'm finished. All I can do is watch a steady stream of fresh gore pour off them. The cave behind me growls from the angry beasts locked inside. They hiss and grind their anxious claws against the stone walls. If another one escaped, all I would do is lay down and die. I barely have the energy to flip them off—but I power through it anyway.

My extended grin (and finger) brings a frustrated growl that makes me believe they can still understand insults like this. The oh-so-satisfying moment is cut short by a stray flicker of cotton streaking in the corner of my eye. The flash turns out to be my rescued girl hauling ass across the mountainside; her burlap dress flapping in the wind. Then, just as abruptly, she's gone... over a damn cliff.

Chapter 9: Run(away)

After this, *ALL THIS,* and it ends like *THAT?!?!*

I can't even.

I MEAN, REALLY???

Words escape me. My level of disbelief is so great, my mind can't even comprehend what my eyes have shown me. Honestly, I'm too stunned to move.

It takes an uncomfortably long amount of time to get moving again. And even then, the rugged landscape makes it hard to hobble across the mountainside quickly. While the broken body is indeed challenging, what's really holding me back is the fear of what's waiting for me over that edge.

The anxious butterflies multiply with each step toward the steep cliff. Eventually, the ground runs out and leaves me standing alone at the end of the world. There's a sharp line at my feet that divides life into two things: mountain and sky with nothing in between. I have to force my apprehensive toes up to the unsettling edge. My mind is desperately searching for any excuse not to look over into the abyss. Surely there's something to delay this inevitable meeting with the truth?

Sadly, no.

It's time.

Past time.

My eyes begin on the rolling horizon and slowly work their way down. I purposely start at the furthest mountain so my eyes can cross the range slowly. My neck turns so gradually, it's hardly moving at all. Needless to say, it takes a very, very long time to finally reach the bottom of the steep cliff. But what I find there is easily the last thing I ever expected.

Of all the possibilities my panicked mind had invented, this unbelievable reality was *certainly* not one of them. Thunderous laughter rolls down the valley from my shocking discovery. Their echoes make it sound as if a chorus of angels are chuckling along with me. My girl is, *somehow,* only a few feet below the sharp cliff face, lying face down in a soft sand pit! Her arms and legs are spread wide as if I've interrupted her in the middle of making snow angels!

My deep belly chuckles quickly draw the wrath of the dusty girl. She rolls over to look—and by look, I mean stare *daggers* through me. "Stop... *spit*...why...*spit*... why are you laughing at me?" she pauses occasionally to wipe clumps of sand away from her mouth.

As terrible as it sounds, not even her scolding look or hateful attitude can hold back my uncontrollable amusement. I *really* can't help it! I want to, but physically can't! All this extreme relief is just coming out as irrepressible laughter! In my defense though, I fully expected to find her at the bottom of a jagged ravine! And now she's gonna walk away from this with nothing worse than a scraped knee!

"Stop it!"

"Damn you, stop it!" She cries in a grief-stricken voice.

"I'm sorry! *Whew...* I mean, I *really* am sorry, but the way your arms flew up in the air was just so funny! They were all *WHA WHA WHA* and then you were gone!" My arms reenact the cartoonish way she disappeared over the cliff. Her bottomless scowl makes it clear she doesn't appreciate the visual aids as much as I do. "See, it's funny now that you're not all splat!" This crude explanation only makes it worse.

I'm the first to admit my sense of humor suffered arrested development around the ripe old age of thirteen. No matter how old I get, it always seems to keep failing the seventh grade. In fact, it takes several more minutes of letting the laughter out before even making another attempt to collect myself.

And when I do, I feel like an absolute dick. The petrified girl is folded into a tiny ball in the pit, utterly consumed by fear, and crying so hard, she doesn't make a sound. While I've been laughing, she's been spiraling down an emotional hole. Why wouldn't she be??? Who knows what kind of torture she's been through? The parts I know are bad enough; waking up in a cave with a complete stranger, being chased by giant man-bats, sharp claws snapping out of the dark in her face, and when she finally escapes, a bat bursts into flames on top of her! No matter how well intended my self-serving laughter was, all she sees is an asshole.

If I had a tail, it would be tucked between my legs. Since there's no possible justification for this amount of cruelty, I simply slip off the rock and slide down in the pit. My injured shoulder makes the brief trip an especially difficult one. The overly clumsy entrance does cause her to raise up long enough to give an uneasy look before cowering so far away, she might tip over.

I'm not totally sure where to go from here. My hands remain awkwardly frozen until—after a lengthy internal debate—the decision is made to gently lay one over her exposed shoulder.

She snaps, *"Leave me alone,"* the moment my fingers touch her sweaty skin.

"Please know I didn't mean to be so cruel. I was just so overwhelmed with relief, it came out in a really odd way. You see, I really thought you were a goner when you went over that cliff."

"I *should* be..." she sounds hollow inside.

"You don't mean that. It's all right now, you're safe."

In the saddest possible way, she responds, *"I know."*

Her bulging neck muscles begin to relax a little bit. She's also not leaning quite as far away as before. I take the fleeting opportunity to give another heartfelt apology. "I really am sorry for laughing at you. I never meant any harm." This display of genuine sincerity finally brings us face to face.

There's an undeniable vulnerability in her flushed cheeks. Never-ending tears have washed long canyons beneath her eyes clean. Hidden underneath the thick layer of dust is a patch of honey-colored skin that's as flawless as still water. I try sweeping the wild curls away from her drawn face, but it takes several more attempts before they finally agree to stay away. The unfortunate result is a much better look at the fear locked in her eyes. They appear heavy and sunken, as if the weight of the world might be carried behind those shiny sapphire disks.

After this comes an unexpected calmness, like a wide valley between two rising waves. There's a wonderful serenity that comes from sitting side by side while not expecting anything more than silent understanding from one other. Time passes and we don't say another word.

We don't have to.

She's noticeably anxious at first. Her feet begin tapping at a frantic pace before settling in to a steady, clock-like rhythm. We stare down the mountain, listening to the hypnotic beat for what seems like a lifetime. And while I know time is not all that relative (it's a rigid set of defined points that pass by at the same rate), when your only source of stimulation is a comfortable melodic beat... I end up drifting off into some strange place where minutes refuse to move along the way they normally would.

I'm free to bounce from one incomplete thought to the next. My brain is desperately searching for a solid place to land, eventually settling on her. I try to imagine her story; what terrible things has she been through? In the single hour before I found her, what could have possibly happened??? How did she get all the way up here without a single scratch? That's a question I intend to ask of her, just not right now.

She's shaking due to the drizzling rain and merciless wind. The only help I can offer is by wrapping my tattered jacket over her exposed shoulders. I do my best to keep the bloodiest parts out of sight. She snuggles into the coat and, consequently, me. Her unintentional touch warms my skin like a campfire on a crisp fall night. The gentle heat melts my worries away for a moment of much needed relief.

Gone are the fears of monsters trapped only a hundred feet away. My throbbing body, with aches and pain pretty much *everywhere,* goes numb. Best of all, the horror show that had been playing in my head simply dissolves. Everything is wiped away from an unspoken moment with a complete stranger. The most surprising part of all this, is that it's not surprising at all. It just feels natural.

She comes up briefly to scan the valley before strong winds force her back under the jacket. Looking at the emotional girl is even more heartbreaking for me now. Her lost expression becomes a moral dilemma I must solve. Is she searching for something? Home, maybe? It's not hard to imagine she could even be from the Points. Honestly, I know maybe three people in the whole damn Colony.

My imagination is eventually forced back into the dark cave. Its particular brand of torture is something I'll never be able to completely wash off. They say there are things you can never un-see... well, today I've had my fill of them. The most unbelievable would have to be the tiny fanged infant. Could it really have been a pure blood? It's been over a thousand years since one of those walked among us, and he's become a legend for all the wrong reasons. Sure, the books had most of it wrong, but he definitely had an insatiable lust for power and a superiority complex that's been passed down the bloodlines ever since.

The girl's cough breaks me from my contemplative mood. I'm not sure if I fell asleep or simply floated off into a hazy limbo. Judging by her glazed-over appearance and the jacket wrinkles pressed into her cheek, we must have fallen asleep, or at least she did. "You okay, tiger?" It's a pretty generic question that should be enough to break the ice. Gazing at the ground, she timidly says, "I shouldn't have yelled at you."

"Trust me, I deserved it. I tend to have that effect on women." The lame attempt at a joke doesn't make her react in any discernable way. Her eyes are still permanently glued to the colorful pebbles by her feet.

Even though moving is the last thing I want to do, we can't afford to go another round with those bats. We need to be safely behind big steel walls by the time the sun goes down. I stumble to my feet, "You probably already know this, but it's time we get off this mountain. I'm sure you're just as anxious as I am to put this place behind us. What you think? Ready to get out of here?" She reaches her hand up, so I'll assume that's a yes.

The shivering girl is still wrapped in the coat that's two sizes too big, and her knees are knocking like a baby deer as I help her up. Between her wobbly legs and my wrecked shoulder, it may be easier for us to roll down this mountain.

"My name's Hayden," I offer as we set off down the trail. After a few silent minutes I continue, "So, what's your name?" She digs her tiny hands way down inside the coat pockets to answer softly, "Quinn."

Chapter 10: Back from Hell

The monolithic Colony walls have never looked so good. Sure, they're still the same crappy old metal, but they now shine with an almost angelic glow. All the patchwork panels, over-protective guards, lingering smell of freshly caught salmon being prepared over a cedar plank fire; absolutely everything is perfect!

The proof is in my huge smile as we round the last set of pine trees. I can already hear the bells ringing at the end of Tin Pan Alley. Everyone going about their daily routine helps me get some mental distance from the cave and all its horrors. While the warm evening sun won't make those memories disappear forever, it does help me see the brighter side of life. Like the fact that we made it here. Making it back was something I didn't believe would be possible on several occasions today. Also, the walk home has been much easier than I thought it would be. So, that's something, I guess.

Quinn has barely spoke two words since we left. Truth be told, she hasn't even spoken one. I have a feeling that a large piece of her has been left up on that mountain. I can relate, it certainly kept a lot of me (and my shoulder) as well. The worst part is that we aren't even far enough away to know just how big these scars will be yet. Time has a way of revealing even the most well-hidden of wounds. See, another advantage to living a hundred years is that hindsight doesn't reveal single mistakes, it shows long trends. One I've noticed *repeatedly* is that my deepest scars never come from where I think they will. All the real damage will always come from an angle I didn't see coming.

The horrific things I've felt today, not just seen, but experienced up close, will haunt me for life. They're the kind of enduring terrors that I'll catch in the stray reflection of a passing car. Maybe I'll see them crawling around in the very darkest shadows. One thing I can guarantee is that those creatures will sneak up every now and then in nightmares, and they'll be so terrifyingly real that I'll wake up to check under the bed for them. While I may have physically escaped, I'll relive this day many, many more times to come.

While my heart debates the philosophical implications of today, a more real-life problem comes in the form of two silhouettes on top of the left tower gate. They're huddled underneath the same tattered blanket to ward off the early evening chill. In the milliseconds it takes to communicate the image to my brain, I already know who they are. It doesn't take enhanced abilities, or even the common sense God gave a squirrel, to know what they want from me. They believe Quinn is the missing girl I went in search of.

They believe I've brought their daughter back to them.

My throat seals at the sight of them. The air is still in there, it just can't leave, and nothing new is allowed in. I would gladly welcome the small delay of a guard search right now. Where are the extensive security scans when I actually want them? Instead, the rusty old gates swing open immediately. My heart wants to beg for forgiveness while my head says to run screaming back into the woods. My body splits the difference by doing absolutely nothing. When the excited couple rushes through the doors, all I can do is stand there.

Speechless.

Useless.

There's already high-pitched squeals of joy coming from the woman. I would gladly take the banshee wails of the demon bats over these unnerving cries of delight. At least they could only hurt my brain. Her happiness rips the heart from my chest, stomps on it, slathers it in humiliation, and shoves it back in upside-down. The man, on the other hand, is stuck in the kind of wide-eyed amazement usually saved for the best moments in life. Both hurt in equally terrible ways.

They believe I'm the answer to their desperate prayers.

They *believe* in *me*.

My heart pounds so hard it hurts, breathing is only a distant memory, my silent mouth has gone bone-dry, so now what? What words can possibly explain that their daughter is *gone!* Her lifeless body will be trapped with those monsters *forever!* How can I possibly say *that???* My lips part to spit out some meaningless words—something, anything—yet nothing but gut-wrenching silence comes out. Although, like I said, the truth always finds a way out.

Even in this excruciating moment.

The man is the first to realize, and he melts like a candle. I don't know if he meant to stop running or if his legs simply quit working; either way, he staggers to a hobbled stop. Decorating his face is a look of disbelief that will enter my personal hall of shame as one of its biggest trophies.

The heartbroken man reaches out to grab the lady without ever turning away from Quinn. He's twice her size, but can barely contain her hysteria. She shouts frantically, "What are you doing!?! What's wrong with you??" while pushing harder than his trembling arms can handle.

What's wrong with him? That's a question with a very simple answer. His only failure was me.

She continues to plead even when he won't let go. He *can't* let go. He's eventually able to reel her close enough to listen to his broken words. They're too soft for me to hear, and that mercy will, *easily,* go down as the best thing to happen today.

He's turned a ghostly shade of pale that exaggerates his swelling eyes even more. Despite his best efforts to hold them back, large tears have forced their way through his blockade. They tumble down and collide with her outstretched arm. That's when the runaway train finally strikes Mom. It begins by freezing her frantic fingers, then quickly sweeps through the rest of her. All her agonizing screams are cut off so abruptly, only a haunting echo remains. Her hands eventually release his crinkled shirt to turn and see the awful truth for herself; this time, without the hopeful eyes.

The bone-dry dirt crunches underfoot as she pivots. I hear the spit gently pop from her mouth falling open. Despite the man attempting to hold her up, the broken woman collapses in front of us. All she does is sit there staring at Quinn as if her eyes will eventually show her something different.

Quinn turns to me for some kind of guidance. She's obviously shocked by this unknown (to her) turn of events. I hadn't told her about the other girl. The one whose parents are lying in a puddle at our feet.

The one whose name I will never know.

The one who...

Ughhh! STOP IT! STOP IT! DAMMIT, STOP IT!!!

Quinn scoots behind me to shield herself from the emotional firestorm. I still don't have the words to make the failure hurt less, so I do what I do best—run. Race through the open gates to leave another devastated family in my wake. Because this is all I know how to do. Fail, then run.

And I don't stop until I'm far enough away to release a violent scream that will hopefully help chase away some of the smothering failure. Then I drop to the dirt, clutch both knees, and let the anguish really pour over me.

"What happened?" a confused Quinn asks from above.

"They..." a huge lump prevents more words from escaping for several minutes. When the words finally do make it out, they sound as if I've gargled rock salt. *"They thought you were someone else."* My disgrace is so obvious that she doesn't ask any more questions. She simply puts her hand on my shoulder, in the same place I did on that bloody mountain, as I grumble almost silently, *"This has been a bad day."* Maybe saying it out loud will make it better.

It doesn't.

I allow myself to wade deep into the murky waters of failure. All the shame that had been carefully tucked away into the farthest, most forgotten parts of my soul, rushes back out to mix with this fresh disaster. This dark place is one that I'm all too familiar with. It may have been a while since my last visit, but it slides back on like a comfy pair of shoes. The only difference is the girl with her hand on my shoulder; she still needs me. I have to put this behind me until it's over, then I'll have the rest of this endless life to swim in gloomy failure.

See, I told you it would be from an angle I never saw coming.

Once the difficult choice is made, I flip the switch that's both a curse and a blessing. On the outside, I'll smile as if nothing happened, but inside, I'll pick at the scabs just to feel them bleed again. So yeah, it's time to dry my eyes, paint on a pleasant smile, and get out of the damn pool.

"My bike is back at the bar," I finally say. This new confident voice is a total departure from mere seconds ago. "It has a first aid kit we could both really use." She doesn't say a word, although her confused expression says plenty. The abrupt switch is hard to understand for anyone who's not me. Trying to explain it would only make me look like a bigger psychopath, so I just put my arm around her, partly for comfort, but mostly for support, and set off toward the bike.

I clumsily transition, "I know this place where they make the best boardwalk fries. Seriously, they're as big as carrots! They fry them in peanut oil, so hopefully you're not allergic? Also, they frown on the use of ketchup, so don't ask. Vinegar is the only way to go anyway. Apple cider vinegar." I ramble on and on, over-emphasizing every word to re-emphasize my own sanity. She gives me the look of a confused girl who's trying not to freak out. Can't blame her though; it's creepy to me, too.

I'll explain it this way: when I was fourteen, I was walking to the courts to play basketball. An old family friend, named Huggie Bear, just happened to be driving by, so he offered me a ride. As soon as we got in, I noticed something unusual, "Bob," I said to the driver, "you don't have a rear-view mirror." The man straightened his dirty baseball cap, looked me dead in the eye, and answered very matter-of-factly, "Well, we ain't drivin' backwards."

Maybe I read too much into it, but something about that stayed with me. He probably wasn't trying to make some grand metaphysical statement on how to live your life. Most likely, he was just a whole lotta crazy, or too cheap to replace a broken mirror, but it was a message I'll never forget. He's the reason I keep going forward, even if I'm not very good at the "not looking back" part.

Chapter 11: Living for Two

I quickly make good on the promise of two orders of the largest fries known to man. We immediately drown them in about a gallon of very pungent vinegar as soon as they're handed to us. There's a common misconception that vampires can't eat regular food anymore. Bullshit. I would've run a stake through my own heart if I couldn't occasionally munch on a New York-style cheesecake. It's only because I like the taste though; it doesn't "feed" me anymore. The vampire virus keeps my metabolic rate so high, I'm basically running on overdrive all the time. That's also where the advanced senses and strength come from.

The downside to this "gift" is the virus literally eats me alive. Red blood cells are the fuel driving the virus, and they're broken down so quickly, a fresh supply is needed almost every week. Of course, how often I have to feed depends on how hard my body has to work. Luckily, I fed last night, so the bruises should be gone by sundown. The deeper cuts will probably be simple scratches tomorrow. With any luck, the shoulder should be useful again in a couple days. Long story short, all this healing will leave me needing to refuel much sooner than usual, maybe just a day or two.

I'll enjoy these fries now, then sneak off later for the real stuff. There's no need to shove the worst parts of my life in Quinn's face. She doesn't seem to be in a huge rush to tell me where home—or anything else—is. There's also a new discomfort between us that won't go away. She wasn't talkative before, but there's definitely an air of coldness to her now.

Adding to the fun are all the heads we're turning from simply walking down the street. People are staring at us like we're made of diamonds. This one is understandable, though—it's pretty obvious we've been through something pretty tragic. We're both covered from head to toe in the most disgusting stuff imaginable. As far as I'm concerned, we can't reach the bar fast enough.

Since the word "quick" is not in my current vocabulary, due to a bruised body and sore legs, I'm growing increasingly impatient with the gawking public. The budding tantrum builds, and builds, and builds, before finally erupting all over the next poor guy that looks at us the wrong way. My (completely mature) response is to hurl the remainder of my fries at the next condescending prick that looks at us the wrong way. They ricochet off his shocked face, sending salt and vinegar splattering absolutely everywhere.

Sadly, the simple act of tossing french fries hurts so bad that it leaves me bent over, on the verge of tears. Quinn busily apologizes to the man, saying everything possible to keep me from getting my ass kicked. She must have a silver tongue, because he finally agrees to walk on after exchanging only a few bad looks.

That's probably a blessing since I wouldn't have been much of a challenge in my current condition. I'll need to check my bruised ego if there's going to be any hope of making it all the way back to Pandora.

My priorities need to be:

1) Beer

2) Not getting ass kicked before getting to beer.

After ten more minutes and dozens more judgmental stares, the dirty old bar shines like a beacon at the end of the alley. There's Ol' Red, still parked out front where I left her. I don't remember taking up two parking spots with the stubby bike, but it is what it is. At least they haven't towed it. I suppose they wanted to see if I made it back first?

It actually doesn't seem to have been touched at all! She's still packed with all the random crap and meager camping equipment I came here with. It seems there was nothing worth stealing, I guess.

"Aspirin?" I offer, digging for the first-aid kit. It's best to be prepared when you spend as much time away from civilization as I do. There's a flimsy sling (which I've used far more times than I care to admit) for my busted shoulder, iodine for our numerous cuts, and the last two aspirins in the tin box.

Without being asked, she snags the sling and quickly sets my separated shoulder. She has a delicate, yet firm motion to pop it back into place. Then she wraps it tight and secures it with medical tape. I'll admit to shedding a few tears during the process, though it's not because she did anything wrong. I fell out of a tree once (tip: don't drink and hunt) and I was convinced the doctor cut off my arm and beat me with it. Compared to that, her treatment is a dainty bee sting. Most surprising is that she does this all without any guidance. This is obviously not her first time around a first-aid kit. What a little box of puzzles this girl is turning out to be.

I reflexively joke, "You want some hard liquor to wash down those pills?" She replies in a deadpan voice that makes it hard to tell if she's joking or not, "I really do."

"Oh... well, um... yeah," I stutter without knowing what else to say. "Well you're in luck, I happen to know the bartender!" I purposely over-exaggerate to hide my sudden confusion.

Swinging the familiar double doors open reveals all the changes since I've left. The collapsed side of the building has become a fresh wall of sloppy plywood. It looks pretty hastily thrown together from whatever they could come up with. Most likely a temporary solution to protect against late night shoppers. Half the tables are already stacked against the wall to make room for the real construction to come. The crowd is understandably small and Shepherd is in the middle with a partially-folded blueprint. "Doing some remodeling?" I shout.

He whips around with a wide-open jaw, "Flynn? Where have you been?" He then works through the mess of tables to bear hug me. I'm pretty sure he isn't, but it feels as if he's trying to break me in half. I growl through gritted teeth, "Aggghhh, easy there, champ... broken shoulder and all."

"Oh, my fault! I wasn't paying any attention!" He apologizes emphatically, and since I don't want him to feel like an ass, I play off the throbbing pain as merely a flesh wound. With crooked brow, he dives right in, "Why would you go after a Eutherian? Don't you know how vicious those things are?"

Trust me, I do, and although this would be the perfect chance to explain my day in graphic detail, I don't take it. There's no need to stifle the little bit of personality Quinn is starting to show. "Ha! Yeah, I followed it back to the nest and found this young lady here." casually gesturing to Quinn. "Shepherd, meet Quinn. Quinn, Shepherd." I scoot back slightly to give him a look that says, "no questions". This obviously isn't the whole story; not even close, but it's the only version I'm comfortable sharing right now.

"Yeah," he offers an oddly brief response. He's still smiling politely, even though there's a thick undertone of uneasiness surrounding him. He has the pale look of a man who's seen a ghost. A BIG ONE.

I hesitantly ask, "Have you met before?" trying to get to the bottom of his abrupt mood change.

"I'm sorry. I don't believe we have." He snaps out of the strange funk to offer Quinn a charming smile. "Shepherd Roberts, but my friends call me Shep," and reaches for her hand. Apparently, whatever crawled up his ass found its way back out again. Quinn obliges, so he leans down to gently kiss the back of her hand.

"Wow! Is it my imagination, or did it just get very Victorian in here! Smooth Shep for the win! I didn't know you had it in you, Mr. Roberts!" I joke while struggling to throw my one good arm around him.

"How about you kiss my ass. Better?" he proclaims with a snide smile.

"Well, you see, I have a problem that only you can help me with, Sir Roberts! I have this aspirin here and nothing to wash it down with. I'm sure a man like you can understand." I grab dramatically at my forehead.

"Of course, my good fellow! A round of drinks for this noble knight!" He commands in a pretty damn good English accent.

"Thank you, squire!" I play along, "Squire? Is that the right word here? It means you're a noble, right?"

"No," he answers. "A squire was the knight's trainee. You basically just called me your bitch."

"Oh. Well, then I stand by it!" I nod with an extra-wide grin. Shepherd laughs and squeezes my good shoulder before excusing himself. We take the opportunity to make our way over to one of the few remaining tables. Running my hand across the bruised tabletop is surreal. All the dents bring a swell of emotions ranging from grateful to utterly ashamed.

A tiny man interrupts my reflective mood to get our drink order. Now the mystery of my (possibly) young alcoholic friend can be solved. "What can I get for you folks?" he summarily asks.

My request is simple, "Let's start with two big amber ales. And please, whatever you do, don't let me see the bottom of the glass for an hour."

"And for you, ma'am?" he motions to Quinn who has sat down next to me—very close, actually. "Coke, please," she responds. So, her drink comment was just some kind of weird comedic timing? It appears her sense of humor might be as odd as mine. Looks like we should get along just fine!

Several minutes later, Shepherd makes his way back over with drinks in hand. He sets each one down on a little coaster that I really don't understand the point of. I felt the deep gouges in the table myself, so what kind of damage will a few drops of beer do? It's exactly the kind of thing I would normally use against him, but I put all jokes aside when he asks for the full story.

I spit out a roughly edited version of our trip through Hell, with only quick mention of the first lost girl. Quinn has a perplexed look that shows she's actively putting this story together with the events at the gate. Thankfully, it doesn't cause her to shy away from the conversation, or retreat back into her shell at all. In fact, she actively participates in the recap; stepping in to describe the flaming bats in a way that paints me as the hero. Given the events at the gate, mountain, and my life in general, that's a role I'm so uncomfortable with that I chug the rest of my beer and then half of Shepherd's.

Chapter 12: The Memory Remains

By the time I rejoin them, I'm in just the right mood to begin a very lengthy rant against the gruesome cave of devil bats. It doesn't take long to figure out that the wounds are still a little too fresh to carry on anything close to an actual conversation. All I'm doing is railing on while repeating the same basic idea; they should all be burned the ground.

There's an excitement to the idea that catches on with Quinn, but appears entirely lost on Shepherd. His total indifference only spurs me to try harder to convince him of the danger living a few mountains away. "Oh, and I haven't even told you the most astonishing part yet! I merged with one of the devils—long story there—and buried in its horrible life was the memory of an infant vampire! A true pureblood baby!"

This news doesn't seem to affect him the way I expect, either! When I found out, it was like a bomb going off in my head! I was sure he would feel the same way, except the news rolls off him like water off a duck's back! Quinn's also tuned out a bit—since she's not one of us, I expected it from her—but not Shepherd! Increased frustration leads me to spiraling into even greater detail. Why is it so hard to get them to understand the impact this could have on the entire world?

I continue trying to describe the infant and group gathered around him. Trying to explain the strange atmosphere is the hardest part. Describing the conflicting emotions of watching him, and watching others watch him, is impossible. There was a complex mixture of love and fear that's hard to put into words. I finish the exhausting report with, "I guess you just had to be there." Hell, I wasn't there, but whatever...

There's still an argument stuck in the back of my craw. It's driving me nuts that no one else seems to care about this life-changing news! A pureblood vampire is living in the Titan colony! That's barely a thousand miles away! What do they not understanding about that? Sadly, the back and forth conversation never comes. I have to drown all the bubbling frustration with the glass of beer in my hand. It, like me, has become increasingly hot during m extended rant. The disgusting drink only pisses me off more on the way down.

After thirty seconds of full-on pouting, there's a firm tap on my shoulder. It's one of those aggressive full-hand-wrapped-over-the-arm kind of attention grabbers. It's likely that some nosy drunk has overheard our conversation and has an opinion to share. Since there's not much going on at our table, I'm tempted to hop over and hear his vodka-soaked observations. At least he'll have something to say about it!

I remove the hand before turning to greet him. Instead of one drunkard, what's waiting for me is a very large, very angry group of armored men. These aren't the wannabe town guards, either. No, these guys appear to be true bad asses. Their military-style uniforms range from black, to darker black, to darkest black.

The closest two are something even scarier than the others. Their outfits aren't freshly pressed like the rest, they're scarred and stitched as if they've been through a few wars. Even their aluminum faceguards have been decorated in uniquely intimidating ways. The farthest one has sharp flames crawling up his mask like a gnarled hand. They flow with the same buttery fluidness of real fire. Even his eyes are hidden behind the intense blazing inferno. The other one is far less mysterious with his appearance; he went in a more *"you're gonna bleed"* direction.

His entire head is encased in a molded chrome skull that would probably slice your finger to touch. Sharp creases run into snarling teeth that look more rabid wolf than human. Sitting above them are deeply sunken eyes glowing an intense cherry red. He continues the skeleton theme with a bulky chest plate of chiseled chrome ribs that proudly display dozens of unpatched gunshot dents.

"You really don't know what she is, do you Flynn?" Shepherd asks while dramatically gesturing toward the stunned girl. His voice elevates as if leading to the punchline of a bad joke.

"What *Quinn* is???" My response is almost laughed out. The dramatic number of guns in the room would suggest using caution with my choice of words, instead I ask, "Are you a princess running away from her loving, yet over-bearing father? How did you get out of your tower again, young lady?"

I'm the only one laughing.

I've clearly stepped into something bad involving Quinn. It seems, as always, I'm the last asshole to the party. I lean uncomfortably close to Shepherd, "She's a kid, that's what she is. I don't know anything beyond that. So now it's your turn to tell me who these men are."

The mood in the room turns to an uncomfortable fusion of anxiety and aggression. I can sense the hulks inching closer until Shepherd finally breaks the dangerous silence with, "You don't understand, my friend. She's merely a gift." His inviting grin has returned, and brought with it a slathered-on fakeness that weakly attempts to avoid the unavoidable. With his last words still ringing in my ears, Quinn leaps from the chair and slams herself into the solid wall of guards. "NO!!! DON'T TAKE ME HOME!!!" she screams hysterically.

Okay, so she's in on the secret, too.

Dammit.

This is clearly not some misunderstanding. That means this will only end in one of two ways: bad or worse.

As hard as she tries, the massive guards easily overpower Quinn. They begin by slamming her down hard enough to leave a steady stream of tears leaking onto the dented table. Welling up in her wide green eyes is the unmistakable look of desperation. She pleads through trembling lips, "Please, please, please, please, please, please." The guards answer with a smooth metallic needle that slows her frantic lips. Eventually, they stop for good, but the desperate look never fades.

My eyes dart back and forth between Shepherd and the girl. I know where my allegiance should be... I mean, I know literally nothing about her and he's one of my closest friends, but I've seen that look before. This is something beyond fear.

"Seriously, what's going on, Shepherd? Is this a kidnapping or something?" He straightens to the stiff stance of a soldier being called to attention. "You really do spend all your time in the woods, don't you, Flynn? Take a look at her clothes. How do you not recognize the uniform of Gas Light Colony?" His question seems more rhetorical than anything.

"They're human cattle that only exist to be what we need. Front line soldiers, body part donors, or—like this one—an offering to the Eutherians! We give them as gifts and the bats leave us alone." His fake charm is completely gone. It's been replaced by an emotionless stare and a matter-of-fact arrogance.

"Why are you giving those monsters anything at all??? They don't need to be pacified; they need to be destroyed!" I shout to anyone who'll listen.

He answers coldly, "I couldn't agree more, Flynn, but a few snacks here or there seem like a small price to keep our other Colonies safe."

"A snack? Are you serious? That's a *person* you're talking about! Dammit, man; it's a little girl! We fought together against this kind of sick shit! What happened to you, Shep? What happened to my friend?"

"Nothing." His face reddens with emotion. "In fact, I've been here fighting that same war, because it never ended for me! I didn't scamper off into the woods and ignore the problems we were stuck with." Resentment is thick in his voice. "You're too idealistic. There's no good, no evil. Only results—and those who get them are doing what has to be done. Can't you see we finally have it within our reach to change the world? This could all be over!"

"Well now, how the happy hell is feeding her to the devil-bats going to change the whole damn world???" I mockingly wave my hands in the air. Shepherd's eyes draw to narrow slits, "Not that insignificant flesh bag! Your problem is you could never see the bigger picture. All these things were temporary fixes; Band-Aids over a rotting corpse, until now. We finally have the real answer! You even saw it with your own eyes!"

I pause, perplexed, attempting to make sense of what he's said. "Wait, you mean the baby?"

"The pureblood!" his cruel grin stretches like a true madman. "Our future is behind Samael!"

"The Harbingers are already rebuilding this fractured world we've created. Have you shielded yourself so much that you can't see the obvious truth? Damn, Flynn, there are colonies that still hunt vampires as you do those dumb stags!" His energy suddenly drops, "Hayden, I'm tired of fighting..." trailing off from honest exhaustion. As crazy as the words sound, I know he believes every one of them.

The passed out girl on the table inspires me to point out the major fault in his logic, "How can you possibly justify the slaughter of kids? I mean you can hear all this craziness coming out your mouth, right?"

"Because I will make the tough choice!" He pounds the table. "I didn't go camping after the war! I put my hands in the bloody dirt to do the real work! People like you don't want to know how things really happen. You just want to go about your pathetic lives without ever having to peek behind the curtain. Peace doesn't just happen, it's bought with violence and paid for with spilled blood. Remember how it used to be? How the Eutherians would swarm at night? All that stopped. How do you think that happened? We asked nicely?" His new smartass tone takes a page from my playbook.

I have to laugh at all the righteousness suddenly flying around the room, "You're no peacekeeper. You're an asshole that feeds kids to monsters."

"And I will continue until the need is gone. Until Samael sweeps across the world to destroy creatures like Eutherians. You know we can't live like this, Flynn. This is your chance to become part of our rising tide. Samael is the phoenix that will burn this diseased world to its rotten core! And from those ashes will emerge a brand-new life! No more colonies, no more hatred, just one united world!"

I'm trapped in stunned disbelief from my friend's cold words. I plead with him, "Now, I won't argue this is a utopia by any means, but any world built on the bones of evil has no place for me in it. I'm asking you as a friend, Shepherd; look at what you're doing here. Look at that little girl over there... You showed me who I wanted to be. You were my example. Brother, this ain't it."

He doesn't even flinch. "You're wrong. This is my mission and I'll destroy anyone that gets in my way. That's who I am. That's who I've always been. Now, you get one more chance, as a friend, to finish this together." He reaches out for me to symbolically join him on his unholy mission. His fingers are deeply scarred, as a true hero's should be. They symbolize all the ugliness it takes to create the beauty of the world.

For a split second, my mind actually bends far enough for the words to make a perverted kind of sense. Killing is the very foundation of being a vampire. Of being me. I kill to survive, that's my truth. Then I remember the desperation in Quinn's eyes and don't care who he is—this is wrong.

"No, Shepherd, you can't justify the slaughtering of children. Everyone wants to get back to something close to happy, but how we get there matters. And building that road on the suffering of others is not an original idea. Neither is having hatred, greed, and rampant hunger for power disguised as naïve idealism. But coming from you? That's brand new."

My heartfelt words don't seem to move him in the slightest. Not even a sideways glance of self-doubt.

"You've made your choice. There's no other option because she's going back." Shepherd nods and the guards instantly rip Quinn off the busted table and drag her toward the door.

I can't let this happen.

I won't let this happen.

Before they make it outside, I flip the table end over end into the crowd. My instinct is to follow and punch Shepherd in his smug face, but my only goal has to be getting to Quinn. And the only one standing in my way is the flaming guard.

There's no obvious weak point in his heavy armor. He's padded from head to toe in thick metal that would only injure me to punch. The thinnest part is where I end up burying the widest part of my foot—right in his twig and two berries. The mountain of man collapses to the floor like broken glass. I can't help but chuckle at his head lying on the ground. His flaming facemask looks more like a calm campfire than it does an intimidating inferno.

As brief as it was, the laugh distracts me from seeing the chrome skull sneaking up behind me. He clamps onto my wrist—the injured one, of course—and painfully twists it all the way around. Every forceful tug feels like it's ripping muscles away from bone. He's still fighting to grab my other wrist, but all I really care about is stopping the searing pain carving through my injured shoulder!

There's no hope of actually pushing him away, so I spin into his padded chest instead. At least this way we're going to be face-to-face. He still has a solid grip on the bad arm, but I manage to create a little bit of separation by wrapping my free hand around his chrome skull, then, with all the pain-fueled adrenaline available, bring our heads crashing together. A monstrous thunderclap echoes across the entire cramped bar.

As soon as my skull cracks against his helmet, the world explodes into a brilliant display of stunning fireworks. Next thing I know, I'm lying on the tile floor, incoherently slurring, "Thaaat baaaad. Thatttt... that nnnot aluminum."

"Pure carbon steel, pendejo."

"Yeahhhhh." I'm not totally sure which of the three said it, but it's usually the middle one. Focusing suddenly becomes a minor issue when the other guard, the one with sore balls, yanks me up by the shoulder, "Agggghhh! Easy, you dick!"

Shepherd says with a touch of remorse, "I wish it didn't have to be this way. You need to understand that this is bigger than both of us." He then signals the flaming guard. By looks alone, I don't think this will end well for me. I don't have to see behind the mask to tell how extremely pissed he is.

In the background, I watch them drag Quinn out of the front doors. When flame boy grabs me, the only thing I have time to think is, this is gonna hurt.

Chapter 13: The Color Red

Ugggghhhhh.

All I smell is wet dog.

Where am I? Even though my eyes haven't opened yet, I'm already pretty confident I won't like the answer. When they finally do flutter open and my new surroundings come into gradual focus, it's just as I thought... I don't love it.

It's dark, dingy, and doesn't smell like the Points anymore. The flickering fluorescents are giving out a piss-colored light that refuses to stay lit for longer than a few seconds at a time. Despite the creep show lighting, I can make out three dirty brick walls, and a fourth that's made up of thick steel bars that have been generously lined with sharp spikes. There's also a small rusted pipe in the corner which I guess is supposed to take the place of a real toilet.

And that's all.

I spill out of the little cot to clutch my throbbing head. The sizable knot on my forehead is the most likely reason for the sensation of long drills burrowing into each side of my brain. That flame-skulled guy was a real dick! But, to be fair, I did kick him in the balls first. Still, he could have caused serious brain damage with a hit like that! Judging by the way I'm stumbling around my tiny cell, that possibility's still open. And it's not likely I'll be receiving much medical attention in here, either. This is the kind of place you put people to die.

Miserably.

The only view of the outside world is the miniature window right above the cot. It's heavily barred and wouldn't even fit a grapefruit through, so this certainly won't be my way out. Plus, life doesn't look too much better on the other side. The only thing out there is a rundown stadium that's a bizarre blend of Roman coliseum with a modern glass building plopped in the middle. Surrounding it are long rows of old benches leading up to large towers at each corner. The only lights in the entire place are the faint blue reflections coming off the sides of the shiny castle. Everything else appears to be made from old wood, steel tubing, dust, and tears.

The entire place seems to revolve around the glass castle. Every sign, step, and chair points directly at it. It sits in the center as the bullseye of this very large target. As for the building itself, it's constructed of dozens of glass rooms all flowing organically into each other. Its design could even be considered beautiful without all the noticeable blood stains. It's clear whatever happens in there, is absolutely horrifying.

"Hey, you in the box," floats in a mysterious voice from somewhere outside my cramped cell.

"Uh... yeah?" I hesitate. Since I've been in jail once or twice, maybe five times, I've learned there are two types of people in here: sheep and lions. So, I step up the macho game, "Yeah, what you want??" Too much, too much. Let's bring it down a peg. I try finding a more balanced tone between "action movie hero" and "don't shiv me in the lunch line" to ask, "I guess this is some kind of prison?"

The disembodied man answers in a thick southern drawl, "Nah. They jus' gone hold you 'til show time come round." Then I imagine the playground of death outside is the stage? Good times.

I half-heartedly ask, "When do the curtains go up?" Even though, again, I really don't want to know the answer.

"Sorry, son. Yours is right soon, I reckon." the brutally honest cellmate says. "You the guy that done stole that girl?"

I concede, "Apparently."

His thick accent makes some of the words hard to understand, but I believe he says, "Yeah, word moves real quick round here. Them bats is comin'."

I had a bad feeling that's where this is all heading. This leads into the next obvious question, "So, I'm in the Gas Light District?"

"Yup" he says very directly.

It's the kind of news that strikes like a lightning bolt to the chest. I fall onto the thin mattress to process exactly what all this could mean. The loud scrape of springs hitting the floor causes the voice to ask, "You okay in there?" My ears register his words, though my mind rejects the optimistic thought. No, I'm not "okay." I'm actually on the opposite side of the emotional scale as "okay."

So, I ignore the question and replace it with one that carries far less emotional baggage, "What's your name?" Mindlessly chatting should allow me to turn off my own bruised feelings for a while.

"Name's Bill, but most folk call me Brain Guy."

It's a struggle to keep my inner child from falling out of his chair with laughter. Seriously though, I doubt the faceless voice got his nickname from an extremely successful neurosurgery practice.

"So, why you in here, Bill? Did you have a failed rescue go ridiculously bad, too?"

"Me? Nah, I got sick s'all."

"Sick? That doesn't seem like a very serious crime." My joking tone is probably lighter than appropriate for our situation.

"You sure is one crazy sum' bitch! Means I can't be in them bloodlines no more s'all." He says this very directly, as if I should know what in the world he's talking about.

"I'm confused. Bloodlines? Like, they won't let you have kids?"

"Boy, ain't got nothin' to do wit them youngins. Can't feed them lords no more, s'what it is." Still very matter-of-factly.

I'm starting to think that the less I know about this place, the better. However, I need to know what I'm up against. Knowledge is power, so I probe further, "They won't let you feed the lords because you're sick? They don't want you touching their food?"

"Hell son, I *is* their food! The sick's in my blood so I can't feed 'em no more." He says all this in what is still a very carefree tone. My head sinks deep into my palms as I piece together what Brain Guy has laid on me. This place uses people as walking blood banks.

Fantastic.

On a good note: My shoulder seems to be working again.

On a bad note: Everything else.

My attention is suddenly drawn to the cell wall where the dirty bricks have taken on a bright new crimson hue. Even from here, I can tell where it's coming from. The sky outside has begun burning with an intensely deep-red glow.

"What's going on out there, Bill?"

"It's a Reckonin'." He sounds much more sympathetic now. "That family gone be put down."

WTF?! Quinn's family is gonna be killed because I saved her? How the $&@# does that happen?

I'm struggling to deal with the madness rapidly exploding like fireworks on the fourth of July. Bill's next words help to fill in some of the blanks, "Once they go, they don't come back. They gone make a learnin' of 'em." His voice never waivers; never drops. Nothing about this is unusual to him at all.

I leap up to the see the changes taking place outside the small window. The once-empty arena is now filling with people pouring into every single row. There are so many, there appears to be one seat for every two flooding in. Each one of them has an anxious energy, as if they absolutely cannot wait for what's getting ready to happen.

Locating the source of the burning sky is easy. There's a room in front of the glass castle that's completely lined with windows, like an announcer's box. Sitting on top of it are two enormous spotlights pointing straight up at the clouds. They are what's turning the entire thing into a thick, bloody soup.

I instantly recognize this.

It was the red sky from the Eutherian memory.

Some twisted trick of fate has landed me in the center of someone's stolen dream. Except he was on a hill overlooking the town, while I'm trapped in a box inside it. Plus, I have a feeling his storm was a totally different kind than the one getting ready to rain down over me.

There's a flurry of action occurring within the castle walls. It's awash with brilliant colors that help spotlight the various intricate rooms locked inside. They also better highlight the many stains adorning nearly every wall. The bloody puddles are left completely intact as a clear reminder (or trophy) of the sick things they do here.

None of the rooms are large and seem to connect randomly. However, after studying it a few more seconds, I notice the entire thing has actually been crafted with careful precision. While they're all different sizes: tall towers, narrow halls, square rooms... they all have one thing in common—destructive toys. Each has a mirror, metal cage, or spikes to entertain the bloodthirsty audience. There's no part of this thing that's not completely see-through. Not even the floors are solid. It's built to be a giant display case to highlight every sick twist and turn. They wanna make sure their viewers don't miss a single thing that happens in the human-sized rat maze.

Quinn is being led into the room overlooking the castle. I spy the familiar masked guards from the bar dragging her along. She's still fighting hard, even though the poor kid looks half-dead. It's easy to see everything happening inside due to the entire room being one giant window. The guards begin by securing her to a sturdy-looking chair that seems custom-built for the occasion. It's firmly bolted to the ground and features heavily worn streaks from all the unfortunate souls who've sat there before.

Standing behind her is another familiar mop of blond hair. Shepherd looks my way and we lock eyes for a brief moment. To my amazement, there's nothing left in his blank gaze. The man I knew, the man I idolized, is simply gone.

A greasy-looking chubby man, dressed to the nines, sits in prestige next to him. His pinstripe suit is already soaked from the sweat rolling down his neck folds. It appears he also slicks back his salt and pepper hair with pure cooking oil. The Governor of this fine Colony, I assume.

While I'm watching the spectacle unfold in the box, a small group of handcuffed people are led into the ring. They've been herded into a tight circle at the entrance of the imposing glass castle. Out front is an older man with distinguished-looking grey hair running along both temples. He's nervously holding a young girl that couldn't be more than eight or nine years old. The only thing I can really see of her is the blue velvet bow tied to a single brown braid. Everything else is buried underneath her dad's worn denim shirt.

Next to them is her mother, clinging as tightly as a person possibly can. Her grip is firm enough to bring light swelling to the father's arm. Behind them stands a barrel-chested young man doing his best to compensate for the biting fear inside. My guess is that he's not too far removed from his eighteenth birthday. While his strong jaw and stiff arms give an appearance of bravery, the trembling hands are a dead giveaway of how he actually feels inside.

The sight of them sends Quinn into a wild hysteria. Spit and water pour from her flushed face. She's ripping at the thick restraints to absolutely no effect. Her intense screams have forced large, bulging veins to the surface of her forehead. She eventually fights hard enough to pop several of the bolts holding her chair to the ground. The guards have to force her back down, but even they can barely contain all her violent convulsions. She's as hostile as anything I've ever seen; human, vampire, or edge-of-death wounded animal.

Almost lost in the chaos is an announcer babbling while the family is shoved into the first room. The steel door slams shut immediately after the last toe crosses the threshold. With the hallow clang still ringing in my ears, every light goes dark. A thumping heartbeat steadily pulses through the speakers.

It begins slow and steady...

Boom   Boom   Boom   Boom   Boom   Boom

   Boom   Boom   Boom   Boom   Boom   Boom

... building to a frantic pace.

Across the coliseum, feet are pounding with the pulsing beat. Large chunks of drywall are dropping from the worn-down ceiling of my cramped prison cell.

Hateful energy visibly leaks from the pores of every person out there. It reaches new heights of disgust when the towers explode into a massive display of fireworks, flames, and shredding guitars. New spotlights shine on the two men ruthlessly banging out the ear-piercing rock chords. Their spectacle helps build the crowd into an even deadlier frenzy. I don't know what to call these people... they're not monsters. As cruel as my monster is, these things are a different kind of beast.

Pure evil lives here.

Chapter 14: Rockin' A Hard Place

Outrageously dressed hunters begin making flamboyant entrances throughout the arena. Each one brings their own distinct version of hyping up the already fanatical crowd. Some do it by beating their chest like rampaging gorillas, one drags claws down the dirty glass walls, while others flip and tumble to show off their incredible athleticism.

And it works to a scary degree. Every face in the crowd has the same unmistakable lust for violence. They pound fists and stomp feet; smash into one another. The kids even hold up hand-painted signs with the name of their favorite hunter. These aren't killers to them; they're heroes.

After the showboating ends, the lights outside the castle disappear. This leaves only the glass prison to shine in the bleak night. The glowing floors flash with the beat of the music. One at a time, the hunters begin entering the maze through hidden portals. The pounding heartbeat slows as each one enteres.

Boom   Boom   Boom   Boom

   Boom   Boom   Boom   Boom   ....Beeeeep.

The eerie flat line is the official start of the hunt. The killers instantly scatter throughout the see-through behemoth in search of prey. Some are ghosts, slipping silently into hidden cracks, while others slam into walls and generally raise every kind of hell. There are many different ways to die descending on Quinn's family all at once.

The young man tries to move in front of the pack as they leave the first room. This, of course, starts a brief argument between the two men. As fathers are apt to do, he eventually wins and the son agrees to move to the back of the group. And that's how they'll begin the game, men surrounding the ladies, with none of them standing a chance.

The first couple of rooms are uneventful. They merely serve to take them deeper into the maze. It's not until the first of the giant towers that they encounter one of the hunters. He doesn't show himself at first, instead waiting up top for a concealed door to snap shut. It traps the family at the bottom of a very tall, but extremely narrow box. It's so skinny that they can barely stand next to each other or even turn around. Because the family is busy scrambling to pry the door open, they never see the man perched high above them.

Planted on a small ledge is a thin figure hidden in the deep shadows. His jet-black hair is pulled back into a tight bun that accentuates the laser-like focus he keeps on his prey. When he shifts, the back of his long black coat drops over the edge like hanging Eutherian wings. An eager grumble rises from the impatient crowd as he drops in silently behind them. His intimidating coat spreads across the floor in a perfect circle from the landing.

The audience stands with the hunter when he makes his first bold move. They hold their collective breath as the assassin calmly strolls up behind the unaware father. A gasp sounds out when the chrome sword is finally released from the sleeve on his back. He drops the tip of the razor-sharp blade to the ground and drags it along next to him. Every deliberate step builds the expectations of the anxious crowd. And all this happens while the family is still painfully unaware the killer is even in the same room as them!

Finally, like a shot in the dark, a piercing scream cuts across the arena to alert the family. The bound, but not helpless, Quinn was able to find enough voice to warn them through several walls of thick glass! Unfortunately, it comes a fraction of a second too late. The ninja was able to make a single slice before the father even had a chance to turn around. The blade sinks into the widest part of his stretched calf, and just as quickly, the assassin's gone.

In the brief amount of time it takes the man to hit to the ground, the silent killer is swallowed by shadows. The crowd roars with excitement. The entire arena chants in one voice,

"RINSHI! RINSHI! RINSHI! RINSHI!"

The assassin was never going for a kill. It's too soon in the game for that. His job was merely to draw out the family's torment for the fans. And it works; they're practically rioting in their seats for the would-be killer.

The doors spring open to release the stunned family before they can even comprehend what's happened. Dad is still helpless on the ground and only Mom seems to know why. The rest never even saw it happen! Mom's busy putting pressure on the wound while screaming for the young man. He's hastily ripping off the bottom of his shirt without yet knowing why. She then wraps the cloth tight enough to force the gashed flaps of skin closed. Although, from the serious amount of blood still spurting around the bandage, it must have been far deeper than I thought.

Dad doesn't let any of this slow him down. He's already struggled back up to his feet by using mom as a makeshift crutch. Their only change is that the brother has now moved into the lead position.

But why?

Why keep moving?

Why not hunker down and fight instead of playing their sick game? Is it a real maze with a finish line to reach? I have no idea, but they sure move like it!

They continue going from room to room with some kind of goal in mind. The young man moves quickly, albeit a bit more cautiously now. He makes sure to survey every room before letting the rest in. The little girl has been so sandwiched by the group, she really isn't visible anymore. Five rooms later, the young man abruptly abandons the family to run down a different passage. Waiting at the end is a stubby dagger mounted in a well-marked sleeve on the wall. It's been painted orange to draw even more attention to it.

So that's why they keep going! There are minor weapons hidden throughout! Probably nothing that could actually help defend against the supercharged murderers, just little slivers of hope to keep them playing along!

The young man's swell of pride is, unfortunately, short lived. He suddenly finds himself stuck between a rock and twin hard places. Specifically, the cramped walls and two maniacs tumbling toward him.

The twin hunters are frighteningly identical in every way, except one wears a jade green vest, while the other's is dark blue. They resemble circus monkeys with entire velvet outfits matching their ridiculous vests. Both are covered in the same scraggly red hair and lengthy beards. One of the only things not covered by the ginger straw are their piss-colored teeth and eyes.

The boy begins shouting frantically for his family to head back down the hall. Although, with the dad hobbled so badly, they're cut off before they even begin. The brutish cavemen tumble around the group like lions circling a wounded elk. The green one smashes off the glass in a show of strength or (depending on your point of view) insanity. His shoulder leaves a spider-web of shattered glass in its wake. The other unleashes a roar that would shame King Kong.

Together, they succeed in herding the family into the middle of the empty room. The bewildered people huddle together for some kind of protection from the snarling beasts. Only the young man remains standing and he's trying to blindly slash at them with that stubby dagger of his. Eventually, he manages to land a lucky cut across the blue gorilla's forearm. It appears to be a pretty serious wound that runs the entire length of his hairy arm.

That's when the young man makes the mistake of letting a smirk of confidence bleed onto his face. He feels as if he's really accomplished something here, except the wild man doesn't even blink. He simply pauses before using a long, deliberate motion to drag his tongue across the split flesh. Watching the beast enjoy the taste of his own blood is like watching a starving man relish every bite of a gluttonous next meal. The animal returns, cheeks smeared with crimson joy. At the end, he turns to give the kid a deliciously crooked smile with teeth freshly painted in the gore of the boy's failed efforts.

Damn.

Cold chills slither down my spine from this gruesome act of bravado. The crowd, however, *LOSE THEIR DAMN MINDS.*

They erupt in an earthquake of applause that shakes the very foundations of the arena. The overflowing malevolence has grown men fighting in the stands. Anything not bolted down, and some things that were, ends up tossed into the center of the ring. Whatever it takes to release their pent-up wrath is fair game. The beastly men feed off the crowd chanting their name, "Wild Bunch" endlessly. It fuels their extended torment of the young man. They spit at his feet and pound the ground to destroy the last bit of his youthful swagger. The roaring crowd and circling gorillas have left him a trembling shell.

That's when the boy defies logic to pitch his only protection, the small dagger, back to his father. He bolts down the hall, leaving the wild men as startled as the rest of us. Either the kid has lost his mind or there's some kind of genius plan in the works. I'm leaning toward the former.

The confused twins pause for a brief moment before storming after him. Everyone howls for the chase and upcoming kill. The Wild Bunch stomp down the hall, although speed is obviously not their strong suit. It allows the much faster kid to get some space before he ducks into a particularly harsh shadow. It's so deep that it must have been intended for the hunters to use.

The wolves split up to surround their separated sheep. The first one to arrive is the green twin, and he refuses to wait any longer for this victory, this kill. The entire arena is on its feet as the lumbering brute strides confidently into the shadow hiding the young man. Not a sound is made while they eagerly listen for the impending death cry.

Except it doesn't come.

The frustrated giant steps out from the darkness as if he's gotten completely lost. The look on his face is one of pure, total, and utter confusion. Even I have to admit to being completely clueless where the kid might have gone. I mean, we all saw him go in the shadows.

Soft hisses trickle from the fickle crowd. The brute dives back in to continue his search and (again) comes back out empty handed. He looks visibly shaken as the disapproving fans increase their ridicule. He angrily thrashes around in the dark puddle with no reward. Just then, the young man drops from the ceiling to catch the wild man completely off guard! He falls from the murky ceiling just as the hunter looks up and drives a steel bolt *directly through his forehead!*

Chapter 15: Bad Blood

The *"POP"* of the breaking skull echoes across the entire silent arena. It drops every jaw in utter shock—except mine. "HELL YEAH, KID!!!" I bark to the scrappy little fighter. Everyone turns their attention to the shouting man up in the little cell. This causes me to yell, scream, and even slam my cot against the wall just to see what kind of horrible noises it will make. Then I send Shepherd a look that will hopefully haunt him in the quiet moments of life.

Back over in the castle, the young man isn't celebrating; he's rushing to escape the corridor before the other twin can track him down. What he doesn't know is that the blue Gorilla isn't even interested in him anymore. He's thrown himself over his brother's corpse like a wet wool blanket. His raspy sobbing is easy to hear throughout the hushed arena. Even now, the fans show no mercy by taunting their distraught killer. Apparently, there's no pity for either side.

The game makers immediately dim the lights to that section of the castle. They obviously want to save their player from further humiliation by the cruel crowd. It doesn't work. They continue heckling the beast mourning the loss of his brother until the young man finally stumbles into a new hunter.

The fans erupt in unanimous cheer as the kid (literally) runs into a mountain of a man. He's a seven-foot-tall reminder that this game is far from over. In fact, the kid's small victory will surely make it worse for the entire family by the time this is over. But for now, he just has to worry about the mountain of flesh and bone waiting for him with clenched fists.

The speedy kid rounded the corner and bounced off his big gut like a rubber ball. A collective "awwwweeee" rises from the crowd when the young man barely misses bashing his head against a set of metal spikes. The collision is hard enough to keep the kid on the ground for an extended time. By the time he's up and ready to go, both exits are blocked. One by the mountain, the other by a nasty-looking freak in a filthy clown suit.

Have I mentioned I hate clowns?

No, seriously... *I REALLY <u>HATE</u>* clowns.

Maybe this is why? I instinctively knew this day would come. The kid must feel the same way, because he goes after the hulking giant instead of the much smaller clown.

It must take the mountain 20 minutes to spread his huge arms, but they stretch wall to wall when they finally get up. While he's a pretty convincing barrier up high, down low is a different story. The kid is able to easily slide through the sizable gap between his legs without much effort. Everything the giant does is so sluggish, he appears to be on a time delay. The kid's already down the hallway by the time he reacts, and then it's only to awkwardly stumble into the wall from his own shifting weight!

Just as things are starting to look up, a new player gets inserted into the game. It's probably no accident that he happens to be put in the exact same room as the family. This new killer is encased in a snow-white exoskeleton. Every inch of him is covered by a slippery-looking pearl armor. Not even his face is visible underneath the mirror-like visor.

His weapons of choice are smooth blades running along both forearms that end in sharp spikes pointing over angry fists. Then I notice some of the subtler tricks hiding up his sleeve. As he moves, light reflects off the skinny razors embedded in each fingertip. Even his boots have been sharpened down to a lethally sharp point. If Apple built a killing machine, this would be it. Beautiful, elegant, and coldly terrifying.

Everything about him screams death.

Slow.

Painful.

Bloody.

Death.

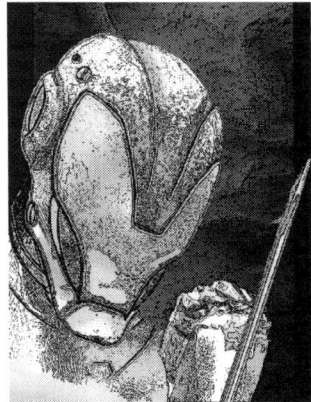

His first move is to point directly at the wounded father like a ball player calling his shot. This helps to get the fading crowd back into the game. They roar as he drags those bladed fingertips across the wall leading up to him. The shrill scraping is too close to the sound of a screaming Eutherian for comfort.

His movements are as accurate as the hands of a finely tuned Swiss watch. There's nothing wasted, just deadly precision with a purpose. He effortlessly strolls up, scoops the father around the ankle, and lifts him high into the air. There's absolutely no sign of strain while stringing a full-grown man up like a fish. Mom tries to interfere and is shoved aside easily. This leaves the little girl exposed for the first time. Even though she's completely alone, for whatever reason, the great white hunter wants nothing to do with either of them. His focus remains locked on the man dangling in midair.

He's too busy running his ivory glove up the father's chest. He relishes in the deliberate process of working along, slowly slicing into the shirt and top layer of skin. The poor man is barely clinging to consciousness by the time he makes it to the bandage around his calf. One smooth stroke is all it takes to sheer that cloth off too. After that, the blood is free to drizzle down his leg in long sheets. Then the sick bastard uses his sharp fingertip to dig into the gaping wound. My stomach churns as the flesh peels even further away.

It's hard to imagine there has ever been a more anguish-filled scream in the history of mankind. It's saturated with such unimaginable pain and suffering that it turns my heart inside out. His entire body quivers from the finger slipping further into the meat. Relief comes only when the wounded man finally passes out. Without any more torment to enjoy, the assassin drops the limp body and uses the fresh blood to draw a war mark down his visor. The crowd roars as he does.

"HEY, DICKHEAD!!!" spits out from behind the killer. Unbelievably, it's the fearless son barreling straight at the snow-white hunter! The silent man extends his stubby forearm blade into a lengthy spear with buttery smooth fluidity. It shoots far out over his fist while, at the same time, he plants his feet and guides the stretched spike directly toward the boy's unflinching face. I look up to Quinn's chair as she fights the guards holding her head straight. There will be no escaping the sight of their revenge.

The audience emits a wave of happiness that shatters several windows along the bleachers. All the destruction pushes them closer to the salivating edge of insanity. They literally jump for joy as the blade inches closer to the boy's cheek. At the last possible second, so close that the tip nips the end of his nose, the young man plummets straight to the ground. Not at the killer, or under him, just straight down.

One thing I've noticed during my drawn-out life is that karma is usually a slow-moving lady. She likes to take her time while delivering her syrupy-sweet vengeance.

Not this time.

This time, the blood-thirsty crowd gets to watch as the mountain of man stands impaled on the pale killer's blade. He had been behind the boy when he fell to the ground, and his own weighty momentum did the rest. It propelled the sword through his ribcage like a hot knife through butter. You can see the tip of it sticking out right below his massive shoulder.

This time, karma was an instant, stone-cold bitch.

My level of happiness should honestly be illegal. I can't stop myself from screaming at the disgusting crowd. Not a single one of them even looks back this time. They're still glued to the (formerly) white assassin wiping red splatter off his visor.

The dying colossus collapses. He gasps for air when the long blade is pulled from his pierced chest. Blood coats the entire room as his trembling fingers reach for help. He manages to touch the tip of the spear, right before it's driven through the dead center of his forehead. As gruesome as it looks, this is the first bit of mercy I've witnessed here. You know, when you're in a place where someone being stabbed in the face is an act of kindness, you should really re-evaluate life.

Which I'm currently doing.

Again.

The boy takes advantage of the chaos by gathering his family. He tucks them away before scrambling to search for the long-lost dagger. With luck on his side, it only takes mere seconds to track it down, scoop it up, and return to the tight family circle.

The young man towers over the group as if he could protect them with intimidation and a butter knife, but it's not the same cocky, teenage-driven ego as last time. Genuine confidence is fueling him. I mean, he did just take down two of the biggest guys out there. Those trembling hands are a direct result of excitement this time around. The kid's good. Hopelessly outmatched, but good.

The makers of this sick game must sense the sudden change in momentum as well. A stern voice sweeps over the mute crowd, "Enough!" The gruff word belongs to the well-dressed Governor. Sweat's really pouring down his custom suit now. He must not be used to the home team being down 0-2.

For some reason, he extends his short T-rex-like arm toward the arena. It doesn't reach very far, and mainly just emphasizes the large pit stains creeping up his sleeve. Then his little sausage thumb takes a dive toward the floor. I don't know exactly what it means, but it can't be good.

Not another word is spoken as the castle's lights turn the same vile color as the sky. The new red wash draws out hidden hunters from their various hiding spots. Some, I've seen before; the mysterious ninja in the long black coat, the grotesque clown, the remaining Wild Man... while others I hadn't. And most of those are even nastier than the ones we were properly introduced to.

Leading the pack is a short, muscular man with a bionic arm that glows between every metal band. He clutches a ruthless-looking hatchet that's been modified to have seven large teeth instead of a blade. Behind him is his polar opposite; a powerful Amazonian lady wrapped in a skimpy black outfit. She's very sexy in a "I'll kill you after we're done" kind of way. Until I see her other eye is a dead grey thing without a pupil. She's so creepy and mesmerizing, I have to force myself to look away before my soul is devoured by her forked tongue.

Stepping from the shadows, and directly from a nightmare, comes a twitchy terror of a man who's been scarred from head to toe. His gnarled fingers clutch two curled daggers. His trick is that he constantly drags the blades across his wrists and they miraculously heal immediately afterward.

This is no longer a hunt.

It's an execution.

The entire stadium is on its feet. None of the TV screens show the different angles of the fight anymore; instead, they focus on a single close-up of the family huddling together in the dirt. This shot captures their fear in the most putrid detail.

In her final moments, Mom holds the little girl tight. She does all she can to shield her from what's coming. The heroic son accepts his fate by kneeling to join the rest on the ground. He clutches his sister's hand, crying for the very first time. Dad is the last to look away. He defiantly stares down the wave of killers crashing over them, and just before they land, he lays himself over the entire family. Then, it's over.

They're gone.

Chapter 16: Burn It Down

The lights fade as the disgraced fighters slink back into the shadows. There will be no applause for them this time. While the bloodthirsty crowd got what they wanted, it wasn't the gruesome spectacle they craved. The family lost their lives, but they died as lions.

I get my first look at Quinn when the lights come back on. She's melted into the chair with every sign of life missing. Shepherd also got what he wanted. She paid the ultimate price for being the unfortunate victim of my good deed. My cowardice prevented me from having to see how my own family passed. I never had to know how their voices were silenced. I wasn't forced to see their pain. Still, that's been its own special kind of torture. No answers means no closure.

My legs crumble from the nausea churning in my stomach. I dribble down the wall, lost in the utter helplessness of the situation. Weakness is not an altogether new or uncommon sensation for me, but this goes far beyond anything I've experienced before. It paralyzes my body like a toxic poison seizing every nerve ending.

The only thing I'm capable of is digging sharp fingernails into the pads of my hands. They carve out four crescent moons that trickle blood onto the filthy floor. My frustrations release as a series of rapid punches to the shrinking cell walls. The rough bricks gladly keep most of the skin from my knuckles. This only adds to the bloody mess that my hands are quickly becoming.

"Sorry partner," solemnly floats in from next door.

"Me too, Bill." My broken, flat voice reflects the hatred I feel for myself. It's hard to think, even harder to believe, but Quinn should've died in that cave. At least there, she was in a trance. She wouldn't have felt a thing and her family would still be alive. In our world, everyone dies; your only choice is how big of a mess you leave behind.

My fidgety body can barely keep still. Every tick of the clock fills me with a brand-new form of guilt. The worst part is that it's completely unearned! How can you hate yourself for saving a life? I've done nothing to bring this evil on any of us! That knowledge doesn't help soothe the fluttering pulse or cure my nervous feet from craving to run again. After all, it's what they do. It's what I do.

I RUN!

I NEED TO, BUT CAN'T!!!

I DON'T KNOW WHAT TO DO!

WHAT <u>CAN</u> I DO?!?!

Pacing back and forth across the tiny cell only increases the panic level. I can barely contain all the thoughts running around my overloaded mind, let alone solve a problem with no real solution.

AGGGGGGGGHHHHHHHHHHHHHHHHHH!!!

I half shout/half growl while crashing my head against the cell door. Instead of my skull cracking, it's the metal latch that unexpectedly gives way. *"POP!!!"* and the exit swings wide open!

"You've got to be kidding!" I scream in astonished disbelief. *"This isn't a strong cell???* What kind of dumbass puts a vampire in a regular jail?" My tone is far closer to genuine rage than happiness.

"They never really hold you guys in here," Brain Guy lives up to his name with a remarkably simple yet accurate answer. I sit in stunned silence until the shock has a chance to dwindle a bit. Then, our new reality punches me square in the teeth. My heart pounds from overflowing adrenaline and endless possibilities. Remember the terrible things I wanted to do to these sick people? All that payback? Well............. *I'M FREE, BITCHES!*

"Time to go, Brain Guy!" I peek around the corner before ripping the door to his cage off. Now I have a face to go along with the voice. It's a very ordinary-looking one that perfectly matches the vanilla tone. He has absolutely zero remarkable features to speak of. Dirty blond hair, faded t-shirt from a band I've never heard of, and a pair of acid wash jeans to tie the entire look together. He's not good-looking or bad-looking, just sorta *there*. The man is so genuinely plain that if he mugged me, I wouldn't be able to pick him out of a lineup.

"Ah, no thanks, bub," he declines my invitation to leave. "I ain't got nowhere to be nohow. They'll round me up again, and..."

"And what?" I interrupt. "Throw you in a cage until it's your turn to be out *there?* That's already happening! At least this way, you would have a fighting chance! Get out of here and see the rest of the world! Most of it sucks, but I guarantee it's a hell of a lot better than all this!"

My plea makes enough sense for him to at least consider it. Somewhere in that vanilla mind, he tries to fathom the possibility of life outside these vile walls. They've thoroughly trained these people to remain as sheep until the ragged end. He squirms from even contemplating my odd-to-him request. I'm pretty sure he goes through all seven stages of grief in a matter of a few seconds. His face contorts between confusion, anger, fear, doubt, and finally coming back around with renewed vigor.

"Shoot, son. Maybe you dead-on. You know what? I gon' give it a shot! Now, how you reckon I do that?"

"You don't worry about that. Just wait for your cue, then run like the wind."

"Right, what cue?" I'm already on my way to find the answer before he has a chance to finish the question. A nearby window provides a quick exit, while the fire escape makes reaching ground level a painless effort.

So far, so good.

I'm transported to a completely different world when my feet touch down on the smooth pavement. Nothing about this charming town is like the ratty, boarded-up coliseum inside. Instead of blood-smeared walls and dirt, there are flawlessly manicured streets running between flat modern buildings. Even the bushes have been trimmed into perfectly sculpted hedges on every corner. Fittingly, all the street lights resemble old Victorian gaslights. Their fake flames burn with a deceptively inviting warmth.

The only similarities between the coliseum and city out here are a shared love of enormous windows and steel beams. Those are nearly identical to the sinister glass castle inside, except they aren't covered in every form of liquid formerly found inside of a human body.

The crowd roars up again, and reminds me of my burning desire to kill everyone inside the arena. Since that's not a thing I can (or should) do, I'll have to settle for getting Quinn out alive. However, accomplishing that will require a serious plan and that's something I'm—admittedly—not very good at. I tend to be more... impulsive.

Fortunately, since the entire town is busy watching the show, I'm left all alone out here. Unfortunately, I just end up pacing back and forth, waiting for a masterful scheme to come to mind. A perfect plan will not only lead to our great escape, but also result in everyone else falling into an active volcano. When nothing comes to mind, I settle for a good ol' smash and grab. Is it elegant? No. But it's literally all I've got.

So, first things first. I find a glossy black SUV parked across the street, calling my name. Its windows are even graciously rolled all the way down. That <u>has</u> to be a sign, *right?* I guess you don't have to worry about theft when your entire town is ruled by mutual asshole-dom. Just in case, I keep both hands in my pockets while casually strolling to the iron giant. I take one more look around before swinging the thick door open, then confidently climb in like the car belongs to me.

Waiting inside is enough tan leather and woodgrain to make me miss my camp back home. It's like a sprawling forest in here! Definitely a stark departure from my very basic Ol' Red. My tired ass honestly feels as if it will never stop sinking into the overly plush seats. I make quick work of the thin plastic surrounding the key hole and, within moments, the engine is spitting out the throaty growl of a fine-tuned V8. Its husky roar gives me a reflexive smile as my foot falls on the stiff pedal. It's a shame this beauty will only be mine for a few more moments. I'm really starting to enjoy this!

The transmission clicks into low 4x4 while I attempt to get back to a more grounded reality. I mentally unfold the plan leading all the way up to the part where I break through the massive gates, then realize that's about as far as I can go. Who knows what's going to happen after that!?!? What good is a detailed plan when all you want is chaos? That thought makes me feel strangely better, so before my nerves unravel again, I pop my knuckles and self-assuredly grab the heavy steering wheel. Staring down the long hood helps keep my mind clear enough that there will be no more thinking.

Just doing.

Chapter 17: Push It

The slightest touch of the gas pedal launches the vehicular behemoth away from the curb. Since I'm a guy who can appreciate a fine automobile, I honestly feel bad for what's going to happen to her next. That being said, I still approach the massive gates with as much caution as a hyperactive child with a triple chocolate birthday cake.

The big black truck bursts through the wooden arena doors, shattering them into a million toothpick-sized pieces. The sound alone is a bomb detonating over the shocked crowd. Watching them scatter like a roach infestation fills me with a devilish delight. I would love to hunt each one down for what they've done, but my goal must remain laser-focused on one thing: getting Quinn out of here.

Spinning the broad truck around in tight circles sprays the stands with even more debris. While I'm at it, I keep an eye out for some of the hunters. It would be a nice bonus if a few of them just happened to slip beneath my tires along the way. Sadly though, they seem to have scattered along with the rest of the terrified crowd.

After enjoying a few more turns, I point the steering wheel in the direction of the nearest tower, unbuckle the seatbelt, and get ready to move on. As soon as the belt snaps back, one of the bright spotlights makes the interior explode as if I'm driving into the center of the sun! The sudden burst leaves me completely blinded to anything beyond the dashboard. But, since I never planned on finishing this trip anyway, the cruise control is set and steering wheel directed dead ahead.

Now, there's only two things left to do:

1) Don't touch the steering wheel during my jump.
2) Make it out past the tires. (This is **_most_** important)

I have to pry the door open against the gusting wind, and it really seems to enjoy fighting me every step of the way. With that big spotlight cutting off my view to the rest of the world, there's no way of actually knowing how much time is left before this big brute finds an explosive new home, but I have a strong gut feeling that this train is about to find its inevitable station.

I reluctantly pull myself from those plush seats and leap from the moving battering ram before I find out too late. The slamming door catches a toe, and while it doesn't hurt, it sends me into a wild spinning tumble instead of a much-preferred slide. This, plus the truck's speed, means I skip across the ground for an unbelievably long amount of time. The sound my body makes bouncing off the arena floor is like banging a drum with a wad of crinkled paper. There are loud thuds, followed by quick crunching noises, then...

BOOOMMMMMMM ...rocks the entire stadium.

A tremendous explosion rips through as the four-wheeled missile finds its target. The massive impact feels as if the entire planet has been rattled to the core. It unleashes a beautifully destructive ball of fire that blooms up from the ground, soaring toward an already burning sky. Waves of intense heat scorch my shoulders with every new roll in the dirt. By the time my skid comes to a full stop, half the arena is on fire. The blaze spreads across the old wooden coliseum like a raging inferno. *Then the fun really begins!*

The burning tower begins to sway under the weight of the massive spotlight up top. One leg went missing in the crash, and the raging fire is already nibbling away at the others. They groan from shifting back and forth in the tall flames.

I seriously never gave a single thought to all the possible directions the tower could fall in (including on top of me), but the goliath decides to sail straight into the heart of the glass castle as if guided by a cosmic hand. All the sharp debris is, at first, sucked down into the vacuum as it slices through the steel beams like plastic straws.

But then it lands...

The enormous shockwave blasts every piece of glass, metal, dirt, and splinter so high that they become flaming rain on the way back down. The drizzling glass and crackling fire mix together into one big symphony of beautiful chaos. Let's be honest, I had hoped to cause some destruction, but this is *WAY* beyond even my wildest expectations!

There's no time to revel in all the anarchy. My ultimate goal is still waiting for me out there under those soaring lights. I quickly carve out a narrow path that should be clear enough to hurl myself across the entire stadium. Now hear me out, launching myself blindly into the air might seem reckless, but I really feel the universe has my back this time around. It owes me one.

This swell of unearned confidence leads to a jump that carries me much farther than it should've. All my anxious momentum has shot me well past the center box; all the way into the arena wall. Two more feet and I would've landed back out in the city!

Thankfully, I didn't. I'm able to safely remove myself from the Hayden-sized hole and immediately get busy yanking out the spotlights. The severed wires create a shower of sparks that tattoo a macho grin on my face. The inflating confidence has me holding them high over my head like a trophy, instead of the weapon they will become. Well, not a weapon, more like a bomb... that doesn't blow up, just knocks holes in things.

Anyway, Quinn is up front by the windows, so the over-sized hunks of metal are launched through the back of the roof. The force instantly dissolves half the ceiling and leaves a fantastic new hole to watch the carnage unfold inside. Through it I can see dense smoke, flashing lights, torrential water sprinklers, and a whole herd of people scattering around. With everyone distracted, I'm free to head over to the front to grab the ledge above the window. Lowering myself down is simple enough, although finding Quinn through the mass confusion is a different story. There's nothing more than blobs of moving shadows and strobe lights in there!

I decide to quit wasting time trying to look through the lava lamp and just get inside. My heels kick twice before being plunged straight through the oversized window. That sounds great, except the fragile glass crumbles faster than a popped balloon! This leads to my body careening wildly through the unexpected hole, and although the speed throws me off a bit, I somehow manage to land going in the right direction.

It helps that most of the smoke has poured from the freshly missing window. Now it's much easier to find Quinn right where they left her. She's still slumped over in that torturous chair, her face behind a curtain of wet hair that hides most of her face. I hardly recognize her when she looks up. Her eyes are so swollen, they're practically shut. It's obvious that she's simply shut down.

The sight fills me with a healthy kind of rage. One that keeps me focused on freeing her instead of tracking down Shepherd and his goons. The first thing I have to do is get rid of the cuffs. This isn't really a problem since I can snap off the chair arms and simply slide her out.

She's standing. Probably not for long, but she's standing.

"I've got you, Quinn." My reassurance causes her head to wobble without ever looking directly at me. She mostly just stares blankly in my general direction without ever actually *seeing* me. I have to scoop her up, shove all that to the back of my mind, and move on. Right now is about pure survival.

Of course, this single-minded resolve has to be tested almost instantly. The moment we set off toward the front window, a pretty fierce tug tries to yank her out of my arms. I expect to find one of the threatening soldiers on the other end, but instead there's only the swollen sausage fingers of the governor. The stumpy little man is practically having a heart attack from trying to pull the petite girl away from me. My monster begs for me to wiggle up his nose until reaching the death button in his brain. I have to calmly remind myself (and him) not to get sucked into those kinds of thoughts.

And it turns out that my resolve is indeed *excellent* today! Instead of folding him into a greasy little ball, I settle for one of the most satisfying punches of my life. I delight in feeling each knuckle sink into that pudgy face. They have to push away several squishy layers before finally finding the hard bones of his skull. The delicate nose cartilage bursts through his thin skin and blood spurts in every direction. After that, the short prick merely stumbles off into the growing chaos. There—problem solved.

Now, with that out of the way, I can finally get back to getting out of here, this time with a fresh grin and a budding sense of accomplishment. Well, that is until I suddenly discover the unexpected downside of a window popping like a bubble... there are shards of glass everywhere! Even on the ledge *OVER* the window!

I clear out as much as possible, but still manage to slice my palm wide open on the way up. My dripping hand becomes so distracting, I almost miss the glowing red eyes lurking above us. In my defense, the light is so dim at first that it can barely cut through the smoke, then gets turned up to retina-searing levels when our climb begins. The entire side of the building is suddenly under a really unwelcome spotlight. The skull-masked guard then reaches down, "Need a hand?" Funny bastard...

I recommend for the all-too-familiar guy to go make toast in a tub as I look for another way out. We're definitely not going up, or back into the chaotic room, so I quietly whisper for Quinn to hold on. She obliges by wrapping around my neck like a scarf that's been tied a little too tightly. I'm forced to shove off from the building before even finding out where the rest of his asshole friends could be. There's no plan or thought involved in launching us out into the flaming unknown.

Only instinct.

What we'll find out here is a nerve-wracking mystery, but staying on that wall was no longer an option. I only hope we don't land in a pile of burning debris; because I'm backward, there's no real control over that, either. All I can do is cocoon myself around Quinn and prepare for the worst.

My ass is the first to find out. When it hits soft dirt instead of jagged metal, I already consider this a victory. I've had the displeasure of rolling across the ground several times today, and it certainly doesn't feel any better this time around. Each bounce hurts a little more than the last. By the time this is over, I'm going to be one gigantic (hopefully) walking bruise.

After sliding to a twisted, uncomfortable stop, I quickly swing around to keep moving. Pulling myself off the floor becomes an unpleasant game of "spot the new aches and pains," and the big winner appears to be a shoulder that's several inches lower than it used to be. The knee that keeps trying to lock up is a close runner up. Nevertheless, our goal of staying alive is still within reach!

I urgently shout to Quinn, "We have to go!" but my warning comes a little too late. An impenetrable wall of shadows is already emerging from the raging flames. Their angry faces are lit only by the burning remains of their precious arena. The swarm swiftly confines us into an ever-shrinking circle.

"You should've just let the little bitch die, Flynn," barks an unmistakable voice.

"Which time, Shepherd? Here in your sick game or back in the cave? Oh, maybe we can still roast her over the fire!" I say, excitedly clapping my hands.

Shepherd responds, "Do you always have to be a smart ass?"

"It's a coping mechanism!" I bluntly answer.

"I tried, Flynn. I tried to get you to see what's happening here. Not this girl's death—that's meaningless—but the big picture. There's change in motion you can't stop. If you would've just run back to your trees, none of this would've happened!"

"It's better than what you assholes call fun around here," I mutter in mocking response.

Shaking his head, Shepherd boldly proclaims, "What we're doing is actually changing things. We're moving away from the apocalypse and finally setting the world right! How is that any different than what you fought for in the Great War?"

I'm shocked at the words spewing from my friend's mouth. "You know, the scary thing is, I think you really believe that."

"Of course I do. *I believe in ending all of this! Why don't you?*" He lets distress slip through this time.

"What you're doing here isn't new, Shepherd. People have been justifying their atrocities for centuries. You can't just defend one evil with another. What's the saying? Two wrongs don't make a..."

He interrupts the tired cliché before finishing, "I'm sorry you can't see more clearly on this. I'm also sorry I can't waste any more time explaining it to you. She's going to the Eutherians and these people are going to kill you. You brought that on yourself." He waves his arms around at the wreckage as if I didn't know what he was talking about.

"You know, Shepherd, you're right. I'm probably going to die today..." The sound of my voice would lead you to assume I had surrendered to his false logic; however, just as the words reach Shepherd's ears—before they even reach my brain—I sink my teeth into Quinn's soft neck. She doesn't have a chance to scream. Only one quiet squeak makes it out before she collapses from the venom spreading through her.

"...but not before I take away your precious little gift."

I make the bold declaration while still not totally sure what I've done or why I did it. There's not much time to figure it out, either. My jaw instantly explodes from a meeting with Shepherd's fist. It's a vicious collision that numbs my entire body and sends me to the ground in a crumpled puddle of floppy bones.

The ringing in my ears makes it hard to hear him shouting above. *"YOU DAMN FOOL!* Why aren't you getting any of this? What are you trying to prove? I'll easily replace her with two of her friends! If one cow gets away, you don't stop eating! *You eat its friend!* Why can't you understand that she *doesn't* matter? *None* of them matter!" He towers over to point down at the girl, then continues making his point by lifting me up by the collar.

"He is the Phoenix! The Phoenix of hope, by rule of the divine. And in order to rise, a Phoenix must burn! *He will burn this whole world to the ground!* It's *OUR* time, Flynn!!!" Slamming my skull on the ground after each new word really drives his point home. I'm fighting against the steady waves of unconsciousness, but they get stronger with every hit. Eventually, there's no option other than drifting out into the murky waters as Shepherd's garbled mess of words fade into the distance.

I can barely make out Quinn lying next to me. She's still frozen from the bite and there's nothing I can do to help her anymore. She'll die just as alone as the lost girl in the cave. At least she'll be the last of my mistakes. I reach out to Quinn one last time and a familiar face stares back at me. I'm sorry I couldn't be there for you, Dru... I'm sorry_yyyy.

Chapter 18: Uncharted

A jarring pain stops me from aimlessly drifting away on an endless sea. The cause is unknown, but it seizes the entire right side of my body from head to toe. It hastily parts the unconscious clouds and commands me back to life. Even with eyes struggling with the hazy fog, it doesn't take much to track down the source of torment. Quinn's delicate hand is quickly turning my fingers into pretzels without the salt! The vampire infection is spreading so rapidly that she's stuck shaking violently on the ground, not to mention, crushing every damn bone in my hand!

The thumb is the first to give out under the pressure. It now has two bends like the rest of the regular fingers; this one just happens to go back in the opposite direction. Several more fingers end up snapping before I can wrangle my hand away from the crusher.

While pain has cleared away the remaining mental cobwebs, my feet are still struggling to escape this stubborn hangover. They slip, slide, and move in every direction but underneath me. I eventually get them to cooperate just enough to reach a safer location to watch her convulsing arms and legs pound the earth. Their brutal force is a clear sign of the horror still to come. I can already see the haunting shade of blue transforming her once hazel eyes. They flutter with the palest color this side of white.

Her body is contorted into shapes that humans shouldn't be able to reach. Legs are where arms should be, twisting and pulling wildly, all while her face shows the most intense burning pain possible. Finally, with one last massive thrust toward the sky, the seizures come to a scary end. Her chest remains bent into a high arch while her feet and skull remain glued to the ground. She's formed a perfect half circle that could be straight from a full-fledged exorcism.

Her angry fingers have chewed up a thick cloud of dust that hides everything except her screaming face. Her pained cries have steadily become the all-too-familiar Eutherian howls. It's no coincidence the circle of people has expanded as well. Even they fear what's going to happen next.

Quinn roars to her feet like an animal freed from its chains. Flames dance in her wild eyes as they scan the crowd. She snaps her teeth; pausing only to taste the burning air. Without provocation, she heaves herself claws-first into the crowd. Those primal new fangs instantly remove the throat of the nearest person. She spits it high in the air, and before the chuck of flesh can even land, she's already latched onto her next target. Furled claws dig aggressively through anyone who dares to come within reach. On, and on, and on she goes until the air is filled with the noxious odor of death.

This is only the beginning of a masterpiece of violence that carries the tiny girl across the entire crowd. She claws through anyone crazy enough to stay. They don't have to be attacking, just physically exist near her. While all of this takes place, I remain carefully hidden away behind the mangled steel to watch it happen.

Nothing is scarier than a freshly turned vampire. The venom fuels our need to eat, kill, or do whatever it takes to satisfy the monster within. Quinn is something different, though. I've unleashed is an emotionally devastated girl onto the very same people who slaughtered her family. The venom provides the strength, but her motivation is much, much darker.

She shreds the mob like paper dolls. Trained killers fall easily at the hands of a small teenage girl. Shepherd appears to have wisely disappeared into the wildly scrambling crowd. Apparently, his desire to feed her to the bats isn't as strong as his need to save his own ass.

The first familiar face she finds is, appropriately, the first hunter that found her family. The tall assassin plants himself like a statue waiting for her. His long black coat flaps dramatically in the billowing smoke. She brushes off a few more insignificant attackers on her unstoppable march to him. They fall quickly, almost effortlessly, into a growing pile. The look on her brow is one of single-minded vengeance.

The hunter doesn't move an inch until the young vampire gets within reach. Even then, it's a crude punch I wouldn't expect from such a skilled warrior. Quinn doesn't even attempt to block or avoid it in any way. Instead, she drives her sharp fangs down through the top of his speeding fist. Blood leaks from the sides of her mouth as she clamps down on the impaled hand. His pain stokes the raging fire in her eyes. When she draws in the corners of her mouth, I question whether it's to keep him locked in place... or to smile.

He eventually frees the pierced hand at a steep cost. It must be pulled directly through her fiercely clamped fangs. On the way, his hand is ripped into thin strips of flesh and hanging meat. Every single muscle is shredded in a gruesome display of power that doesn't stop there. After this, the unrelenting Quinn drops down to *unexpectedly* slice the back of his leg. His calf splits like a busted melon. This is the first time she's slowed down for even a second. She's obviously taking her time to enjoy every drop of his ghoulish agony. She even drags him back by the same injured leg when he tries to crawl away. Safe to say she remembers *exactly* what he did.

She's fighting wild but calculated; she wants him to hurt. Apparently not for long though, since three lightning fast moves later, it's over.

<u>First</u>: She lifts him up by the throat.

<u>Second</u>: She slams him down with enough force to shake the ground all the way back to my hiding place. He shatters so completely; his entire body loses shape. The impact turns him into a bag of mushy jelly with disconnected bones floating around inside.

<u>Third</u>: She brings her heel straight down to collapse his chest like a popped balloon. The remaining fighters are either fiercely loyal or nuttier than squirrel shit; either way, there are still plenty of them to keep the vicious show going for far longer than it should. No matter how many that try, she puts each one down. Gruesomely.

We eventually reach another person who interests me. The surviving wild man is the next familiar face to challenge her. Outside the ring, he fights differently than the rampaging gorilla routine from earlier. He actually moves quite gracefully for such a chunky guy. He's also the only one who's carefully stayed outside her reach. He waits for her to make a mistake—the longer they go, the wilder she fights. Her patience (if she ever had any) is quickly slipping away.

He eventually finds an opening large enough to wrap those tree-trunk sized arms around. Several other attackers move in to take advantage of her newly trapped position. All the crazed twin has to do is stay locked in place while the mob attacks with blunt rocks and sharp blades. She can only shove them away with a few well-placed heels to the chest, like a rampaging bull.

Quinn is desperately trying to buck the attached strong man, but he still manages to forcefully twist both wrists behind her. The crowd is growing bolder by the second. She's helpless without her claws and they know it. They're dipping a bit closer to the hogtied girl each time. One of them even manages to land a rough-looking cut that opens a flowing river of crimson. That's when I realize she's not going to make it back without my help.

Now, I'm not crazy enough to go in there empty-handed, but since everything here is either sharp or on fire, a weapon shouldn't be too hard to find. While the selection might be plentiful, my time is not. I end up grabbing the closest thing that looks destructive; a long piece of mangled steel that should make for a fantastic spear. I then simply line up the jagged end with the Wild Man's laughing head and connect the two together.

The sharp spike penetrates his skull while he's in mid-laugh. His abrupt stop leaves a haunting echo lingering in the burnt air. It only takes another half second for the lifeless body to reach the ground. It falls with a heavy thud.

That's still too long for Quinn.

She refuses to even let the newly dead fingers release before removing pieces from every remaining attacker. Some fall instantly, while others bleed out slowly. Within minutes, none are left. The unintended consequence is that I'm suddenly left all alone with her. Judging by her rising claws, this won't be a friendly reunion.

While there's a slight delay instead of instant decapitation, it's not long before she's coming after me. "*Whoah* there, kid!" I try reasoning. "Quinn, it's me! *You remember me!"*

My desperate plea doesn't keep the fierce girl from shifting into full-on Olympic sprinter mode.

"HOLD ON!"

"HOLD ON!!"

"HOLD ON!!!"

Now, I generally consider myself a fast person, but compared to her, I'm a three-toed sloth with two broken ankles. She removes a long strip of my skin before I manage a single step. The burning sensation of canyons being carved into my back is ample motivation to return to my shelter *much* quicker. But what happens when I get there??? She's still gonna be just like this!

I leap into one of the corners with some weak notion of fighting off the irrational wildcat. Although, how to actually defend against something like her is completely beyond me. One foot stays up to knock her back, if possible, while my hands are reserved for offense only. They remain up even after it becomes plainly obvious she isn't coming after me. I peek across the flames to find she's already balls-deep in a new group of pathetic attackers. It turns out that my best defense is her very short attention span.

We need to end this. I can't just wait around until it's my turn again. She's worse than a dog backed into a corner—a dog with a hurt leg, a thorn in its paw, and any other stereotypes that could possibly be used to describe a pissed-off animal. So, what do you do with a rabid dog?

Cage it.

A long section of metal from the fallen tower would make the perfect wrapper to turn Quinn into a human burrito. Bending the corners in should make it easier to fit her squarely in the middle and, hopefully, the steel will be strong enough to keep her there.

I charge full speed ahead as soon as her back is to me. Within seconds, a Quinn-shaped outline appears in the creased metal. I wrap the sheet all the way around and bear hug the little blonde tornado with all my might. Several rips and tears quickly appear from her kicking around like rocks in a blender. The thin barrier was only meant to be a protective layer between us. And a *very* temporary one at that.

Lifting her off the ground relieves most of the problem. She can't kick nearly as hard if there's nothing to push against. As an added bonus, I get to use the rolled steel as a bat to swing at the remaining townspeople. It works, but more rips begin to appear in the metal after only a few hits. We need to get out of here before it splits all the way. Although the carnage—walls of flames and fire—have made the location of the gate a complete guess.

I try making up for what I lack in knowledge with sheer determination. Our direction will be based purely on the space available to build up the needed speed. Three short jumps later, we're sailing out over the arena wall with no one following us!

Our escape is actually going *shockingly* well! This positive turn of events makes me almost ignore my hip tagging the concrete on the way back down. Compared to the other ass beatings I've had today, this one is a mere scratch. The only real damage it does is shaking the wiggling kid a bit looser.

We're only taking turns bending the fragile metal. She'll push it out; I'll press it back in. I have to plead between jumps for her to calm down. The words fall on *predictably* deaf ears. All I can do is keep on jumping and hope it holds out long enough to do... *something?*

One way or another, she's coming out of this thing soon. I figure I have about two minutes to figure out what to do with the pint-sized tornado between my arms.

Maybe less.

Chapter 19: Hold On

I don't even get the full two minutes before she makes it out. While my momentum keeps me going forward, she drops straight down into a dense group of trees. She takes another sizable chunk of my left shoulder on the way.

I eventually land on a riverbank that would be serene, except for the string of obscenities spewing out of my mouth. Partially from losing the girl, but mainly from the steady stream of blood pouring from what's left of my shoulder. It's fairly easy to see the alarmingly large puddle accumulating underneath me. Here's where a choice has to be made:

1) Go back in and get the insane vampire child?
2) Get really, really, *really* far away from here?

She's probably busy biting the head off a rabbit, so I wouldn't want to interrupt that. Plus, I don't stand a chance against her in my current condition. I can barely stand up, and thick blood is leaking from pretty much everywhere.

Unfortunately, the leaves are already shaking from the kid plowing through the forest. The growing rumble makes it painfully clear that the choice has already been made for me. She's coming out.

I anxiously watch the line of dark trees for some sign of my approaching doom. Tense moments click by while I watch for some sign of where the angry little wrecking ball will be coming out. Finally, I spot a shadow that isn't swaying like the rest... it's moving in a more forward direction. She isn't coming out, but an *entire tree* is!

Mostly by luck, the largest parts miss me. Only a few of the thin outer branches actually make contact. Some crack like a whip, while others connect more like a Louisville Slugger. However, it's not the physical pain that hurts me the most. It's the knowledge that *"she threw a damn tree at me"* that ultimately sends me stumbling out to deeper water. I go out in search of some kind of protection, but the slippery rocks make standing, let alone running, impossible. They're coated in a thick slime that keeps me splashing around instead of focusing on the hostile woods.

My eyes can't even make sense of the dark puzzle. The gentle rustling leaves disguise the dangerous secret hiding inside. They're the perfect canvas on which to construct imaginary creatures crawling from the void. Could she be torturing me? This doesn't feel like the wild, uncontrollable girl from earlier. That's when I remember all the sick things I did to my first victim, and I have to wonder, *"Am I her mountain lion??"* Will I die in the same cruel fashion my monster came to life?

Also, shouldn't I be feeling acceptance for my impending death? Aren't people supposed to get some kind of grand awakening in their final moments? Well, that's the last thing I feel right now!

Quinn doesn't wait for my internal struggle to finish before roaring out of the shadows. She rips back the shadowy curtains by leaping from the top of one of the tallest trees imaginable. She's up so high, it looks like she's falling in slow motion. Even with the extra time, all I can do is sink deeper into the slimy water. There's no way to avoid the coming collision, so I just throw my hands up in desperation. That's when the arms that were supposed to block her end up buckling and sending us both deeper into the river.

The only thing visible through the cloudy water is a mess of thrashing limbs and tangled bodies. Quinn moves so fast that it looks like eight arms are attacking me at once. Thankfully, after a few seconds, our fight stirs up so much sediment she can't seem to find me anymore! I take advantage of this by quickly sliding over to where only an occasional scratch can reach me.

The tide officially turns when I find a sturdy rock to anchor against. Using my newfound footing, I simply reach in and pluck the little wolverine from the muddy blizzard.

While I have to pause and take a much-needed breath, her constant violence never skips a beat. She, on the other hand, actually gets faster! Most of the skin on my forearm disappears within a matter of seconds! All concern for her well-being vanishes immediately when I have to basically heave her off in any direction just to end the assault.

The blind throw ends up sending her toward the middle of the rushing river. She flips end-over-end a few times before being swallowed by the swift current. I rush to sneak in a few quick breaths while waiting for her inevitable return. The pressure of breathing pushes my fresh cuts wide open, exposing them to the freezing water. Crouching is the only relief I can find. It's cold, but at least the raw flesh isn't being forced open anymore.

Minutes pass without a stray ripple to signal the start of round two. The little beast has been gone for way longer than she should. Either she can breathe under water now—or she can't swim.

Shit.

I tear off toward the spot where she went under, but each rapid step drives the icy river into my open wounds like sharpened icicles. The immense throbbing brings on the familiar twinkling stars and tunnel vision of a rapidly approaching blackout. Diving under only intensifies the overwhelming sensation of swimming down a dark hallway.

I can only trust that my hands are still pulling me into the abyss. The ability to see (or feel) them went away as soon as I went under. But that's not the worst part; it's the thought that she could reach out of the darkness at any moment. Her deadly fast fingers could pull me under, and I would never see it coming. However, those fears are put to rest when I find the two dim candles at the end of the long tunnel. I barely have enough vision left to even see her eyes glowing in the dark. The angry girl has fallen all the way to the moss-covered bottom of a deceptively deep river. Still, that hasn't stopped her from continuing her one-sided rage-filled fight.

Nothing's changed. She's the same wild maniac that's chewed me up and spit me out several times now. My body goes limp without hope to keep it driving forward. Watching her struggle to reach me with those swatting claws drains all remaining life from me. The spreading poison, her monster coming to life, the mental torture she's endured; all of it has created this rampaging creature in front of me.

So, what *has* to happen now… Hayden Flynn could never do. I cowardly retreat to allow the monster to return. He has no guilt or shame holding him back. He's survival in its purest form. An emotionless tyrant that will keep my arms locked when they desperately want to reach for her. He knows she can't be pulled up like this. It would threaten his survival, and he would *never* let that happen.

The monster only permits me to float along next to her. I have to watch as her movements grow slower, more pained, for what feels like an eternity. I remain stuck, trapped in this underwater hell, forced to watch the life fade from her hateful eyes.

Eventually, the waves from her snapping jaws subside. She's become nothing more than a puppet guided by invisible hands by the time the last air bubble is carried away. Her body softly sways from side to side in the current. It no longer moves on its own.

Quinn's gone.

Now the countdown to pull off a miracle begins. My arms and legs strain to close the distance between us.

It takes *four seconds* to reach her.

I lose time when my hurt hand slips while pulling her in. One meager second doesn't sound like much, but it could be the difference between life and death here.

Two more seconds slip away.

My numb fingers can't even tell what they're grabbing anymore. They just dig at whatever's within reach.

Five seconds.

I'm kicking with legs too frozen to be of much use anymore.

Three seconds.

Finding the surface takes another setback when the broken thumb can't keep its shaky grip on the girl.

Five seconds.

Precious seconds tick away as I simply try not to completely drop her.

Five seconds.

I tangle the busted hand in her dress so my fingers won't slip again.

Seven seconds.

My lungs heave from the stale air rotting them from the inside out.

Four seconds.

The harder I kick, the farther away the surface gets.

Three seconds.

My lungs reject the decomposing air.

One second.

My cheeks *FINALLY* shatter the rough surface of the river! My mouth is so eager to take in the fresh air that it forgets to clear the choppy water. I end up choking down a few gallons of the foul-smelling river.

Two seconds.

The frigid air burns my lungs like hot fire. Surprisingly, any body part that's not completely numb, is ablaze.

Five more seconds

I'm shaking so hard it's impossible to control most of my body. It's seizing violently while trying to wrap the crushed hand back up in the dress. Getting it to stay will free up my good arm to help get us ashore quicker.

Seventeen seconds.

Her face won't stop dipping underwater. I don't bother wasting the time it would take to rearrange her; just keep pressing forward.

Six seconds.

At this point, my numb legs barely move anymore.

Seven seconds.

Honestly, I can't even tell when my feet drag across the rocks close to shore. It's not until I'm smacking my hands against them that I notice.

Two seconds.

The slimy rocks, hard enough to navigate earlier, are virtually impossible now; mostly because of the dead legs flopping around underneath me. Digging my knees in the mud is the only way to get the leverage to toss her ashore. It's not a good throw, but good enough.

Three seconds.

Without the added weight of the girl, plus being able to use of both hands, the crawl from the watery grave goes much quicker. Still not "fast" though.

Five seconds.

I end up flopping around the choppy surf, desperately trying to pull myself in. I eventually use her dress as a rope to literally pull myself ashore.

Eight seconds.

I waste no more time in tilting her head back and yanking her jaw open. Her chest rises and falls with every forceful breath leaving my mouth. I've gambled her life on being able to pull this off.

Six seconds.

Her blue lips and pale face show no signs of life.

Sixteen seconds.

What have I done?!?

Twelve seconds.

I watched her drown right in front of me!

Let it happen!

Why didn't I *pull her up???*

I could have fought her off!

It's that fictional thought that pulls me back to cruel reality. We would have both died if I tried that. She would have slit my throat and ended up drowning anyway. No, I reluctantly have to accept that this was the only way we could have both reached the surface. It still doesn't help much with the crushing panic.

I desperately search for any small sign of life after each new breath.

Ten seconds.

Nothing!

My unnerving terror is resembling anger more than concern. That fevered mindset leads to smashing into her frozen chest with both closed fists. They don't even stop after feeling the unmistakable shift of a dislocated rib. They just keep beating her like a madman, never accepting the possibility she's already gone.

Five seconds.

All that unwavering belief is *finally* rewarded with the most beautiful eruption of vomit ever! A steady stream of wonderful muddy water is dribbling out with every new cough. I set her up to clear out the rest while attempting to regain the composure needed to only tap hard enough to remove the remaining fluid. What follows are several lengthy coughs, each growing deeper, and *darker*.

Chapter 20: Hold On, Too

Nothing has changed. Her eyes reveal the same furious glare as before. As we speak, there's a hard valley carving across the ridge of her furling brow. It runs down to perfectly blend with a wide, snarling mouth. Her lethal fingers begin crawling their way back up my still-bleeding arms.

Really?

After all this, it's going to happen *again???*

My fist instinctively buries itself between her pale blue eyes. I didn't tell it to. I don't think the monster did, either. Maybe it's simply as frustrated as I am? Either way, it had to happen. That single, desperate punch, is enough to leave her an unconscious ragdoll on the edge of the desolate river. Then I turn into a hysterically screaming fool, "Where do we go from here, *Quinn?*" My voice breaks from the physical and mental strain. What happens when she wakes up ready to kill again? Then what?

Kill her???

How would I even do that????

Serendipity is defined as "The occurrence of events, by chance, in a happy or beneficial way." As odd as it may sound, my serendipitous moment comes in the form of a comically overweight beaver sitting just a few short feet away. The chubby little fellow drags me from the sticky tar pits of insanity just when I need it most.

I suddenly go from screaming at the unconscious girl to calmly watching the silent creature watch me back. We share a look that makes it pretty clear we're both surprised to have found each other. The rotund rodent's hilariously large eyes are so ridiculously funny that I can't help but burst into tearful laughter. His tiny head resting squarely on top of a *massively* round belly makes him resemble a Hershey's Kiss or jolly snowman more than a living creature.

The abrupt laughter causes him to spill the branches he'd been meticulously gathering. That's when he makes the difficult decision to abandon his hard-earned loot to make a not-so-quick escape. It takes several adorably awkward rolls to make it back onto his petite feet, but after that, there's no looking back! His chunky tummy sways back and forth like a half-filled water balloon as he makes his frantic getaway. Although he stumbles a few times from the shifting weight, he keeps moving forward, making loud clicking noises that echo all the way down the valley. They make it sound as if there's a dozen beavers instead of just the one.

The fun distraction comes to an end as his flat tail and fuzzy butt slip into an extra-tall patch of grass. It served its purpose, though; my mind comes back from the brief comic interlude in a totally different place. All the anger and frustration is gone. In its place is a more realistic view of our current situation and, realistically, we're still screwed.

The dull moonlight paints everything in a shade of grey that makes it feel even more desolate than it already did. There's also a growing sense of dread like the other shoe will drop at any moment. Seriously though, why haven't we seen the townspeople yet?

They could have *easily* followed the noise we've been making. I mean, she threw a damn tree and I've been ranting loudly for over five minutes. I guess we should take advantage of this unbelievable head start instead of questioning it. I begin by rolling Quinn up into a neat package and clumsily staggering to my feet. At first, I blame the slippery rocks for throwing my balance off, but soon, a whole new wave of nausea kicks in. One I know all too well.

Hunger.

The extremely rubbery knees make it obvious I'm fading fast. My last meal should have lasted much longer than this. Normally a feeding that size would've lasted for weeks! My body must've used it all up trying to heal from the countless beatings I've taken lately.

Another disturbing trend is the volume of blood still leaking down my side. That should have stopped a long time ago, too. I try using a ripped section of shirt as a makeshift bandage to slow it down. It helps, but there's still a decent amount oozing around it. The blood loss could account for some of the nausea, along with the sensation of wading through wet cement with every pained step.

Since passing out here is definitely not an option, though, we need to keep moving. But to where? I guess that, for now, our best answer seems to be *"not here".*

Life usually demands a definitive answer: Yes OR No.

This way OR *That way*.

Right now, my choice simply has to be *ANY way.*

So, I heave the (mostly) dead girl off the ground and take off in a random direction. It only takes about five steps before figuring out that carrying the extra weight won't go very well. My arms refuse to lift any higher than shoulder height, so the best I can do is sorta pull her along. She slips further and further down with each uncomfortable step. After five minutes, she's fallen to about mid-thigh. By ten, she's close to knee-level, and I'm basically dragging her. Then, two minutes later, she's yanked out of my arms by a small weed! *A WEED IS STRONG ENOUGH TO PULL HER AWAY FROM ME!*

We're going absolutely nowhere fast. To put it mildly, I'm as worn-out, exhausted, and broken as a living person can be. I flop my defeated self down on the ground. My damaged body can no longer combat the virus, so it's simply shutting down. I can feel it eating away at my tired muscles. Just sitting here hurts.

I go ahead and playfully toss a handful of dirt on myself to symbolize my upcoming second burial. This one will certainly be more successful than the last. Maybe I'll even stay in the ground this time? It's a funny joke until the searing pain of moving ruins the amusement. After that, I lie back down and wait. I only hope death finds me before the crows do.

The selfish wallowing is interrupted by the quiet clatter of a diesel engine. It's only a small ticking at first, so tiny that I almost can't hear it over my own bitterness. But even I can't ignore when a calm morning is suddenly interrupted by the booming sound of pistons rattling through trees. I know there's a good chance that whatever it is will be filled with people we don't want to see. People who want to kill us. However, from where I stand (or rather, lay like a rotting corpse) it may be our only choice. We either take our chance with whatever's coming up the road, or I eat Quinn myself.

And that won't be good; vampires can't eat each other. Our viruses are not compatible. Like, at all. Sometimes, if they come from the same family, it's okay. Quinn and I might be able to cross because I infected her, but that's still no guarantee since different blood types mutate the disease in a variety of ways. That's also why some of us have different abilities. (Example: the hypnotic spell she was under.)

If there is conflict, you'll die all kinds of awful ways:

Best case: My nervous system will shut down and leave me paralyzed for life.

Average case: My temperature will get high enough to boil several internal organs. Usual result is a slow, painful death.

Worst case: I'll expel every foreign object in my entire body. Basically, crap myself to death.

Even knowing all this, I still have to hold the monster back from feeding on the lifeless girl. Facts don't matter to him. He sees a body and wants its blood; that's all.

From a mental standpoint, the decision is easy. The hard part is actually dragging Quinn through the heavy brush. That turns out to be one of the *hardest* things I've done in my extra-long life. There's no way of stopping the skinny branches from lashing against any bare skin they want. With my hands currently occupied, I have to just take it and keep moving.

Several permanent scars later, we finally reach the edge of a deserted road. Well, it's not much of a road, more like a tightly packed gravel trail that barely looks wide enough to fit a compact car.

I pause one last time to reconsider the (possibly) tragic idea. The engine doesn't have an industrial military sound to it. It's quiet, like a commercial engine—at least that's what I tell myself before exiting the safety of the trees.

My reward is the dim yellow headlights of a retro-looking bus slicing through the early morning fog. Beautiful sleek panels flow seamlessly down the sides of the silver aluminum fox. It appears to be an expertly crafted tour bus that's been forged from a solid block of steel. This kind of craftsmanship is something you really don't see anymore; especially bouncing around the potholed backroads of a small mountain town. She's certainly a welcome throwback to a much better time.

Stumbling into the road looking as we do brings the bus to a sudden halt. The squealing tires trigger the abrupt flight of several flocks of birds from the surrounding trees. The ruckus also brings about a dozen people inside up to look out the windows. The weight of a thousand worlds lifts when all those curious faces turn out to be extremely wrinkled. The chance that these pruned people are trained killers is pretty slim. I feel pretty secure as I pull Quinn up to the unfolding door.

"Everything all right, son?" the driver asks in a deep voice. True concern drips from the raspy words. Coincidently, his hair is the same glossy silver as the bus he drives. Judging by the loose stitching of his houndstooth cap, it could be just as old as he is.

His kindness is contagious when I catch myself laughing at the colorful moose adorning his sweater. The quilted animals are the same cheerful shade of blue as my room growing up. Anything that reminds me of home gets an automatic smile or two. This is going *far* better than I could've ever hoped for!

I try to briefly explain our situation, "forgetting" to mention a few details; the horde of people chasing us as well as the fact that Quinn *might* wake up and try to kill everyone on board. Midway through, I get the distinct feeling that even if I had told the whole story, it wouldn't matter. His comforting voice says, "Of course, son! You get that girl on up in here. We'll take you anywhere you need." By mid-sentence, I'm happily limping up the short steps.

They've already cleared us a seat in the back by the time we make it up all the way up. Since the narrow aisle won't let me carry Quinn any farther, two of the more (relatively) muscular men spring up to carry her for me. She's already lying next to the window when I finally make it back there. With any luck, she'll sleep off the rest of the harsh transformation. That's especially true when the bus bounces down the road again and her head falls into my lap. I want nothing more than to sling it off like a hot rock, but I turn my jacket into a makeshift pillow instead. Partly to not alert the passengers that anything's wrong, but mostly because she needs me now.

Without the jacket, the full extent of my injuries is shown to the world. The worst of which are claw marks down two *extremely* bloody shoulders and a thumb stuck firmly in the hitchhiking position. A sweet little lady peeks around the seat and at first glance, my bloody state causes her to gasp.

She quickly replaces the shocked look with the kind of polite smile only a grandmother can make. "Would you and your lady friend care for a sandwich? It's peanut butter and honey without crusts. *Harvey doesn't like the crusts!*" she whispers.

All I really want is blood.

Lots of it.

However, I'll settle for the perfectly trimmed snack. By the time Rita finishes handing me things, I'm loaded down with two sandwiches, a travel pillow, four caffeine-free sodas, and several *mostly* current issues of *Cat Fancy*. The outpouring of kindness is both overwhelming and much appreciated at a time like this.

"Oh gosh, Rita, this sandwich is amazing! How did you get that little bit of crunch in there?"

"The secret is to top off the peanut butter with some freshly chopped almonds!" She winks as if letting me in on a closely guarded secret. It feels good to have a casual conversation, even if it's over something as trivial as peanut butter. I truly embrace the moment and thank her for everything she's given me. Not the sandwich or cat magazines, but for the temporary respite from a very worried mind.

Taking a quick peek down the aisle makes it abundantly clear we're the only ones on that bus under seventy. Yes, I'm actually a lot older than that, but for appearance's sake, I'm fifty years their junior. I turn to the lady across the aisle whispering, "Excuse me, ma'am. Where is this bus heading?" She enthusiastically replies after adjusting a hearing aid, "Young man, don't you know? We're going to Vegas!"

Chapter 21: Soul Suckers

The days on the bus crawl by at a painfully slow pace. At our first stop, a small truck stop diner that barely fits everyone, I found a raccoon rummaging in the dumpster out back. It definitely wasn't a glamorous meal, but quick enough to pass off as an extended bathroom trip. I have to blame my newfound grin on the damn fine cup of coffee and cherry pie.

Since then, my wounds have healed slightly. The small snack should keep me from having to scavenge again before we reach Vegas. My newest fear is that my nose has been permanently stained by the overpowering smell of prunes, muscle rub, and baby powder that saturates this entire bus. The origin of smell is only one of the mysteries bouncing around my brain. Mainly, why was there no pursuit from town? It's not like Shepherd to cut and run like that. Of course, I could end up eating those words if this all turns out to be some elaborate set-up.

I've seen Shepherd's vicious side up close. He has a way of disconnecting that leaves his entire world in black and white. Back then, I respected his hatred of messy grey areas; now things are looking different from the other side. Though my most urgent problem has to be, which Quinn is going to wake up? The one who wants to maul my lap or, well... anything other than that?

The folks on board have graciously agreed to let us go the whole way with them. Vegas is in the general direction of Titan, so we will at least be closer to where we we're going. And what a great group of people they are. They've been so incredibly warm and inviting in every way imaginable.

Each of them has stopped by to offer food, drinks, or words of encouragement. Turns out they're a bridge club from Eureka, California on their annual trip to Sin City. It seems that the Michael Bublé experience is the hottest ticket in town! It's about the only thing all these little old ladies want to talk about. Like Elvis before him, once the Canadian crooner died a few years back, the Bublé impersonators seem to have really taken off. Maybe if everything goes well, we can catch a show? I mean, we need to rest anyway, so why not take in some holographic tigers and dancing monkeys? They sound like a great distraction, even if I have no clue what they have to do with love songs and swing music.

I've overheard a few of the ladies whispering about Quinn. They've become understandably worried because she hasn't budged an inch in the last few days. The lead chatterbox, a gossipy redhead named Flo, is convinced that she's dead and I basically won't accept it. She's kind of right, I guess.

Thankfully, the old crow is eventually proven wrong. Quinn finally begins to stir in the cutting morning of day three. Everything begins innocently enough, with soft little grunts as she stretches muscles that haven't moved in days. I proactively rush a hand up by her throat after one particularly loud squeak—you know, just in case.

She's softly rubbing eyes that are straining to focus on anything. Several funny mumbles leak out as if she's busy fighting off a bumblebee. Before long, she calmly grabs the seat in front to help pull herself up to the window. Her peaceful demeanor helps settle my nerves enough to risk lowering my hands... a bit. Well, she hasn't eaten me yet, so we're off to a pretty good start.

"Where are we?" she mutters blankly while staring outside at the passing cacti. She's obviously confused by all the rolling sand in place of the usual evergreen pines. Her face looks as if it's been through a brutal 20-round boxing match. Her eyes look particularly sinister from the deep, dark circles surrounding her new baby blues. Up until the moment I spot the hair sticking straight up from the back of her head like a peacock; once I do, she's not quite as terrifying.

"We're on a bus headed to Vegas," I say hesitantly, unsure how she'll take the news. She didn't make an appetizer of my twig and berries, so I'm pretty sure I've already won this battle.

"Vegas? Oh…" and that's all she says about it. The way she sits calmly looking out the window is disarming. Or maybe alarming… I can't tell. Either she is the most laid-back person—or she's in total shock. It's not like she was that talkative before, so maybe this is just her way of dealing with things? I always think everyone should ramble on like me, even when they never do.

I talk for a few more hours, mostly to myself since she doesn't seem to want to converse. Every now and then, I'll catch a few tears in the window's reflection. After a while, I decide to give her a break from my constant yammering and respect that we'll talk when she's ready. The silence leaves me trapped in a very scattered mind. I wish it would focus on something other than the last few crap-tastic days. Not that I want to avoid reality completely, but it does me absolutely no good to constantly stew in the anxiety of what's yet to come. I've had more than enough time to dwell on it during my solitary days on the bus. I could really use a small mental break from all the turmoil.

Desperately searching for a positive thought sends me down the rabbit hole of chasing good memories. There's not a lot to choose from in the last fifty years, but I have tons from before I knew how to appreciate them. About the time I reach the memory of my sixth grade trip to Williamsburg, Virginia, I glance over to see Quinn staring at Rita like a veal cutlet with cranberry sauce.

"*Quinn!* Look at me right now! You absolutely cannot eat Rita! She gave us *peanut butter sandwiches!* I mean, don't eat any of these people, but especially not Rita!" Her eyes have retreated further into their hollow sockets. She's so completely imprisoned by the hunger that she's looking right past me. Absolutely nothing can break her laser-like focus on the octogenarian meal.

"Did you hear me? I know what you're thinking, and *no,* Quinn!" Planting my face directly in front finally breaks her trance. She snaps back long enough to plead, "I'm hurting, Hayden! It feels like my skin is shrinking around me! I want to peel it off!" I know where she's coming from. I remember what it was like crawling out of that grave. The worst part was fighting against cravings that were *totally* unimaginable before. Back then, I would have been willing to do anything to make them go away—including eating little old ladies.

Her restraint is pretty amazing considering that she's freshly turned. Right now, she's the worst kind of junky; wanting terrible things and loathing herself because of it. The need to feed is *consuming* her in a real way. And the longer she has to go without blood, the worse it will get. Tunnel vision has probably already started seeking out anything with a pulse. Eventually, she'll start tasting the air. When that happens… let's just hope we're off this bus.

The only help I can offer is asking Rita for more snacks. Salty ones, preferably. She of course grins like a fool, delighted to help, while passing over countless bags of travel-sized nuts. They go straight from my hand to Quinn's determined lips. Her eyes reluctantly shift from the eighty-year-old entrée to the crazy guy shoveling things into her face. "Try to taste the salt on these. It will make you feel better until we stop again. I promise."

It won't.

After finishing the last of the bag, Quinn's gaze returns to the juicy old lady. She continues to mindlessly eat and salivate over the silver-haired meal. I hardly recognize the withered shell she's become. The olive skin that was so vibrant before is now pale and cracked. It looks brittle enough to rub off like old paint. The only colors left are the large red canyons of chapped lips and bloodshot eyes.

For now, I'm helpless to do anything about it. All I can do is anxiously watch the miles go by. A few magazines do help pass the time, but Quinn wants nothing to do with those, either. She's too busy sniffing people as they walk by. I have to keep grabbing her chin and tilting it back toward the window. Occasionally, she'll snap at my fingers, or shoot a look that sends my testicles turtling for cover.

She scolds with an angry growl, *"I have to go to the bathroom."*

I happily answer, "Of course! Maybe splash some water on your face. That will definitely make you feel better!"

It won't.

This is another lie.

I'm just hoping that all these little distractions will keep her busy until we can find a real solution. Judging by the way she sluggishly walks down the aisle, touching every seat, taking long sniffs of every person—it won't.

And she's not discreet about it, either. Everyone gets a turn with the strange little girl smelling them up and down. I want to explain, but what's there to say? "Sorry, she thinks you would be delicious with gravy" isn't particularly reassuring. Without a reasonable excuse to offer, I simply bury myself in the folds of another gossip magazine. They do a good job of hiding my embarrassment and become a nice diversion, too.

I lose myself in an article about UFOs found hiding on the dark side of the moon. Vivid fantasies of exploring the universe unfold while reading the far-fetched story. How cool would it be, to be a starship captain, cruising the galaxy with a bunch of colorful friends and a foul-mouthed raccoon? Imagine being able to say goodbye to the Earth, and living among the stars as a sailor on an endless sea!

My instinct is to share the funny idea with Quinn, until I realize she never came back. Also, I don't really know how much time has passed. Fifteen minutes, maybe? I usually try not to barge in on people in the bathroom, but this seems like an exception. I don't even make it out of the seat before my mind is hijacked by all the terrible possibilities. Could she have passed out? Worse yet, could she have jumped from a window!? Full panic mode sets in by the time I reach the flimsy door.

What if it's too late?

Can I get her some blood on here?

Do I need to kill Rita???

No, not Rita. I can find someone else. Maybe that gossiping redhead... Okay, so I might be getting a bit carried away here. I need to slow down and just take a peek inside. Perhaps there's a simple explanation for what's taking so long. Maybe she's simply crying it out?

Of course the door is *locked*. Fortunately, it's one of the cheap plastic ones that opens with a simple tug.

"Hey kid, you okay in there?"

"OHHH FFFFFFFUUUUUUuuuuu!" blurts out before I can cork my own mouth. The bathroom door is half blocked, but it's more than enough to find Quinn curled up next to a mangled, bloody corpse.

Chapter 22: Many the Miles

"What the hell!?!? I thought you had to pee?" I struggle to keep my scream at barely louder than a muted whisper. Franticly flipping over the body reveals that yes, this lady is dead as hell, and the entire room is now a major crime scene. Blood's splattered so thick, it drips from every wall and low ceiling. The wrinkled old lady appears to have been mauled by an entire pack of hungry wolves. Luckily, her face is one of the only things left unharmed. For what it's worth, I don't recognize her.

"How am I supposed to live like this, Hayden?" she cries without looking for any kind of comfort. It's nothing more than the blunt words of a harsh new reality setting in. She's realizing that what just happened will continue for the rest of her now endless life. The worst part is that I don't have an answer for her blunt question. The harsh truth is, for us to live, others will die.

"I don't honestly know, Quinn." I attempt to give the same naked truth she deserves.

"I killed that woman, HAYDEN!!! I watched my hands doing it; I tried to stop them, but they *WOULDN'T STOP!!!* I *couldn't* stop them from tearing that lady into *pieces!* OH GOD, I can still *taste* her blood in my *mouth!!!! What did you do to me?!?! You made me one of those..."* She tapers off hopelessly.

"Monsters..." I finish for her. I'm shamefully speechless except for that single excruciating word. She's dying inside and for the first time, I'm speechless.

My heart splits open as the uncomfortable seconds fly by. Even though I'm probably the least qualified person to give advice on loving yourself, since I'm a professional pessimist with a self-defeatist attitude to match, she needs some reassurance right now. She craves to hear the sun will come up tomorrow and life will go on.

"You know how you're gonna keep going? With me."

I clinch her bloody hands in mine before continuing, "I won't tell you this is a great way of life. Good people are not meant to live this way. You're not supposed to have to constantly fight back the devil telling you to do evil things. But the one thing I can promise is that you'll never have to go through it alone. I'll be with you every single step of the way.

Together, we can be broken things.

When my family was taken, I had no one. I was lost in a world that wanted nothing to do with me anymore. Well, eventually, that pain twisted into the worst kind of self-loathing. I hated myself for being so cowardly. I hated myself so much, I honestly didn't believe I should ever be happy again. How could I be? I didn't deserve to be happy when I couldn't even save my own family! That's the kind of permanent shame that will always stay with me. Even when I someday see them on the other side, that disgrace will still be mine.

So, that's why I've removed myself from the entire world and everyone in it. The last time I even remember feeling anything was during the war. It gave me purpose, you know? Who you fight for, who you fight with, defines you. And now everything we fought for—died for—is going to be for absolutely nothing! The war is going to begin all over again and those mongrels will be unstoppable behind the pure blood.

Think about it, every monarch has two things in common: they believe their life is far more valuable than yours, and they have something to unite behind; a symbol or cause that bonds everyone together. Samael will be that figure they're willing to die for.

Think about it this way, Shepherd is the very tip of a coming wave that could drown us all. That's why we have to take advantage of our chance to stop it before it can even begin! We must take their symbol, Samael, and use him for good. As an added bonus, we'll get to make those assholes pay for what they did to you. I know this is hard to believe right now, but what you are, *your monster*, can be used for good. That devil inside will let you accomplish some really amazing things if you let it. It won't always be pretty. Honestly, we'll probably do some terrible things along the way—vicious, cruel, ugly things—but sometimes the world doesn't need another hero. Sometimes it needs a monster."

Was it a Patton-worthy speech? No, but hopefully the sincerity trickling down my cheeks will convince her that her anxiety is a shared one. My rare display of vulnerability does succeed in wiping most of the hopelessness from her face. We get to sit in a comfortable silence while our tears fade naturally. Well, mostly comfortable, since bloody ooze is still dripping off the cheap plastic paneling around us.

After a few minutes, there's a simple nod to signal she's ready to begin the lengthy clean-up. I waste no time in pulling out every roll of soft-as-gravel toilet paper. Her skin is easy enough to clean; it actually looks better than when she came in. Life has returned to her sunken cheeks and hollow eyes. Our biggest problem seems to be that her cotton dress has become a sponge of incriminating stains. She already had a few, but this is *sooooooooooo* much more than a couple spots.

Covering them with my jacket hides most of the really nasty bits. The bottom still has some splatter, and there's one extra-large spot over her hip, but overall it should work. Maybe no one will notice if we rush back to our seats quick enough? So then, what do we do with the pruned corpse? As unappealing as it is, my teeth ache just looking at it. I still haven't eaten anything more than a raccoon in days, and my monster is getting impatient. Like it or not, he needs to eat.

I ask Quinn to turn away. Partly for her own good, but mostly due to my own embarrassment. I then drain every last drop in the withered body. There's not much left; just enough to make the shame worth it. The fresh blood does help to take the edge off. Rational thoughts are definitely coming a lot easier now. Like, since no one has checked on the missing lady, there's a good chance she's traveling alone. Maybe there's still a chance we could ride this one out? We can jam the door closed, but the body certainly can't stay here. The smell alone would quickly give us away. It seems getting rid of it is our only real option.

Realistically though, given the cramped room, that's pretty limited, as well. There's really only one possible direction to go, and this will definitely not be one of my finest moments. I throw open the roof vent and measure it with my forearm. It's not wide enough to fit her yet, so a few sections will have to be peeled back like a banana. I stop to re-measure after each new slice until I'm sure she'll fit all the way through. I then say a prayer of thanks and tack on an apology for what's getting ready to happen.

Lifting the body isn't too hard since she weighs around sixty pounds now. And my measurements were so accurate that the upper body slides through without even touching the sides. Then, once the waist is out, the wind does the rest.

The strong vacuum easily pulls her the rest of the way out. Everything is going perfectly until one shoelace catches a jagged edge of the peeled roof, then all that quiet, cautious work is rendered *utterly* useless as the withered body starts banging off the top of the bus like a damn bongo drum!

Shit! Shit! Shit!

I scramble around the small room for several seconds with no actual goal in mind; just a wild panic and desire for the gut-churning noise to stop! The wind continues picking up the anchored body and slamming it back down every few seconds! Each new collision makes our cramped room explode with the ringing sound of thunder! It must be echoing across the entire bus and alerting everyone here! They manage to detonate seven or eight more times before I can wrangle the wedged foot free! Even then, of course, it bounces a few more times on the way down the roof.

Like I said, shit.

I slip out of the hole and mentally prepare for the rush of people coming through the door. It's not that they scare me; I mean, most of them can barely walk, but hurting them is the last thing I want to do. Maybe it would be possible to push our way off the bus? Although, that's not ideal either, since they could easily break a hip or something.

Fortunately, all my worry appears to be for nothing when no one ever charges through the flimsy door. There's not even a casual knock of concern to check on the sound of several bombs exploding in the toilet. For some mysterious reason, no one seems to care about all the obvious destruction that's been going on in this small room! Even so, I allow a few extra minutes of caution before getting back to Quinn.

And what I do find is a girl buried so far in the corner that the paneling is bent around her like a bubble. "It's finished." I reassure her (and myself) with a confident voice and outstretched hand. She's shaken to the core, but still breathing. Right now, that's all we can ask for.

Where do we go from here? Quinn's still covered in blood, I played a furious drum solo on the roof, and we'll have to find a way back to our seats eventually. Well, since no grand ideas come to mind, let's just open the door and see where it goes!

Could we fight our way of here? Yes.

Do I want to? No.

I straighten my windblown hair one last time before facing the jury outside. I carefully position Quinn so we won't have to open the door any wider than we have to. We'll butter up and squeeze out of here if it means no one's going to be able to see around us.

Funny enough, opening the door carefully actually takes great effort! I have to inch it along to keep it from spilling all the way open. When I turn my attention back to the bus, I notice the curious folks in the back are staring right at us!

And the next row.

Then the next.

And the next.

It quickly becomes apparent that every eye is firmly locked on us. The entire bus remains glued to our every move while the old folks whisper quietly. Do they know what *happened?* Since they're smiling, probably not. This would be a *very* odd response to murder. *So, what is this then?!?!*

Quinn remains in the bathroom just in case we need to exit out the vent, too. I try forcing a smile to hide my shock and confusion. When only half my mouth lifts, it ends up looking more like an awkward family photo than radiating joy.

The anxious tide shifts by catching a couple of their muted conversations. "Oh, she *must* be feeling better!" snickers one couple. "The color has *certainly* returned to his cheeks!" observes another. "I swear, kids these days will do it any ol' where!" protests one dusty old crow.

They think we were screwing in the bathroom?

WHAT!?!?

Our imaginary fling even causes one couple to reminisce their glory days of doing it on a plane ride to Denver. That conversation paints the unkind picture of the two dirty, wrinkled fools joining the mile high club. It's mentally damaging, but far better than the truth. I turn to Quinn and give my best *"go with it"* smile. If sex will explain all the disturbing noises, we're gonna play right along!

I'm suddenly inspired to release more fake chuckles, along with a big sloppy cheek kiss for good measure. Anything that helps paint the picture of two horny kids who just can't keep their hands off each other. It probably helps that we already have the very authentic red-faced appearance of a truly embarrassed couple. A firm smack on the ass only adds to the over-the-top theatrics. It also distracts everyone while I break off the bathroom door handle, then shove it back through the wall like a makeshift nail to keep the door closed. I give it a few gentle tugs to check how well it might hold up over the next few stressful days. It doesn't budge, so *hopefully* it will hold long enough to get us off this bus.

I turn back to boldly proclaim, "We were just so happy she's feeling better!" Another solid ass slap gets cheers from some, eye rolls from others, but none suspect us of anything more than boning in the bathroom. Quinn's eyes are two perfectly round circles during the entire thing. She was speechless already, so this just drives her further down that silent hole.

On our walk of shame, we get cat calls, congratulations, and several high fives before reaching our seats. "After you, dear." I continue playing the role while methodically positioning her bloody dress away from the crowd. I don't take an actual full breath until she's made it all the way into the protective seat.

Once everyone has gone back to their business, I ask the still-trembling Quinn, "You all right, tiger?" She's stuck upright with her head frozen straight ahead; glaring at the seat in front of us as if she could set it on fire. "If it's any consolation, that's the way I would want to go. You know, out the roof of a speeding bus." As soon as I say it, I regret it. Even I know it was too far. It's the rotten result of a sluggish mind and blazingly fast mouth. I try smiling, but it comes out as one of those, "What can I say, *I'm a dick*" expressions.

Suddenly, Rita swoops in to save me from my purgatory of discomfort, "Care for a soda?"

"Bless you Rita, I would *love* one!"

"Thought so. I bet you're *exhausted.*" she speaks with a noticeable grin. Nice to know she's like me, a real asshole.

Chapter 23: Lucky

The wheels on the bus go round and round, round and round, round and round, for what feels like an eternity. I don't even believe it when the clock says it's only been twenty hours since the bathroom incident. The entire time has been spent with one eye on the broken door, and one on anyone who gives me a strange look. Constantly going back and forth has kept me a fraying ball of nerves. I have to carefully study every face for some hint that they're onto us. Call me crazy, but our only punishment so far has been a guilty conscience and having to stop at every rest area along the way.

I eventually force myself to sleep just to break up the maddening routine. Sadly, the naps never last long because of the aforementioned pee breaks. The entire group has to slowly shuffle off and on the bus every twentyish minutes. Quinn hasn't said a word or even looked at me yet. She's remained glued to the window, lost in her own world. That leaves me with nothing to do except drift in and out of my frustrating slumber for hours. By the time Rita shakes me awake, I barely know where I'm at. She mumbles something, although it's not until Quinn repeats, "we've pulled into the terminal" that I actually comprehend what's happening.

My slow-moving mind isn't really a problem since we clearly won't be going anywhere for a while. Even though we have no baggage—nothing except restless legs—the old folks do, and they're in no rush to get them. I decide to use the extra time to show Quinn the grandeur of the Vegas skyway. Resting right outside is the ship that will take us up to the cities. Maybe I should explain that Vegas has changed, too...

Vampires had a serious numbers problem at the beginning of the war. While they were *far* more powerful than humans, there simply wasn't enough of them. Like, not even close. The vampire plague was a wildfire spreading across the globe, and yet they were still outnumbered 500 to 1. So, they solved their complex problem with a pretty simple solution; simply dismantle the _entire_ infrastructure of the country.

Their destructive plan was to isolate us from each other, completely dismantle the government, and remove any form of organization we ever had. That plan would keep us fighting on a local level, and it worked pretty damn well.

We became victims of our technological dependence. Electromagnetic pulses (EMPs) took out all digital communications, as well as most air and ground transportation. Anything with a computer became an expensive paperweight. This effectively separated everyone into small geographic areas, breaking the global war down into thousands of tiny wars, each with its own ending. That's why we have separate colonies now. Some battles were won by humans... most were not. And once we were broken, there was no going back.

The United States were gone.

Only the Colonies remained.

Their next step was to cut off food supplies. That meant systematically destroying every major dam and levee used for irrigation. Dwindling food supplies brought starvation and further divided an already brittle population. People began killing over a single loaf of bread. That's also when vampires started trading food for loyalty, and hell broke loose. It was win-win for them because they had no need for actual food.

Lights were the next to go. That kept us fighting in the dark so they could come in the night to wipe us out. Even after they stopped, humans couldn't sleep anymore. They feared the boogeyman (or mongrel) that might be hiding in the shadows. Our side was divided, paranoid, starving, and losing fast.

Vegas enters the story when the hydroelectric plants were destroyed. After Hoover Dam was destroyed, Las Vegas withered up like an old prune. Without water, it quickly reverted back to the barren wasteland Mother Nature always intended it to be. Nothing was left except ghosts, goblins, and empty buildings buried in the sand.

Long story short, after the war, some entrepreneurial types wanted to rebuild, but the old city was too far gone to bring back. So, in true Vegas style, they went straight up—two and a half miles! From down here, all you can see are the huge pillars supporting the massive new city. Those things stretch all the way from sand to sky! The only trace of the city itself is the massive round shadows it casts down on the clouds.

Of course, none of this stopped Vegas from becoming the epicenter of decadence and glamour it always was. I went many years ago, and though my memory of that trip is *fuzzy* at best, I remember the layout pretty well. You start down here at the gigantic column supporting the main strip. Think of it like a really, *really* tall table. Everyone lives and plays on the top, and right now we're at the bottom looking up. Over the years, three more floating cities have been built around the original. Each one is a different size and meant for a different audience. Some are for entertainment; others are only for the hardcore gamblers.

One of the most unique things about the cities is their total lack of roads. For a place known for its "strip", these new cities are built without any streets at all. Instead, there are massive tracks on the underside of the tabletop that carry suspended trams, shuttles, and individual cabs. Some of the best ones have glass floors that let you see all the way down to the ground. Think of it like a subway without walls. Plus, it's the only way in and out of the city.

Now, of course, as long as you play by their rules, there will be no rules. It's the only city where you have to pass a credit check before being allowed in.

Ironically, when New Vegas was constructed, it brought the old one back in a very unexpected way. The new cities act as umbrellas to partially shield the desert from the unforgiving heat. That's made the original into something of an oasis for any stray desert dwellers and mutants looking for a place to live. I've never been there, but it must be pretty bad because they've had to relocate the loading docks several times to avoid the creatures living there.

So, that's where we are at now, looking at the arched gateway that marks the very beginning of our long climb. Honestly, it has to be seen to be believed. While every other bus stop in the world is a simple old boring terminal, a modest utilitarian object to get the job done, that's not how you would ever describe *this* place. Simply put, it's grand.

And it's not just one specific thing that makes it so awesomely incredible; it's the entire package. At first, you're drawn in by the flashing lights that lead up to the colossal arch. Mind you, this isn't some standard half-circle buried in the ground, either.

This beast of grand architecture begins with curvy golden walls that gradually rise from the ground. From here, it closely resembles two long, flowing trees merged in the center. The curve of the arch is fluid, almost like the broad shoulders of a slumped giant. It climaxes in a massive hanging ship they call a shuttle, but because of its titanic size, should only be called a ship. Maybe I shouldn't use the word "Titanic" since I'm getting ready to get on board... Anyhow, its engines are already humming on the triple beam track above.

And what's on the other side of the mighty arch?

Absolutely nothing.

The entire thing rests on the edge of a steep cliff with nothing more than sand and air behind it. And of course they call the station "the Stairway to Heaven." Modest, they are not.

I say a fond farewell to several of the folks who have been so kind to us. Rita, who shared everything she owns with me, gives us one last hug and makes me promise to keep in touch. Then she slips another of those delicious sandwiches in my pocket for the road. The little old ladies continue waving all the way down the long walkway. Just as we enter the double sliding doors, I overhear the bus driver shout, "What's this mess? We must have hit a coyote!" My toes curl while I shove Quinn through the doors a bit faster.

The guilt still weighs heavily on my mind when stepping through the grand entrance. But, once inside, I'm magically transported to the distracting world of a tacky genie's lamp. Wall-to-wall cherry velvet covers everything but the faux marble floor. Several rows of columns, straight from a fevered Greek fantasy, effectively divide the room into six long lines. At the beginning of each row is a gold cherub that welcomes us with a pen and basket of forms to fill out.

We scoop up the financial paperwork before claiming a spot to wait our turn. Soon, a beautiful red head in a tight black corset appears out of nowhere to offer us free drinks. Her skimpy outfit ties my tongue so tightly, only a caveman grunt manages to make it out. I try recovering, but end up saying, "you're welcome" instead of "thank you." It's time to cut my losses, lay a few bucks on the tray, and slump off in shame.

Quinn's judgmental eyes are anxious to share their critical opinion of me. In fact, they can barely contain all the tearful laughter welling up behind them. She's clearly amused by the whole thing, even if she won't admit it out loud.

Fortunately, they've got processing the paperwork down to a fine art, so our time in the embarrassing line is mercifully short. People are checked off as fast as they can sign their name. Some are turned away for bad debts, while others are given a gold house card and a personal assistant. My credit score will get us neither of those things. It will only land us a tote bag with a pocket calendar missing the month of September.

With the prerequisite financial checkup out of the way, we're free to track down the shuttle for the main city of Nexus. The rest of process is just like any other public transportation; find a line, claim a seat, and wait.

Luckily, this wait is also ridiculously short. We barely have time to stretch out before the ship lurches forward and we're on our way. They seem pretty anxious to get us, and our money, up to the great cash machine in the sky. We're told the entire trip should last twenty-seven minutes and fifteen seconds. (They really do have *everything* worked out here.) We decide to pass the time with slot machines and a few table games. I have no idea what the object is, but I win twice! Then I lose fourteen times in a row.

That's when I decide to try my luck at the bar instead. Quinn settles in with another big bag of salty peanuts and a diet soda with lime. She stays almost silent until the conversation turns to Vegas, then her natural curiosity asks for every little detail about the place.

This conversation clearly shows the different lives we've lived. Not just our ages, but the vastly different worlds we come from. I remember life before the war, real freedom, while this restrictive place is all she's ever known. I mean, humans had absolutely no rights where she's from. They weren't even allowed to step outside of the city due to the risk of infection. Every aspect of her life has been based around "the Lords".

She was never allowed to just be a curious kid. All seventeen years were lived as a prisoner, where independence would be rapidly snuffed out by public execution. The time on this boat has been the most engaged I've seen her, and Nexus should be even better! There will be an incredible amount of reckless fun and less violent ways to control our hunger. They have world-class plasma shops filled with amazing stews, pastries, tarts, smoothies, coffees, and cherry wines that you could get lost in.

Trust me, I have.

All of them are infused with the blood she craves, without any of the additional guilt. She wants to be disgusted as I describe them in detail, even as a bead of saliva forms on her shimmering bottom lip.

Chapter 24: Chasing the Sun

It takes a while to accept this new way of life. I mean, you live as one person, with certain rules of how to sleep and eat, then all that leaves in the blink of an eye. The monster seeps its sticky black fingers into every little crevice of your being. Concepts like murder and morality become innocent victims to the altar of satisfying it.

True story: I once knew a guy who was a vegetarian his entire human life. Well, after the change he couldn't control that anymore. He would literally go vomit after every bloody meal. He was so disgusted that he'd refuse to eat until his monster would eventually make him. He woke up from these blind rampages with no memory of the terrible things he had done. There were only countless pools of blood to let him know that it definitely wasn't good.

This tragic cycle played on until he absolutely couldn't take it anymore. One random day, when he felt the dreaded hunger coming back, he calmly laid his things on the sidewalk, gave his favorite coat to a passing stranger, and chewed through his wrists right there in the middle of the street. I suppose my point is that everyone has to find their own way, though it's easier for some than others.

My somber mood is interrupted by a soothing voice over the intercom. She alerts us that the ship has broken cloud cover and the best views will be off to the left side. Quinn abruptly bolts from her chair with a fistful of my sleeve. The girl tugs my jacket (with me in it) all the way over to the huge window.

Her over-enthusiastic hands spill my freshly made drink along the way. Even though it's uncomfortable, it's easy to laugh off since it will easily blend in with the rest of the dark stains. Quinn's honest smile, as the clouds tumble away from our ship like cotton balls, make my freezing-cold clothes a distant memory. Her eyes twinkle from the sparkly white peaks spinning into magnificent new shapes every few seconds. They appear to be solid enough to scoop the fluffy mountains up into a delicious ice cream sundae.

In the middle of all the natural beauty is a rising monument to human construction. The massive stalk grows out of the thick clouds and finally gives us our first view of the four silver behemoths. This first city, appropriately named Prime, looms large over us. The ship purposely slows to allow us time to enjoy the passing spectacle. At first glance, the bottom layer appears to be one big mess of jumbled steel, but it's actually an expertly crafted maze of tunnels with brightly colored shuttles running the labyrinth. Some are in enclosed tubes, while others merely hang down in the wide-open sky. All the precise routes remind me of a slow-motion game of Pac-Man.

We pass so close by another shuttle that its passengers wave to us. Quinn reaches out to the friendly people by pressing a hand to the glass. The window steams up under her lingering pressure. She refuses to look away from their kindness for even a brief moment. It's not until the shuttle is completely gone from view that she finally decides to remove her hand from the steamy window.

Even though Prime is the smallest of the four, as we sweep by the middle layer, I'm astonished at how deep the city is. Its foundation is *at least* four hundred feet deep and coated in a dark chrome on the outside. Running around the center is a wide golden ring that gives it a very classic look. Great care has been taken to make the entire city appear built from one solid piece of steel. There are no visible seams or bolts on the entire thing. I'm such a sucker for architecture that I would have loved to design these mega structures in another life. The sheer amount of engineering it takes to turn metal and bolts into such a gorgeous piece of work is astonishing!

The strong midday sun cuts through the cabin as soon as we emerge from underneath the massive city. I have to look away from the blinding light, while Quinn remains fixated on the rising dome. She's mesmerized by the towering casinos, grand buildings, and glowing billboards that make up the unbelievable little planet. Even the grass shimmers in an unearthly way.

Off in the hazy distance are the other smaller cities; Argo and Tetra, but they're mere infants compared to big daddy Nexus above. If you put Prime, Argo, and Tetra together, they still wouldn't match the gigantic size of Nexus.

Quinn drapes herself over my shoulders to get a better view of the growing giant. This is the first sign of warmth she's shown since we've come down from the mountain. If I didn't know better, the way she's wrapped around me is dangerously close to a hug. She's most likely caught up in the moment and I'm reading too much into it. But maybe, just maybe, there's a small crack in her impenetrable shell.

While I'm contemplating the significance of a very simple act, she stares intently at the hovering giant as if it were an invading UFO. Its massive size swallows everything including the sun. This has to be what it's like coming up underneath a planet! My head must have been really far up my ass on the last trip here; I don't remember any of this! Actually, I believe it was focused on the fiery red-head at the roulette table. You know what they say: red on the head, fire in the number two men's bathroom stall.

What is it with Vegas and red-heads, anyway?

Also, why don't I visit here more often?!

While my mind is on a very bright-haired lady, our ship coincidentally plunges into the all-consuming shadow of the city. Two chimes and a soft voice later, we're instructed to return to our seats for docking. It takes some of the more *mature* passengers a lot longer than us. We're already enjoying another bag of peanuts by the time the ship slides into an even darker loading bay.

Now, this next part I *DO* remember, and it should really blow her mind! It begins with the same pleasant announcer asking for everyone to please remain seated. A few seconds later, some bright flashing lights and horribly loud sirens ring out. Suddenly, the entire left wall drops away, and waiting inside is a completely blank room. White walls, no pictures, and very cramped. I'm really starting to hate small places.

When a confused Quinn glances over at me for direction, I refuse to spoil the surprise. Not the grand entrance she was expecting, I guess? A couple stewardesses come by to aid the mobility challenged among us into the empty room. One of them happens to be the attractive redhead from earlier, so a few extremely awkward glances are exchanged. I grin and she gives me a look that could peel paint off the wall.

Anyhow, when the last wrinkled toe finds a place to stand, the wall closes and lights abruptly shut off. When a few anxious "eeks" come from the intense dark, I have to wonder if scaring a bunch of centennials is really the best idea???

"ARE YOU READDDDYYYYYYYYYY!!!!!!!!!" blasts out with a thumping beat. Green and yellow spotlights begin crisscrossing the crowd and everyone's knees buckle slightly as the chamber starts raising. The club atmosphere doesn't last long, though; daylight is already flooding in from a small crack running down the middle of the ceiling. The split grows quickly, so the two halves fold away like a box without a top.

For a brief time, we're stuck in the strange position of being bombarded by loud techno music inside a crazy small room, with the midday sun shining in from the missing ceiling. It's not until the elevator stops that the rest of the walls join in the origami magic.

One thing's for damn sure—all these mechanical clinks, clanks, clunks, and pounding music are real torture on the enhanced senses! Within seconds, the entire room has disappeared, leaving us standing in the very center of the Vegas strip.

"They do it in style around here, Tiger!" I'm still shouting even though the music is long gone. *"Pretty cool, right?!?!"*

"It's BEAUTIFUL!" Her wide eyes reflect the vibrant colors of this dreamlike town. Best of all, she's wearing the first genuine smile I've seen on her.

The excited crowd is quickly (for them) spreading out to go their separate ways. All of the sudden, it's *us* in *their* way. Since we don't really have a destination in mind, we move to a nice patch of neon grass to get out of the slow stampede. There's a sprawling tree not too far away that seems like a good place to hide from the passing mob. It seems unusual to have such a natural beauty in the middle of all this fakeness. It does make complete sense that it would be the first place I would seek out, though.

Quinn makes herself at home by stretching out on the smooth grass. I one-up her by taking off my shoes to let the silken strands run between my cramped toes. Who knows if all this is fake, but the talking squirrel in the tree surely is. Our furry friend breaks the ice with a very unusual joke, "There was once a very successful man from Chicago. He had a beautiful wife, three wonderful kids, and a great job making plenty of money. Then one day, he heard a voice in his head saying, 'Quit your job, sell everything, and move to New Vegas!'

It wouldn't stop! All he could hear was that voice in his head and it was driving him crazy! Every day, 'Quit your job, sell all your crap, and move to New Vegas!' Well, this guy couldn't take it anymore! This crazy voice *HAD* to be his calling!

The next day he quit his job, sold everything, and moved to Vegas! He didn't even unpack before the voice commanded him to go to the Bellagio. There was no turning back, so away he went! At the casino, the voice directs him 'Go to the roulette wheel, and put all your money on red thirteen.' He immediately shouts to the dealer, 'Put it all on red thirteen!' The man behind the wheel is shocked that someone would bet all their money on one spin, but does as the man says. The ball drops into the wheel as a large crowd anxiously gathers to watch. Even management and security come over to check out what's happening. The heavy ball bounces around, and around, and around... until finally landing on black twelve.

The inner voice says, 'WELL, DAMN!' and he never hears it again."

The weird little squirrel then laughs with all his mechanical might before giving a final advertisement as the next group moves in. "Thank you folks. I'm here all week! No, seriously, I'm bolted to this tree! Could someone get a wrench? I know where to find one. Try Sky Daddy's Gaming Emporium, open twenty-four hours a day, and don't forget to order the veal! So, has anyone seen my nuts?" the furry comedian finishes.

I pause for a few minutes to contemplate the very confusing story. Was it about gambling addiction? Or a PSA about mental health? To me, it will just be a funny story to tell the next bartender.

I can't get my shoes on fast enough to escape the weird squirrel's pleas to help find his "nuts." We decide to leave the neon green pastures behind and hit the main strip instead. As fun as all the shops look, we decide to get something to eat first (she still isn't calling it blood), then head off to a hotel to get cleaned up.

The hardest part of finding food here is deciding where to eat! There are shops and street vendors on almost every corner. "Muffin's Shake Shop" is our obvious choice since, well... could there be any better way of adjusting to the vampire lifestyle than *MILKSHAKES?*

Unfortunately, the resulting concoction resembles pink cottage cheese more than delicious happiness in a cup. While the pictures on the menu may be deceiving, I've certainly eaten way worse. Quinn, on the other hand, looks as if someone pissed in her cup. "Not quite what you were expecting, huh?" She watches the glop like it's getting ready to attack. To her credit, she does get in a few sips before gagging and dropping the rest to the ground. I ask if she would like something else while scooping the mess off the pristine ground. She can't quit coughing, so she holds her arms up in a big X to let me know that no, in fact, she would *not* like any more of these delightful shakes.

Eager to put the diet disaster behind us, I suggest finding a place to lay low and relax. Looking at all these glamorous hotels has my ego craving far more than my meager budget will allow. We end up standing at the front desk of a ratty little hotel, talking to a man in a heavily stained wife beater. He doesn't ask for names or info, just how many hours we'll need the room. When I inform him that we'll need it for three days, he actually has to open a book to find what their daily rate is. We're *not* off to a good start here.

But I reluctantly grab the key to our temporary home.

Third floor.

Room thirteen.

Awesome...

It takes a few seconds of standing outside the door to prepare to open it. As long as there isn't a chalk outline on the floor or man-sized cockroaches flying gang colors, it's gonna have to work. When the courage finally comes and the door creaks open, it's honestly not as bad as I feared. Tacky as all hell, but I can get over that. The terrible wall paper of hundred-dollar bills has an authentic Old Vegas feel to it.

Over on the lopsided table is a plastic plant in a cracked vase. At least they've tried to class the place up some? The hardest part is playing dumb to all the stains on the used-to-be green shag carpeting. It's not really even multiple stains anymore, just one *big ass* stain.

Quinn is walking around, trying not to touch anything. I excuse myself to visit another very cramped bathroom. This one consists of a giant toilet, miniature shower, and one extremely cracked mirror. There wasn't room for a sink, so they simply decided not to have one.

I didn't really need to use the restroom, I just want a few minutes where I don't have to keep a forced smile and fake confidence. I want a few minutes where I don't have to be strong for anyone else. It takes a wrong turn when I look into the cracked mirror and don't recognize the man looking back. This is the first time I've seen all the damage up close. Some of my wounds are healing; most are waiting for a fresh supply of blood before committing to the idea.

I look like I've been colored with every shade of purple and green crayon in the deluxe-sized box. Everywhere I look is something new. Fresh scratches over half-healed ones, bruises under busted blood vessels; there are even cuts in both arm pits! The missing chunk of shoulder has healed better than most, but it still looks deflated. How thoroughly I examine myself would be creepy if anyone else watched.

By the time the self-examination is over, I'm wearing underwear and a half-crooked look of revulsion. Everything else is bundled up into a sloppy pile on the filthy bathroom floor. The brief moment for myself turned into a twenty-minute journey of self-discovery, seeking out every flaw on an extremely damaged body.

It hurts.

A lot.

I begin my uncomfortable return back to reality by wading through the soiled mound of clothes. It quickly becomes apparent that getting redressed in the cramped room is not going to be as easy as stripping down was. My elbow must hit the same damn towel rack, in the same damn place, at least a dozen times. Just when I think a sore arm is going to be my worst problem—the common act of picking up a jacket drops a bomb on me. More specifically, three little ones.

The trio of coins plummet from some lost pocket with the force of Earth-shattering boulders. Flakes of dried blood paint the floor on impact. The metal lets out a piercing wail that skips the ears, and heads straight down into my heart. The miserable souvenirs seize control of my every breath; constricting them into gasps that do little more than tease me with oxygen.

My mind does a full swan dive, with a full gainer and half twist, into the cesspool of failure. It replays the dissected girl that laid on top of these very coins. The blood on the floor has me running from the tiny coins as if they were actual bombs. I want nothing more than to flush them down the toilet, or heave the little bastards into an active volcano, but that would require touching them, and I never want to feel their cold bite on my skin again.

The tiny room won't allow me to get far enough away from the cursed things. The best I can do is toss a grimy towel over them so they're out of view. Hiding them allows me to get some mental separation from the humiliation and guilt. My irrational side wants nothing more than to walk out the door, lock it, and burn this place to the ground. But the longer I look at the little knots on the ground, the more I realize what I actually have to do. It's the same thing I asked of Quinn... I have to make a deal with the Devil.

Realistically, we're flying blind out here. No one's on our side. We have absolutely nothing and even less to lose. We don't have even the slightest clue what we could be walking into. Hope and willpower will only take us so far. For the rest, we could really use some leverage. Though it sours my soul to even think it, having some financial insurance could make a huge difference. I told Quinn to use her monster for good, and I need to do the same. These little round bastards can be made into more than monuments to my personal failure. I don't know how yet, but my gut says so.

The renewed spirit gives me the courage to (eventually) remove the towel. The very sight of them fills the toilet with the contents of my stomach. No matter how well-intentioned, I can't make peace with the idea of those bloody things. Trembling fingers have to carefully unwind an entire roll of toilet paper to bury the damn golden devils under again. It's unnerving because either way, tossing them or taking them with me, they have to be moved. I might as well do the smart thing. As much as it makes my skin crawl...

I decide it would be best to bundle the entire wad of toilet paper around them. I then shove the hefty pile into the deepest pocket before I have the chance to change my mind. And as soon as the last piece clears, I try to forget they ever existed. Somehow, I hadn't noticed the extra weight before, but now they're all I can feel.

A last glimpse in the mirror reveals that I look even more crazed than when I came in here to relax. The cracked glass splits my face into three distorted pieces, each more disturbing than the last. I could let them bother me, rip away my confidence, or use every bruise as motivation to leave this room a better man. I've earned each one, and the job's not over yet.

The sudden attitude upswing launches me out of the little room with a vengeance. I round the corner with a fire in my belly, only to discover that Quinn doesn't share my revved-up emotions. The exhausted kid has passed out right by the front door. Seeing her curled up in the cheap chair is both heartwarming and heartbreaking. She's still here, but I wouldn't wish what she's gone through on my worst enemy. The heartache she's experienced in a few short days is more than enough for an entire lifetime. Putting all macho crap aside, I couldn't have done it. I would've given up long ago.

The least I can do is not let her sleep on the rickety chair. Not that the bed will be much better. Its stiff sheets and course comforter could be mistaken for a poorly paved road. It works, though.

I find myself gawking at her little hands on the way over to the bed. It's amazing to think that those delicate fingers have torn through entire armies of trained killers like paper dolls. They're the reason I'm still alive to be able to lay my face on these scratchy overstuffed pillows.

My muscles celebrate being able to finally stretch out after being crammed into a narrow bus seat for so long. My brain is the next to attempt to relax. It tries shrinking all the worried feelings into a single, hopeful thought. While I have no idea what the rest of our journey will bring, I'm simply going to enjoy this moment because, for once, I'm not alone.

Quinn Chapter 1: Come in from the cold

A churning stomach keeps sleep as nothing more than an unobtainable dream. I might have gotten an hour or two of actual rest, but that's about it. The rest of the time I've been making plaster constellations out of ceiling cracks and praying for sleep to take me away for a little while longer.

It never does.

I'm trapped in this living nightmare instead. After a while, I simply refuse to close my eyes anymore. Why should I? They only show me terrible things. Miranda's shaky arms wrapped around Daddy bleeding in the dirt. Morgan is down there, too, with that stupid little knife of his. Then there's Mom, who—right before being pulled into the murderous crowd—said, "I'm sorry."

To Me! *Why???* It was supposed to be *me!!!*

Her face had the same ghostly expression as the day this all started. Everyone heard the door, but only Mom knew it was different. I don't know how; it was only three ordinary knocks on our worn-out door. Not even the dog thought they were special enough to bark at. But Mom knew, and each knock sucked a little more life from her.

The first froze her solid.

The second removed all color from her paralyzed skin. She became a ghost looking at a plain wooden door.

The final one stole the sparkle from her bright eyes. If you've ever seen a corpse up close, you'll know what I mean.

I saw the same look years ago. Mom was feeding Miranda in the kitchen when I came home. My usual order of "hellos" was Mom, Miranda, then grandpa. Morgan and Dad usually didn't get home until way later in the day. Gramps would always sneak me some treat that Mom wasn't supposed to know about. I would grab it on the sly and enjoy it in my room. It was our thing. He really loved having the ultimate power of a grandparent; doing whatever the hell you want because you're the parent of the parent.

That day, he was resting in the living room, watching his favorite TV show. It was some old space western that had only lasted one season. I thought he was sleeping... then I saw his eyes and their dull appearance. Mom had that same look the day the men came. The knock was redundant; her eyes told me what was coming.

I was dead.

My body just had to catch up.

Dad swung the door open without a care in the world, with no idea what was waiting on the other side. That would quickly change.

The bastards didn't even wait for Miranda to leave the room before explaining their compensation. $5,452.55. I'll *NEVER* forget that number down to the penny. How could you forget the exact value of your life? And why that amount? Is it the same for everyone? Am I more or less valuable than others?

Mom strained to hold back the inevitable tears as the soldiers explained the details like I were an old pair of shoes. Their money was all the sympathy my family required. The Lords made it known that when the guards come, you go with them. Anything beyond that is a *gift*.

We had all seen what fighting against them would do. Years ago, a boy from my class tried to hide under the bed, and he was strapped to a pole in the center of town within the hour. The poor kid got to watch the bats eat his entire family before being sent to the arena. Of course, not before suffering on that pole for another long week. He was our warning. I never knew his name, only heard him called "violatore della legge" by our neighbors, but he's the reason I didn't say a word that day. It was just my turn.

The next hour was a blur of anger and tears, and none were mine. I had already accepted my fate. Only a soulless mask was left behind to say goodbye.

I was cold and hollow because I had to be. I even stayed steady when Morgan refused to leave his room. How could I be mad at him? He was angry, scared, and miserable like me. My only slip-up came when Daddy called me "pookie bear." Several painful tears broke through my hardened shell. That was his nickname for when I'd been in trouble and he had to explain why. He would always say, "Now pookie bear, you know you can't... (followed by whatever goofy thing I'd done that time)."

The lingering smell of his cherry tobacco is one of those things I never knew I would miss. I can still feel his famous hugs. The way he would pull me in with one arm, wrap the other over my shoulder, it felt as if nothing could ever hurt me inside that protective bubble. I even miss the weird things, like Miranda's high-pitched laugh. She would sound like a chipmunk on helium. Or how about when Mom used to drag me to the cheap movie theater every Tuesday? I'd only go for their extra-buttery popcorn. How much would I give for any of those lost treasures again?

The worst part was knowing that everything I did would be for the last time. A person should _never_ know when it's their time to go. I tried to burn those memories in so deep they would have to go to Heaven with me.

That single tear was still drying when Miranda gave me a handful of berries for the trip. She didn't really know where I was going, and certainly didn't know I wasn't coming back.

At least, I wasn't supposed to.

So, I bit my lip when the soldiers returned. I even opened the door for them myself. The sun was so bright, the men were only flat silhouettes on a burning background. That was perfectly fine with me; I didn't want to see their disgusting faces again. I was as close to total acceptance as a dying person can be. All I wanted to do was enjoy the warm sun on my face one last time. The dirty pricks couldn't even give me that.

They interrupted my bliss with a hot glove on my shoulder. The scorching leather squeaked with every twist of his crooked fingers. He shook me, demanding that I look him in the eye. My stubbornness wanted to fight, but knew the consequences my family would suffer. I gave in and let the two vivid eyes crawl out of the dark and swallow me whole. Then I was gone.

...Until I wasn't anymore.

Because, somehow, I woke back up. And now I'm here. Stuck in a place with nothing left for me! I had already made peace with death! So, what now? What's left other than _more_ death, and not mine, either! All the deaths it will take for me to keep living this pointless life.

The only things I feel anymore are anger, hatred, and rage! About the time I look over and imagine slicing the tip of Hayden's nose off, I figure it's time to get up and shut this out for a while. And I want to do it without his rambling mouth!

Slinking off the bed is extremely easy, since the stiff mattress doesn't flex at all. Hayden doesn't even skip a snoring beat. I do stumble a bit while putting my feet down in the plush carpet. I'm still waiting for my body to feel normal again. Everything works so well, it's like learning to walk again. My leg muscles want to push so hard that I'm almost skipping around the room. It's odd to feel so fragile and yet crush everything I touch.

And hearing, don't even get me started on hearing. It takes serious concentration to *not* pick up absolutely everything! Every scurrying bug, whistling nose hairs, grass growing... EVERY. DAMN. THING is amplified so much that it's hard to hear *any of it!* It's all one big tangled mess of noise.

I gently pry the door open to go in search of distractions. My hand, predictably, crushes the handle into a crumpled wad of aluminum foil. Not even this wakes the hibernating Hayden. Good. The last thing I want to hear is how unsafe going out alone is. Before I accidently do something that does stir him, I quickly slip outside and shut the door quietly behind me.

The moment I reach the fresh air, the crazy train is derailed. All the irrational thoughts melt and float away on the glorious breeze. The best thing about this city is the way it smells. It always smells fresh, like a spring shower has just swept through.

My fingers embrace the warm railing as it soaks up the perfect midday sun. Sliding them around allows me to sense the slight temperature variations between the screws and metal itself. I enjoy following the slender crease where the handrail was welded together. The little bumps flow like a river rushing to the ocean. Things that should be impossible to detect, like the steel pores expanding in the heat, are now unmistakably clear. None of this feels right anymore, but it's all uniquely wonderful.

The scratchy concrete makes it apparent that I forgot shoes. Instead of risking knocking the door off the hinges going back in, I decide to skip them all together. Going barefoot shouldn't be a problem in a place that's a perfect climate-controlled 72 degrees all the time. Plus, there's something energizing about the way the ground feels on my naked toes.

I leap up onto the warm railing and assume I'll tumble right back off. My old body would have slipped off the thin railing almost immediately.

Not this new one.

It's a magnet.

There's no more balancing. I'm free to stroll around on this narrow beam as easily as flat ground. Forward, backward, jumping, sliding; it doesn't matter. After that, dismounting and dropping two stories onto solid pavement is as effortless as breathing.

I feel so alive! Every direction has some fantastic new treat to enjoy! All the hypnotic colors, smells, and sounds are living creatures in this brand-new world!

I allow my eyes to drift closed in the middle of a busy crowd. People rush by and immerse me in all these new sensations; heartbeats, sweat, perfume, drumming feet, clanking ice cubes, all creating a beautiful symphony of life. They paint a brilliant picture of a hidden world that's always existed without me. It's as if there's been this beautiful masterpiece buried beneath my dull grey life all along!

Well, not anymore. The curtains have swung wide open and all her secrets are spilling out! From the slight tug of gravity, to the low hum of flowing electricity; even the machines clicking away in precise synchronicity. The distant buses, grinding hundreds of feet below, could be buzzing along right next to me! The magic of my new reality is wildly intoxicating, and that's *before* I open my eyes!

The entire world explodes into the rich colors of a vibrant dream. When I reach for the neon lights casually wandering off billboards, their beams bounce off in a million different directions. Everyone stares at the giggling girl, but I don't care. They can't see these wonderful creatures the way I can. This alien world is mine alone to explore. All I wanna do is chase the neon pixies from building to building. Dance along as the brilliant signs release more and more of my magical friends. In this blissful moment, there's only me, twirling across rooftops, swaying to the soundtrack of life while the heartbeat of Earth intertwines with mine.

My hair whips carelessly on the perfect breeze. The cool tips slash against my hot cheeks. Down below the scribbles of people are frantically trying to discover what I'm doing up here. I can hear their conversations; most have decided I'm going to jump.

Am I?

Can I fly?

Maybe.

I can do *everything* else!

If not, that's okay, too! There's nothing left for me here! I toy with the nervous crowd by dancing along the high ledge. I continue teasing them by dipping one foot over and enjoying their collective gasp. All of creation spins as my senses fire to incredible new heights. My heels rock along the steep edge. Their screams pushing me closer to the brink every time.

Their fear is beautiful.

Their fear is *addictive.*

Balancing along the sharp ledge allows me to enjoy it all. I slowly lean in to find just the right balance between sky and ground; the delicate center of the scale where the weight of a feather could either push me back to safety... or hurtling off a cliff. In the end, it's the weight of my shifting smile that tips the scales. I'm ready to fly.

There's no more self-doubt. The last bit of skin leaves the security of solid concrete. This feeling is the first real freedom I've ever known.

Freedom from Pain.

Control.

Weakness.

Gravity's mighty grip.

Even freedom from time itself as the endless fall continues.

The sea of lights shatters from my body slicing through it. My skin senses the slight temperature change of the rapidly approaching ground like hearing water reaching the top of a filling cup. My hand mindlessly reaches out to a grab a tree, then swings me effortlessly from branch to branch.

THIS. IS. FREAKING. AWESOME!!!!!!!

I can do incredible things without knowing how or why. They just *happen!!!* Like gliding through the tree, the only choice I make is to kick the talking squirrel on the way by!

A mob of astonished people have gathered to watch me. They marvel over my perfect landing, and I soak up every second of admiration. I'm grinning from ear to ear while being swept away in a blanket of pure ecstasy. My whole life has been lived as a mouse scurrying away from stomping feet. I've never been anything special, just something to shove aside for someone more important or powerful.

NEVER.

AGAIN.

My power burns inside like a fire that refuses to be contained anymore. No one will *EVER* push me down or make me feel weak again. NOTHING will ever be able to…

A jarring scream, unlike all the rest, suddenly yanks me from the whirling tornado of bliss. Without the blinding happiness, I unexpectedly find a young boy locked at the end of my unbreakable grip. The shocking discovery comes as teeth are already snapping toward his exposed neck. I force them away, but not before they carve a shallow valley from the underside of his chin. The taste of blood threatens to send me into a frenzy to cure the craving.

I'm fighting to cling to what little control I have left. The panicked crowd doesn't help by weakly attacking me. The only thing they're hurting is my *already* loose grip on reality, and shoving me away from a kid I already wanted away from! I try carefully swatting them back before this gets even worse than it already is.

They wisely choose to leave me alone after the first few fly off. The diversion gives me an opportunity to escape during the madness of rushing bodies. On the way through a startling revelation hits; I don't see people anymore—only meat. No faces, just the salty blood in their veins.

What's wrong with me? Is this all I am now?

I hurry to find the darkest alley this sunny place has and bury myself in its deepest shadow. In my freshly scrambled mind, time passes with no regard. Five minutes, maybe five hours, go by while I desperately search for any shred of stability. My only comfort comes from submerging myself in the bustling sounds of the lively city. I enjoy listening and making up my own stories about them. Like, if it's a bus I'll decide what color it might be. Or why someone is walking in uneven steps—are they hurt or old? Anything to keep my attention off the frequent murderous impulses.

And it works for a long time, too. It's not until the sound of approaching footsteps that I'm finally yanked away from my solitary trance. But once the calm feeling is gone, it's *gone.* I burst out of that happy place with a vengeance that frightens even me. It turns out the feet belonged to a guy who simply wanted to check on a crying girl in a dark alley. How do I know that? Because, just before my hands connected his face to the brick wall, he politely asked if I was okay.

It seems the same urges that guide me through trees and over buildings, will also kill anything that comes in reach. *Thankfully,* not this time. His nose is definitely broken, and shards of brick are stuck in his face, but he's still alive. There's so much blood gushing out of the fractured nose that I have to fish out old napkins from a nearby dumpster. Shaking off bits of food increases my already immense guilt. The extra shame helps to rid me of any lingering desires to drink his dripping blood. Well, most of them.

He doesn't look much older than me, and the side of his face that's not bleeding is quite charming. I can feel my cheeks blushing at the thought. Thankfully, none of his wounds seem bad. There's a nasty gash cutting across the eyebrow, a deep lip scratch which hopefully won't scar, plus a few more that—once you get the rocks out—should heal just fine.

Since I'm stuck holding the leaking nose, there's plenty of time to study all his colorful tattoos. My favorites are the red and blue samurai stretching all the way down his forearm. Actually, my favorites are the koi fish playing right below them. It's amusing how blissfully unaware they are of the intense battle raging above them.

My semi-creepy obsession is broken up by a rustling garbage can at the far end of the alley. I'm already on top of the dumpster before my mind can even catch up to what's going on. I sling the metal box aside, ready to maul whatever's hiding in there, only to find a skinny orange cat with terrified eyes. I certainly must have been drunk on power earlier, because as I'm fangs-deep in alley cat—all that's gone. Tears stream down while draining the unfortunate creature of every last drop. My hands are sloppy from the buckets of spilling blood. When I'm finished, the soft body melts to the ground, and all I want to do is dissolve with it.

At least there's a moment of clarity that should last long enough to get me out of here. I begin by wiping myself with more random trash pulled from the dumpster. It takes Herculean effort not to melt into a blubbering puddle of tears while scrubbing the cat away with used tissues and coffee filters. I then slip into a large passing crowd once I'm clean enough to blend in. The "blending in" part is likely just self-delusion, since I'm covered in smeared blood and trash. No one would look at me and think this was normal.

I can't control myself. That much is becoming fatally obvious. My only option is to fight back the crazies long enough to reach the crappy hotel room. Like it or not, I have nowhere else to go. While he isn't family, or even a friend, Hayden is the last thing I've got left in this world.

Chapter 25: Gold on the Ceiling

I lazily drift back from some of the best dreams I've ever had. There's a grinning bobble head on the bedside table that perfectly fits in with my calm mood. The cheap trinket, an Oriental-style cat that looks stolen from a Chinese take-out place, welcomes me back with its constant nod of approval.

How much time has passed? The fog of my blissful sleep still has a powerful grip on me. First, I stumble into a wall, then get my toes tangled in the shag carpet. I eventually find the light switch, mostly by luck, and watch it flicker on with an ugly florescent color. The grey/green glow helps to highlight every cut and bruise in painstaking detail. The haze finally lifts enough to realize the reflection is showing me two things: a bruised man and an empty bed. It takes a couple more seconds to grasp the big problem with that...

Not again.

I skip across the bed and rush to the door. The crushed handle is an obvious sign she went this way. A long list of bad possibilities is already stacking in my brain before I even make it through the flimsy door. The thought of Shepherd dragging her out (even though I was sleeping a foot away) actually makes sense in my hungover state.

I run out, barking in a raspy morning tone, *"QUINN!"*

"Shhhhhhh! I'm up here!" a little voice floats down from over the doorway. A quick stretch of the neck finds her delicately perched on the low rooftop. She seems to be up there enjoying a spectacular view of the sloping dome I hadn't even noticed before.

"What are you doing up there!?!?" My heart is still pumping from all the frantic excitement.

"Just watching."

It takes a few more seconds of settling nerves before I'm capable of continuing our conversation. She's obviously fine, and I'm more spitting words out than saying them. After the anxiety drops enough to talk without sounding chastising, I ask if there's anything worth seeing up there.

"Not really. I ate a cat," she explains. The odd, unexpected statement immediately draws me onto the roof to join her.

"Wait, you ate a cat?"

"Well I didn't eat it, but you know what I mean."

"Oh, trust me, I've eaten *way* more pets and rodents than I ever wanted to. Not that I ever really *wanted* to eat *any,* but you know... that didn't really work out, either." It's the kind of clumsy explanation that forces a lengthy pause after it.

"So, how long was I out?" is apparently the best transition I could think of.

"Two days, I think. Although I'm not sure how long I slept, so maybe more."

"Damn. I didn't think it'd been that long! And the doorknob? That was you?"

"Yeah. I'm still trying to get used to this stuff." This time, there's more irritation in her voice. She's also leaning in as if she's preparing to say something important.

"Hayden, I'm angry..." Her voice trails off, even though there's obviously more on the way. "I don't know why. There's been this crushing hatred poisoning everything I do. It's made me sit up here, watching the sun rise and fall, debating on the best way to end this. I even went down to the docks to stare over the edge for a little while. All I could do was stand there, looking straight down, picturing what it would be like to fly through the clouds one last time. There's worse ways to go, you know?"

She has a far-away look that's different than before. The words might sound ominous, but her face tells a different story. There's a resolve she didn't have mere seconds ago.

"...but I couldn't do it."

And that's it. No other explanation than a simple, "I couldn't do it." Luckily, she doesn't need one with me; I understand. These are the first bricks of the wall she'll need to keep her life separate from the monster.

I offer honestly, "Some people embrace the hatred and it utterly consumes them. I'm certainly one of those. I let it drive me to some dark places that took a really long time to leave. Quinn, what you've been through is beyond evil, and the vampire virus won't be making it any easier. See, the disease has the same effect on your emotions as it does your body, meaning that everything will be amplified to extremes.

Therefore, when it's good, it's going to feel *REALLY* good.

But when it's bad, it's going to feel *EXTREMELY* bad.

The one thing I won't do is lie to you. I'll be honest even when it hurts. So, when I say we're going to get through this, believe me. Sometimes it'll be ugly. You're gonna screw up, but that's all part of it! Trust me, there's no mistake I haven't already mastered. Just don't punish yourself like I have. You don't have to lock yourself up in that prison of solitude."

I could go on and on about the challenges ahead of her, but there's no need. My point isn't to scare her, it's simply to be honest. And real, naked truth, usually contains things that hurt to hear.

She watches me intently the entire time I talk. Despite all the focused attention, her only reaction is a tiny fold in the side of her cheek. She's not very open with her feelings... or anything else, really.

The stale air stretches on between us until I break the ice, "Want to go drain my bank account at a casino?" Have I mentioned I'm not very good at being serious? Judging by the continued silence, I'm not very good at joking, either. I'm not sure if it's wearing my heart on my sleeve, or suddenly ripping it back off, that makes people more uncomfortable.

We stay trapped in the silent prison until the warden finally releases me with a casual nod. I take the cue to immediately hit the shower and scrub off the grime of the last few days. The moment I set foot in that water, the weight of the world runs down the drain. I lean against the wall to let every sin wash away with the built-up dirt. Before I know it, the once steaming shower has become an ice-cold bath.

Then comes the part I hate the most—having to put those damn clothes back on. It honestly takes more courage to drag those filthy abominations across fresh skin than it took to blindly leap into a cave of monsters. Needless to say, we're at the souvenir shop across the street within minutes.

Given the lack of available options; Quinn ends up with a serviceable violet shirt and grey hoodie. I, on the other hand, get to leave with an *I heart Vegas* t-shirt straight from the $5 rack. Admittedly, it's not a great look for anyone, but far better than the Hawaiian floral that was option two.

Even with the fresh clothes, I'll occasionally get a whiff of rotten that unwillingly draws my mind back to dark places. It seems the miraculous shower couldn't wash away all the foul remnants of that cave. I guess it shouldn't be much of a surprise, though. I'm sure both our souls have been stained by its rancid wickedness.

Piss-poor wardrobe and fowl stench aside, I think we're doing pretty darn well. I try to keep the positivity flowing by taking a trip to a new shake shop. One that will, hopefully, have something Quinn finds a little more appetizing. And while these are much easier to drink, it still takes several painful minutes for her to gulp down the frozen treat.

With our spirits filled and wallet still full, I leave it up to Quinn to decide where we go next. She picks a place called "Moxxee's" due to an apparent love of double letters. It's not nearly as big and lavish as most of the places here. It's also funny to consider a building being guarded by golden lion statues as *modest*. Beyond the twin cats is a traditional neon casino with a glass roof that mimics the city's dome.

The large bouncer out front pretends to card us, before waving us through. I'm not sure what Quinn showed him, but he didn't look at it, so I guess it doesn't really matter.

Once inside the red double doors we find crowds of skimpily dressed dancers grinding away on a bunch of sweaty men. The music is loud and drinks are flowing, so it should be easy to blend in with this group. I pause when Quinn's light touch briefly disappears. Being programmed to fear the worst, I turn to fight, only to find her blocked by a wheelchair that's stopped in the way.

It's been an eternity since I've relaxed. Even now, I'm looking around for the nearest exit. It reaches the official height of ridiculousness when a crippled man (oxygen tank and all) looks too long, and I find myself ready to fight. If the entire point of being here is to show Quinn life *isn't* over, I'm definitely not doing that by constantly making up problems. We should be taking advantage of the atmosphere instead of poisoning it with imaginary fears. The way I see it, I might not be alive in two days, so why not live a little?!?!

We plop down at a poker table and trade in every dime I have. I'll admit my ego takes a bit of a hit when the dealer hands back a surprisingly small amount of chips. We'll have to be really good if there's going to be any chance of stretching this feeble stack of coins out more than thirty minutes. Though it might not be too tough, the entire table appears to be filled with ancient ladies whose husbands are occupied with the inappropriately young cocktail waitresses.

Quinn seems to take to the game like a fish to water. She shoves me back into my seat after only a few quick tips. One by one the drinks fall, while I become more and more convinced that I'm a real poker master. Maybe this is just the universe's way of shifting some of our bad luck back around? A few great hands later, it's confirmed.

I am, in fact, ***THE* POKER MASTER!**

Quinn laughs off a large bearded man who was already making his way to the cash prize. His cigar drops to the floor when she flops a straight flush right down in front of him. *Somehow, she's a card shark, too!* Within ten minutes, we've not only tripled our money, but collected a swarm of fans along the way! I spot several familiar faces from the long bus ride. Even dear old Rita has found her way into our cheering section! They must not have found the one lady we threw off the bus! This really *must* be my day!

I shout to a nearby waitress for a round of drinks for all my friends—two for Rita! Although, this isn't as high roller as it sounds since the drinks are free. That doesn't stop me from raising the highest glass in the room to make a sentimental toast to a new day! Hopefully, one filled with less murder.

Almost immediately after that is when a rather large man plops down awkwardly close to me. He's the first unfortunate thing to happen since my lucky streak began. I'm also not sure why he bothers me so much. Perhaps it's his cheap cigars that force me to breathe using my hands as a filter. Plus, he's sweating like a marathon runner even though it's a perfect 68 degrees in here. Every one of his wheezy breaths is an epic struggle that usually ends in a phlegmy cough. And to top it all is the unmistakable stink of blood. *He's a vampire?* How? It's almost impossible to be *this* unhealthy with our metabolism!

I wanna be nice, and maybe it's the liquor speaking, but something's just off about him. I offer, "Can I get you a drink, buddy?" in hopes of scooting him back out of my bubble. "Why thank ya' kindly," he replies in a thick Texas drawl. He then proceeds to order a scotch that should really add to his growing collection of grossness. I do my best to shake off the man before returning to my card game.

The dealer shouts "Twenty-one!" as my amazing run of luck comes to an official end. From that moment on, I either bust or lose on a 16. Every. Single. Damn. Time. Each passing round makes it more and more clear that it's past time to walk away. I need to turn these cursed cards in and just go find a redhead... except my stubborn pride has to right this sinking ship!

My next hand is obviously a 16; plus, since I decide to stay, I lose to the dealer's 17. Now it's time to walk away, right?

Wrong.

Arrogance leads me to double up the next bet instead. And again, the cards add up to 16! I defiantly lay two fingers on the table to signal for the dealer to give me one last hand. Guess what happens? That's right, I bust!

DAMMIT!

My growing anxiety can only be comforted by a cute cocktail waitress with a fresh new drink. I quickly bow out of the next couple rounds to slam back the much-needed beverage. I actually end up sitting out enough hands that the same cute waitress threatens to cut off my accelerating beer orders. But before that can happen, the putrid Texan leans in, "He is the Phoenix. The Phoenix of hope by rule of the divine. And in order to rise from its own ashes, a Phoenix first must burn." Even through my alcoholic haze, I recognize the words.

They're the same ones Shepherd used back in Gas Light. Even the vile tone of voice and smug appearance are eerily similar. Then I notice the cowboy's grave look is not confined to him; the entire room has ground to a sudden halt. Only my tumbling barstool dares to make a sound in our sudden standoff.

The silent mass eventually parts like flowing water around an unmovable rock. Emerging from the hushed stream is a tall man shrouded in a long leather coat that sways the same way he does—deliberate and irritated.

He's physically imposing, rising several feet taller than I am. I find myself staring up at him as if I were a tiny child when he comes to an impactful stop in front of me. The first thing I notice is the overhead lights perfectly reflect off his smooth, bald head. His chocolate skin is so dark that his eyes appear to float in their cavernous sockets. The second thing I notice is that the air around him is thick with the unmistakable sensation of utter despair. And that's before he speaks in a crackling voice that's both deep and hollow, "Hayden Flynn, you have been far more trouble than we ever expected."

Shit.

He knows my name.

In my experience, when you first meet someone and they already know your name, well... it's not good.

"I have that effect on people, Mr...?"

"Forgive me. My name is Silas, but most call me the Keeper."

Chapter 26: Heat Wave

I'm no scholar, but then again, it wouldn't take a genius to figure out he's the leader of this merry band of assholes. And it seems that, somehow, everyone is part of his silent army. It's clear these people are not the trained killers from the Gas Light Colony, as most of them are ancient *and* out of shape. Alone, the human raisins wouldn't stand a chance against me. Which is probably why there are hundreds of them.

They're literally standing shoulder to shoulder to form an impenetrable wall of flesh and bone. And right in the very center is kindly ol' Rita. My heart breaks at the sight of the syrupy-sweet grandma waiting with fangs out.

My monster instinctively scans the group to find a weak spot. "Now, Mr. Flynn, you're not thinking of leaving us, are you? I can assure you my Harbingers will not let that happen," Keeper demands. "You caused quite a ruckus over in Gas Light, didn't you?" His tone is almost approving. "Lots of fire and carnage from what I hear. A bit flashy for my tastes, but overall, I must say well done. There was even talk of converting you after that little show; however, I convinced them it would only delay the inevitable ending of your story. As it shall be for all nonbelievers; where we go, only death follows."

Well, he doesn't mess around. No flowers, no chocolates, no foreplay, just straight down to the filthy business. Although it's funny to hear this random group of oldness described as "Harbingers of Death."

"I really don't think..." I begin until he interrupts.

"Honestly, it doesn't matter. I know your type, Mr. Flynn. You're all mouth to compensate for a terribly delicate ego. For some reason you delusionally believe you're unique or special in some way. Maybe Mommy told you that you were her special boy and you believed her a little too much. I promise you, I've met thousands like you, and each one ends up on their knees. Sometimes I'll even let them walk away before I slit their throats. But not you, Mr. Flynn; I want you to see it coming. I want you to know that all you've accomplished is becoming another stain on this filthy floor."

Damn.

This guy's a dick.

The circle of obedient people tightens with a quick wave of his gnarled finger. Well, let's not waste any more time, since it appears words won't be getting me out of this. That doesn't stop me from giving him a smirk while securing a tight grip around Quinn. Then I lock eyes with the revolting man, grin a little bit wider, and hurl a chair straight up through the glass ceiling. The metal legs burst through the clear dome, sending a razor-sharp downpour over the surprised room.

Before the first shards of deadly hail can arrive, I yank Quinn underneath the nearest poker table I can find. From our crouched position, we hear the screams, see blood collecting on the floor, and smell fresh air wafting in through the newly opened hole in the roof.

We have to patiently wait for the man-made hailstorm to pass before attempting any kind of escape, but as soon as the last piece lands, we're already up on top of the large central chandelier. And from there, it's only a short leap through our brand-new ceiling exit.

The echo of hundreds of revenge-hungry feet pound the battered rooftop behind us. They form an unrelenting wave that sweeps from building to building along with us. The tenacious pursuit matches us down to the rhythm of each frantic step. No matter where we go, there they are. In my head, outrunning the thundering mob would be child's play. They're a bunch of old people, right? In reality, they have a clear advantage no one saw coming—they don't seem to care if they live or die. Like, at all. They tumble out of the air, get thrown over buildings, and gladly get trampled under the mob with no reaction at all. They merely die without ever making a sound.

Quinn doesn't seem to notice any of this. She's still running full speed ahead, while I've slowed just enough to put some obstacles in their way. I start by tossing a medium-sized billboard into the front of the overly persistent hoard. It successfully knocks a few out of the chase, but as one falls, two take their place. I try throwing more and the same thing happens—the wave simply absorbs it and continues on. It seems the only thing I've accomplished is allowing them to catch up. Their feet are already crunching the pebbles right behind me. They continue nipping at my heels all the way to the edge of the building. Maybe I can lose them in the jump?

Nope.

A stray hand clamps around my ankle midair and sends us both spilling out onto the next rooftop. I glance at the attached man to find the only real threat he poses is in lost time. One solid boot heel is all it takes to send him flying back into his friends. The small fish crashes into the big wave right at the peak, causing a chain reaction of falling bodies between buildings. Hundreds of them spill over the edge like a tilted cup.

The victory is, unfortunately, a short-lived one. I only get to enjoy it for a very brief moment because the mob's already swelling for another jump. Plus, Quinn is almost completely out of sight now and I'm completely clueless on how to catch her! Motivation certainly isn't the issue; I'm literally running for my life, but she's just so much faster than me!

She runs like a graceful sledgehammer, leaving behind a trail of shattered concrete that cuts straight across the entire city. I can't even run the same path as her because of all the slippery wreckage. Large chunks of brick and broken glass cover everything she's touched. I'm in the tricky position of having to close our gap while making sure not to trip over any of her wreckage!

I decide my best option might be a shortcut when she starts chewing up the side of a particularly tall building. Instead of going over the building, I'll go through it!

It's such a spontaneous plan that I almost forget to cover my face on the way. It's not until the very last second that I remember to fold into a loose cannonball to help protect myself from the window at the end of the jump. My knees dissolve the pane of glass into jagged diamonds on impact. The accompanying explosion pulls all the little shards along with me into the new room.

My body ricochets off several blurry objects before coming to rest in the middle of a *very hard* hardwood table. Judging by the sloppy pile of mashed potatoes under my elbow, I've interrupted dinner service at (what used to be) a very nice restaurant. Luckily, the crowd in here is not the same as the one chasing us. They seem far more concerned about saving their own asses than beating mine.

The smell of perfectly cooked steak tempts me to swing by the kitchen on the way out. I resist because doing so would defeat the entire purpose of this detour, not to mention result in my brutal murder at the wrinkled hands of old Rita, who I'm wildly disappointed in... She must be far less caring and grandmotherly than I was led to believe.

I stay focused so that I reach the exit just as the herd explodes through the remaining windows. The good news is that the cramped room is far more effective than I could ever be against the crowd. I don't have to do anything more than watch them trip over tables, chairs, and each other. I could enjoy this with a big bag of popcorn if I didn't have a Quinn to catch up to. I decide to settle for one last peek at the chaos, then return to trying to find the nearest exit.

Two long hallways and one cheap wooden door later, I'm just in time to catch Quinn leaping across the gap. My timing couldn't have been better! Not wanting to miss the moment, I quickly hurl myself through another window and pray it will be my last.

The glass wall quickly melts away, leaving me surrounded by nothing but clear blue sky. Being out here, disconnected from the world, is a rush that's equal parts ecstasy and pants-filling terror. That is, until I join Quinn for a moment that feels more like destiny than luck. Gliding along side by side over the crisp Vegas skyline fills me such unshakable confidence, it deserves an epic soundtrack. How cool would the restaurant have been with loud music pumping over it? Imagine perfectly choreographed parkouring over tables *AND* people, with the bad guys charging in behind me. Slow motion of scattering debris and then, just as I reach the climactic window, **BOOM!** The world goes dead silent.

Only shattering glass, rushing wind, and an awesome quip can be heard as the brave hero meets up with his long-lost partner. Instead, "Good to see ya!!" comes rattling out in an almost Irish accent. What the balls was *that?* This was my *one chance* at an epic one-liner, and that was the best I could do? If this ever reaches movie theaters, change that line!

Tormenting myself over the blown quip actually allows for a brief moment of blissful ignorance. One that lets me almost forget about the massive horde trying to kill us. *Almost.*

But then I'm sucked back to reality by a rapidly approaching wall of curved glass. This means two things:

> 1) Our pursuit has taken us across the entire city.
>
> 2) The end of the dome is here.

Number two is the most important since it also means we've come to the literal edge of our world.

Quinn instantly vaults over the edge of a slanted rooftop. This time, I follow without hesitation. I watch as her personal assault on the property of New Vegas continues as she digs her hands into a previously smooth wall. This allows her to slow her fall, so I grab the same concrete she's already softened up for me. The entire drop becomes a delicate balancing act between trying not to lose grip (and fall off) or slam into the wall (and be impaled by jagged bricks).

But it works. We eventually make it all the way back down to solid ground. Even then, there's not enough time to wipe off bleeding hands or take a short breath before we're hit with another wave of maniacs. It's starting to feel like we're trapped in a never-ending game of whack-a-mole. When we knock a few down, dozens more pop back up.

The major issue is that all the hysteria is making it difficult to tell who the real villains are. You don't know who's trying to kill you until they're already doing so. Some of these people are barely teenagers! They shouldn't even be home from school yet, let alone out here trying to kill me!

But the longer it goes on, the more I realize it might be *them,* trapped in here with *Quinn.* There's an unnerving beauty to her violence. Take away all the other people and she could be dancing the most stunning, elegant ballet ever seen.

The never-ending onslaught doesn't allow us any kind of second guessing or hesitation. We both have to rely on feral instincts that are just as vicious as they are necessary. She leads the way, tearing through the crowd with the same tenacity and precision as back in the Gas Light district. As we battle side by side through the swarm of zealots, I can't help but feel that this is where I'm supposed to be. For better or worse, and however this ends, everything in my life has led to this.

Chapter 27: The Mighty Fall

Even though we don't have the numbers, we make up for that with twice the heart. Still, the wave continually crashes, no matter how many times we beat it back. Mostly by luck, we eventually find ourselves at the entrance to the railway system below. It's not a great option, though it's got to be better than the wide-open street fight up here.

Quinn leaps down the stairs with the grace of a jungle cat. Her smooth stride is fluid and every attacker is pushed aside with effortless ease. She's a mother tiger playfully pushing her cubs around. The only difference is that when she pushes them, they become craters in the subway wall. Her agile dance continues all the way down into the belly of the mechanical city. Surprisingly, the lower levels are almost vacant. There are a few random people here or there, but nothing like the ant colony above. Rows of electronic booths are set up to buy tickets, except there are no damn *trains!* And peeking down the tracks reveals that none are on their way, either!

No buses.

No taxis.

Nothing that will help us escape the pounding footsteps growing louder by the minute. Strong voices boom off the tight tunnels right around the corner. "Okay now, hear me out," I begin in the most rational tone possible. Maybe she'll agree if I don't sound *too* crazy. Although, if her wide-eyed desperation is any indication, she'll go along with just about anything right now.

"Jump on my back." The growing stampede and lack of better options convinces her not to argue. I immediately rip a metal "no pets allowed" sign out of the concrete ground. The thick post is then bent into a large U shape that should hold both of us. Quinn stares, still clueless, but trusts me enough to climb onto my shoulders. I warn her to hold on *extremely* tight before I leap blindly onto the empty track.

Both of us scream as the bent pole wraps over the metal rail. The force of our landing propels us down the tunnel much slower than I had originally anticipated. We have to kick our legs just to scoot down the almost flat railing. Soon, our momentum picks up enough steam to release a banshee wail of grinding metal on metal. That's when our gentle slide becomes more of a moderate slope. Then the walls disappear and everything goes right to crap. With the tunnel walls gone, we're left dangling in the great wide open with only clouds under our feet. I won't lie, I'm pretty sure I just shit myself.

The only relief comes from Quinn burying her nails in my sides. Normally that wouldn't be such a great thing, but it's a very welcome distraction from the vast expanse of nothing underneath us. Even worse is when our ride takes an abrupt turn toward the ground... that's when we find out that this is not one of the many, *many* railways leading around the city. Nope, my luck has landed us on a one-way trip all the way back to the ground!

Plunging down the steep hill isn't like riding the biggest rollercoaster on Earth, it's like hanging on to it by the wheels. Our runaway train is picking up speed by the second, and there's not a single damn thing I can do about it. All the friction is shooting a ruffled rooster tail of sparks behind us.

Within seconds, we've hit the wall of puffy white blindness known as clouds. As soon as we enter, the temperature nosedives and starts biting at every piece of exposed skin it can find. The dense, frozen, soupy clouds are a stark contrast to the glowing hunk of metal in my hands. The signpost is radiating a burning orange color—the only thing still visible in the suffocating blizzard.

As proof that it could always be worse, the end of the clouds eventually arrives. Waiting on the other side is what could only be described as complete and absolute horribleness. At this speed, it's like going from completely blind to being able to see in every direction (including straight down) for miles. At this speed, the giant mountains and unending sand have blended into one infinite sheet of tan.

As if that weren't enough, we have a more pressing problem ahead of us. Actually, directly ahead of us is a small taxi leisurely moving down the one-way track. It's so close, and so slow, that I don't even have a chance to come up with a curse word strong enough to describe my feelings before we're buried into the back of it.

The brutal collision hurls me all the way across the tiny car. My only detour is to bounce off several hard seats before smashing through the windshield. It's not until reaching the very edge of the short hood that my hand finally locates something sturdy enough to keep me from going all the way over. The wild ride has left me buried up to the bloody elbow in shredded metal, but alive.

Still, that may just be a temporary condition... only that one wedged arm and a small sliver of my upper chest is anywhere close to touching the car. The rest is dangling perilously far out over the hood.

My heart is beating so hard, it actually lifts me away from the crumpled hood. And for some reason, my feet won't stop kicking as if there were something down below, other than clouds, to grab on to. The adrenaline also inspires an endless string of urine-soaked expletives to spew out of my panicked mouth. Some are real words, but most are just random sounds that are only meant to relieve my over-flowing fear.

My free hand is desperately reaching to find additional grip, but it only coats everything in more of the slippery blood. The grasping fingers leave behind so many slimy red prints that finding any kind of real security virtually impossible. I'm at the mercy of one weary arm, and it's fading fast.

A feverish panic sets in, and it's not the kind that will add additional strength or motivation, either. No, this one drains the last bit of life from my already tired muscles and spins the world on its head. The car groans as one of the clamps holding it to the track gives out. The unexpected lunge dislodges my wedged hand, flinging me to the other side of the hood. My monster manages to find a piece of the windshield frame before I tumble the rest of the way off. While that may sound like a good thing, my new grip consists mostly of broken glass and twisted metal.

The agony of holding on to such a torturous thing gradually releases each finger one by one. When all but two have slipped off—at the very peak of my torment—comes last-second salvation in the form of a fleshy vice grip around my failing wrist. An unmistakable voice says, "I've got you." Her usually soft voice is filled with a new air of confidence. My head flops back to see Quinn leaning out of the car above. The sun glistens off the track steel behind her. It spreads like wings around the glowing girl. While I may not believe in angels, I believe in *her*.

Another failed support rocks the taxi just as she pulls me in from the abyss. The jolt slings Quinn into a few of the angry passengers. I end up stumbling forward into the driver's lap. By my count, there are six in here besides us. Three of them were knocked out and the others are up moving around the cabin. The driver is one of the unconscious ones, but since the car is falling off the track, he wouldn't have been much help, anyway.

"*Snap*" goes another support.

And another.

Each new break is causing the car to scream down the track even faster. There's a shrill scraping sound (like spoons in a meat grinder) that comes with it. Plus, the entire car has dropped to a pretty severe angle now, so everything, including people, is trying to fall out the busted windows. Quinn snatches up a few and the rest tumble into a sloppy pile on top of me. There's not much else to do except pray this bucket can hang on long enough to reach the station.

More supports break. Suddenly, the car is almost pointing straight down. We're a lot closer to the ground than before, but I still wouldn't want to fall from here.

I *must* be psychic, because just as I think it, the jarring final break rings out. All the intense grinding and relentless racket dissolves in the actual blink of an eye. The stack of people that were on top of me gradually floats away as our car finally separates from the last little bit of track. I can feel our trajectory changing from falling forward to dropping straight down. My hands are the first to escape gravity, followed by knees and legs, then the contents of my stomach.

The wind howls mockingly through every broken window as our car goes from a gentle sweeping arch to the steep drop of a thrown rock. Then, with the force pushing us all to the roof, the absolute strangest thing of all happens... the entire cabin fills with a light green jelly!

I close my eyes, then open them again, only to find that the entire car has been encased in a giant ball of Jell-O! I can still breathe through the green gel for some reason; not well, but enough to make do. I can also still hear the wind whipping around of our little ball of goo. Even though there's no room to bat an eyelid, we seem fine, just frozen in place! Inches from my cheek is a leather briefcase stuck in the slime like everything else: papers, people, and clothing are all trapped exactly as they were during the chaotic fall.

My brief examination comes to an abrupt halt when our falling bubble finally reaches solid ground. The brutal impact is what it must feel like to be crushed by two jelly mountains. The front and back of my body are squeezed so tightly, they want to meet in the middle. The air in my lungs asks to leave, but there's nowhere else to go.

Then, abruptly, the merciless pressure leaves. It's replaced by uncontrollable spinning and the feeling that every internal organ is trying to find a way out. The speed I could handle, but this? This is a completely different kind of torture. The world swirls in a blurry mess of vomit-inducing circles.

Eventually, another impact comes along to slow us down. This one is smaller, yet still crushes my hollow lungs. It seems our car has turned into a rubber ball, bouncing along the desert floor. It repeatedly collides with the ground every few seconds. Each time the impact gets smaller, until it doesn't feel as if it's trying to squeeze out a kidney anymore.

My eyes are still rattling around as we come to a sudden stop. I want to blame them for the sensation of continued falling, except the ooze actually does seem to be melting away. Mad hysteria erupts when the goo drops down far enough to uncover every mouth in here. That's when all the passengers decide to express their extreme hatred of me. They scream repeatedly while sloshing around in the sloppy jelly pools.

I look around to find that Quinn is just now reaching the ground. She's gotten flipped upside down, but still managed to keep ahold of the two passengers she'd stopped from falling out of the car. Since our car is still at a pretty steep angle, they slide into the corner with the goo when she finally releases her tight grip on them. She prevents herself from slipping along with them by clinging to a hanging seatbelt.

I let the angry passengers continue venting until it starts to have a negative effect on our efforts to get out of here. It's really hard to concentrate with all the loud voices bouncing around the inside of this cramped ball. I try politely asking them to calm down. When that doesn't work, I rip out a chair, and shout all of them into a compact pile in the corner.

Fear can be effective, too.

The peace and quiet allows me to finally focus on the strange sphere that's trapping us. While the goo's mostly gone, the thick outer shell still remains. It seems to be built out of several large interconnected plastic panels that surround the entire car. Imagine the view from inside a hamster ball and you've pretty much got it. Moving around in the goo doesn't help, either. We're all coated in a lovely film that makes any attempt at standing more like a semi-controllable slide. We look like baby deer walking for the first time.

The passengers have begun mumbling as if they're plotting a mutiny. What they don't know is that *I'm* not their real problem. I want to get out just as badly as *they* want me out. Also, if they knew what was coming, they might be a little more helpful since I sincerely doubt the army of assholes will discriminate much between us and them. So, for their sake, we need to get far, far away from here. At least dropping out of the sky should buy us a few minutes' head start. You can't find a faster route than straight down.

I quickly return to examining the outer shell. My hands slide from top to bottom, trying to find a weak point. Quinn doesn't mess with my intellectual approach. Instead, she crawls up to the plastic and makes an instant exit with her claws. On her way out, she gives me a look that's equal parts arrogance and skepticism.

Hum, guess I overthought that a bit.

I turn back to the pissed group before leaving. "Look, I'm sorry to crash your party. This wasn't what I planned, either. But don't worry; you'll never have to see either of us again." Their collective cold shoulders don't do much to relieve the heat already pouring in through the flapping exit.

Chapter 28: Attack & Release

There's an unnerving crunch when I step onto the scorching sand for the first time. The gusting wind swirls the grains around, and they burn like tiny bits of charcoal every time they find my naked arms and face. The leftover goo doesn't help by trapping them tight against the bare skin. As a result, the pain lingers even longer than it normally would.

I seek shelter behind one of the massive beams that our car has been wedged against. The severity of our situation comes into better focus when I notice that the metal is actually one of the legs of the Eiffel Tower. Well, not *the* Eiffel Tower, but the Vegas-sized replica of it. The soaring beams loom high over us and—besides being an impressive monument—serve immediate notice that we didn't even come close to clearing the wastelands.

I'm not completely sure where this will land on our growing list of problems. I've only heard rumors of what goes on here, but even those are scary enough to get me scanning the abandoned city a whole lot faster. And that doesn't take long since there's not much left of it. The hungry desert has already reclaimed most of the former metropolis. All the best parts have been buried beneath deep mountains of sand. From where I sit, only a few of the taller buildings are still left poking out of the ground.

That doesn't mean there isn't plenty of evidence of the hellscape waiting for us: bullet-ridden walls, razor wire, graffiti tags, and ground-up bones are all mixed in with the gritty sand.

The gravity of the situation seems completely lost on Quinn.

"We need to go, *NOW*. There's no time to explain, so you're going to have to trust me on this one."

While my lips are still unfurling from saying the word "one", the sound of the first body hits. The strange noise takes several more moments to even register as something to be concerned about. We're trained to instinctively fear the crack of a gun or squealing tires, but the solid "thud" sound meant almost nothing to me.

Then the second one crashes down.

With many, *many* more to follow.

Bodies are dropping from the sky like autumn leaves in a thunderstorm. Every few seconds, another one collides with the hard-packed sand. The steady trickle quickly turns into a cascading waterfall of human raindrops. Some of them ricochet off the metal beams and are instantly split into several pieces. I watch in shock as they slam onto the ground, following the path of the tracks above. But the *undeniably* most horrifying, soul-trembling, gut-wrenching part is that they're watching me right back.

They keep their dead eyes locked on me...   All.

The.

Way.

Down.

None of them scream, yell, or really do anything more than stare at me. Their cold faces show absolutely no fear. Instead, they seem almost curious in nature, as if they've all been possessed by the same quizzical demon. It's so unnerving that Quinn has to pull me back inside the car to escape the approaching stream of bodies.

I'm still trying to shake off the fear-induced numbness when the bodies start crashing into the top of the already crumpled cab. The rest of the passengers have no idea what's actually happening, let alone the bone-chilling way they're doing it, but their screams easily make up for the herd of silent jumpers. Quinn and I have to drag them away from the windows while the human rainstorm finishes passing over. Dozens of violent collisions strike the tiny car during the fast-moving storm. By the time it's safe to look out, the tranquil desert has been turned into a horror show of torn bodies.

Quinn grabs my unconsciously shaking wrist and says in a steady tone, "You were saying it's time to go, eh?" I look around and find that every direction looks equally horrible. We obviously can't follow the terrifying storm, so...

One direction down, three to go.

The roaring rumble of unknown engines cracks to life from somewhere behind us. They sound raw and full of venom, as if they've been patched together from old scavenged parts.

Two directions down, two to go.

It's a fifty/fifty shot at this point. There probably isn't really a *good* direction, so we just head off toward the dark alleyway to the left. Everything goes pretty well for the first few blocks. We agree to only take streets that have lots of trash or shadows to hide in, but this plan unintentionally takes us deeper into the heart of the city.

I catch a shadow scurrying into a huge pile of garbage out of the corner of my eye. Quinn lets out a small scream before I can cover her mouth. If her eyes are any indication of what's over there, it's nothing I wanna screw with. I give the shadow a gentle smile in hopes it doesn't become the newest addition to our list of problems. Three eyes rapidly blink back from inside the trash cave.

Blink blink blink　　　*blink blink blink*　　　*blink blink blink*

The hidden creature lets out a deep, crackling hiss that raises every hair on the back of my neck. I try to keep the forced smile even after several bottles come hurling out toward us. While they smash harmlessly against the wall, it's more than enough for Quinn to already be halfway down the block.

She wisely doesn't choose to stay out in the open for very long, dipping into a nondescript-looking building in the middle of the next street over. By the time I catch up, she's hidden behind a loose piece of metal sheeting. I take a step back to look at the bland structure. It's not much more than a square block of concrete with no cool architecture to catch your eye. All in all, it's just a plain ol' brown box.

I've spent a lot of time hiding, so trust me when I say the best spots are always right out in the middle of everything. It has to be some place that you would never even look at twice. If it looks like a good hiding spot, it isn't.

This spot seems to fit that bill perfectly. One whole side is covered by a steep bank of sand, while every other door and window has been securely boarded up with scrap. By the looks of it, no one's been there for a very long time. There are no prints in the thick dust or tracks going in or out. I lean against the door and it sounds just as empty as it looks.

Suddenly, six loud booms echo off the side of the building.

"Pop"   *"Pop"*   *"Pop"*   *"Pop"*   *"Pop"*   *"Pop"*

Six gunshots—six people were in that cab. Don't think for a second that I'm not aware of how they got there, either. The group would be off living happy lives if it wasn't for me. On purpose or not, I brought them here. Their blood is on me.

I have to fight back the instinct to shut down and wallow in guilt. It may sound cold, but I have to push it down with the rest I carry and simply move on. One unusually deep gulp is all I allow myself before whispering for Quinn to smooth the sand behind us. She retrieves some garbage from a pile and methodically covers our tracks with it.

The motorcycle engines fire up again, so I give the door a solid hit with my least injured shoulder. When it doesn't budge, I move back further to give it another try.

Nothing.

I scoot back a few more feet to give it a bit of a run this time. *Damn!* Still nothing more than a bruised shoulder! This is one solid door! I signal Quinn and we both hit the door with everything we've got and the damn thing finally surrenders!

Just as the loud springs snap, an overwhelming rush of mold spews out from the coal-black room inside. I reach in and the first thing I notice is how bizarrely cold the door is. How could anything out here possibly be this cool? It's a fascinating mystery, but not one that will keep me out today.

I examine the broken lock and the mystery grows even deeper. No wonder it didn't open easily. Hidden beneath the very normal-looking exterior are thick steel rods that look as if they could be straight from a secured bank vault door. Now, I admit this does give me some serious hesitation, however, the nearby engines are rumbling proof that whatever's in there will be much better than what's out here.

That being said, I do make one last attempt at peering into the mystery room before committing my toes to moving any further. Sadly, yet again, the dark void refuses to give away any of its hidden secrets. Still, there's nothing *visibly wrong* with it either. The only thing really holding me back from leaping inside is the churning nervousness in the pit of my stomach. And that's a feeling that's easy enough to put aside, because there's no other choice. We *have* to gamble on whatever is waiting inside the unknown room.

I hesitantly slide through as Quinn covers the last of our tracks. Once inside, I slam the door and seal it tight. We broke off some of the steel rods trying to gain entry, but turning the crank still plunges the rest in with beautiful precision. I can hear them slide several feet into the dense walls, so whatever was in here was pretty damn secure. Hopefully they'll keep us safe, too.

Not even a single beam of light is leaking around the sealed door. It leaves us submerged in a pool of darkness so thick you could almost swim through it. I ask Quinn to look around for a light switch while my fingers search the mostly smooth walls. The only textures to be found are flat metal walls with extra-large rivets poking out. There are so many that it appears this might have been an industrial warehouse of some kind, even though it *certainly* didn't look like it from the outside.

"Any luck?" Her only answer is a rapid heartbeat. And something else is new—the low hum of a pulsating machine.

"Do you hear that humming?"

"Quinn?"

A synthetic voice answers from the void, *"That's me."*

Chapter 29: Waiting for My Rocket to Come

A retina-searing beam of light joins the artificial voice. The sapphire laser punctures the darkness, spreads out, and works up the entire length of my body.

"What's your business here, outsider?" the harsh voice commands. This mysterious creature doesn't sound even close to human— more like a pissed-off ATM. I still haven't heard a peep from Quinn, so maybe it's best we handle this delicately for now.

"Easy, friend. We just needed a place to hide and accidently stumbled in here," I answer in an almost comically soothing voice. "We're looking for a quick way out of town. See, there's these people looking for us and they..."

"So, you bring a war to my front door then?"

Balls.

"*Yeah*, well, about *that*..." I stumble through words trying to find a reasonable explanation to calm the voice back down. Maybe it wasn't such a great idea to mention the band of psycho nuts after us? The blue beam quickly shifts to illuminate the side of Quinn's cheek. It also highlights the shiny metallic fingers that are pressed firmly over her mouth. Unfortunately, I still can't see anything hidden past the blinding light.

"Outsiders have no place here. Take your problems elsewhere or I will crush her skull into arrrr... auggghhhhh..." he groans before the light abruptly drops to the floor.

Quinn bursts out, "Hayden, I hit 'em in the balls!"

It seems the angry flashlight is human after all. I hastily shout, "Get him while he's down! Whatever you do, don't let it get back up!"

"No problem," she answers savagely.

Thump.   *Ping.*   **CLANG**.   ***Bang.***

The spotlight finally flickers all the way off. It leaves me in utter darkness, listening to noises straight out of a bad joke. Each one sounds totally different than the rest. It's hard to tell whether she's punching a side of beef or a rattly tin can. I'm stuck blindly walking around trying to find them; which should be easy in such a small room, except the echoes make it sound as if they're everywhere at once.

Then, out of nowhere, fake new synthetic voices cry out, *"Daddy Daddy Daddy!"*

That's it.

My mind's snapped.

This is all just one big hallucination coming from a broken brain that's simply making shit up now. I'm already settling into my comfy seat aboard the crazy train when the lights finally come on, and not one, but two baby robots run in. One boy. One girl.

Well, that's certainly not something you see every day. They both cling to this half human/half machine *thing* on the floor. I don't know if he/it has been in an accident, or some kind of freaky experiment, but it appears that most of his body has been replaced with mechanical substitutes. The only real flesh left is on the right side of his face and arm. He even wears goggles that blink while trying to adjust to the light.

The clinging "children" beg me, with big blue digital eyes, to not hurt their "Daddy". Quinn staggers away at the sight of them. "I uh... I don't know what to do here, Hayden." She's looking to me for some kind of guidance, except I'm just as bewildered as she is.

Another adult-sized robot adds to the confusion by storming into the suddenly cramped room. This new one is female and obviously the "Mother" because of the way she instantly protects her children. The "Father" appears to be the only one with any actual human parts; the rest are 100% metal.

"Please don't hurt my Daddy, mister," pleads the sympathetic robot boy. There's genuine emotion rooted in his artificial voice. This is clearly his dad. And this really is his family; a tad different than what I'm used to, but who am I to judge? Not to mention, *we* were the ones who invaded *their* home.

"I'm sorry." My fists unfold at the sudden realization of who the real assholes in this situation are. The tension in the room lowers along with my hands. Those of us with lungs take a deep breath as the standoff ends. I suddenly have the burning desire to make it very clear that I would *never* have intentionally put this family in danger. Maybe it's because these kids actually seem scared of me. I can't stand the thought of children, even metal ones, being afraid of me.

My olive branch is reaching down to offer Dad a hand up. "Listen, we invaded your home because we were in a really bad spot out there. My intention was never to harm you or your family. I'm only asking this because we're completely out of options and desperate; is there any way you all can help us?"

All eyes turn to the man. He takes his time helping the kids off his lap and they, in turn, help him off the floor. Every few seconds, he'll give a sideways glance as if he's trying to form some opinion of me. Then, after calmly smoothing his shirt, he stands mutely in front of me.

I add, "My name is Hayden Flynn and this lady is Quinn." (*Side note:* I just realized I don't know her last name. I should really ask about that the next time no one is trying to kill us.)

"Servo," says the man.

"Servo?" I repeat.

"Name's Servo." His voice has no inflection or emotion. Just the cold tone of an automated message.

"Great to meet you, Servo." My hand reaches out again, though he still shows no interest in touching it. He only gives it a quick glance before walking away.

"I'm sorry for my husband's attitude. He doesn't like humans too much," Mother explains while approaching us. I'm having a really hard time digesting the last sentence. The *"female"* robot just explained that her *"husband"* doesn't like me because I'm human. All the while, he's the only one even partially human. Plus, there's a few "baby" robots clanking around. So, yeahhhh...

"Where are my manners?!" she exclaims. *"I'm Nila, this is Kylea, and that little man over there is Colin."* She affectionately pulls them in close to her. *"And that grumpy Gus over there is Tom."*

"Servo!" shouts robo-man.

"Your name is Tom!" she snaps back.

Nila acts like any typical flesh-and-blood woman who's agitated with her husband. Complete with attitude and a swing in her hips. She even bats digital eyes while sternly correcting him. Without saying another word, Servo presses a small panel to reveal a hidden door along the far wall. He wastes no more time on us and stomps bullishly from the room. This leaves it up to Nila to invite us in their home, which she joyfully does.

Stepping over the threshold is like traveling back in time. My heels are in a dingy aluminum room, but my toes are all the way back in 1957. The entire place has been meticulously decorated exactly as you'd imagine a 1950s home would be. The walls are plastered with a classically tacky pink wall paper that's been out of style for decades. A mint green sofa and accompanying ruby chair are the highlights of the room (they actually hurt to stare at too long). My favorites are the studio portraits of the entire family wearing matching green sweaters. They're even wrapped in the cheap golden photo frames of the Sears and Roebuck era. Humans doing this is funny; robots doing it is *freakin' hilarious!*

All these monuments to a lost time have been carefully arranged around a tube-style television up front. Of course it's playing a black and white show from the same era we've magically been transported to. While the TV is definitely intriguing, what I'm most drawn to are the long, frilly curtains that frame four window-like screens. They show an entire computer-generated neighborhood waiting right outside. That imaginary world is complete with a perfect sunny day and a well-manicured lawn. It's filled with everything I know isn't actually out there: passing cars, neighborhood children playing ball, big billowy oak trees, and there's even dust accumulating on the window sill!

The entire place could have been plucked directly from one of my happiest dreams. It's pure serenity, wrapped in a blanket of absolute perfection, and deep-fried in good ol' fashioned nostalgia!

My cheeks tighten from the sun's warm kiss coming through. I've only been here a few minutes, yet I'm already fully immersed in the innocence of this place. If there's a glitch in this digital perfection, I can't find it. Pressing my hand against the window allows me to fully delight in the heat of the day outside. The gesture causes the playing children to pause briefly and wave to me before returning to their game of catch. I can't help but affectionately return their cheerful wave.

"Can you believe this place, Quinn?" I excitedly turn, only to find her buried under a pile of metal kids. They're anxiously showing off their wide variety of simple toys. None of those are modern or complicated at all, they're just humble wooden or plastic dolls that have obviously been hand-painted with great care. No matter how advanced their own bodies are, their lives are innocent and completely uncomplicated.

While the eager children are excitedly welcoming their new friend, Servo is toiling away at a workbench with stuff that will (hopefully) help us get out of here. He folds the sleeves of his old-fashioned white dress shirt and covers his pleated khaki pants before diving into a box of oily tools. The deep grooves of his hands are heavily scarred, most likely from the not-so-innocent world outside. Shockingly, the rest of the family is nothing like him. There's absolutely nothing human about them except the way they act, which, funny enough, seems to be the one thing completely missing from Servo.

The mother guides me gently by the hand over to the couch. She's dressed in a traditional tea-length dress with a red velvet bow pulling in at the waist. She asks in the soft tone of any caring mother about the *"nasty people chasing us,"* and if *"cookies would make it better."*

"They won't be here long enough for that, Nila" interrupts Servo.

His rude tone leads to a few more verbal jabs between the amusing couple. I interject that, "While we really appreciate the hospitality, we have to get going." This must have been music to Servo's ears since a large section of the floor retracts almost immediately. The smell of fresh-cut wood drifts out from the new passageway. At the snap of his fingers, ugly florescent lights reveal a steep staircase to nowhere.

"You want out? I want you out. Let's go." Not even looking back at us, he grabs a large wrench and disappears into the tunnel. I don't usually follow strange men, who *obviously* hate me, into a pit under their house, but this seems to be an exception. We say goodbye to the bouncing metal children and they act genuinely sad to see us go. The little girl proceeds to clamp onto my leg with the strength of a miniature grizzly bear! I have to gently pat her head while holding back a river of painful tears. Quinn mistakes my swelling eyes as sadness, but it really isn't. It's just the normal reaction of someone trying to snap your bones in half.

The one thing I will actually miss is the fake utopia outside. I limp back over to the window to have another lingering look. The friendly children wave a long goodbye that fills me with a burning desire to find a place like this of my own one day. If places like this still exist.

This sudden revelation let's me better understand Servo. There's no need to know who he is or where he came from, to recognize what he wanted. Quite simply, he couldn't find happiness, so *he built it.* No wonder he's so pissed! I'm a threat to the dream he's worked so hard to perfect!

As if on cue, *"Hurry up, asshole!"* erupts from the tunnel below. *"Watch your language in front of the kids, Tom!"* Nila unleashes in a fit. This launches them into a new round of sitcom-style squabbling. After landing a couple great verbal jabs, Nila hands us a small olive-green knapsack stuffed with water bottles and snacks of every kind. *"Please be safe out there. I've heard stories..."* Concern trickles off every word.

Quinn leaks several tears as the metal matriarch hands over the bursting satchel. In return, she gives Nila a tight hug that leaves a large dent where her ribcage would be. Even though Nila doesn't seem to notice, I quickly shuffle Quinn over to the hole in the floor—you know, just in case.

"I'd tell you we'll come back and visit, but I don't think Tom would like that very much," Quinn tells our hostess, cautious eyes gesturing in Servo's direction.

"Oh, don't you mind that old cranky pants! You come back as soon as you can! Bring a hammer and you'll be best friends for life!" she laughs. I don't know if you've heard a robot laugh before, (I certainly hadn't) but it's the weirdest, most insane noise in the entire world. It's as if an accordion is being played through a drive-thru speaker!

I know the winds of life won't blow us back this way; however, it's a nice parting thought. I wave goodbye again while attempting to navigate the steep stairs into the mystery hole. As the door seals shut with a vacuum-sealed drag, I turn my attention to Quinn. "I haven't felt this good in a long time. My insides just feel all warm and fuzzy!"

"Me too!" she giggles. We continue to rant and rave down the narrow tunnel as the dull florescent lights grow noticeably dimmer. I completely ignore all the obvious red flags and continue along the creepy hallway to nowhere without a care in the world.

A soft whistle from Servo changes the ominous hall into a dazzling display of lights blooming like wild dandelions. They float along gently, burning with a kind glow, to lead the way. Every step brings new batches of the sparkling fairies out of hiding. Walking amongst them is to cross a magical field of low-hanging stars. It's so mesmerizing that I forget to keep moving and simply stare in wide-eyed amazement at the surreal beauty unfolding all around.

After a not-so-gentle reminder from Servo prompting me forward, I discover what's waiting for us at the end of our magical walk. Resting down low in the center of the room is a bulging blue vehicle. The fantastic fairies wander up to let their warm light reflect off its glossy paint.

Our chariot awaits.

And it's a damn rocket!

Chapter 30: Ground Control

Well, maybe not the outer space kind, but I'll be damned if that's not a rocket car! An audible giggle squeaks out from the excited 5-year-old in me. The fireflies continue blooming, revealing every sexy curve. She's sitting down on the tracks, taunting me with wide hips and a soaring tailfin. Her finely sculpted nose points down the tunnel as if ready to pounce on some unsuspecting victim.

My fingers glide down the buttery smooth sides of the curvaceous navy blue ship. Masterfully sculpted vents blend seamlessly with the golden stripes running from tip to tail. Out back, there's a chrome engine peeking out to hint at the vicious power underneath. Servo brings her to life by uttering a single word, *"breathe."* There's almost emotion in his automated voice this time. The throaty engine happily sings back from deep down in its eight-cylinder belly. Every happy note sends sharp flames shooting out behind her.

The entire machine becomes a concert of moving parts. While the exhaust is spitting dragon fire, the cockpit and chairs swivel to greet us. The cabin inside is wrapped in a rich, absolutely flawless leather. Silver buttons, chrome switches, and glowing gauges wash everything in a cool light that makes it feel straight from the damn future.

"How cute!" I exclaim. "It has four seats! You have a family rocket car!!!" Our cyborg host is clearly not as amused by this observation as I am. There's a look of utter disgust etched across his stern face.

What?" I say when my enthusiasm is not responded in kind. "Really! It's so cool!!!" I attempt to explain my genuine sincerity only to get an annoyed grunt in return.

He bends down to trigger a wall of lasers tracing the outline of our bodies. My constant fidgeting forces the scan to start over several times. That, in turn, leads to being yelled at even more by Servo. And this leads to the wrath of Quinn coming down on me as well. In my defense, all this bottled up enthusiasm has me wound tighter than a knife fight in a phone booth!

When they've both finished shouting and the scan finally has the chance to complete, the entire cabin launches into a mass of moving metal. The whole thing flows like molten lava until two seats magically disappear and the remaining ones fit us perfectly!

The impatient cyborg instructs us to sit down and, *"for tits' sake, don't touch anything."* Guess you gotta respect he's gonna be a real curmudgeon to the bitter end. "You know, Servo, even though you're getting ready to shoot me off into some mysterious black hole, I gotta say, this is a really nice place you got here. You're such a lucky guy! All those shiny steel faces, plus you'll never have to worry about cavities or braces!"

"It's the pheromones I pump into the place, asshole," he says in a monotone voice. *"They keep me happy,"* then slams the dome shut over us.

"Bwah ha ha ha! That was him *happy!?!"* Quinn and I both erupt in euphoric laughter from the admittedly mild joke. The automatic belts can barely contain our irrational hysteria.

"I mean can *you* imagine...." The rapid thrust of the rocket taking off cuts me off mid-thought. My open jaw releases a dog whistle scream that would be embarrassing if Quinn could possibly hear it over the roar of the engines.

WHOOOOOOOOOOSSSSHHHHH!!!!!!!!!!!!!!

The speedy car zooms down the track at such incredible speed, the feeling is akin to having an obese gorilla sitting on my chest. The force folds little ripples in my cheeks, while the sudden rush leaves my stomach behind at the station. It also embeds the seat bolts into my skin. I can even feel the welds digging into the bulging bones of both shoulders.

We continue picking up speed until the tunnel lights become one long, blurry line. The air beats against the car's slippery exterior and Quinn screams along in perfect harmony. I can't even tilt my head to the side, let alone turn around to check on her.

At least the intense ride is a (mostly) brief one. The pressure eventually eases enough to begin taking full breaths again. As it does, I notice my head wobbles on my shoulders like it's either five pounds heavier or lighter than before. My entire body has the distinct feeling of being ripped apart and put back together again—loosely.

My attention is stolen by a wonderful rainbow pouring in through the expansive windows. Our shuttle exits the enclosed tunnel, leaving us with the perfect view of the last little bits of daylight slipping away. The fading sun has reached the delicate tipping point where it will soon spill behind the mountains for the rest of the night. But for now, it's leaving behind a sky that's been painted with the richest of reds and only the most glorious purples.

The glorious sunset is a great example of the deceptive beauty of this place. All this perfect weather and picturesque sky will soon become a bitterly cold night that will attack us at every opportunity. Deserts are places of devilish extremes, with dishonest perfection stuck in between.

For now though, it's fantastic.

The powerful car glides to a casual stop, finally giving my stomach a chance to catch back up. Even the queasy feeling doesn't stop me from leaping out as soon as the top slides open. Quinn though, is much less motivated. It takes her several more minutes before she's ready to leave the comfort of the soft seats. I decide to use the extra time to explore our harsh new surroundings. Unfortunately, it doesn't take long, simply because there's infinite sand and colossal mountains. That's it.

The entire world has become eerily quiet with absolutely nothing in sight. Not even plants are stupid enough to live out here. There's not a single thing, living or dead, in sight. An apprehensive lump forms in my throat at the thought of venturing off into the barren wasteland. So, when I see Quinn carelessly chugging a bottle of water, I quickly tilt it back down for her. It's safe to say the gesture is not well-received... My explanation of the value of our water is met mostly with eye rolls and attitude, but it's eventually put back down in the knapsack with the rest.

Maybe it's best for me to handle the food and water for now. While the pack is currently bursting at the seams, it won't be after a few days. At least our path seems to be pretty clear. The lengthy mountain range leave us with two directions: forward and backward. Since we obviously won't be going back into the city, forward it is.

They say a journey of a thousand miles begins with a single step. So, with that nugget of optimism, we launch off toward the wastelands without any more delay. The flawless weather will only last for maybe another hour, so we need to make as much headway as possible. Quinn is dragging behind in her typical quiet fashion. I try to draw some mindless small talk from her since the crunchy sand isn't very entertaining. I start with a question that should've been asked long ago. "You know what? I don't know your last name."

"Really?" she sounds surprised.

"No, seriously; I never asked you. In my defense, we've had a lot going on lately."

"Merrin," she says quietly. "Quinn Alexander Merrin. My parents thought they were having a boy, so they kept Alexander, and tacked Quinn in front of it. It fits, though. I've always been a tomboy." We ramble on for hours, diving into favorite stories and lost memories that would have been far too painful to dredge up alone. The conversation hurts us both in some extraordinary ways. She pushes on through the monsoon of tears; laughing, crying, and even shouting to ease the pain.

I've had decades to deal with my grief, yet somehow managed to completely avoid all of it. What she achieves in a few short hours is both comforting *and* demoralizing. In a single story about a broken baseball bat, she goes from not being able to string together two words to a tear-slathered smile that refuses to fade. She doesn't hide from the grief like I do. At first it was shame that tormented me the most. Fear of who, or what, I had become. Eventually, it became the one emotion that never diminishes—guilt. No matter how hard you scrub, it's a permanent stain on your soul.

For the first time, I'm not the one filling the air with words. The barren landscape perfectly matches with the emptiness I feel inside. The only positive I see is the full moon tonight. It casts an extra-long shadow that follows everywhere I go. Real or not, knowing that there's something that can never leave me helps.

A little.

Quinn Chapter 2: House of the Rising Sun

My feet hurt from the regrettable combination of cheap boots and hours of walking absolutely nowhere. Hayden hasn't said a word in an unbelievably long time. He's spent most of that time staring at the ground. Not to be rude, but it's been a welcome break from the constant dribble. For a person who talks all the time, he never really says much.

The unexpected break gives me time to focus on things like the slight warming of the air. There's been an icy breeze my thin hoodie hasn't been able to keep out, so I'll celebrate even a few degrees' change. It's also a sign that the long, cold night is *finally* coming to an end. Feeling can now return to my long-frozen cheeks. They savor the subtle warmth coming in from a rapidly changing sky. In fact, everything changes so fast out here that within minutes, the entire sky is on fire.

My eyes twitch when the sky reaches that all-too-familiar shade of crimson. I have to force them away to enjoy the rest of the transforming world. Like the jagged mountains breaking the morning light into spectacular beams scattered across the valley floor. They lay on the ground like fallen stars waiting to be picked up.

The heat is rising much faster now. Frost doesn't even have the chance to melt before it's turned into steam. Somehow, I'm already forming a bead of sweat. There's a thick blanket of haze rising from the desert floor like low-hanging clouds. I try relieving some of the warmth with a ponytail, but my hair is just short enough to refuse to stay up. After five more unsuccessful attempts, I surrender and just tuck it behind my ears.

Of course, our path is leading us straight toward the blinding sun. I attempt to block it with my hand, only to find the reflection off the gritty sand is just as bad—maybe worse. The ball of fire seems three times its normal size, angry as hell, and ready to swallow us whole.

Within the blistering heat is another major surprise: something on the horizon seems to be moving! It appears to twirl, swirl, and dance right out of the sun itself! The rolling waves of heat and distorted light may be playing tricks, but I swear a solid silhouette twists to life right before me.

Should I be frightened or relieved?

Is it even real?

I snap Hayden back to reality to be a second set of eyes. He confirms that yes, it's very much real, and yes, it's definitely moving. His paranoia is already plotting an escape route into the high mountains. While I certainly understand the caution, my curiosity shrugs it off. We can't avoid the only living thing out here for absolutely no reason.

He reluctantly agrees after I promise to run at the first sign of trouble. But when he attempts to move in front of me, I shove him aside as a gentle reminder that I can hold my own against whatever it is. For now, it's only a half-formed silhouette against the raging morning sun. One with two heads, apparently.

Even as we get closer, both heads stay in place. Recent flashbacks of the three-eyed creature have me suddenly reconsidering our course. Fortunately, one of the heads eventually spreads large feathery wings. It appears this is a normal, one-headed person, with an unusually fat bird on its shoulder. And the details get even stranger the closer we get.

The man is so lanky, he could be a stick figure come to life. His rigid posture gives him a prim and proper appearance that seems wildly out of place in such a dusty hellhole. By comparison to the skinny man, the stubby bird looks to be as round as a bowling ball. In fact, it's not until we're almost right on top of them that I finally get a complete picture of our mystery couple. And they're the exact opposite of what I expected to find in such a desolate place.

I'll start up top with his rounded bowler hat; it's the grey felt kind with a bushy white feather poking out. His long, rust-colored coat has the thick chocolate elbow patches of a professor's jacket. Resting in his thin hands is a beautifully crafted walking stick with a golden lion head as a topper. The stick looks too delicate to actually support a person, so hopefully it's just for show. Every bit of him is dusty, yet perfectly put together. From his wing-tip shoes that appear to have no mileage on them at all, to the suit perfectly tailored to his leggy frame.

What I mistook for a plain fat bird is actually a splendid white owl with burning golden eyes. Tiny tan freckles decorate its otherwise pure-white body. She stares right through me as we approach. The man, on the other hand, just stands there, talking to thin air. He's engaged in a passionate conversation with an invisible partner that leaves him totally uninterested in acknowledging me.

This is all Hayden needs to see before trying to push me away from the seemingly distinguished man. Of course, this leads to a small shouting match while standing awkwardly close to him. Not that he seems to notice.

What's the harm in talking to a man standing alone in the middle of nowhere? Really, what harm *could* he do?

I give the occupied man a slight tug to get his attention. "Hello, sir! Please excuse my rude friend here, but we're completely lost. Is there a bus, or road, or something nearby you could direct us to?"

He eventually drops his invisible conversation long enough to focus on me. "Good day, young miss!" he proclaims in an excited cockney tone. "And what can I do for you this fine evening?" I'll pretend the "evening" comment has more to do with a preferred greeting than mental stability.

"We were wondering if you knew a way out of..." before I can repeat the question, he interrupts.

"My name is Sir Charles Wilfred Templeton the third and this is Bobo." Now, I'm not sure if he just introduced me to the owl or his invisible partner, but since the owl nods, I'm going to assume it was the bird.

"Well, it's great to meet you Mr. Templeton. Now, if you could tell me if there's a..."

"And Bobo," he blurts.

"Excuse me?"

"And Bobo, dear. She's very sensitive, you see."

"Of course she is, Mr. Templeton. It's nice to meet you, Bobo." The cuckoo expression Hayden makes over his shoulder forces a chuckle out at the end of my sentence. Interestingly, it's the owl that turns to scowl at Hayden. I press on with my question, "Like I said, we've gotten kind of lost and need..."

"We are all a bit lost, dear. Why do you think we're here? It's to get found." A rising excitement enters his voice.

"Yes, well thanks. So, as I was saying, is there a road or maybe some other form of transportation that got you here?" The easy question obviously can't hold his divided attention; he's already engulfed in another round of conversation with the invisible man. As much as it pains me to admit, Hayden was probably right about this one. The poor guy seems to know his bird's name, but that's about it. We're clearly on our own in getting out of this furnace.

I give the confused man a deflated thank you before turning back to Hayden. The look on his face screams, "I told you so," which makes me want to wipe it off with my boot heel. The only small satisfaction I get is from bumping his shoulder on the way by.

For some reason there's still this nagging worry that I can't get rid of. The crazy guy and his fat bird will die without food or water. I doubt they would even make it through the day. Insane or not, no one deserves that. Part of me wonders if he's too crazy to drink it anyhow, or if he does make it through today, what about tomorrow? I try rationalizing a good reason to keep our water, but there isn't one.

I quickly remove several large bottles and a few snacks from the overflowing backpack. I fill one bottle cap with water as a peace offering to the stern, fluffy bird. For several awkward minutes, all she does is continue making her untrusting scowl. But in time, the chubby owl finally shifts her ruffled chest down next to me. Her vibrant yellow eyes, inches away, speak loudly. It's as if she's accepting me and threating my life all at once. Then she dips her beak in for a hesitant first sip, eventually followed by a few longer ones, prior to checking me out again. I hold steady as she takes her time gobbling down the rest of liquid.

After the last drop is gone, she begins proudly bathing herself on the man's shoulder. I take this as my cue that she's finally done with me. Who would have thought that giving an owl water could be such an intense experience! Without a doubt, there's something special about that bird. It has me curious how such a magnificent creature came to be paired with such an equally odd man. It has to be an absolutely bizarre story!

I plant three water bottles at the man's feet. The whole exchange seems lost on the man as he's still chatting up his imaginary friend. It's not, however, lost on Hayden. I hear him screaming as I walk away from half of our supplies. His scolding tone reminds me of when I was ten and Dad caught me stealing toys from the market. "Are you crazy?" he asks. "That's all the water we have!" blah blah blah. But when he reaches down to snatch the bottles back, I bluntly snatch his wrist. "We have more and he had none." Hopefully, he can tell by the sharp edge on my words that I'm serious. This is the first time I've felt anything other than anger since becoming this monster, and dammit, I want to enjoy it.

None of this sits well with him. He grumbles under heavy breath while storming off to finish his mild temper-tantrum. Tiny mushroom clouds puff up under his feet from stomping in the dry sand. It's so over-the-top that it would be funny if I weren't so pissed.

The sweat rolling down my face is a reminder to not enjoy the show much longer. Even though he's only a few feet in front of me, Hayden's already disappearing into the dust and heat. A few quick tugs ensure that the backpack is tight enough for the long hike ahead. As my toes take the first step, "Miss," drifts in over my shoulder.

I turn to find his long arm held out to me. At the end of it is a small chain dangling from the tip of his finger. It holds a petite locket that's leisurely spinning in the vivid morning sun. Light bounces brilliantly off its smooth silver sides.

"This is yours, Miss." he warmly says. "It will help you get found." My lips part to decline it, to tell him to keep his pretty trinket, but it's already somehow in the palm of my hand. The aged chain is strangely cold in the scorching heat of the day. Delicate etchings and swirls flow gracefully down both sides. Every new look reveals some masterful new detail I missed before. Engraved on the back is a lovely inscription in a language I can't read.

"Patris amor. Amor patris."

The words flow beautifully, even if I can't understand them. They lock my cheeks into a frozen smile just from speaking them aloud. It's the kind of feeling that transforms the world into a fresh place. "I don't know what to say, Mr. Templeton. Thank you isn't enough for such a wonderful gift!" Stumbling through words to fully express my gratitude.

"Say you will live a long life, dear." All the previous confusion is long gone from his voice. "You had better go now, Quinn. Your friend is almost out of sight." It's sadly true. As much as I would love to finish this conversation, and solve the mystery of his new clarity, Hayden is barely a blip on the horizon. I don't know if he doesn't know I'm not with him, or simply doesn't care.

"And don't forget to go to the left," The distinguished man concludes confidently. I have so much to ask Mr. Templeton, including the meaning of "go to the left," but he's right, I have to get going if there's any chance of catching up to the pouting prince.

I secure the brilliant locket around my neck before running to catch up. As I turn to wave at the puzzling man, I find that he and the bird are already engulfed in a concentrated gust of wind that devours them completely. The sand forms a tight cone as if a tiny tornado has touched down directly on them. Then, just as mysteriously as they arrived, they're gone again.

Chapter 31: Blossom on the Tree

What the hell was she thinking!?!?

The old nut bag was visibly crazy! So, what does she do? Give him half our water! Look, I'm as understanding as the next guy, but come on! We gotta look out for ourselves!

"Who knows how long we're gonna be out here, Quinn!!!!" Of course, my screams get no answer. It's because she knows there's no excuse for it! My frustration builds with each step we take into the bleak landscape. The more sweat that falls, the more rage I throw in her direction. She owes me an explanation, *AT THE VERY LEAST!* There has to be a reason why she would do something so irresponsible without even asking me first!

"Okay, in the future, when you make a decision that could get us killed, could we talk about it first?" I spin around to find absolutely nothing behind me. I've been wringing my hands in disgust at *no one!* Where did she go? I'm positive she was behind me when... *oh no.* Don't tell me she stayed back there with Capt. Crazy-Ass and the winged volleyball. Maybe she had to give him her shoes or something, too!

Whatever.

At least I can stop wasting my time worrying about her and concentrate on getting out of this furnace. But *ughhhhhhh,* she still has what's left of our supplies! I only have a half-full bottle and it's going fast. At least she didn't give that away! Well she can keep them! She'll need them if she's staying with that maniac! Besides, I'll travel faster without her, and it will be nice to not worry about someone else for a change.

All this sounds great, but the farther I walk, the more my legs want to turn around. I slow to a crawl while my head and heart battle for control. Does she really need me? I've seen what she's capable of, but the enemy here isn't something you *can* fight.

My feet have already unconsciously turned around. I guess there never really was much of a choice. Besides, I can just scoop her up and we've lost maybe twenty minutes. The whole "I'll travel faster without her" sounded tough, but let's be real, I would be dead with only half a bottle of water.

Within minutes, a tiny speck appears on the horizon. It seems to be heading toward me before it stumbles into a small sandstorm. All I can see now is a blonde poof of hair inside the intense storm. It's a good thing I did come back. She *never* would have caught up to me with this thing! For a selfish moment, I wonder if this could be karma for her wasting so much of our water.

Only for a moment though.

One long...

Sweet...

Delicious moment.

Once that's over, I get back to figuring out how to help her. Going headlong into a cone of swirling shrapnel doesn't seem like much fun, although it looks like that's what's gonna happen. I charge in without another thought and find it even worse than it looked from the outside. "Kneel down, then put the pack over your face!" I scream to the stuck girl. She shouts something back that I can't hear either.

I hastily rip off my jacket (it's seen a lot of use lately) and throw it over both our heads. From inside our new bubble, I'm free to repeat, "I said, put the pack in front of your face!" She doesn't respond to my snide smile and seems content to huddle in silence while the sand finishes lashing our cocoon.

Holding the jacket up exposes my stomach to the raging tornado. For the most part, it's like rubbing fine grit sandpaper against my soft belly, although it will occasionally hit a spot that's like grinding salt into a fresh wound. Fortunately, the storm doesn't last long enough to do much more damage than fill every crack in my body with sand. Behind both knees, between every finger, even the folds of my eyelids get filled with grit.

Quinn has an entirely different problem. Her wavy bob has become the best afro you'll ever see! Judging by her expression, the same could be said of me. Our shared chuckle sets a positive mood to return to the desolate road to nowhere. But it's not long until our refreshed spirit is thrown into a blender—this time by Quinn.

"Turn left," she declares quite forcefully.

"All right; why left?"

"The last thing Mr. Templeton said was to go left."

"Well if that pinnacle of knowledge says to..." Safe to say the good mood is gone.

"Trust me, I think he knows what he's talking about. Let's try it." I wanna disagree just to spite the crazy ol' bastard, except this appears to mean a lot to her. Besides, what do we have to lose? We don't have a clue where we're going anyway. If it makes her feel better, let's go left!

"How left would you like to go? Like a gradual tilt, or full ninety degrees?" Judging by the wrinkles crawling across her nose, she isn't amused.

"I don't know. Just go left." She instructs while rubbing a silver pendant with her thumb.

"Well that's new, isn't it?"

"It was a gift from Mr. Templeton," she answers briefly.

Fair enough. No matter how much I really want to start a new verbal brawl, I suck it up and work on getting us out of here before we kill each other.

"Is this okay?" I ask, pointing slightly off to the left.

We're back to our silent march under the scorching sun. Small talk comes rarely, and when it's there, it's forced. Mostly by me. To make matters worse, the scenery never changes. The mountains always look the same, no matter how far we go. Nothing we pass says "living things are here." Time is the only thing left crawling in this desolate place.

Chapter 32: Wildfire

Hours pass with no sign of anything good for us. This is a place where even vultures don't scavenge. My forehead is the first to beg for relief from the merciless, unforgiving sun. It's grown tight enough to move as a single sheet of thick skin every time I squint. Of course, there will be no break today. The only shade is the soaring mountains, and they seem to run further away the closer we get to them.

Our time in the sun has taken a heavy toll on us. What little remaining water that's left has been tightly rationed, except it still hasn't gone very far. Two sips every fifteen minutes has turned into one every thirty. Dehydration was tolerable when it was only a dry mouth, but now it's a dull ache pulsing through my *everywhere.*

Each step directs a fresh bolt of pain to rip through me. Nothing is left out. My feet hurt from walking, eyes from straining to block out the sun, and even the tips of my ears are burnt from baking so long. We can't even distract ourselves with some tasty snacks because the salt burns our chapped lips. Plus, they would make us crave the cooling relief of water that much more.

If we were ever making progress, that time has long passed. Now we're stuck at a grinding pace that feels slow, cruel, and pointless. Needless to say, my frustration grows with every finished bottle of water. *What if* we had those other bottles? Why didn't I just take them back? Could she really have stopped me? What right did she have to decide that for us? The "what ifs" are really starting to pile up.

Why am I not at Shepherd's place, still clueless to all of this!?

Her.

Why am I out here?

Her.

Why are people trying to kill me?

Her.

Why am I cooking in this oven?

Her.

And LEFT? Why did we go left???

Her.

Why risk our lives on the words of a lunatic?!?! That psycho gave her a necklace, yet couldn't manage to tell us *how he got here?!* He didn't drop out of the sky, so where's his car? Not even the owl had enough good sense to fly far away! To top it off, she's fiddling with that damn silver locket every time I look over at her!

I'm really struggling to remain silent. I try shoving a large protein bar in my mouth to force it to stay shut. And yes, I can feel every grain of salt between the glacier-sized cracks in my lips. The thirst has gotten so powerful, it feels as if it's trying to pull the moisture from my very eyeballs. I'm also pretty convinced that if I tried hard enough, I could shed my entire skin like a molting snake. And the bleak horizon isn't doing much to cheer me up, either. It's nothing but one giant view of depressing nothingness. There's one spot of color and it's only a tall, lanky green cactus.

The dumb thing has two branches spread out in the shape of a hitchhiker with his thumb up. There's a plump flower in middle of one of his "hands" that appears to have a million tiny orange petals. My delusional mind quickly begins to transform the prickly plant into something that challenges me with its very existence. Mostly because his one arm is pointing off to the left. To the #@$&!*% *LEFT!*

Something inside me snaps. The anger that was buried just beneath my thin, hard-baked surface, comes boiling over in a fit of unhinged madness. My shaking hands snatch up the tormenting green arm. I watch as the long thorns sink deep into the palms of my fists. The numbing hatred prevents me from feeling any of it. I feverishly smile as my fingers dig into the hideous creature's flesh. Maniacal laughter erupts as stringy chunks of meat pour from the wide holes they make.

I rip the tormenting arm off, and heave it across the barren desert floor. *"There was nothing to the left, asshole!"* Not much is left of my voice. Then, my attention returns to the soulless flower in the other hand. How could this lovely orange thing thrive in this God-forsaken place? That kind of beauty is nothing but a cruel mockery in a valley of death.

Nothing has the right to live out here.

I remove the delicate antagonist before desperately choking the life from its colorful petals. "It's just like us, Quinn!" I don't even have to turn around to sense her mocking gaze. "We were never supposed to make it out of here alive! I've never been anything more than a cog in a machine! Why did I think I could ever be anything more than that??? That kid was the answer! They took everything from me! It didn't have to be like this! I never even got to say goodbye!" My scattered thoughts are starting to fly out in random order now.

Experiencing your sanity crumbling away is both terrifying and liberating. Everything binding you to society's rules: manners, kindness, compassion, giving a shit; it all melts away. I turn to the little tyrant that threw our lives away. *"Don't you see, Quinn?* That water was our life, and you *threw* it away! You took *my* life! We're going to die out here today!!!"* She stands in a slumped curve, hiding behind a wall of blonde bangs, guarding herself by staring only at her feet. *She can't even look at me!*

"You don't have *anything* to say? I need a reason! A simple explanation for *you* wanting to kill *me!"* Her hands are glued to the straps of our empty pack. The wind pulls back the curtain of hair far enough to catch a tiny glimpse of her melted, pouty face. When the shielded eyes refuse me, I twist her trembling chin around so she has to face the man she's murdered. Tears splash my arm as she fights to turn away. There's enough of me left to know this is wrong, but not enough to care, or stop. Using all the evil from the darkest part of my soul, I say something I'll never forgive myself for.

"Your parents weren't enough? You had to kill me, too???"

The last echoes of the wicked words are still poisoning my mouth as her fist destroys the entire left side of my face. It seals both eyes shut, numbs my legs, and hurls me through a galaxy of stars. My feet lose touch with the ground, and it's not until my shoulders collide with something rock hard that I assume I've landed again.

The lengthy air time also knocks some sense back into me. I consider myself extremely lucky when I wake up on top of the ground instead of under it. She somehow stopped at only one—admittedly solid—punch. I don't know if I could have done the same.

The landing stirs up a thick cloud of dust that leads to repeatedly coughing out of a (most likely) broken jaw. Just one blurry eye is brave enough to open and see what's coming next. Among the thousands of blue sparkles is a dark silhouette moving in over me. The recognizable shadow yanks me up by the throat to finish what my mouth started.

With only one working eye, all I can see are quick flashes of screaming lips or threatening extended fangs. Occasionally, a nose will come into focus, but mostly there's just the impact of large, rage-filled spittle splattering my face.

"You know why I gave him the water, Hayden? *Because he needed it!* It was *the right thing to do!* Isn't that the *bullshit* you're always spewing? All those dumbass stories are all about how *YOU* want to do the *RIGHT THING!* Isn't that why we're even out here? So *YOU* can do the *RIGHT THING?* Well, how was leaving him to die the *RIGHT THING?* You don't get to pick and choose who lives! That's what *THEY* do!"

Her words strip away the last shred of my self-worth. I'm now guilty of doing the exact things Shepherd and his people do. I judged that man and decided he wasn't worthy of life.

Quinn collapses in the sand, whispering, "I'm fighting to keep some part of me alive. These aren't my thoughts anymore! Every waking moment is filled with the most vile hatred imaginable! The only thing I can think of is eating! Killing!"

There are a million things to say, but the only words that come out are, "You're right." The resulting silence threatens to burst my wanting eardrums. Even though my heart begs me to find the words to make this pain go away, all I'm good at is running. I'm never strong when people need me to be. That's what I admired about Shepherd; he was never afraid.

I still don't know right the words, let alone how to say them, but the silence is killing us both. "I... I can't take it back, Quinn. It was purposefully evil and only meant to hurt you." The shame tries to draw my eyes away from having to look at her. This time, I don't let them hide. I don't let myself run.

Quinn Chapter 3: Say Something

I hate crying.

Always have, always will.

It leaves me feeling so naked inside.

His words still play on a constant loop in my head. Each new time around, they hurt a little more. My guilt wants to accept them as truth, even though I did my part! I tried to die!

My role in this thing was clear long ago. Still, the moment he pulled me off that mountain, we were all dead. Maybe it *is* my fault. I'm the one who couldn't even throw myself off a cliff right... So, when I let him take me back to that town, I became responsible for everything that happened after that. The only part I didn't ask for was being made into a monster. Besides that, every minute of suffering, every drop of blood, is on me. All of it.

I can't be here anymore. Just looking at him makes me want to shove my finger through his brain. Before that happens, I need to be somewhere else. Anywhere but here with him.

That's when I turn my back defiantly and just start walking.

To the left.

Hayden did say one thing that's undeniably true, and oddly it's the one thing that doesn't bother me at all. "We won't make it through the rest of the day." That's true. I know it should bother me, but as far as I'm concerned, I've already lived a week too long.

He says something behind me.

He doesn't want me to go.

He didn't mean it.

I don't care.

When he makes the mistake of touching me, I sling him over my shoulder like a squealing pig. His sudden flight, and face-down plunge into the dust, releases an extended grin that remains on my face long after it's finished. I walk on without giving him another thought, until the pitter patter of a desperate man eventually creeps up from behind me again. Without turning, I pause to warn, "You still have one good eye, so don't touch me again."

"Fair enough, Quinn. I just want you to know…" and the crap begins again. I turn to meet him, ready to shut his mouth with both fists, and he doesn't skip a beat. Lucky for him, my desire to break his cheekbone fades. Sadly, this results in a one-sided conversation that lasts for twenty minutes.

He trails along like a lost puppy through the wide-open desert. I may not be able to stop him from following me, but if he gets too close, I'll swing at him. If he's close enough to get hit, that's not my problem.

He stops talking for almost a whole minute after an hour or so. I make the mistake of checking to see if he's still back there, which of course he is, so this starts the repeating record over again. The verbal assault continues during the slowest, most miserable chase in human history. It's not just the blistering sun, either. The worst part is the endless heat boiling my lungs. Every breath pulls in fresh steam, so it's a never-ending cycle.

He eventually runs out of useless words. The rest of the time, we're left with only our heavy breathing as a soundtrack. Trudging under the cloudless sky makes it easy to tell what time it is simply by what body part hurts the most. Morning roasts my face, midday moves to the neck and shoulders, evening takes its toll on the slit between my t-shirt and jeans.

To make matters worse, the last water bottle has been gone for hours now. My lips hurt too much to even open anymore. The skin snaps instead of stretching the way it should. I try keeping enough hair over my face to block out the worst parts of the blistering sun, but nothing really helps. It's made worse by the fact there's nothing to keep me going anymore. There's no finish line. I'll eventually just surrender to the inferno, and who will care? Seriously, who will even know?

My head stays trapped in the darkest places possible. Scanning the bleak horizon only confirms all those hopeless feelings. The only thing pushing me forward is not wanting to deal with Hayden. I don't want to even look at him.

Occasionally, a random object will spring up, although it always turns out to be another mocking cactus or rock. But they're enough to keep my emotions riding an exhausting rollercoaster of exhilarating highs and devastating lows. Sometimes I'll build them up to be another Mr. Templeton, and by the time I get there… it's a plant.

Since it's physically impossible for the day to *never* end, the sky is forced to finally fade back into a lovely shade of pink that doesn't scorch my skin. It's an extended moment of needed relief, right until it hits that shade of heartbreaking red that comes just before nightfall.

FML.

The final nail in the coffin comes from a surprising "THUD" hitting the ground right behind me. My reaction time isn't quite as swift as it once was. It takes genuine effort to turn around and find Hayden face down in the sand. I try saving myself from having to bend over by gently nudging him with my foot. I'm not lazy, it sincerely does kill to move in any direction other than straight ahead.

But when my toes sink deep into the lifeless body, it becomes apparent our real problems are beginning now. He doesn't move a single muscle. Lifting his face shows that the un-punched eye is completely rolled back in his head. It seems that his clogged nose is barely taking in enough air to keep him alive, although for now, he's just mostly dead.

The raspy voice of a 90-year-old man finds its way out of my mouth while shaking him back and forth. "Wake up, Hayden. We've got to keep moving." I'm grasping for else what to do. It doesn't take long to realize that if I couldn't walk away from a stranger, I certainly can't walk away from him.

The idea of being needed actually gives me a burst of energy. He suddenly becomes my missing reason to keep going. A few minutes ago, I didn't care if he died, but now that he's actually on the verge of it, I'm hoisting up his limp remains to drag him out of here.

While my ego might have a renewed sense of purpose, my body is still running on empty. Hauling the extra weight really starts taking its toll after a few hours. Concentrating on one step at a time helps a little. I shut down every part of my brain not related to moving steadfastly forward. We realistically won't make it through another day, so we're either going to escape tonight, or we'll find a nice place to die.

The morbid deadline allows me to rediscover my long-lost step, but it doesn't help much with the discomfort of hauling Hayden's dead weight around. One positive is that the moon is shining with the same intensity as the sun did during the day. *If* there is anything out here, I'll be able to see it coming.

These are the first true emotions I've had since becoming this... *thing.* I'm genuinely pushing forward with everything left in my withering body. Before, I simply pretended to feel the way I used to. I went through the motions without any real desire to actually be doing them. Faking it because that's what I thought I should be feeling.

He's on some kind of weird moral crusade, but what am I doing? Why am I here? My biggest problem is how absolutely out of control I've become. It doesn't help that all we've done is react to all these shit storms exploding around us. That's fine with Hayden since he's not really the planning type, but that's not me—at least, it wasn't.

So, how did I get here? I guess it doesn't matter anymore. The only thing that matters is what's going to give out first: my feet, spirit, or mind?

There's a blip on the horizon large enough to gather my divided attention. It's far away, so there should be plenty of time to get my hopes up before crashing them down again. Nevertheless, it's a nothing I have to follow. At least I'll get to enjoy unlocking the mystery of a new puzzle.

It's a long, low flat mound.

It's not natural; definitely man-made.

It looks as if there are holes all over it.

All these clues add up to a whole lot of nothing to me. And it's starting to feel like getting close enough to solve this might kill actually me. Each step is getting more impossible than the last. Even blinking hurts.

Hayden's got it easy. He gets to ride along without a care in the world. Truthfully, it's a surprise the floppy man is even still alive. "We're almost there, Hay." I know this information won't help him. It's meant more to encourage my weary legs than comfort him. I'm also not sure why I called him Hay? Maybe it was to conserve the tiny amount of energy the last syllable would have cost me.

The puzzle pieces finally come together and, like I thought, it's nothing. Just an old school bus. Definitely not the salvation I had dreamed of. Honestly though, what really could've made much of a difference at this point? Even the pain in my head has gone silent. It's accepted the end is here. Pure stubbornness is the only thing keeping me moving now.

"Jack," My mother's sweet voice echoes down the halls of my mind. She always called me Jack. It was short for Jackass. Not in a bad way, though... It came from being stubborn as a mule. The name came from an old donkey named Jack. Of course, calling your mule a jackass is one thing, but mom took it to eleven by using it on me. Why would I worry about this now? The meandering thoughts of a dying mind, I suppose. Maybe I just wanted to hear her call me Jack one more time.

Almost without noticing, I'm standing in the door of the rusted-out bus. Well, there isn't a door, or windows, or anything, really. It's nothing more than a rotted corpse that's been picked over by the vultures of time. At least crawling inside should be pretty easy.

I heave Hayden's heavy ass up the stairs. His floppy body makes a not-so-graceful landing in the middle of the narrow aisle. While the frames of some seats are left, they're pretty much just rusty springs these days. Honestly, the floor looks much more comfortable than any of those torturous chairs. I wisely decide to stretch out next to Hayden on the flat floor.

One last time, I check his weak pulse and find it slow and steady. Ironically, he's doing better than I am at this point. Simply lying down is like fighting back full-on rigor mortis. Most of my muscles are so dehydrated, they simply refuse to straighten out anymore. I feel like I'm paralyzed, or maybe frozen in a solid block of ice.

Because my eyes are the only things that don't hurt to move, they're free to enjoy the graffiti-covered bus ceiling. They sluggishly roam around, exploring the vivid messages from people I'll never know. I really didn't want to die under a colorful "Keith was here" drawing, but it seems like that's how it's going to happen. Well, Keith, I hope your life ended better than mine.

The last bit of comfort I have is the silver locket. It soothes my brittle skin to rub its silky-smooth surface. Tracing the peaks and valleys of the inscription helps steady my labored breathing. Its message is permanently engraved in my heart, "*Patris amor. Amor patris,*" The unknown words help me accept what my body's known for hours; it's dying.

I'm dying.

That's when my eyes finally draw to a reluctant close. My last lingering thoughts are about all the other times I should've died, and this, *this* is how it ends? Shit.

Quinn Chapter 4: One More Night

My fingertips gradually grow just as numb as the rest of me. At least my encroaching death is soothing relief for these long, aching muscles. They had been absolutely throbbing from the strain of pushing on for miles past their breaking point. The dry fibers felt like the brittle threads of an unraveling rope.

The numbness eventually ceases enough to wipe all that away. As it does, the murky bus surrenders to a brilliant show of dazzling white lights. The colorless fireworks explode too perfectly to ever exist in the real world. Real or not, I'm welcome to casually float among them. All these happy little clouds release me from the grounding chains of my never-ending pain. In this blank landscape, I'm not happy, or sad, or anything else. I simply am. It's as if I've gotten lost on the way to some far-off dream.

The spotless canvas begins to sprout tiny golden flowers that bloom in entire bushels. Then, as if they had been here the entire time, tall green grasses fill in the rest. Within seconds, the blank landscape has been colored in by the most colorful crayons in the box. The result is a stunning meadow that's as real as anything else in this surreal place.

There's a faint breeze playing conductor to keep everything flowing in perfect harmony. Growing amongst the swaying blooms are crowds of wonderful people dancing along to the same unheard song. Their faces light up with heartwarming smiles as soon as they see me. It's the kind of loving outpour usually reserved for the most important people in your life. The fact that I'm a stranger seems totally irrelevant to them.

There's an invisible energy to this dreamlike place as tangible as warm summer rain. Every new second is a celebration that saturates my soul with an unearned happiness. It pulls me in with a simple kind of magic. Things that shouldn't be possible just feel completely natural here. Nothing about the instantly blooming flowers, or even the blooming people, seems out of place. They fill my heart with a guilty joy that makes me want to scream, cry, and sing all at once!

Every ounce of worry melts away while I wade through the waist-deep grass. When I manage to get close enough to the contagiously happy group, my ears finally find the lost tune. And it's unlike anything I've ever heard before! Maybe "heard" isn't the right word, more like *felt* deep inside my chest. There are no actual words or melodies, but this song is as much a part of this place as the grass, air, and people. The melody merges with my soul, bonding me to this wonderful world and everything in it.

I want to live in this feeling.

A small boy breaks away from the group to personally welcome me. He's no one I've ever met before; however, the look he gives is what you would expect from a long-lost friend. He has a shaggy mop of blond hair that's as golden as the endless field. His beautiful mismatched eyes beg me to join him. One is the color of the deepest oceans, while the other is the radiant green of a forest morning. He tells me they've been waiting for me. Not with his voice, but with something hidden in the music. And by "they", he means my family.

Could it be?

Are they *really* here??

I grab the small hand without hesitation. The moment I do, what can only be described as pure joy washes over me. The best way to explain it is that I feel complete for the first time. I rejoice in the magnificent moment by dancing through the sprawling meadow. Velvet plants tickle the soft skin between each spread toe. There's a fresh lightness in my legs as if I'm floating, except I'm not. At least I don't think I am.

I remain lost in the infinite paradise for hours, maybe days, or even weeks. No measurement of time could ever capture what it means to be here. I experience emotions that are more powerful than any words could ever hope to describe. My heart is pounding to the same song of this charmed place. Voices whisper in my ear like angels welcoming me home.

Through the peaceful chorus comes the unexpected rumble of a giant waking up underground. The quake stands in stark contrast to the perfect melody, like thunder drowning out a baby's laugh. The mighty growl shatters our carefree mood and every smile falls away.

Terror seizes our small community as the rumble quickly grows into a raging storm. The kind breeze transforms into a furious hurricane that mercilessly snaps off the tall flowers. Delicate petals swirl around like snow in a blizzard. Even the crystal blue sky has become a murky black hole in the world. The destruction is complete and _devastating_.

Everyone and everything is sucked into the all-consuming vacuum. The frightened people, and worst of all, my golden-haired child. I _desperately_ scramble to return to the safety of his touch, except he's always out of reach!

"Please don't leave me! Don't go!" I repeatedly beg. A biting panic develops from the thought of never seeing this place, or feeling this way, again. No matter how far I reach, and my bones are stretched farther than ever before, we simply can't touch! His soft fingers are right in front of me, yet some invisible barrier keeps us apart!

"Stop fighting, you little shit!" rolls in over the crashing thunder. In a show of raw, unchecked power, lightning spreads its prickly fingers across the black sky. This growing storm seems on the verge of ripping apart the entire planet. The vengeful hurricane rages until the last ray of light is gone. All that's left now are dull grey smears of nothingness. The mystical fields, smiling faces, fluffy clouds, even the blissful beating in my chest has been silenced. Only the violent hurricane and angry voice remain.

Quinn Chapter 5: Goodbye Yellow Brick Road

I'm lost, floating in limbo, while the harsh voice assaults me. It spews long chains of cruelty that slowly chew on my sanity. My only comfort is the ghost of the boy still lingering in the darkness. Soon though, even his sweet face begins filling me with a deep bitterness.

He's gone.

That fantastic world, *gone.*

I try taking my anger out on the supernatural voice, only to find the intense pain of moving my dehydrated body has returned. Frustration leaves me stuck between these two worlds; my heart belongs to the beautiful meadow, while the venomous voice anchors me in this desolate hole. If it would only shut up, I could return to the warmth of the golden boy.

The poisonous words have me imagining things slithering in the darkness. They plant ideas that have hateful creatures crawling out of the inky pools like snakes in mud. Finally, a shape evolves that's so vile, so gruesome, that it has to be real since my imagination could never create something so revolting. The dark shadows have twisted into a face so wicked, it could only belong to the hateful voice.

It emerges from the void with bloodshot eyes set deep in hollow sockets. The face around it is so sickly that it could be mistaken as skin stretched over a chiseled skull. Large veins bulge from its forehead that throb intensely, almost hypnotically, during each scream. Heavy smears of black paint run in a colossal X across the entire haunting face. What few teeth it has left are stained the color of rotten meat.

The rest of the skeleton-thin man eventually emerges from the darkness. What had been hidden is a thin freak of nature that seeps hatred from his very pores. It's not anything particular that makes him frightening; it's the whole ruthless package. His tattered outfit, which covers him tightly from boot to neck, appears to have been sewn together from black leather scraps, and (barely) held together by rusted metal clamps. And there seems to be several iron scales scattered almost randomly throughout the otherwise dark suit.

He's so tall that, even bent over, his green mohawk scrapes against the bus ceiling. But his most noticeable features are the two large tubes erupting from right under his jaw. They lead down into a backpack that's pumping an endless stream of green slime into them. The glowing tubes slither like constricting snakes around his skinny neck, and bathe his face in an eerie light. You can even see the radioactive ooze flowing through the shallow veins of his face and hands. When he squeezes my arm, they wiggle like neon worms.

I push back against the bony chest, which only pisses him off more. He slams his spider-like body down on top of me in response. Those long, spindly arms choke my wrists into an unwilling submission. He squawks, "Oh, we got us a live one here, Crow!" My fist reaches out, but it's easily smacked away before it has a chance to reach him. I'm too weak right now to have done much damage, anyway. Another voice chimes in from somewhere out of sight, *"Throttle up and get 'er, Rat!"*

"Hells yeah, boy! We gon' have some fun with this one!" Rat joyfully squeals while bashing several large buttons on his forearm. The tubes in his neck immediately turn an angry shade of red. As they do, a morbid howl explodes from his mouth. The big brute dips down low before launching into an uncontrollable fit of shaking that rattles the entire bus.

He rises with a very satisfied, "Aaaaaaaaaaaaaaahhhhhhhhhhhhhh" while dragging his scabby tongue across dry lips. His eyes are now the same haunting shade of baby blue as mine.

"Now where was we, girl??" in a terrifying new voice. *What the???* What *is* that thing? Even if I could identify it, I couldn't do much to stop him. I get to helplessly watch as he snatches me up by the throat, slings me into the ceiling, and laughs in my face. One of my arms goes all the way through the rusted metal so I can feel the cold wind blowing outside. And coming back down isn't much better either...

I stir up enough rust to paint my entire body in a thick layer of chocolate brown flakes. Inhaling the sharp snow instantly seals my throat shut and, suddenly, defending myself isn't as important as merely finding a small breath! I desperately try sneaking in a little air by pounding on my heaving chest. Rat doesn't seem to know (or care) I was beaten way before this fight ever started. He absolutely refuses to let up, even as I struggle to simply breathe! Instead, he angrily gathers me back up to toss through several rows of skeleton seats.

The impact knocks more of the rust free, but I'm still urgently trying to cough up the rest. I fantasize twisting those tubes all the way around his bulging throat, while helplessly lying on the ground. In reality, though, I'm stuck upside-down on this rotten bus bench, wishing the world would turn right-side-up again. I'm completely powerless to do anything other than watch him come get me, again. Stomping feet are the only things can I see. Three rows separate us—then two. Every few seconds, another set disappears.

One. By. One.

Quinn Chapter 6: All Time Low

My inevitable meeting with the rampaging beast comes when the last seat disappears. I rip and tear at his scruffy boots since they're the only things within my low reach. Sadly, the soft outer layer is about as far as my dead fingers can dig. He just laughs and drives his foot deeper into my ribcage.

The beating pauses only so I can vomit on the floor. Then it resumes by scooping up my mostly dead body and hurling it through the back window. There's no glass, but plenty of metal remaining. I feel the flaky steel slice under my skin on the way out. It hammers in further with every tumble across the hard desert floor.

I can't fight anymore. My brittle arms collapse while trying to pull myself from the sand. The best they can do is drag my nose out far enough to breathe again. Unfortunately, it lands right next to a big pair of black boots.

"Do it." I command with a tired voice. *"Kill me."*

"Now, why would I waste a fresh young thing like you?" Rat sneers and, for some reason, doesn't actually kill me. Instead, he straps large bands onto both wrists. It should be pretty obvious that I don't need to be restrained. I'm not going *anywhere.* He punches a few more buttons on that forearm screen of his. They trigger deep tremors in both wrists, as if they're being electrocuted. I can feel the static charge raise my hair before, *"Schink!"* suddenly snaps the bands together.

A powerful magnet has turned the simple metal straps into unbreakable handcuffs. Though, at this point, the weight of the metal would have been enough to keep me on the ground.

I'm simply done.

"That was disappointing, kid. I really thought you'd put up more of a fight than that."

Yeah. Me, too.

The freak's spindly arms attach another band to each leg and once again, *"Schink"* locks them together. I wish I could make this harder on him, I really do, but I really don't care what his plan is. What can he do to me? There's nothing left to take away. There's absolutely no way he can punish me any more than I've been punished already.

Whatever his plan is, it begins by using those bony fingers to pry open my jaw. They taste like sulfur and dust while they root past my tongue. I'm actually surprised at a couple things when a few tears roll out:

1) That I care enough to cry.
2) That there's enough moisture to still make tears.

Next, he tilts my head back and shoves a giant rubber hose down my throat. The rough plastic scrapes against the soft flesh on the way down. Each ripple triggers a new gag as it plunges deeper. All I can see is the dark night sky and grubby fingers shoving the fat tube further. I can feel it stretching out the bottom of my stomach like a rubber band by the time he's finished.

There's a few more dead moments of anticipation before a dark crimson ooze begins flowing through the tube. When some of it leaks out the top, I get a better look at the mystery ooze. This stuff looks different than the neon liquid flowing though Rat's tubes. There's no radioactive glow or surreal coloring to this one. I try fighting against whatever's being pumped into me, although without hands or feet, it does little more than spit some of the liquid onto his ugly face. But it's his reaction that really scares me. Rat absolutely *freaks* out from just a few drops touching his skin! What is this stuff???

Then the ooze reaches my own taste buds and I absolutely can't believe what it is... BLOOD. Fresh, salty blood. I have to pause and make sure my mind isn't playing some cruel trick on me. But no, against all belief, it's the most wonderful thing my lips have ever tasted. I quit fighting the impulse to vomit up the tube and let the savory syrup restore my body, which until now had been deflated like an old balloon.

My muscles shiver from the fresh plasma soaking in. The feeling is so incredible, so completely irresistible, that it almost makes me forget about the gigantic feeding tube shoved halfway down my body.

Almost.

Along with the returning strength comes the rage. The fangs that ache for one more round with the heavy metal asshole. And this time, I promise not to disappoint.

My revenge plans suffer a setback when the prick clamps a new collar around my neck. This one is the thick leather kind used to leash wild dogs. He makes sure to put it on the end of an extra-long pole to keep me, and my aching fangs, as far away as possible.

My feet clamps come undone as soon as the leash is secure. The shocking development makes me completely miss Rat's partner sneaking up behind me. He presses one hand down on my shoulder, and uses the other to rip the tube out. The fat torture device, *somehow,* feels much worse on the way back up. Every tiny ridge seems to catch a spasming muscle this time around. It's a level of pain far beyond anything I've experienced before.

At least with a cut or bruise, you know what to expect. That's familiar pain; this on the other hand, hurts *so bad*, it's confusing. I can't actually tell what part of my body hurts. The shock runs from toenails, to eyeballs, and everything in between. When the tube finally falls out, I collapse on the ground with it. The leftover ooze gushes all over and Rat leaps out of the way as if it were hot lava. I must instinctively chuckle because he suddenly yanks at my leash, "What you laughing at, bitch???" He tugs at the rigid collar and every twist of his angry hand collapses the leash a bit more. But, his humiliation has caused him to accidently bring me within biting distance.

That's a <u>BIG</u> mistake.

I take a chance by driving my teeth toward his noodle-like neck. The attack is way too fast and sails far off course; managing to miss everything except for the bridge of his crooked nose. He stumbles back to reveal the new valley carved into his slimy snout. While the wound is only superficial, streams of blood are gushing down both cheeks. I would love to bottle up his stunned expression and eat it with a spoon. Rat quickly pushes me back out of reach again. I doubt he will give me another chance as good as that one.

When his brow plunges, I brace for the coming payback. Sure enough, he swings the leash (with my head attached) into the side of the rusty bus.

"I'm gonna make sure they treat you extra special." My restraint tightens even more after he's finished taunting me with that darting tongue of his.

"Get your ass up here." This time I don't struggle; visibly.

Fearing the loss of my ability to breathe again, I test the limits of my restraints a little more casually. Little things, like stretching to see how secure the collar is, or tugging at the cuffs while walking to see how far they'll reach. But, sadly, I'm already by the side of a large truck before finding out if any of it would've worked.

This is also when I get my first view of Hayden. He has the same fresh blood trails leaking down his chin. His feet and ankles are also tied like mine. However, Rat's partner hasn't bothered with the leash because he's still out cold. It's easy for him to drag Hayden up to the rear of an oddly shaped truck. While the front is standard desert runner, the rear is made out of two thick sheets of steel that have been leaned against each other in the shape of a tent or upside-down V. That's all. No bed, no storage, just this funky metal wedge.

The thin freak types on his forearm the same way Rat had. This time, all of Hayden's cuffs separate. Regrettably, he's in no condition to take advantage of this newfound freedom.

The scavenger takes his time in carefully arranging Hayden into a giant X on the desert floor. After each floppy arm and leg is spread to the farthest corners, his entire body is thrown toward the steel slab by some invisible force. He collides with a loud metal-on-metal thud that exposes the secret to their magnetic magic. It seems these cuffs will turn us into puppets on unseen strings.

Not me.

The second my leash drops, I'm out of here. Or I'll rip his damn arms off trying!

So, Rat repeats the process when my turn comes. He leans me against the opposite slab and commands me not to move. I meekly reply, "No problem." What the sniveling mutant doesn't know is that I'll be miles away in just a few minutes. But for now, I don't want to look overly anxious while waiting for the little prick to hit the button.

No eye contact.

Nothing too unusual.

Keeping my head down, I concentrate only on waiting for the tiny tremors in my cuffs to end.

It's not long before my wish comes true. I keep just enough tension in the cuffs so my hands fly apart the second they release. I instantly whip my neck forward and the thrust yanks the leash from his hands. The pole only bounces once before I snatch it up and smash it into the side of his skull.

The sound echoes across the valley. **CRACK!!!!**

He drops to the ground so hard there has to be a crater left behind. I don't waste time going for another hit on the already collapsed man; instead, I choose to get some much-needed distance between us. That turns out to be extremely easy thanks to the fresh infusion of blood. My legs are able to tear across the sand like never before.

...until they're suddenly not anymore.

The familiar tremors start in the base of my thumbs, and quickly work their way up. That's before my arms experience the abrupt stoppage of a dog finding the end of a short chain. The impact drops me to one knee, but I continue digging in the sand to keep moving forward. Nothing will stop me from crawling my way out of here.

Except, even buried deep in sand, the tremors eventually overpower me. My churning legs have stopped. When they do, I'm up in the air, sailing backward toward th—

BAM!!!

Quinn Chapter 7: Remedy

I don't wake up until a particularly harsh bump bounces my sleeping head off the steel slab. The abrupt awakening leaves me struggling to make sense of the endless smear of blurred colors rushing by. It seems my mind is having a very hard time recovering from the extended forced nap. Even the basics are gone, like who I am and how I got here are completely lost in the fog.

Discovering the lifeless Hayden helps to fill in some of the missing pieces. Falling out of Vegas, Mr. Templeton, those crazy cute robot kids, the Rat bastard, and of course, my family. That part, I wish I could forget again.

One major difference is our location. This certainly isn't the lifeless desert anymore. There's actually stuff here. Not good stuff, though—most of it is on fire.

The worst are the barrels releasing fiery debris into the air. They're real-life fireflies floating around, looking for a place to land. And the swarm bites at my frozen skin every chance they get. Then, when I'm paying too much attention to them, my head will bounce off the truck again. These cuffs have me pinned so close that almost any little bump will crash my skull off the solid steel wall.

None of this matters to the assholes up front. They're too busy shouting at each other to actually drive. They also seem really fond of swerving off the road every few minutes. Every time they do, gravel sprays up my bare legs. The extra pain in my left foot probably means I've lost a boot somewhere along the way.

When we drive into a pitch-black tunnel, it comes to mind that I'll be wiped off the side of the truck if we swerve in here. This causes my heart to skip a beat from every twitch of the fidgety steering wheel. I can't tell how close we actually are, but the echo makes it sound as if we're right along the edge.

A plume of sparks erupts from the front fender after another collision. The metal shavings give off just enough light to illuminate the wall only inches away from my nose. The deafening wind, burning metal flakes, roaring engine, and fear of becoming a long smear on a wall make me consider just leaning forward to get it over with. Thankfully, before I can make peace with the idea, the punishing tunnel ends.

The shot nerves have left me hanging off the side of the truck in a melted mess. I'm stuck somewhere between unconscious and insane. Probably about as close to crazy as you can get while still being aware of it. I fantasize about floating away to leave this all behind. Simply abandon my body and let my spirit blow free on the wind. It's surely a hallucination, but I swear I see myself hanging off the truck from several feet away. I'm floating high above, looking down on myself in sympathy and disgust.

How long this mental limbo lasts is impossible to tell. The next real thought that comes is the realization that feeling is finally returning to my frozen fingertips. That means the icy wind has stopped. It means our truck has stopped, too.

It's an actual challenge to lift my head to greet whatever fresh hell this will turn out to be. I *need* to know, but don't really *want* to know. When the courage finally does come, I find something completely unexpected. I had imagined those filthy bastards were taking us to some run-down shack in the middle of nowhere. This is *definitely* not that.

It's more like a chemical plant than anything else. Every building is meticulously maintained and spotlessly clean. They could best be described as sterile-looking, even though dozens of giant smokestacks are busily shooting massive balls of fire out every few seconds. Surrounding the entire thing is a thick row of razor wire that leads to a *VERY* closed front gate. *"VERY"* because of the *extremely* uninviting spikes covering the whole thing.

Crow flashes the lights four times as some sort of signal to the guard shack. After the fourth flash, a large number of automated guns spring out of the previously blank wall. They form a tight grid of red dots down the length of our truck. The men scream franticly at the radio between hitting each other Three Stooges' style. Apparently, the fourth flash was a big mistake.

They shout, "Runners! Night runners, dammit!!!" when the entire cabin lights up in a spectacular laser show. Several of the dots have migrated to the center of my chest now. Even though they aren't applying any actual pressure, it feels as if they're shoving me against the hard slab. Luckily, before something stupid happens, an all-clear sends the guns back to their hiding spots.

Air refills my starved lungs the instant they're gone. Not everything is good though; my head clumsily falls back and cracks the steel wall again. I'm still reeling as the truck sputters through the open gates. Maybe it's the minor concussion talking, but everything about this place says "STAY AWAY." Even the way the doors slam shut behind us is ominous. They close with the force of two colliding cars. I worry I'll never see the other side of them again.

Quinn Chapter 8: Love Don't Live Here

The wide-open doors unleash a foul smell from inside the building. My stomach churns as the overpowering stench of rotten blood pours out. This odor is nothing like the salty sweet smell of regular plasma. Whatever this stuff is, it crawls up my nose like corrosive acid.

Rat threatens me with a cocky, "Ah ah ahhh, kid. Don't cha go tryin' to run away." His voice has lost the devilish growl. "I'll have ta' snap them pretty little knees of yours." Obvious joy pulls his leathery face into a sarcastic smile that has me aching to carve him up pumpkin-style. Crow is too busy working to join in Rat's game of threating me. He swipes his finger four times and Hayden drops off the side of the truck. There's still no sign of life when he pours out over the filthy concrete ground.

Then, from seemingly nowhere, a tiny machine hovers in over the lifeless body. The silver robot is as round as a Frisbee and just about as wide. There's a small antenna on top that wiggles as it makes weird clicking noises like a cricket. After a few seconds, a hidden panel slides open to release two lengthy cables from the bottom. On the ends are round disks that automatically seek out the metal bands attached to Hayden's wrists. They continue searching until the familiar *"Schink"* sound rings out.

A loud whirring sound begins when the bottom of the mini droid abruptly lights up. The noise surges as it struggles to lift Hayden's limp body off the ground. By the time it revs high enough to take off, the scream could be mistaken for a crying baby.

A matching droid flies in for me a few seconds later. Just like the last one, two cables drop down and search for my wrists. Rat's careful not to let me touch the ground this time. It seems I'll be leaving directly from the steel slab. I helplessly watch the cables snap on my cuffs, all while imagining myself wrapping them around his tube-filled throat. Then the new droid revs up to peel me off the side of the beat-up truck. Rat flicks his tongue through cracked lips, "Bye bye now, lil' mama. Maybe I'll swing by later to give you a little *taste.*"

Nasty son of a bitch.

I kick toward him, but that only makes me look even more helpless. The freaks relish in my misery by catcalling while the little bots carry us away. The humiliation sharpens the fangs of my rapidly growing anger.

This suffocating helplessness remains as we fly over the grimy factory. Below us are dozens of people rushing around like crawling spiders. Every one of them is as nasty looking as Rat and Crow; same bloodshot eyes, skeleton faces, and they're all covered in *whatever* is in those tanks. This whole place is nothing but huge vats of the gross smelling ooze. Giant paddles constantly stir the foul concoction, sending fresh waves of it into the air. This is definitely not a smell I could ever get used to.

The little droids are really picking up speed as we enter a new section of the building. At least this part smells slightly less disgusting than the other. Most likely because the vats are completely missing. The only things in here are countless rows of frosted glass tubes stretching from wall to wall. The tubes, almost coffin-sized, are connected by endless pipes and hoses.

A young voice breaks in from behind, "Slow up, TTs," and we drift to a gradual stop. A floating chair, piloted by somebody that couldn't be much older than me, glides up beside Hayden. The occupant is a homely looking guy with the same sunken face, but with a much dumber outfit. It may sound weird to notice how a person is dressed in this life-or-death moment, but he's just so ridiculous looking, it couldn't be ignored. He seems to have gotten the black leather memo; however, his stiff jacket is two sizes too large, while the striped polo underneath it is two sizes too small. And I'm not even sure what his pants are made of. They appear to be stitched together from several sets of equally terrible curtains. Still, his defining feature has to be the slicked-back hair that leads away from an acne-ridden face. The crazy amount of grease sitting on his forehead reflects the florescent lights with mirror-like accuracy.

Then he opens his mouth, and every other word cracks like he's in full-blown puberty. Turning his attention to Hayden's bot, "You know we can only use live ones! TT-K, did you run vitals? Which runner was responsible for the feeding?" The bot responds with two quick beeps and a pop-up hologram of Crow's ID.

"Were the proper vitals run?"

"Beep beep" chirps the bot. The picture converts to numbers that the nerd swiftly moves around in midair. He grabs and shuffles them with amazing speed to decipher Hayden's vitals. He clicks through screen after screen, reading charts and tweaking settings, until he's finally satisfied. "All right; this one passes, but just barely. Make a note if he doesn't survive the spike, it was runner Crow's catch."

After that, his attention turns to me.

"So, what do we have here? Don't you just look full of life!" His chair moves in ridiculously close. Close enough to appreciate every sad hair randomly poking out of his chin. Close enough to get drunk on his musky cologne that's somehow worse than all the other putridness in here.

He attempts to lower his voice and it cracks even more under the strain. *"Well, hello laaaaaadddy!"* He draws a few fingers through his oily hair at the same time. After it's been slicked completely down, he attempts a dreamy, smoldering look that comes off as confusion with a touch of constipation.

"Now, aren't you a sight for these sore eyes!" he croons while rubbing my cheek. The sludge from his hair smears my face with every stroke. Dangling here leaves me no actual way of avoiding his filthy touch, so I smile and not-so-patiently wait for him to make a mistake.

The pitiful smooth talk continues, although my attention has turned to Rat and Crow. They're clumsily strapping Hayden into a large mechanical spine sticking out of the floor. Its giant centipede arms look ready to wrap him in a dozen rigid steel bands. His wrist cuffs clamp onto the prongs, then the spindly legs bite down to hold him upright. Rat shoves another feeding tube down his throat after this is all finished. Crow mutters under his breath, obviously still fuming over what the nerd said about him, but the grease ball is too busy stroking my hair to care.

I keep my repulsion buried since he seems like the key to getting out of my own cuffs. I bite my lip to look overly sexy. It also helps choke back the disgust. My mouth manages to vomit, "Hey yourself, good-looking." The words are more spat out than said.

"I really like, that... that jacket." I slather on lies and watch him eat up them one by one. "And that hair! Are you a bad boy, handsome? What's your name?"

"Nick," he responds with a sharp squawk. He's obviously not used to anyone flirting with him. Like, ever.

"...but my friends call me Diesel."

"I'm sure they do! And I see why! Look at those big, strong muscles!" I worry about laying it on too thick, except it doesn't take my super senses to hear his racing heartbeat, or see the tiny bulge forming in his pants. I continue to spew more sweet-sounding lies, "Would you flex those big muscles for me? I want to see that strong body!" He stammers while flexing the little mounds of sadness on both arms.

"The right muscle is so much bigger than the left!"

"That's my gaming hand!" the silver-tongued Romeo excitedly exclaims while circling me. It rolls from his tongue as smugly as a Shakespearian quote. I can feel his unblinking eyes trace my body. They make my skin crawl, but at least I don't have to worry about him seeing me watching the other two assholes. They've begun latching several smaller tubes onto Hayden's cuffs. After they're secure, dozens of tiny prongs spring out from the edges. They're curved under like fishhooks and point around the bottom of his hands.

Rat activates the machine and the entire thing becomes a flurry of activity. Hayden's body is instantly lifted in the air, then laid inside one of the large glass tubes. The hooks bury themselves deep into his wrists as soon as he's in place. This causes a steady crimson stream to begin pouring into the smaller tubes. Nick Diesel yells over his shoulder, "It's your lucky day, Crow! Looks like he made it after all!"

"Wha... What are you doing to him?" I ask as non-desperately as possible.

"Oh baby, he's going to make me a whole bunch of cash! You play nice and maybe he'll make *us* lots of cash! *You like that, don't you?*" I want to remove the bastard's heart through his ass. Instead, I force another pained smile, "Well, how is he going to make us all that money?"

"Not just him, honey—all of them." He points down the rows of frosted glass and I finally see the faces watching me from their crystal tombs. Thousands of them. Most are little more than skin, bones, and pumping veins.

And they're ALL alive.

Quinn Chapter 9: Money Maker

The bottom of my chest abruptly falls out. All these people are living blood farms! It brings a sudden rush of traumatic memories from the feeding lines back home. I've been on the wrong side of a bleeding needle before. The feeling of someone slowly draining your life is an emptiness that never fades.

Nick snaps me back to reality with a limp-wristed pinch. "Don't you be scared, honey. Maybe we can keep your sweet cheeks out of there?" He doesn't even pretend to look at anything other than my breasts.

I unintentionally break my pretend-to-be-sexy act for only a moment. Either a disgusted look, or hateful smirk, leaks out and causes the slimy prick to back away. I'm going to be in those things next to Hayden if I don't recover quickly. He needs to be convinced that I could *somehow* be interested in anything he has to offer. Thankfully, all it takes is one good smile and he comes fluttering back with stars in his eyes.

"We make V from these blood suckers. That V equals cash money for Nick Diesel!" This guy's ego will give me all the information I want as long as I play along. "You like that, don't you?" He slathers those filthy fingers all over me again. "Why don't we head up to my room so I can show you a King-sized mattress in search of a Queen?"

Ughhhhh...

This conversation is quickly going in the wrong direction. In an effort to steer it away, "Oh, V? All my friends love it!"

I've never heard of it.

"So, then, how do... how would you spend all that money? Buy me nice things?" I'm grasping for anything to talk about other than his bedroom, and this seems repulsive enough. I need more time to figure out how to get Hayden out of that blood-sucking machine.

"Does it kill them?"

"Certainly not! We couldn't filter the V through them if they were dead. It's a beautiful process of pumping blood in through their mouths, then taking it back out with those prickly bracelets." He pokes my cuffs to simulate the needles I saw stabbing into Hayden.

The longer he goes, the higher his squeaky voice gets. "And what comes out is V. People will pay out the ass to be a vampire for just a few minutes! Everyone wants to be able to do the things you all do. Want to climb buildings? Bench press a car? A shot of V is all you need!"

He ends by boasting, "Not that I need it" while flexing those puny muscles again.

So, all these workers look like they're out of their minds because they really are. They get high and it eats them alive. That also explains how Rat went from zero to rampaging hulk back on the bus. Hayden had said something about V-heads back in Vegas; this must be them.

I might be new to being a vampire, but one thing I know is that it's a disease. So, how can they be a vampire for only a few minutes? That stirs up a question that may be a little too smart for the bimbo role I'm playing. "Why aren't you infected after drinking our blood?"

Luckily, it appeals to his geekiness instead of giving me away. "Oh, I knew I liked you! Brains and beauty in one! You would be right, except we've already thought of that. See, I don't go in through the fangs to harvest the blood. We go through the wrists! That way, the hyaluronidase in your teeth can't activate the venom. So, without activation, the effects are only temporary. Like catching a cold versus the flu!"

His explanation destroys the last sliver of hope I had for a cure. How could I have ever believed that this sniveling bag of diarrhea weasels could have a way of freeing me? Until the end of time, I'll be this.

This *monster.*

"So, would you like to slip out of those cuffs for a while? Or are you into leaving them on?" He picks an extremely poor time to deliver the slimy words. I was already struggling to hold the rage back, and his pathetic words land like a sucker punch to the gut.

His hands are busy exploring further and further down my waist. Every slithering finger sends a bolt of disgust shooting up my spine. His hot, sticky breath causes me to bite down too hard on my lower lip. I feel the liquid result leaking from the corner of my mouth.

He's getting too bold while searching my exposed skin. He eventually gets the bright idea to bite at my throat and joke, "Is this how you do it? You know, when you kill a man." He walks his spindly fingers down my trembling chest. "Women like power..." pausing on the bone between my breasts, "...and now *your* life is in *my* hands. Does that turn you on? What does it make you want to do to me?"

I'm not even breathing anymore. Still, he won't quit. "I know what I want to do to *you*." That brief sentence shatters the last piece of me. Several sloppy tears break through my hardened exterior. Not even that phases him. "Many beautiful women have come through here. Of course, I've been with them all. Most have gone on their feet, some on knees, but they all go. You understand, don't you?" The devil hides behind that high-pitched voice.

"Now, which kind are you going to be?"

I've learned several things about myself lately. Most of them involve coming to terms with the awful things I do to survive. They've tested the very limits of how far a soul can stretch and still be called mine. However, letting this nasty sack of shit touch me, will never, *ever* be one of them.

I scrounge up the widest smile possible, while bringing my wrists together. He's so wrapped up in humiliating me that he doesn't even notice when I make long slashes across both palms. The delicate skin splits open easily. I have to ease up on the pressure when a nail digs too far in and a few painful tears slip out. It's okay though; I got what I needed. Blood is pouring out, yet my fake smile never fades.

Twisting back and forth ensures the slippery liquid covers every inch of my wrists. I can't see them, but can feel how easily my hands are moving around now. When I think it's good enough to set me free, the forced grin becomes an actual smile. A confident promise slips out, "I'm gonna show you exactly what kind of girl I am." His sweaty cheeks burst with a flushed cherry pink. All the hormone-induced courage leads him to abruptly wrap his body around mine. His filthy hands are greedily crawling as if they can't decide where to start.

I try pulling my hands out of the slippery cuffs. My wrists slide down easily, but still won't fit through the tight bands. Several folds of bunched skin are keeping both thumbs from going any farther. I shift over to find better leverage and he takes it as a sign to attack my neck. His darting tongue nauseates me as it moves further and further down.

I can't take any more.

I. CAN'T. TAKE. ANY. MORE!!!

The boiling hatred erases every bit of doubt I had left. It brings me to a place where I'm willing to do *anything* to be free from these suffocating cuffs. That includes folding both thumbs in and *squeeeeeezing.*

The lethal combination of panic and disgust keeps me going until the bones snap from their sockcts. Two loud pops are heard as the thumbs slide freely out of the way. A bolt of lightning-fast pain rips down both arms. It pushes out an unexpected scream that accidently alerts Nick to my not-so-stealthy plan. The sudden cry forces him to drop his lip-based assault on my neck. While my plan might not be a secret anymore, that's fine with me. I slide easily out of the hanging cuffs now.

It's only a few feet to the ground, and you would think such a short fall would be easy. I mean, I've jumped off buildings. Yet this one still manages to go all wrong. I crash down on the floor with the grace of a dead cat. First to hit are my hips and elbows, followed by every other exposed bone possible. The grand finale was bashing my soft skull against hard ground. That caused my entire body to revolt against me. I lay motionless, trying to convince myself to get going again. Not even the army of approaching feet will get me moving.

Leading the charge is slick Nick in his gliding chair. Even though my eyes are barely working, I can see his stretched, smirking grin from here. I'm drawn to the whites of his teeth. I want to rip them out.

His obnoxious laugh is, for some reason, the only thing I can hear. Just as his obnoxious cologne is the only thing I smell anymore. My entire world revolves around him. Every nasally breath, clogged pore, and pit stain pushes me past my breaking point; the reasons why are no longer important.

I feel the monster gently creeping up inside. This time it doesn't snatch control, but settles in like a long-lost friend. This is the first time it's worked with instead of against me. Its return has contradictory effects—relaxing me to the point of ultimate violence. Even time can't escape my unbreakable monster. It slows the world down to a widespread halt. In the time it takes for a bead of sweat to fall from Nick's greasy brow, I make myself all he can see.

Now, he gets to experience *real* power.

MY POWER.

Everything he thinks he is...

I AM.

I've hurt a lot of people and it's torn me apart inside. This time, with a massive grin that stretches from ear to ear, I'm going to enjoy every second of it. The little coward in the chair shouts for the dirty desert crawlers to come get me. He wants them to put me back in those chains.

Never again.

Before Rat can move a toe, I have Nick out of the shiny chair. He doesn't act like such a big shot when removed from the false throne. In place of his false macho performance, he's become a timid mouse, stuttering uncontrollably, squirming to escape my firm grip.

He begs for forgiveness.

Says he was kidding.

It was all a *joke.*

"Most have gone on their feet, some on their knees, but they all go." I echo the unforgivable words back to him. "Does that sound *funny* to you? Did it make you smile? Laugh? Because, to me, it sounded like a worthless piece of shit who strips the soul away from everyone unfortunate enough to cross paths with him. Sadly, nothing I do to you today will ever make up for that. There's no punishment that could ever make up for what you are."

"But, I'm going to try really, *really* hard."

I drive the point home by tossing him to the ground and stomping his nuts. It crosses my mind to rip them off as a constant reminder of what he's done—what he would've done to me—except I can't. It's impossible to keep myself from snatching his puny neck in an unbreakable grip. I tower over him to make him feel as helpless as I did.

My thumbs squeeze in just far enough to feel the soft tube in his throat collapse. The stench of his fear is inebriating. His tears please my violence-loving monster in ways that are as immoral as they are satisfying. But it's still not enough. The monster craves *violence. Real* violence.

This brings me to the tense moment right before you give into your deepest desires. The one where you pretend to weigh the options, even though you already know exactly what you're going to do. The only reason I haven't yet is because I want to draw out his addictive anticipation for as long as possible.

I breathe in the panic and let it soak into every fiber of my being. It gives me a rush of power that unintentionally squeezes my fingers together a little bit tighter. A drop of salty sweat lands on my bloody wrist. It washes a tiny spot of the crimson hand a little bit cleaner than the rest. I raise him high into the air so that I can stare into his coal-black eyes. He needs to see the fire raging inside me.

I want him to see *me*.

At the climax of his horror, and my satisfaction, my monster plunges fangs deep into him. They clinch tight, feel the rush of vile blood running out, and rip his damn throat out.

Quinn Chapter 10: Where the Light is

A bubbling pool of gore swirls down the drain beneath me. It takes with it the last breath of a soulless person. The world is a better place without him, so this kill won't stain like all the rest. Some sins are forgivable. His were not.

Even after the evil creature (I can't call it a man) is gone, my monster craves more. It needs further violence. All I want is to unhook Hayden and make our escape. All it wants is to taste all the salty treats running for their lives.

I tame the inner beast by concentrating on the pale Hayden hooked up to countless tubes and wires. It sends the monster back to whatever hidden place he calls home. While it's gone, it doesn't go far. I can still sense him occupying my thoughts. He tempts me to do the destructive things *it* wants to do.

The allure of carnage doesn't make it any easier to sort through the vast ocean of wires and unmarked buttons. My distracted mind is far more likely to kill Hayden than set him free. Fortunately, I know the morons that put him in there. Unfortunately, I'll need my thumbs to get them back here.

Pinching the floppy thumb between my pointer and middle fingers feels exactly how I imagined it would. I'm already on my knees trying to keep from collapsing all the way to the floor. After several failed attempts to "pop" it back into place, the pain becomes *blinding*. I can't even see where I'm recklessly pushing it anymore. I'm just shoving down where I think the thumb should go.

It takes several more nauseating attempts before getting the stubborn finger to *finally* slide back into place. And when it does, the relief is miraculous! Don't get me wrong, it still burns like fire, but it's much, much, *much* better than it was. Repeating the agonizing process with the other hand is easier. Maybe it's not such a surprise this time around, or maybe I just luck into it faster. Most likely, it's because I get to use an entire hand instead of chopstick fingers.

Whatever. It's finished.

Completely lost during the sloppy process is the mob that's moved in to surround me. It's filled with the sickliest people this side of a graveyard. They're walking skeletons with no possible chance of stopping me from simply walking out of here... except I forgot about those damn ankle cuffs.

There's a split-second tingling in both ankles right before my legs are ripped up to the hovering bot. My chin smashes the floor and triggers the monster in a scary new way. The vicious hit causes my body to disconnect, and vision to blink on and off like a slide show. I only get to watch the choppy movie of what my body is doing without me.

My legs are kicking wildly to swing me back and forth on the cable.

Darkness.

Sharp claws sink into the top of the flying disk. They split the thin robot straight down the glowing middle. A shower of electrical sparks flies from inside the break. The tiny bot falls from the sky and suddenly the world isn't upside down anymore.

Darkness.

The crowd cracks me with several large electric prods. They circle around and manage to pin me down. Their bloodthirsty looks make it clear what they intend to do. I have to thrash violently to fend off the repeated electric lashings.

Darkness.

Everything's changed. Now, a man begs for his life in front of me. Blood is pouring from the rod shoved through his right shoulder. I'm back on my feet as bodies litter the floor.

Darkness.

Rat's face is inches from mine. My fingers are straining to keep his rampaging teeth away. His eyes shine pale blue from the V flowing through them. The red tubes are busy pumping the poison that transforms him into this juggernaut.

Messy webs of blood splatter his cheeks.

My blood.

We rip and tear at each other like savage animals in an extended, merciless fight to the death. Desperate howls of pleasure and saliva blast me with every snap of his jaw. I'll claw at every piece of flesh within reach, and he beats the living hell out of me in return. Shreds of his black leather suit, and my clothes, cover us both. Thick blood coats it all.

Darkness.

I'm yanked up by the leg and everything turns upside down again. Rat is busy destroying my ribs while I bite at air, just hoping to bring something back with me. Nothing stops the rampaging man. Not even the large chunks of flesh I've removed from him. He doesn't even seem to notice those.

My fingers start clawing their way up his back. They dig in to find something solid, like a bony rib, and climb all the way up until I'm folded into a perfect U behind him. I wrap one arm around his throat and reach the other over to my ankle. The cord and half a droid are still dangling from the cuff, so I wrap it swiftly around his neck.

Once.

Twice.

Three times it goes around.

My grip moves to the end of the rope when it's secure. Stretching my leg pulls one end and reaching back tightens the other, while his scrawny throat is stuck in-between. His mouth makes the sucking sound of water circling the drain. I release the arm holding me up and use my full weight to squeeze the rope even tighter. He thrashes wildly before finally releasing me. I stretch my entire body out like a bow pulling the string tight.

His windpipe collapses. He does, too.

Darkness.

No one's left. Only the brooding monster, howling at its kill, "COME ON! COME GET ME!!!" It's still taunting Rat, even when he's face-down with his neck twisted at a sharp angle. The rest of the crowd is a hazy mess of lab coats running for distant safety.

Studying the disfigured body makes it alarming to see what damage I'm capable of when unleashed. Rat has been made into a jigsaw puzzle with a bunch of missing pieces. Long canyons of peeled flesh and sliced muscles are scattered randomly throughout. As shocking as it is to see, what I'm feeling right now is complete satisfaction.

The cable slips from my hand and clangs on the floor. I'm regaining some feeling in my fingertips again. They wiggle as if the sensation is brand new to them. The monster must be satisfied as well, since it's already crawled back to wherever it calls home. After only a few more seconds, I've regained complete control of my body.

With all the distractions either dead or hiding, I'm free to return to getting Hayden out of the tube. Buried down in the mess is the forearm computer that Rat liked to use so much. It still works, although without a "release Hayden" label, it's utterly useless to me. I cautiously try pressing a few buttons. They create some random clicking, but nothing helpful. Both my ankle cuffs and Hayden are still firmly in place.

What I need is for someone to do it for me...

By the smell of it, Crow's still around.

The air from his particular brand of funk still lingers heavy in the air. Actually, smelling like that, I doubt there's anywhere on Earth he could hide from me. It's so thick that I can almost physically see the trail leading me behind an overturned table. The little coward has, appropriately, buried himself in a huge mound of trash.

He wisely decides not to put up a fight when yanked from the rubble. He just holds up both hands, repeating, *"Okay okay."* I don't say another word, just point to my ankles and squeeze the base of his skull. Within seconds, there's rapid typing and my cuffs spring open.

"How do I get that one to wake up?" I say, pointing at Hayden.

"I don't know. Slap him?" the sarcastic-ass answers. While I prepare to smack that smug look off his face, he shouts, "Wait! Seriously, hold on! You mean the guy you came in with, right? Yeah, he's just passed out. He hasn't even been given the injections yet!"

"So, he'll wake up on his own?" I ask suspiciously.

"Yes! He's all yours!" He franticly bangs the pad and Hayden tumbles out of the steel cage. "Now I can go, right?" His voice discovers a new humility. "I did what you want."

The amount of bodies left behind won't show it, but I'm no killer. Maybe I am... I don't know. My state of mind changes every few seconds. All I know is that right now, I'm not.

"Go, before I change my mind." Of course the rodent wastes no time in finding another hole to crawl back into. I hope he was telling the truth about Hayden. His shackles may be gone, but they're definitely not forgotten. Blood still trickles from the dozens of holes circling his wrists.

Even his older injuries have not healed the way they should. I bounced back almost immediately after the feeding. Why hasn't he?

The adrenaline hangover makes removing his feeding tube as awful as possible. My fingers are still shaking and slick with blood, which isn't helping. Several deep gags make their way up (all of which are mine) before finally wiggling the lengthy tube free. My only thought while looking at his pale, thin face is that he looks dead. I'm not sure what to do about it, either. I can't risk giving him any of the blood in here. The only thing left to do is get out of this place as quickly as possible.

On our way out, I see all the hidden workers tucked into the shadows. I choose to leave the roaches alone since my only concern now is, *"where did they leave that desert runner?"*

Quinn Chapter 11: Moving On

Our time on the road has been endless and nerve-wracking. The lifeless Hayden has bounced off every hard surface in the compact cabin. I try not to obsess, yet I still find myself checking on him after every big bump. Partly from concern, partly from the mind-numbing boredom of being stuck on an endlessly straight highway.

My only distractions have been the countless dashboard switches. This truck looks like scrap metal on the outside, but it's actually loaded with every kind of gizmo you could ask for. Most of them are still a complete mystery to me, although I've managed to start the truck and find navigation, so I'm feeling pretty good about it. Up to this point, my plan has been push a button and wait for something to happen— that's been *mostly* successful. There were a few loud noises like I had ejected something from the back, but we've kept moving, so I guess it was okay.

It doesn't help that there isn't a simple radio in this thing. I've even resorted to making music out of the rocks skipping off the underside of the car. I'll speed up or slow down to create rhythms out of the otherwise terrible noises. Anything to keep busy, I guess.

Five minutes later, I find myself fiddling with the navigation again. This straight road is not a good release for all my pent-up nervous energy. Luckily, the abundant amount of information on this screen could keep me entertained for hours. According to this, the Colony we're coming up on is strangely named "Blue". Not "Fort Blue" or "Blue Waters", just "Blue".

It appears to be more of a trading post than a place where people would actually live. There are a few stores, a general council, and governor that are all on Rat and Crow's payroll. In fact, there are so many corrupt officials, it reads like a Christmas list. Everything you could ever want to know: access points into the small city, population breakdowns, distribution points, and more. Much more.

It holds my interest until the next place on the map shows up. Only a few short miles away is the climax of everything we've worked toward—Titan Valley.

For the vast amount of information they have on Blue, there's absolutely nothing available about Titan. No extra info, no notes; nothing at all. It's a blank area with a name. I don't believe they were very welcomed there. Then again, I doubt we will be, either.

Rounding the crest of a particularly tall mountain reveals the intimidating size of the problem to come.

The city in the distance is a modern steel jungle, sprawling confidently across the desert floor. A concrete labyrinth that's been constructed of low slung buildings resting at the feet of a soaring goliath. The astonishing tower cuts a harsh shadow across the entire valley. The rising three-sided building literally towers above everything else.

There's been a constant nagging doubt echoing in my mind, *are we going to the right place?*

Not anymore.

The gnarled piece of rubber in my hands is a direct result of that revelation. The former steering wheel is also the reason why our truck has rolled to an abrupt stop in the middle of the road. This must be my brain telling me not to go any further. Doubt is flooding in and I'm sinking fast. I can't even operate a simple door handle anymore. When the stubborn thing finally opens, I clumsily pour myself out of the truck.

I'm chewing air rather than breathing it.

My jelly legs can barely remain upright.

Our situation has never been clearer. I've known all along what we were doing, where we were going, but it's never been so *real...* until right now. That concrete mammoth is the period at the end of a sentence. I don't know if there will be another, but this one has come to an end.

Quinn Chapter 12: City of Black and White

There are no walls surrounding the city; nothing is keeping us out except the nervous sensation creeping down my spine.

The city lays low in the valley and every road converges at the soaring tower. It seems that out here this place really is the center of the world.

Hayden is still slack-jawed and drooling back over in the car. For once, I would welcome a stupid joke to break up the nausea swirling in the pit of my stomach. I consider hopping back in the car and turning us around. We could stay lost in the desert and Hayden would never know! Except that won't change what's going to happen here eventually.

We'll be back.

Titan will still be here.

My eyes are so consumed by the towering colossus that they never even notice the car approaching behind us. It obviously didn't see us either, but the thunderclap is difficult to miss. The unexpected impact is a sucker punch that shoves me down into the gritty sand. I get to watch from the ground as the small car launches over our truck in one direction, while its front wheels go one direction and I another. Swirling tornadoes of flames follow both.

In the midst of it all is a narrow blur shooting directly out of our truck's windshield. The missile—Hayden—soars for fifty feet, skips down the pavement another hundred, bounces a few more times, and skids along the solid concrete for a painfully long time.

Hayden eventually stops, but the other car continues flipping end over end into the desert. It drips pools of fire every time the front end smashes into the ground. My body refuses to move while watching it all unfold. My monster simply won't let me go toward any of it. It refuses to release my body until it suddenly sees the whites of Hayden's eyes.

He's awake!!!

After that, it only takes seconds to reach the delirious man mumbling, "Wha.. wha... blar... enough... yeah." The side of his face is missing long strips of skin and pooling blood on the right side.

"Hayden! Can you hear me? Hayden! Talk to me!"

"Ye... almost. *(cough)* ...I hear you... *(cough)* ... please stop shaking me."

I hadn't realized I had been shaking him like a Christmas present the entire time. I restrain myself long enough to shout, "It's so good to hear your annoying voice again!"

"Th... Thanks?" He says with a quizzical, bloody brow raised halfway up his forehead.

There's enough skin left on the road to see the exact spot where he landed. I try pressing a shirt against some of the deeper cuts, but it only makes him shout louder.

A small explosion serves as a reminder of the other car that bounced off. I have to pause all my exuberant fawning to follow the trail of busted metal and flames out into the desert. It's a long, gut-wrenching walk, and at the end of it, I'm absolutely devastated to find how mangled the other car is. Even the color is hard to make out now.

Fire is already chewing on it, and the overwhelming smell of gasoline is a clear sign it's only going to get worse from here. The front and back have completely broken off, with only the passenger section remaining, and it's been twisted in every direction at once. It's deflating, but not surprising to see. Nothing should be able to walk away from this.

That's why the sound coming from inside it is so shocking.

I scream through the flames and only get silence in return. Seeing inside is impossible due to the black soot covering the scorched windows. I quickly scoop up one of the detached wheels to use as a shovel for dumping sand over the wicked flames. This extinguishes a narrow path leading to the red-hot door. The wheel comes in handy again as a blunt hammer to bash in the blackened window. I try to rein in my strength to keep from harming whoever's on the other side.

Turns out there's only one person inside and he's face down across the steering wheel. The small flames, already dancing at my feet, means I'll have a *very* limited amount of time to get him out of there. Forcefully tugging at the handle does little more than burn my fingers and pull the entire car toward me. The vicious wreck has turned it into a single ball of tangled steel that groans under the strain. I try pulling him through the window, but he seems to be stuck on something down low. A leg or foot must have gotten pinned up underneath the compacted dashboard.

I start peeling the car away layer by layer since there appears to be no other option. The outer shell is the easiest; its only challenge is how sharp the ripped edges are. However, the next layer gets a little trickier.

It appears the internals have become a solid web of tangled metal. One that has to be sorted carefully, but quickly, without doing any more damage to the trapped man. Every steel scrap is either thrown aside or cautiously bent back far enough for me to wriggle my way in. This all goes perfectly until I remove the small section covering the man's arm. My heart sinks at the sight of two colorful dueling samurai. It's the beautiful man from the alley in New Vegas—the one I'd punched in the face when he asked if I was okay.

How...?

How could this be!?!?

I've already slammed him into a wall and smeared garbage all over him, now I've hit him with my car! The universe must really *HATE* this guy! That's the only explanation for almost being accidently killed *twice* by the *same* person!

Looking him over reveals no obvious wounds, even though there's blood everywhere. He's clearly bleeding, but now's not the time to figure out from where. The flames have already found the new holes and they're anxious to explore the cloth interior. While rushing to undo his seatbelt, I stumble on the source of the constant noise. It's a little black plastic box screaming in a static voice, *"Repeat last transmission. Subject is on target? Repeat, subject is still..."*

So, it was no accident that I kept running into him. He's been stalking me the entire time! And if he's found me...

As I head back toward the truck, I shout in a commanding voice that doesn't sound like mine, "Hayden, we need to get out of here, *RIGHT NOW!*"

Hayden, still sitting in a daze, asks, "Can I have a minute, Quinn? I went through a windshield and now it feels like half my face is missing..."

"Normally, yes, but see that car right there?" I charge up, pointing at the mangled steel carcass. "The guy in it has been following us."

"That's good!" he says, still not able to shake off enough cobwebs to spot the problem. "*No, not good!* They know we're here! I mean *here,* here. See that city over there? That's Titan! RIGHT THERE!"

He wants to put the words together with their meaning, but they just won't click. Instead of wasting more time with useless talk, I simply drag him up and off the ground. I carry him back to the truck when his feet can't keep up with my growing anxiety. But his wobbly legs crumble completely when I have to set him down to open the car door. He collapses in the slowest, most awkward fall of all time. Although, when he looks up at me, his helpless expression gives me the closest thing I've felt to sympathy since becoming... this.

The warm, fuzzy mood calms my destructive hands long enough to delicately place him in the seat. Considering the shape of the other car, our truck is in pretty good condition. From what I can tell, the thick metal plates on our truck must have basically ramped the smaller car right over us. Our worst damage is a warped steering wheel, and that came well before the accident.

The real moment of truth comes with a few anxious turns of the key. At first, it's only *"weerrrr werrrr werrrrr"* and sweaty palms at the thought of being stranded here. Maybe there's more damage than I originally thought? A few more tries get it to sputter for a second before it suddenly dies again.

Hayden's come around enough to give me a concerned look. It seems he's finally starting to put our situation together with the possible consequences.

I grip what's left of the wheel a little tighter than before, swallow the lump scuttling up my throat, pump the gas, and crank the key. On the fourth try, the ancient truck finally rumbles to life!

"There was never a doubt!" Hayden cracks a sideways smile. I press the gas pedal and the throaty little motor barks back with a raspy growl. "You should hold on." I tell the now googly-eyed passenger.

"Or what? There's no more windshield to go through." At least his sense of humor is back. That's what I wanted, right?

"You love that necklace, don't you?" he abruptly chirps.

"Yeah, I guess. Why?"

"Because it's always in your hand."

Guess I hadn't noticed my thumb had found its way back over to the silver locket, spinning tiny circles over the smooth surface to help ease my fraying nerves. I explain, "It just takes my mind off things." There's no real reason for why it comforts me. At least, nothing I can put into words.

Without feeling the need for further justification, I stomp the gas until it reaches the floorboard. The tires howl as they rip off toward the imposing city. All my deep anxiety converts to rage as the truck gains speed. It finally reaches the point where I feel that the massive city needs to get out of *my* way.

Everything not bolted down is blowing around in the cabin. The surging wind, coming in from the hole that used to be a windshield, makes my eyes tremor. I go to slam into another gear, but find none remaining. My heavy foot is demanding much more from the metal box than she's got left.

The damage from the wreck has our truck shaking so badly that the crooked steering wheel has to be constantly fought to keep us on course. It's just like the rest of us at this point, pushing on to the finish. Broken, but not dead yet.

Chapter 33: Season in Hell

I'm not sure if everything is spinning because of my recent trip through the window, or from the wind aggressively punching me in the face. Either way, it's gotta stop before it makes me black out again. Asking Quinn to slow down accomplishes nothing. Steadying myself against the door only brings the increasingly bad situation into clearer focus. Her appearance is scary, bordering on psychotic. She looks like an unflinching hawk fixated on its prey. Now, I've only been awake a few minutes, so I'm not totally caught up, but I'm pretty sure smashing into the city is *not* our best option.

I don't want to use the word *CRAZY*, but.......

Physically prying her fingers from the wheel doesn't work, either. They're clamped so tightly, not even a pinkie moves. Her foot is buried so far on the accelerator, our truck is sputtering to keep us under ludicrous speed. Nothing, I mean absolutely nothing, changes our course or slows us down in any way.

"QUINN! What's the plan here??? Could we maybe pull over and talk this out?"

Our course remains the same.

It seems that my options, along with the road, are running out fast. As a last resort, I decide to punch her in the jaw. That should get her attention, right?

Well, it does.

She reacts so quickly, all I see are skinny knuckles and stars before leaving the truck again. There are two hits:

1) Her fist buried in my face.
2) My head bouncing off the doorframe.

The impact jars the door open and speed does the rest. In fact, the vacuum sucks me out before I really know what's happening. The wall of wind really accelerates my plunge to the ground once I'm outside. It picks me up and slams me down into an ass-first slide that ends in a full body tumble across the hard desert floor.

Sky.   Sky.   Sky.   Sky.

    Sand.   Sand.   Sand.   Sand.

I do this over and over, round and round, until eventually coming to rest in a low sand dune. It takes several minutes of facedown drooling before the blur fades enough to focus again. Even then, my body refuses to do anything more than watch a determined ant drag a little ball of dung past my nose. It walks like if I'm not even here. I'm either in shock, or I just need a few minutes to reset my brain.

Quite simply, I shut down.

The deadness is actually welcome relief for someone who hears, sees, and feels everything in intimate detail. The fury and madness are gone. All that remains is the mindless ant marching across the glistening sand in utter silence. Every now and then, an actual thought tries to come ashore in my mind, but it's quickly pushed back out to sea. Not even the foot slamming down in front of me pulls me from my state of total ignorance.

Suddenly, the slow crawling ant and gritty sand disappear. They're replaced by a frantic mouth spitting words.

My eyes see them.

My ears hear them.

My brain doesn't digest them.

My skin tells me about the guilty hug pressing against it. About the immense pressure changing the angle of my breathing. About the soft blonde hair tickling my cheeks. They're just more things that mean absolutely nothing to me. I'm content swimming in the happy oblivion, enjoying every second of the conscious unconsciousness.

The peaceful bubble holds out the real world for as long as it can. It takes the information, chews it up, and spits it back in the face of reality.

All except one.

The crack in this bliss comes from words lingering too long to be ignored. *She knocked me out of the truck.* The angry thought echoes all around the peaceful silence. It repeats over and over and over again. At first, it's nothing more than leaves in the wind or a song in the background—empty noise. Eventually though, the words repeat so many times, they start making sense.

knocked out the

She me of truck.

"SHE KNOCKED ME OUT OF THE TRUCK!"

The angry realization shatters my happy state of mind. Ugly truth pours in through the cracks to wash away the rest of the blurry mess. My eyes snap back into crystal sharp focus as the blanket of numbness is yanked off like a warm comforter on a cold morning. That rebounding pain quickly grows into a *very* sharp resentment.

"What the shit, *Quinn?!?!*" I scream while clumsily lifting my broken ass from the dirt. *"You punched me out of the TRUCK!"* While I'm busy yelling, Quinn grinds to a halt as if she's run out of batteries. No more tears, no more sadness; only a tiny smile that creeps across her folding cheeks. She has the look of someone trying to keep the worst-kept secret in the world.

That's when the usually reserved Quinn erupts into crazed laughter and waves her fingers high in the air. All she says is, "You were all like, *Weeeeeeee....*" before falling over laughing.

All my useless anger disappears without hesitation.

I get it.

That's what I felt at the cliff. She was scared, and now she's not. A large part of me still wants to smack her in the teeth, but I get it. I split the difference by just leaving her on the ground to finish the obnoxious giggle. Even if I wanted to laugh, frown, or anything, I can't. It hurts too much for me to move my jaw.

She's still chuckling loudly as I slink back to the truck. It's the kind of infectious belly laugh that would normally make me want to join in; instead, I settle for sweeping the broken glass out of my seat. She actually takes so long that I have time to clean off both chairs and find an adult magazine in the glove compartment.

While thumbing through the "articles", she stumbles back up, still giggling slightly. There's a bursting-at-the-seams look to her as if she's sucking in her cheeks to hold back more caged laughter. After a few minutes of extended awkwardness, I finally give her the permission she's been looking for.

She basically explodes, "*Let me tell you!* Your cheeks were all scrunched up when you fell out! They actually flopped over my knuckles and then you were all like, *Weeeeeee...*" She revisits the waving hands thing while motioning toward the open door.

"No need to rub it in. I get it. Hahaha." I promptly slam the door shut behind me with sarcasm firmly in place.

"No, but seriously!" She pounds the flimsy steering wheel with those damn tiny fists between each word.

"Really, I get it!!!" My agitation is clearly showing through now. I have to remind myself where all the laughter comes from. I mean, of all people, I should understand. It would honestly be a lot easier if her little pounding fists of fury weren't such a constant beacon of irritation. Maybe it's stupid, but it's embarrassing to have been knocked out by a hand that *small!*

I decide to do the *completely* mature thing, and turn away from the giggling girl. Our tables have turned, that's all. The logical side of me knows this. I need to suck it up and move on, but for whatever egotistical reason, I can't. Even when the loud engine revs back up to drown out the incessant snickering, I know it's still there.

It gnaws on my mind as the tires chew through the desert toward Titan. The only distraction is when the massive central tower swallows the entire sun. Its cold shadow helps my mind finally move on from the embarrassment. The insecurities get shoved even further back when we reach the entrance to the intimidating city. We're greeted by a massive sheet of metal bolted to the first building. On it is a wild-looking bird with sharp, circular wings. I don't know what it is, but it doesn't fill me with optimism for what's to come.

It's been a good life, right?

At least it's been a long one.

Chapter 34: Welcome to the Jungle *(You're gonna die)*

Nothing about this place sits well with my growing paranoia. Strangely, it's the total lack of guns, guards, and gates that freaks me out the most. I don't know if it's that I've grown so accustomed to them, or perhaps my expectations were just so completely off from actual boring reality. There should have been ravenous hordes roving trash-littered streets, angry mutant beavers, and bad guys punching fluffy kittens on every corner. Instead, there's regular old streets filled with people rushing off to who knows where, while barely even noticing each other. Just like every other big city!

The only oddity here is that the wild bird symbol from outside is EVERY. DAMN. WHERE. It's on street signs, graffiti tags, tattoos, and a whole lot of very colorful clothing. Some only have the giant bird, most add the word "Harbinger". The name sounds familiar, even if I'm not exactly sure why. Whatever it is, they sure take a lot of pride in the menacing avian symbol. Another oddity is that no one has even bothered to look twice at our beat-up truck cruising along. My crushing sense of dread has consequently lowered to more of a moderate suspicion of disaster. Similarly, Quinn's white-knuckle death grip on the wheel has become more of a casual ten and two.

We haven't said a single word since entering the city. A permanent silence has settled over our uncomfortable truck cabin. Occasionally, we'll exchange an uneasy glance, but that's about it. There's certainly not the same special connection as before. That was so strong, it made me believe a complete stranger over my best friend. Hell, it's probably the reason we've been able to make it this far.

We've hit a few rough patches, to be sure. Turning someone into a bloodsucking killer is a bump on any road to friendship. The crazy rant in the desert probably didn't help much either... My mind continues searching for meaning behind our extended silence. The only other thoughts that can board the philosophical train are nagging questions of familiar self-doubt. Why did we come here? The memory we're following could be a week, year, *or* decade old? This is where he *was*, but where he is *now* could be totally different!

My first instinct is to regroup before making any decisions. We need to find a place to hide, heal, and figure out what to do next. This is basically my plan from Vegas with an extra emphasis on healing, due to my frequent—*unexpected*—trips out of the speeding truck. I could also use some answers from Quinn. Like, "Who was the guy from the wreck?" and, "Why were you so freaked out about him?"

Maybe my mistake was getting too comfortable with the idea of having any kind of control at all. How could I have ever thought life will be anything more than an endless pinball game? Whatever the reason, all that's gone in a flash.

The shape appears too quickly to be anything more than a blur in front of our truck, but that doesn't stop it from hitting us with the strength of a runaway train. The truck's bumper is instantly buried deep in crushed pavement, while the rear is launched skyward. The already small cabin folds in even tighter as everything lunges forward. I tumble onto the plastic dashboard so it can fill the space my lungs used to occupy. The painful groans are eerily easy to hear since they occur during the silence between impact and our inevitable return to the ground. But the calm doesn't last long.

We get immersed in a hurricane of swirling sparks and grinding concrete the instant we land. The severe impact makes it almost impossible to even remain in the car during our wild inverted slide. I somehow manage to secure myself in a corner while Quinn locks onto the steering wheel. The entire cabin lights up from the fireworks pouring in through the holes that used to be windows. They force my eyes shut, and without the visual stimulus, I'm left listening to the unbearable racket of the roof grinding away on the road. The larger sparks bite my naked arms, although there's not a damn thing I can do about that right now.

The relentless slide lasts so long that my teeth are still vibrating after its eventual stop. I try opening my eyes, but the tense muscles won't release more than one at a time. My entire body has the disoriented sensation of being flipped completely upside down.

Because it is.

In fact, the entire truck is lying dead on its crumpled roof.

I go through the checklist to make sure everything still works. Breathing must be fine since my nose is filled with the sweet acidic smell of radiator fluid. My ears, which I thought were ringing, are instead hearing the loud buzz of free spinning wheels. Both eyes are finally open to see just how much smaller our cabin has suddenly become. Now there's only inches separating us from the crushed roof and shattered concrete. The front of our truck appears to have been buried beneath a large mound of crushed grey concrete. Only the side windows are left free of debris, and they're triangular slits at this point.

So, it's safe to say they know we're here...

"You *okay,* Tiger?" I attempt. It comes out as a pre-teen squeak due to the knees that have been firmly pressed up into my throat. It doesn't matter since she doesn't waste time answering me, anyway. She's already rolling into a compact ball to flip herself back upright. After a quick second of almost accidental eye contact, hunks of seat and metal begin flying throughout the truck. There's no method to where the ripped pieces go. She simply slings them aside recklessly.

Eventually, enough pieces go missing to make our dark cabin appear a lot brighter. It's safe to say that whatever hit us won't have to wait much longer to meet her. I obviously need to work on getting out of my flipped position much faster, which is much easier said than done. My attempt at her effortless roll is more drunken bear than graceful jungle cat. By the time I finally make it over and manage to crawl out of the narrow hole, she's already found our wall. And it's not what I ever expectcd.

At all.

Standing directly in front of us is a very angelic-looking guy. I mean, he's absolutely captivating! He has these intense, burning eyes that draw you in with some invisible magnetism. He radiates so intensely that you almost ignore the one feature that should be instantly noticeable—his lips are completely sewn together with thick brown thread! The skin is fully grown over, so it must have happened long ago. Oh, and that damn bird is tattooed down his side.

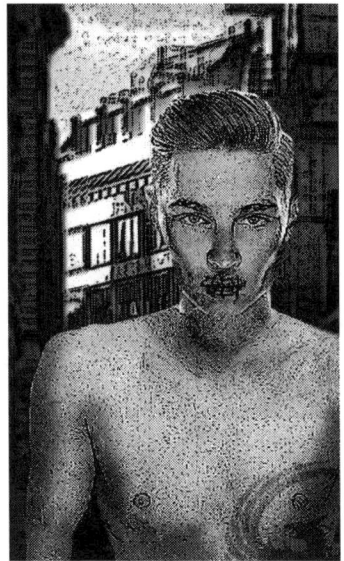

"Well, who the happy hell are you?" I say, obviously forgetting the problem with asking him any type of question. He answers by stretching one long finger across his sealed mouth in a "shooshing" motion. I impatiently answer with a different finger of my own. He doesn't respond in any noticeable way except for taking one intimidatingly large step toward me. I can already tell that this is not going to end without some (probably a lot of) *extreme* violence.

Quinn decides to shoot first. She instantly rips off one of the mangled truck doors and flings it in his direction. The speedy man calmly swats it away as if it were a simple buzzing fly. It unfortunately has about as much of an effect as my raised finger does. None.

"Whoa! Silent *and* deadly!" The obnoxious pun is a desperate attempt to disguise my own steadily declining confidence. Somehow though, the little wildcat is completely unfazed by the unexpected block. She already has another door, and a warped tire, on the way. But they meet the same sad ending as the first. His brutally swift hands brush them aside without even altering his casual pace. Each step has stayed the same length, stride, and speed. Not even his eyebrows flinch while destroying everything Quinn throws at him.

"Is there someone else we can talk to? Or maybe we should just come back later?" My jokes continue to go unappreciated by the silent man. You know, trash talking is not nearly as fun when there's no one to talk back.

Although my frustration seems minor compared to Quinn's. She hurls a few more things: a nearby stop sign, more tires, a passing car, and eventually, herself—in a visible fit of rage.

The way she lands is almost too disturbing to watch. She cocks her thumbs out into perfect little wedges that slide down into the corner of his eye sockets. The rest of her body is folded into a compact cannonball that slams into his bare chest. The impact must crack several bones, but you would never know by looking at him. He doesn't even try to stop her! She's squeezing so hard, the veins of her hands bulge and dance, yet all he does is stand there!

You get the feeling he's letting her finish before taking his turn. She obliges by continuing on until her arms drop from exhaustion. After that, she's tossed aside with the same kind of casual pitch a kid would give an old toy. There's nothing about it that's meant to harm her in any way; it's simply get rid of her. Now, all that's left between us is... well, nothing.

There are suddenly no more jokes waiting on the tip of my tongue. My mouth is drawn back into the tight pucker of sucking on life's newest lemon. He clearly sees this anxiety as well, because he cocks his head to taunt me into coming closer. I take the bait, and before I know it, I'm lying on the ground next to Quinn. Well, *technically* she was back on her feet when I came bowling through and knocked her over, so *now* we're both on the ground. Whatever.

It's becoming clear that there will be no winner to this fight.

Only survivors.

To increase the odds of that being us, I gladly surrender all control to the monster who's been impatiently waiting. The minute he takes over, there's a brand-new dynamic to our fight! Instead of me, it's my monster getting his ass kicked. Not even he can phase faze the angelic man playfully dodging every punch, kick, bite, and scratch with ease.

At one point, when Quinn and I are thrown against the same wall, I recommend running as fast and far as possible. She *again* doesn't bother talking and stubbornly charges back in for more. This time, my feet don't move quite as quickly. This guy terrifies even my monster in a way I've never seen.

I have to watch from the sidelines as Quinn returns alone, although she seems to stay in the fight much better this time around! It's almost good enough to unfreeze my cautious monster, until it notices that the silent man isn't even trying. He's merely playing as Quinn goes full-on psycho. Even worse, his facial expression and heart rate never change.

My feet finally release. Not because I'm happy to rejoin the fight, but because if they don't—she's not coming back. I have to completely unleash my monster. No restraints, no rules, and certainly no morality; just do whatever it takes to bring down the unstoppable man.

This time our monsters stay in perfect harmony. Quinn and I move in a flawless dance of untethered violence that finds every fault, flaw, and opening in his defense. Amazingly, it works! For *exactly* eight hits... then the silent man stops playing and comes up swinging.

HARD.

After those lucky few shots, his casual speed disappears and all I can see is the ghost of where he used to be. Then he casually steps back to let us marinate in staggered shock. The corners of his mouth are drawn back into the first sign of emotion I've seen in him. It doesn't pull back far enough to wrinkle the skin, but clearly shows his great satisfaction. No matter how coordinated, fast, or fearless we fight, he's just a totally different beast than us.

Quinn and I look toward each other at the same time. Judging by our shared expressions, neither of us has any clue what to do. I happen to notice the three perfect cuts running across her forearms. They're evenly spaced, straight as an arrow, and equally spread between wrist and elbow. Then I notice a burning sensation of my own. Sure enough, I have the exact same incisions, in the exact same places. They're not deep enough to do any real damage, only meant as a warning to play by the rules.

His rules.

He's the cat; we're the ball of yarn.

After our lesson, he takes two calm steps backward, and cocks his head to the side again. This time, it's directed at Quinn. I remember how this show ended last time. Before it can play out again, I snatch up the little wolverine and run.

Very fast.

Very far.

It's not glorious to turn tail and haul ass, but it's better than being cut into little sushi strips. Besides, it's not as easy as it sounds. She's leaking slippery blood, pissed off, and really doesn't want to go anywhere with me. Finding any kind of grip is absolutely impossible. At least her attacks aren't directed at me this time!

So, the question of the day has to be, "How do you stop an unstoppable man?" Can he even be stopped? Then, after a few blocks, a plan forms that's so damn crazy, so completely ridiculous, it *HAS* to work! Mainly because it's nothing that he (or anyone) could ever see coming!

It all starts with getting some distance between us. And, for some mysterious reason, that doesn't seem to be a problem! He's following us, just not very closely. Next step is to find a tall building with a flat roof. Since there's a few to choose from, I settle for the closest and dig right in. Quinn decides to make life easier by not struggling during the entire thing. Pointing up is all it takes to get her to start climbing along with me.

We chew up the formerly smooth wall, making sure to keep an eye on him the entire way. Every thirty seconds I'll check his progress. It does seem he's picked up the lazy pace a little bit. He's steadily made up ground each time I've looked back, but fortunately, it won't matter. We've already reached the top with plenty of time left to bring my plan to life.

To keep the violence-loving Quinn out of the way, I sling her through the exit door and down a flight of stairs. Sure, it's a bit extreme, but I'll really need twenty uninterrupted seconds to make this plan work.

The final step is to remove the weathered, two-ton behemoth of an air conditioner sitting across the roof. There's no chance of lifting the whole thing, so I simply remove one of the crate-sized motors that should make for a perfect anchor. This sloppy surgery results in a quick shower of electric sparks, then lots of clattering gears grinding to a halt. My best guess would be this big hunk of steel weighs in at about three hundred pounds. That's not as heavy as I'd like, but given the lack of options, it should do. And with all the miniature explosions working their way up the building, it appears the silent man is almost here.

Ready or not.

Tremors from his forceful climb shake the soles of my shoes. I peek over to line myself up with the little puffs of brick dust wafting out. I can feel every muscle swelling with mounting anticipation. My muscles are so anxious, they accidently crumple the hunk of steel in my hands. Not that a few extra wrinkles will matter much.

The sound reaches the lip of the building.

Three.

Pebbles begin falling over the edge from the vibration.

Two.

I see the first finger rise above the concrete ledge.

One.

Every muscle surges to scnd the heavy motor on its way. I want to scream, "Catch!" as the metal behemoth collides with the man, but only a strained grunt comes out. The loss of the funny quip doesn't stop the throw from being a perfect shot that lands in the dead center of his chest.

Like catching a falling star, all he can do is wrap his arms around and go along for the ride. For a brief moment, I get to enjoy genuine terror in the emotionless man. His fearful eyes leave me with the kind of satisfaction that's bittersweet to taste. By the time I reach the edge, his journey is already halfway over. He's nothing more than a speck dropping between two extremely tall buildings.

Of all the plans I've pulled out of my ass lately, this one goes down as the one that shouldn't have worked, yet did anyway. He was a vicious, insanely skilled man, and now he's nothing more than the bloody center of a concrete crater.

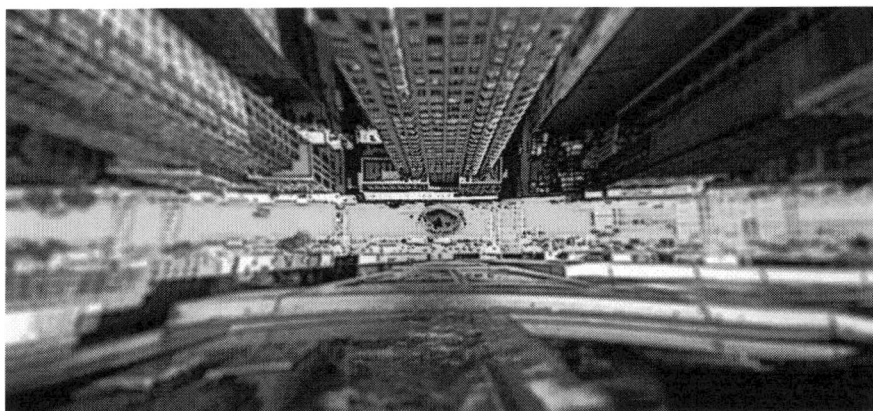

Good riddance.

Chapter 35: HARD LOVE

Quinn throws the door open while I'm busy looking at the mess on the street below. And by "open", I mean send it shooting off the hinges. I'm amazed the shock doesn't send me over the edge as well. My own pounding heartbeat almost drowns out the terrifying breathing of the girl in the doorway.

Almost

She would be spitting dragon fire if it was physically possible. "Hey there, Tiger… how ya doing?" I try to diffuse our tense situation before becoming a second crater on the street. She's having none of it. There's no screaming or shouting, although I wish there was. We could use something to break our rigid standoff. It looks like she's trying to find someone else to direct the rage at—unfortunately, there's only me.

I finally get my wish when a mysterious cracking noise echoes across the city.

Then another.

And another.

And several more.

They appear every few seconds in a constant loop. The slight delay of the echo makes each one reach my ears at a different time. This makes them seem even more haunting than they already are. It takes an embarrassing amount of time to identify the common sound of two hands coming together. That's right, it's simple slow clapping.

Every television, phone, and radio broadcasts the same condescending sound. There's a low voice in the background, too muffled to comprehend, but audible nevertheless. My hair stands on end from the building static charge. Something's coming. Something so unmistakably evil that it's as tangible as the pages of this book.

As if on cue, every screen in the city flickers on. Even the electronic billboards show the black and white lines of a video without picture. Dozens and dozens of empty displays blink on with only the hissing sound. Large crowds are gathering below. They silently stare at me without fear, anger, or judgment. They actually seem devoid of any kind of emotion at all. It's as if they're blank canvasses just waiting around to be painted. They don't even change when the mysterious screens begin filling in line by line.

The slow reveal is far worse than anything that could be waiting on the other side. My eyes dart manically between buildings as if one of them already has the complete picture. The creature gradually forms from the bottom up. By the time it reaches the snarling jaw, I don't need (or want) any more to appear. The slender chin and glistening teeth could only belong to one person.

The Keeper.

I watch as the face contaminates every screen in sight like a virus. Although it's not really possible, his piercing eyes seem locked on me. They look right into my soul and pull out my greatest vulnerabilities. His penetrating stare leaves me wanting to crumble down to the ground, melt, and blend in with the dirty concrete.

Quinn's unnerving rage is gone as well. She's spinning, watching the screens, just as speechless as I am. Neither of us knows where to go from here. The massive faces have us trapped on a virtual island by the snarling man.

"You continue to surprise me, Mr. Flynn," cracks the Keeper. His tone is not nearly as approving as the words would imply. I instinctively launch into a joke about compensating with the size of his screen, but he doesn't react to it. Even though he ignored me in Vegas, this seems different. He's delivering a speech instead of having a conversation. I shout several more pointless, totally random things at the screen to confirm my theory he really can't see or hear us. I don't know how this information helps, other than make me feel better, but it's good to have, anyway.

I let Quinn in on the discovery and she couldn't care less. She's mindlessly rubbing her locket in the same worried way as usual. The wider the circle her fingers make, the higher the stress level. She's almost tracing the rim at this point.

For some reason, the Keeper isn't nearly as threatening as he was back in Vegas. This sounds more like a recruitment pitch than the "I'm going to watch you die" speech. I wonder if this is all flattery to lure us out, or maybe something more?

A sudden thump, like a fallen statue, crashes next to me. An abrupt wind and several little pebbles pelt my ankles. At first, I thought it might have been a gunshot that barely missed, but I find nothing by looking around. In fact, I find nothing, and no one, including Quinn. Then, I look by my feet...

Quinn's down.

Chapter 36: Troublemaker

Should I scream or cry?

Both sound equally great.

A mad scramble ensues to drag the limp body away from the edge. There's no blood, and her breathing is steady. The only thing my relentless shaking has achieved so far is causing her hair to sprawl across tightly closed eyes. Nothing about her tranquil face reveals any kind of pain. By any normal measure, aside from being in a coma, she's fine!

I continue searching high and low for a clue to the terrifying new mystery. What's happening now??? There are no cuts, bumps, or bruises. Nothing is out of place. The only hint of injury is the almost dried spot of blood in the very center of her palm. How this pin-sized prick even stands out in the first place, I don't know. It's so insignificant that it couldn't possibly be the cause of a total collapse like this.

Could it?

I know I really need to move on to find the real source, but something keeps drawing me back to the insignificant spot. There's a biting suspicion that makes my eyes linger on the perplexing spot for longer than they should.

Then I find it. Maybe...

Circling her palm is an indentation about the size of a coin. The familiar ridges, firmly embedded in the wrinkles of her skin, lead directly toward the tiny hole like the rings on a target. They're right where she was holding that damn locket!

I rush to find the little pendant laying innocently by her side. It's flipped over and all I see is some writing, *"Patris amor. Amor patris"*. The words certainly couldn't have caused it, so I treat the delicate locket like a ticking bomb that's ready to blow any minute. I watch it dangle from the end of my shaking finger; it spins slowly as the sun traces its smooth valleys and ridges. The thing seems built from a solid block of steel. There are no cut marks or seams. There's no beginning or end to the flowing inscription. It's as if the metal formed around the elegant words. The thing has survived living in the scorching desert with a crazy man, yet there aren't even any scratches on it!

It takes several careful rotations to finally find the one piece that doesn't belong. And it's the flash from the tip of the needle that eventually gives it away... Poking out of the center is a thin spike, no larger than a thorn, and barely thick enough to be visible. *That son of a bitch POISONED HER!!!!!!* I knew something was wrong with that creepy bastard! Who else would be standing in the middle of a goddamn desert, in a suit and pimp hat, with a fat-ass owl? *Son of a bitch*! Son of a bitchin' bitch bitch!

The insults flow fast and loud. My hands twitch at the thought of wrapping them around his wrinkly neck and twisting until it pops! I wanna walk back across that inferno just to shove that big round bird all the way up his crazy ass!

Keeper doesn't pause his monotonous speech throughout my meltdown. He doesn't take a breath or skip a beat while giving a long list of reasons for all the shitty things they do. The yammering voice, combined with a comatose kid, drives me to launch into a profanity rich collection of insults at the floating head. This time, he reacts to them.

Somehow, some way, the angry man heard me. His speech takes a sudden hiccup before coming back far more agitated. He still isn't talking directly to me, but his big recruitment speech is clearly over.

Quinn's still motionless on the ground and nothing will wake her. This isn't the first time we've had this sleeping problem, either. The first round of hypnosis was a real pain in the ass, this one isn't looking much better.

A new rumble comes up through the floor like a minor earthquake has started. I peek over to find an entire horde of vampires climbing the side of the building like the silent man did. The Keeper's patience has obviously come to a *very* abrupt end. It seems there's no more time to diagnose the mystery illness here, so I'll just have to scoop up the mostly dead girl and figure it out later.

I head toward the open staircase with the sound of another chase to keep me company. Most of the actual steps are skipped, instead leaping from landing to landing, floor to floor. Quinn bounces hard over my shoulder with each new jump. It's not ideal, but there's no other choice than to protect her head and keep on going. That system works great until they start coming *up* the stairs, too!

Can't go down.

Can't go up.

Going *sideways.*

I crash through a security door leading into a hallway where every door is individually numbered: 412, 413, 414, 415, etc. Some have personalized welcome mats, so I would guess they're apartments.

The way I see it, I can keep running and get trapped in a tight corner, or get into a room that could at least be a choke point. Maybe we could luck into finding a place to barricade ourselves in? Or maybe even a fire escape to crawl down? Long story short, there seems to be way more choices inside.

So which door?

Duck.

Duck.

%#@$' it...

Goose.

My hip makes quick work of the flimsy lock. The door flies open and scares the hell out of the two ladies waiting inside. I slide in, trying to extinguish their screams before they attract the horde outside. "Shhhh shhhh shhhhh—it's ok. I'm not going to hurt you."

One of them is holding a newborn baby tightly against her. My usual instinct would be to lash out to shut them up, make them fear me, except the innocent baby is keeping my claws locked. Even the monster isn't *that* big of a monster. So, other than fear, what's the only other emotion I can possibly appeal to?

Greed.

The glistening gold coins silence the ladies the moment they slide out. It won't buy me much time (pun firmly intended) so this needs to be quick. "I'm Quinn and this is Hayde... err... I'm Hayden and this is Quinn." So much for a speedy resolution.

One of the ladies is in the kitchenette warming up a bottle. The other is sitting on a couch with the tiny person it's intended for. For some reason, the baby doesn't seem troubled by me at all. He's stuck with wide eyes and pursed lips as if I've interrupted him midsentence. He looks to be more intrigued than anything.

The smaller of the women, the one who'd been making the bottle, returns to her wife and baby. When she sits next to them, I notice they're both wearing matching oversized sweatshirts and PJ bottoms. The only major difference is that one shirt has a dog, and the other a cat.

"I know this looks bad, but we're not going to hurt you. My friend and I are in a world of trouble. There are people right outside looking for us, and we didn't do anything wrong. Actually, we're running from the same people who killed this girl's family. We're desperate and will gladly pay for your help." If the money doesn't work, maybe sympathy will.

A forceful hand bangs on the door at that exact moment. Screams to be let in are flowing through the thin wood. The ladies take advantage by scanning us up and down to find any kind of hole in our story. We're battered and bruised, so if they're judging on looks alone, I like our chances. Precious seconds tick by without any kind of response to the group. I hold the gold coins up and mouth the word please. Appealing to their sympathies alone isn't enough when our lives are on the line. There's no trust with a stranger, only mutual self-interest.

The smaller lady in the cat shirt opens her mouth—only to close it again. She leaves us all in suspended animation until piping up in a strained voice, "We... we're feeding our baby. Hold on."

She stares at me the entire time. We never lose our uneasy visual truce while scooting out of the cramped living room. The closest exit ends up being their windowless bedroom. So much for having a backup plan.

I gently nudge the door closed and lock it behind me. I'm not sure what protection the weak wood will offer other than making me feel better, except it doesn't even do that. Quinn is quickly laid across the bed so I can return to listening to the events unfolding outside. I lean my ear against the wall just as the front door is forcefully thrown open. The knob slams into the wall before the mob shouts at the ladies. Almost instantly, the newborn cries at the top of his lungs. After that the conversation is hard to hear, but I get the most important part, "There's no else one here."

Chapter 37: Dream On

I finally get to expel the stale air I'd been clinging to when the front door slams shut. Still fearful of a trap, I barely crack the door to make sure they've actually gone. Thankfully, the ladies are the only ones waiting for me, but they've relocated to the kitchen with shiny new knives in hand.

"Sit," they command.

I slowly do as they say, putting my hands up to further diffuse the tense situation. "No problem. I told you, we don't want any trouble." My promise doesn't seem to make them feel any better. They still have the protective scowl of distressed mama bears.

"Where did your friend go?" by the end of their question, I'm already pointing at Quinn draped over the bed. She hasn't moved an inch and I really don't expect her to anytime soon. "She's hurt. Poisoned, I believe." This immediately deflates the shoulders of dog-sweatshirt lady with the baby. I get the feeling she's holding herself back from running to help Quinn right now.

The women were obviously in the middle of a casual Sunday when we interrupted. Cat pajamas lady is a brunette, almost my height, with well-defined cheekbones that plainly express her strong disapproval of me. Dog lady, on the other hand, is a petite blonde with a high ponytail that matches her more forgiving nature. They seem to be at the very beginning of their adult lives together. Photos confirm that college isn't very far in the rearview mirror, and neither is their wedding.

So, this makes the second happy family we've invaded in the last few days. Awesome...

The baby has slowed down his crying and the ladies have shown an interest in hearing my story, even though they still haven't reached the lowering of knives stage yet. My mind is pulled in a thousand different directions while filling them in on the details. I'm trying to juggle worrying over Quinn's mysterious condition, creating a plan to get out of here, listening for the mob to return, and keeping these ladies happy. As a result, the story comes out a bit scrambled, sounding like a lie, even though it really isn't.

I'm still in the process of attempting to win them over when the lights go out. The mechanical hums throughout the entire building grind to a sudden halt. Every fan, buzzing lightbulb, and whirring motor go instantly silent. In their place is the deep voice of the Keeper. "That was a very convincing disappearing act, Mr. Flynn. I could have my men keep searching for you, or I could burn the entire block down. Do I seem like a patient man to you, Mr. Flynn?" I make it to the window in time to see the subtle grin of satisfaction on his usually grim face. There's a twinkle in his eye at the mere thought of burning down his own city.

"You have five minutes to show yourself, but I'm going to blow up the first building in three. You don't want to know what happens if I make it all the way to five." It takes ten seconds to comprehend the need to physically move. It's clear where I have to go, though Quinn's fate is a bit cloudier. That will depend entirely on these two strangers.

I stagger away from the window with legs numb from shock. I'm trying to keep it together, but already fraying at the edges. One knee gives out completely, sending me crashing back into the coffee table. I'm stuck in a daze and drunk on fear. I seriously need to get my shit together and, at least, make it outside before falling apart entirely.

"Ple..." My tongue gets stuck while pleading with the ladies. "Please." is about as far as my mind can go. One of them, I don't even know which one, approaches with kind eyes. She gives the baby to her wife and takes my hand. Her gentle touch makes me want to break down, except the countdown has already started, and I've wasted a full minute.

"I have no right to ask this, but I'm out of options—her life depends on you all now. If I don't go out there, many people will die; including everyone in this room. You don't know me, but you know that much is true." I lay the three gold coins on the broken coffee table. Even though it's slanted, somehow, the cursed treasures don't slide.

"Please."

During that last word, I'm not looking at the women anymore. My eyes have been drawn to the helpless Quinn instead. She's stranded here and there's nothing I can do about that. All we've done so far is to kick the can further down the road, barely making it through each day. That ends here.

I look back at the ladies who unexpectedly have so much depending on them. As usual, the words aren't there, but the sincerity is. I give one final "Please" as I run out the door one last time.

Chapter 38: Let It Be Me

By the time I make it to the hallway, I have no idea how much time is left. I also haven't figured out exactly what it is I'm going to do yet. My monster is the one who usually guides me through this stuff. This time, it gets to be Hayden Flynn in control when it matters most. One thing's certain: I need to get as far away from here as possible. Would he make good on the promise to blow up these buildings? I don't know for sure, but the chances seem pretty good. It's also a solid bet that he'd start with the last place they saw me.

Even before reaching the stairs, my plan takes a hit. A small group of people are lined up at door like bowling pins ready to be split. My legs hesitate for a second before hitting full speed to plow right through them. Luckily, and for some weird reason, the entire group steps aside; I mean, completely at once. As in, their feet move as one.

They also wear the same blank expressions of the crowd outside. Looking at them is like staring into the dead eyes of a mannequin. There's even more of the same waiting in the cramped stairwell. Several small groups have gathered to watch me in the same detached way. Every head follows in perfect unison as I run by. As extremely freaky as they are—and they're *extremely* freaky—they'll have to be added to the list of things to worry about later.

I finally reach the bottom of the stairs and fling open the door leading to the main floor. Another group is waiting; same dead look, same crooked neck, except they're pointing as if to give directions. Which I follow with (almost) no hesitation.

They lead me into another wall of people that cut off every direction except one. I again don't fight the tide and just keep running. The story is the same at every turn. Every place I could need guidance, they're there to show me the way. They never steer me wrong, either.

<u>Without them:</u> I would have gotten lost several times.

<u>With them:</u> I'm standing at the exit leading to who knows what.

I shove both of the grand doors wide open to accept whatever fate lies on the other side. That turns out to be rows of hundreds, no *thousands*, of people lining the street. There's a mob on each side as deep as the eye can see. Familiar dead expressions and all. Carved down the center is a narrow lane meant only for one person—me.

I step out into the crowd and it closes behind me. After each new step, they seal the gap to keep pushing me forward. The mob is so tight, I'm shoulder-to-shoulder with them most of the time. They're careful to only leave one direction open. Straight ahead.

So, onward we go with the mindless mass leading the way. They don't rush or slow me down in any way. I'm allowed to walk at my own nervous pace. And it is *very* nervous.

My anxiety grows with every forced step. Their path is ridged and unforgiving, barely wide enough to fit through, and they don't let me see more than ten feet ahead. It's also a sure preview of the terribleness to come. One thing's for sure, nothing good is waiting at the end of this line. The old song runs through my frantic mind, "You can check out any time you like, but you can never leave."

We make it through several twisting blocks before making the turn I should have seen coming all along. Straight ahead is the soaring tower, and we're walking straight down its long shadow. The sun disappears behind the massive building, leaving behind an inappropriate glowing halo. If I thought my nerves were wrecked before, well... I was wrong.

I lean back into the crowd. This is the unconscious result of sudden, overwhelming panic. For the first time, they push me along, and it feels as if they're suffocating me without ever actually touching me. The notion to fight my way out enters my mind, but leaves just as quickly. I'm literally drowning in an ocean of bodies. How could I fight my way through this?? I try pleading with them out of pure desperation. That only causes the entire group to stare at me with those dead eyes. That instantly silences me.

Now, I've never walked death row, but it couldn't feel much different than this. Even the temperature drops as we get closer. Maybe that part is all in my head, but I'm shivering by the time we reach the last block. Each step is getting infinitely harder to take. My monster is only putting up a half-assed fight now. Even he has no idea what to do. Neither of us knows what the pot of shit waiting at the end of the rainbow will be, but I'm pretty sure it will be a really, *really* big, steaming pile of it.

Chapter 39: A Change Is Gonna Come

The bottom of the tower isn't as solid as I assumed it would be. The center is actually wide open, almost like a medieval courtyard. There are massive columns running down each side that have to be the size of red oak trees. My escorts guide me all the way up to the arched gateway. As nervous as I am, some small relief comes from just being out of the funnel of people. They've stopped closing in, so these last few steps will be mine alone.

The tight courtyard opens up as soon as I pass through the restrictive gate. As far as I can tell, there's one way in, one way out, and a whole lot of bad in between. Aluminum fencing surrounds the entire thing. Not the chain-link kind, but thick bars filled with spikes and thorns. Massive dents reveal the raw steel buried underneath the faded black paint. One detail really bothers me about all the damage—all of it seems to be on the inside. This wall keeps people in, not out.

Up top is a narrow walkway lined with huge canisters lighting up every inch of the massive courtyard. Waiting at the back of the room are two men clustered tightly around a small boy on an actual throne. I can identify all of them easily: the floppy blond mop belongs to Shepherd, the smooth bald head of the Keeper glows in the artificial light, and the last is actually easiest to identify, even though we've never met.

Samael.

The pureblood.

He radiates authority all the way from back here. Merely walking into the same room brings a swell of emotion almost like the guilt of inadequacy or shame. This young boy, still hundreds of feet away, makes me feel insignificant by comparison. He couldn't be much more than ten, but he already has the presence of a grown-ass man. A warrior.

He sits regally with perfect posture. His delicate hands are folded neatly over the arms of the chair, while his legs are cocked as if they're prepared to spring up at any second. The entire upper half of his face is muddied by a powerful, inhuman glow coming from his eyes. The rest of him is completely cold. Like, intimidatingly emotionless. None of the others sit along with him. There aren't even any chairs available for them. I get the sense that Samael tolerates them, but nothing more.

Nobody has said a word yet; they've only stared down from the elevated platform in judgement. I can only work up the courage to occasionally glance up, just enough to keep myself on course. Anything more makes my guts curdle. I mainly stay focused on my own forced footsteps, which are far shorter than normal.

"Not much to say this time, ah, Flynn?" Shepherd mocks. It's true. My usual sense of humor has been missing for some time now. In the past, I would have at least flipped him off; now, I can barely muster the confidence to look him in the eye. Even I know my limits, and walking alone, surrounded by thousands of zombie-looking bastards, is beyond them. Then, about ten feet out, Keeper signals me to stop. He doesn't say anything, just holds his hand up to glare me into submission. Shepherd makes up for it with, "I told you to let her die, Flynn." Still nothing. My mind has no brilliant comeback to offer his cocky smirk.

"Look at me when I'm talking to you, Flynn! Is this really how you want to go out? Kicking your feet like a moody child?" I hadn't noticed my fidgeting legs before. They're sweeping side to side as if they're clearing off a path. My nervous energy decided to come out that way, I guess.

Shepherd continues, uninterrupted by me, his voice rising a noticeable level after each ignored sentence. Who knew I could piss so many people off by *not* talking? The amusing thought must put a grin on my face, because Shepherd goes completely berserk after that. He jumps off the platform and charges fists-first toward me. The only thing stopping him is the melodic voice of the Keeper saying, "Not yet."

"First, we need to know where the girl is, Mr. Flynn." Keeper licks a single snarling tooth. "She's caused us a significant amount of trouble and we simply want to return the favor. We think Kaneda tower, level four? How am I doing so far?"

Wait a second. How could he possibly know that? "How do you know..." but he interrupts me again. I'm not sure if I've ever completed a sentence to this man.

"Samael sees all. There's nowhere you ca—" This time I cut him off, "Oh come on. You're not going to give me that bullshit, are you? He's a kid, not a damn god." That seems to shut him up pretty well. Soon, his expression changes to that of a man keeping a great secret. One that benefits only him.

Keeper looks to the boy king and slides in behind his throne. Samael rises as if he's pulling something from the ground. He dips down low, arms stretched all the way forward, reaching from the floor to the sky. Immediately, the walkway fills with people. They move from the shadows as one large mass of bodies. Samael steps forward with them.

Every mouth in the room speaks the same exact words, "I've been watching since you stepped foot into that bar, Hayden Flynn. Everywhere you've gone—Gaslight, the bus, Vegas... everywhere. When you speak to my Harbingers, you speak to me." I look over at Shepherd's blank stare and he's speaking along with the rest. The only mouths not moving are the ones belonging to Keeper and (strangely) Samael himself. "This is my Hive, Mr. Flynn. I am them and they are me."

The ground shakes from the harmony of voices. Samael raises his hand and the crowd outside joins. The choir takes on a new, defiant expression. "We are the Phoenix of hope, by rule of the divine. In order to rise from its own ashes, a Phoenix must burn." The rage-filled words echo throughout the city. "Your world will burn!" Their chants rumble buildings, shake walls, and generally finish destroying the rest of my already fragile confidence.

After the quake ends, the tiny boy gloats with a subtle smile. He says nothing, just stares with these nebulous eyes that seem to look right through me. They pry open my soul and infect it with his sticky black venom. I can feel him spreading across me, poisoning my thoughts. It's as if he's whispering directly into my mind. Only at the last second am I able to break away from being lured deeper into his *hypnotic* world.

Chapter 40: Only the Good Die Young

The experience leaves me feeling permanently stained inside. A chill settles into the base of my spine while I watch the crowd of mindless zombies from a fresh new perspective. I only brushed up against the bleeding edge of the control he has over these people. I felt him grasping for me, heard the voices creeping around my mind. I didn't really understand before now—I believed these puppets were only dancing on invisible strings—but they choose to do this. Samael makes you *want* to do his bidding.

Somehow, he embeds himself in you. Unlike my monster, who's almost a completely separate part of me, Samael becomes you. He owns you. He invades your soul and permanently bonds with it. As a person who has felt helpless to the drug of my hunger, that was nothing compared to the temptation of what Samael offered me. It was everything I've longed for: security, comfort, love, acceptance... they were all mine for the taking. A huge chunk of me begs to join his sanctuary, no matter how false it is.

My voice trembles as I reason with him, "Listen kid— Samael—you don't have to do this. These men don't own you. You don't have to..." The Keeper (as usual) interrupts. Not to defend himself, but to laugh uncontrollably.

"You believe this is our doing?" he barely gets out between breathless giggles, "As if we could control *all these people??*" He laughs harder. "I appreciate what power you believe me capable of, but it's *extremely* misguided. No one but our lord is capable of molding an entire civilization!

He's the resurrection of Vlad Dracul!

Drank from the Sangraal!"

None of this means a damn thing to me, but it seems pretty impressive to him. My apathetic appearance infuriates the Keeper to scream further details. "Our kind, *your* kind, have waited hundreds of years for his return! Samael is the direct descendent of the Lord Dracula! He's been endowed with all his powers and memories. Do you know what this means for our people? The power he wields could..." I interrupt to ask, "Hold on just a second. How could he have the memories? The kid's like ten or twelve. I seriously doubt he was around back then to..." Keeper cuts me off again.

"Didn't you hear me? He's drank from the Sangraal! This body is eleven years of age, but the blood flowing through it is hundreds of years old!"

Literally, holy shit. That kid drank the *actual* blood of *Dracula!* He merged with the vilest creature to ever walk the planet! Those memories came from the bowels of the deepest wickedness imaginable! There was certainly enough in there to permanently stain his soul with an enduring evil. It takes less than a second to absorb the scope of this life-changing information. In short, I'm completely screwed.

But in the grand scheme of things, it doesn't matter who he is. It matters who I am. The only thing under my control is what kind of person I leave this world as. Pride straightens my spine and stiffens my resolve.

"You know this changes nothing, right? I will never worship your kind of evil or join this merry band of assholes." Saying this out loud is an admission that my chances of walking out of here are not great.

Samael's eyes roll back in his head just as Shepherd says, "Joining me was never an option. You're not welcome here." The kid's voice now comes directly from Shepherd's mouth. The eerie speech was merely an appetizer for the two hands currently wrapped around the base of my skull. Before I can stop it or brace for impact, he serves up the main course of our heads colliding together.

The impact sends me to the ground in a messy heap of bones, meanwhile, it does absolutely nothing to him. It also leaves a giant hole in my vision that makes it easy for him to come get me again. He marches forward with a chillingly dead expression, only stopping to toss me in the air by the ankle. The world rotates once again before being brought to an abrupt halt by a clenched fist around the throat.

My hands reach out to pound on everything within reach. They make a solid enough connection with his left check to instantly force one eye shut. The fat swelling should warrant some kind of visible reaction, except he doesn't even blink. The vastness of my problem is suddenly made much clearer. Either Samael is controlling Shepherd and can't feel his pain, or he can take away his ability to feel it. Either way, this kid could make the entire crowd into unstoppable killing machines!

Darkness is gradually eating away at the edges of my sight. It's the unwelcome result of a hand crushing my trachea flat. I clumsily search for some way of dislodging the hand before my vision disappears entirely. Since the only thing within reach is the underside of his elbow, I drive my fist directly through it. The resulting pop of tendons ripping is music to my ears.

Three fingers release automatically, while the other is pretty easy to break away. My throat and vision return to normal as soon as my feet touch solid ground. I arrive just in time to witness the backward horror of his arm bent in the opposite direction. It's unnerving to see someone twisted into such a shocking position with a completely blank stare on his face. Seriously, the arm is so far back, he could scratch his own back, yet he's still faster than me in every way. It seems he actually *can* kick my ass with one arm behind his back!

I continue retreating, and he continues to advance. Then he hits the dead center of my chest. <u>*HARD.*</u> I hear the bones snap way before I feel them. The collapsing lung triggers a pained scream, but only a wheezy squeal makes it all the way out. He takes full advantage of my crippled position by quickly delivering several direct shots to the face. They land on my cheek at a fast and furious pace. The sound of his cracking knuckles rings out like automatic gun shots.

The taste of blood is coming from everywhere. A loose tooth or busted lip would be my best-case scenario. One eye has already swollen completely shut. With it went all my depth perception. That doesn't stop me from being able to see the massive amounts of blood splatter collecting on his cheeks. Unfortunately, none of it belongs to him. His mouth is drawn into the same slender smile as the boy earlier. That growing satisfaction drives him to hit me harder, and harder, and *harder*, until it *finally* leads to my lucky break.

Literally.

The turning point comes when he hits me hard enough to actually break his own wrist. While my jaw takes a beating, it's his hand that comes back flopped over like a dead fish. He already had the other bent completely backward, so now—without hands—the fight turns rather quickly. I grab a good fistful of his curly hair, cock my shoulder, and drill down for what should be a solid knock-out punch. However, my knuckles have a different plan. They decide to ricochet into a cheek bone and land in the broadest part of his shoulder instead. Even though there's momentary disappointment, it doesn't slow my fists at all. Desperation is still fueling them to dig in further and faster with every new hit.

Breaking Shepherd feels wrong in the worst way. Even after all he's done, what he's become, that face belongs to my best friend. As each successful punch lands, Hayden Flynn has to slip farther away. I have to let the feral monster take complete control because he'll do what must be done. He'll guide my fists into the right spot without mercy. See, that's what ultimately separates me from the vampire. Hayden will have pity even when they deserve none.

It won't.

Shepherd is left writhing on the ground like a malfunctioning robot that's clueless as to why it can no longer stand. Samael's still using the body, even though he can't physically move it anymore.

He's broken.

I've broken Shepherd.

The actual boy king is only a distant blur in my periphery. He's a static shape living on the furthest boundaries of my centrally focused vision. My only concern so far has been completely demolishing the threat directly in front of me. The tiny kid occupying a throne four times too large for him hasn't interested me in the slightest. So, when that blur disappears, I don't think anything of it. Right up until I feel a sudden warm sensation spilling down the center of my throat, similar to swallowing hot coffee on an ice-cold day.

At first, I have no idea what it is. But my head feels different; lighter, looser. I look around to find the young boy standing over my left shoulder. He has the same familiar shit-eating grin he put on Shepherd's face. Then I go to take a breath and find my lungs are utterly missing. I start heaving in terror-induced spasms and the spurting blood covers my reaching hands. A sound, like water being suctioned from a drain, comes from some part of my neck. Air is flowing, uninterrupted, through the fresh new hole in my throat.

My legs give out from shock. Falling to my knees puts the boy and me at the same level. You see him relish the exact moment my horrifying realization hits me. Possibilities and plans rush in, but my short-circuited brain cancels them out immediately. Tears are the only emotion that can break through the intense panic. I'm unable to speak; I can only move my lips in incoherent hushed mumbles.

In my final desperate moments, I'm drawn to a little golden-haired boy in the crowd. Something about him doesn't fit with the rest of the anonymous group. He stands out like an actor that doesn't blend in well with his digital world. It's as if I can see him due to some mistake or glitch, since he simply doesn't belong here. If nothing else, it's because there's sympathy in his blue and green eyes. This lost little boy speaks to me in a silent voice. He fills me with, and I know this sounds weird... hope.

I was never here for Shepherd, or this fight, or even Samael. I came for redemption. To recover the part that died all those years ago. There's no real reason for me to feel as if I've accomplished that goal, but I do. My soul feels as full as a belly on Thanksgiving. Like I'm an artist putting the final strokes on his masterpiece. Again, I have no reason to believe this other than the unspoken words, but why does 2 + 2 = 4, or why is the grass green? Because you accept that it is. Because it's truth. *Well*, this is *my* truth.

The part of my brain controlling balance dies. I have no other option than to fall backward with a stupid grin on my face. It stretches from ear to ear, even as white clouds swallow the entire world. There's not an ounce of fear left in me. Not because I'm brave, of course. Would you consider falling in love to be an act of bravery? Or taking an unknown road for the first time? No, those are just the chances you're willing to take because of hope. Because of the belief you'll always make it back home.

That same faith tells me a brand-new day is waiting on the other side of the coming night. This unexpected optimism wants me to know that everyone dies twice: once when you stop breathing and the last time someone says your name. Well, what Quinn and I started, won't die with me today. We've changed the world and stumbled onto it from an angle I never saw coming.

Because this was <u>never</u> *my* story.

Epilogue:

Draped over the corner of a soft bed, the sleeping finger of a powerful girl twitches. One who will change *everything*.

Note from the author:

If you liked this book—even if you didn't—please share your opinion with me (Ben @redskyseries.com) for a chance to win absolutely nothing except my gratitude & appreciation. I sincerely hope you enjoyed your first trip to the world of *Red Sky* and will join us again in "Red Sky: Nightfall."

"Red Sky: Rising" by Ben Archer

Edited by: Monica San Nicolas

Charleston, WV 25313

www.RedSkySeries.com

Made in the USA
Columbia, SC
24 October 2018